Praise for Misty Evans' *Operation Sheba*

"...the best book I have ever read. OPERATION SHEBA is not at the head of the class, it is in a class by itself..."
~ *Susiq2, CataRomance*

"This is a top notch romantic suspense...... Ms. Evans takes you on a wild ride, one that you will hate to see end. I will await her next installment of Super Agents with great anticipation."
~ *Loloty, Coffee Time Romance*

"...a heart-pounding, super-hot read...continuous nonstop action and blazing sexual interactions. Overall, OPERATION SHEBA was a thrilling, erotic spy game that I enjoyed playing."
~ *Contessa, Romance Junkies*

"Ms. Evans writing style is superb. If you read no other book this season, read OPERATION SHEBA. This author is TOPS"
~ *Carol A. Spradling, Writers and Readers of Distinctive Fiction*

"Bad guys, bombs, and bullets pop up everywhere...The CIA's internal politics are fleshed out beautifully... With non-stop action and a fantastic heroine, Operation Sheba is a great kickoff for a debut writer."
~ *Bramble Nymph, Literary Nymphs*

"...Misty Evans' debut effort *Operation Sheba* is an interesting romantic suspense story......"
~ *Mrs. Giggles*

Look for these titles by
Misty Evans

Now Available:

Witches Anonymous

Super Agent Series
Operation Sheba (Book 1)
I'd Rather Be In Paris (Book 2)

Misty is the niece of Ruth Stoggs

Misty's last name is Fanderelei

Operation Sheba

Misty Evans

Hot shot spies never die... they just slip undercover.

Misty Evans

A Samhain Publishing, Ltd. publication.

Samhain Publishing, Ltd.
577 Mulberry Street, Suite 1520
Macon, GA 31201
www.samhainpublishing.com

Operation Sheba
Copyright © 2009 by Misty Evans
Print ISBN: 978-1-60504-326-5
Digital ISBN: 975-1-60504-082-0

Editing by Sasha Knight
Cover by Angela Waters

First Samhain Publishing, Ltd. electronic publication: September 2008
First Samhain Publishing, Ltd. print publication: July 2009

Dedication

For Mark...this and the giver are yours forever. Thank you for loving me tall all this time and showing me how to spread my wings and fly.

People in an author's life give so much and never realize the depth of what they've given. For my parents, who believed in me and told me to write what I wanted to write and not worry about others' opinions, I offer my deepest love and gratitude. For my sons, who waited patiently while I wrote *just one more line* and who tagged along on endless trips to the post office, I promise to squeeze out more mornings for coffee on the front porch and reading Harry Potter stories.

I owe oceans of appreciation to my dear friend and early reader, Angela Vogel, for her three-hugs-and-a-kick-in-the-pants whenever I swore I was giving up. Along with her, the rest of the Charmed Girls—Cyndi, Angi B., Kate and Lisa—supported my dream of being a published author since the beginning. I can't thank you all enough.

I am blessed with friends who are also talented writers—Chiron, Nana, Carol, Tessy and Ree. I would not be the writer I am today without your guidance.

An author is lost without her resources. For this novel, I owe special thanks to Deb Duhr, librarian *extraordinaire*, who hunted down out-of-print books and other elements for me on everything CIA.

This circle of gratitude is not complete without thanking my wonderful editor Sasha Knight and my dedicated agent Elaine English.

Prologue

Berlin

"I've got a bad feeling about this, Con." Julia frowned at the boom box parts lying around her crossed legs on the bed.

She had dissected the electronic box, cleaning out its internal organs, and was now carefully repacking the frame with C-4 plastique explosive. The boom box would offer her partner an easy way to carry the bomb into the heart of the enemy in the approaching early morning hours.

"What do you mean?" Conrad said.

Julia looked up, the frown still creasing her forehead. "I don't know. Something's not quite right with this mission. Something's off." *We're off.*

"Getting cold feet, are you?"

She expected her partner's cocky grin or a wink with the comment. What she got was his back as he began filling the inside pockets of his black leather coat with extra clips of ammunition. Something was definitely off. Ever since she'd arrived in Berlin the night before, things were strained between them. Conrad was distant and at the same time seemed to watch her every move.

Julia had witnessed Conrad's metamorphosis from good guy to bad guy several times during their five-year undercover stint in Europe. As a highly trained CIA operator, he was capable of changing his physical appearance and personality in seconds with a minimum of tools.

All you need, he would say, *is a one-degree shift.* Extreme changes in your normal looks, posture, or personality were difficult to pull off for any length of time, trapping you in your own deception. To lie well, the lies had to be built on truth; your cover had to be controlled and disciplined.

Sometimes the lies become the truth, Julia thought, watching her partner now cleaning his Heckler and Koch P7. Conrad Flynn had been undercover for months, attempting to flush out yet another gray arms dealer in Germany. As usual, Julia knew little of the details. She was his backup when he needed it but spent most of her time in Paris at the U.S. Embassy under her own cover, working on her own operations. That suited her just fine. She hated Germany and hated what it was doing to Conrad. She had already walked through this nightmare once before with him, providing the explosives he needed to blow up a warehouse six miles outside the city limits. Tonight she was here to do it again, but what she really wanted to do was pull him into bed with her and hold him close.

Eyeing his naked back from her seat on the bed, she could see he had lost weight. The muscles in his upper back and arms had moved past the point of well-defined. He was now ripped. His hair was longer than she'd ever seen it, skimming his shoulders as he moved. Who were the criminals he was after this time and what had they done? More importantly, what had *he* done in order to gain acceptance among them?

When he turned to throw his jacket on a nearby chair, she continued to watch him. Curls of black hair hung over his forehead and his chiseled jaw sported a week's growth of beard. He stopped for a second, staring at the table in front of him but seeming to see nothing. His stillness signaled deep concentration. *He's running the plan again in his head.*

If only they could be somewhere else right now. She wanted to trace the deep lines between his biceps and triceps, wanted to kiss the scars on his back. Run her hands down his rock-hard thighs. Make him smile and laugh and forget the things he'd witnessed, the things he'd done. But the concentration on his face kept her still. What was his secret this time? Was it really the operation or was it something else? Another woman? Anxiety stabbed her heart like a sharp knife.

"How much longer?" he asked, critically surveying her work on the bed.

She looked down, flustered at her previous thought. "Almost done." Placing a layer of plastique in one of the speaker boxes, she stuck in a detonator and a pager. "Each speaker is detachable and each is loaded with explosive. When you page the main box the others will blow too. Give yourself plenty of room before you send the page."

He nodded and she began to screw the cover back onto the box. "God, I hate bombs."

There was always this intensity around Conrad right before an operation went down. It was intoxicating and at the same time it made her want to shiver. "I'll deliver it for you," she offered.

His dark eyes flickered up and locked with hers. After a moment's hesitation, he shook his head. "I know you would, Jules, but I can't let you. It's too dangerous. This is my gig and if I do it right, everything will be okay."

She nodded and finished putting the boom box back together. Moving it off the bed, she brushed dust off her worn Levi's. "Do I have time to take a shower?"

He studied her for a minute and then shook his head. "No," he said, and there it was, finally, the cocky grin. "But we do have time for something else."

She quirked an eyebrow at him. "I thought it was bad luck to have sex before a mission. You always make me wait 'til the dust has cleared."

He moved toward her. "Tonight's different."

She stepped into his arms, wrapping hers around his neck. "Oh yeah? How's it different?"

"Full moon," he whispered in her ear, his lips finding the exact spot on her neck that made her shiver. She let him lead her to the bed, let him undress her first with his gaze and then with his hands. Giving herself up to him, she fought the nagging voice in her head.

Something's off.

Chapter One

Arlington, Virginia, seventeen months later

The man sat perfectly still in the semidarkness watching the woman sleep. Only a sheet covered the slender body on the queen-size bed. Long hair stretched out in waves on her pillow, and he tamped down the urge to reach out and touch it. He watched the rhythmic rise and fall of her chest and slowed his own breathing to match. Resting his gun, a suppressed Heckler & Koch, on his right thigh, he wished he had a cigarette to calm his nerves.

Cigarettes, like his true identity, had been given up years ago, but every once in awhile he caught himself craving the feel of the stick between his lips, the smoke curling around his face. At thirty-two, he'd lost track of all the things he'd given up to become the man he was at this moment. He'd played too many roles, led too many lives, losing his sense of duty and fairness only to find himself becoming the enemy he was supposed to search out and destroy.

But he'd never lost track of her.

She continued to sleep deeply, a sight he had rarely witnessed in their five-plus years together. Her demeanor when awake was calm and unshakable. She was analytical and calculating, sizing up any given situation and devising two or three options to keep herself, and him, alive. But in sleep, nightmares tormented her. Nightmares that gripped her so hard she would cry out, making his blood run cold. He would pull her close and murmur reassurances in her ear, stroke her face and rock her in his arms. Anything to scatter the demons that terrorized her mind and raped her soul.

Seeing her at peace here in the early morning hours gave

him comfort. *I shouldn't have come. I should have stayed dead to her, left her in whatever conciliation she has found.* But he needed her and the hand was already dealt. If he failed he would be dead, for real this time, and someone else would come for her. He couldn't fail. Her life depended on it as much as his did.

A memory of their escape from Berlin the first time he'd used her knowledge of explosives surfaced in his mind. After he had detonated the bomb and eliminated the warehouse, he had pulled her into a hotel in the Mitte District and paid for a shabby room. There they had spent those first few hours after the explosion making love under the goose-down quilt, needing the affirmation they both still lived to wipe out the pain they shared. Hours later, after he had slept and she had stared out the window at the stagnant Spree River, they wired a car and drove to Tegel Airport. Both had changed their appearance and, traveling together, never raised a single eyebrow as they passed the airport's security and boarded a plane to Venice. Only then in the safety of the sky did exhaustion take over and afford her sleep.

The woman stirred, bringing her legs up into a fetal position. The room was starting to gray with the approaching sunrise. Her hand slipped under her absent lover's pillow and he smiled, the familiarity of her movement sending ripples of anticipation rushing through his veins. He struggled to keep himself from whispering her name in the silent room. Pulling himself back a step from the edge, he took a deep breath, slid his gun into the waistband at the small of his back and willed himself to be patient and savor the moment. After all, he had waited seventeen months for this.

Julia Torrison sensed two things upon wakening. Michael was gone and there was another unidentifiable human presence in her room.

Maintaining her deep, even breathing, she kept her body motionless as if still in sleep to give her mind a few more precious minutes to filter through the probable identity of her visitor.

The options were cataloged in her brain. Enemies of her country and of her own making were widespread. But who these days cared whether she lived or died? She was simply an analyst now, lost in the windowless, cubicle-induced maze of the CIA's Counterterrorism Center. From her four-by-six bunker of space, she did what they asked her to—analyze terrorists. Fieldwork was behind her now. Years of training and self-discipline, invisible orders and covert operations lost in the blink of an eye, in the explosion of a bomb, in the abrupt and complete silence of her partner.

No enemy could have found her easily. The CIA had created a new identity for her, Abigail Quinn, and plunked her in their ultimate safe house at Langley. She had thought she would go mad from the sterile confinement of the CTC office, but filtering through the endless pools of information about the disciplined madmen trying to bring America to its knees had actually pacified her. It had become meditation, freeing her brain from the racing thoughts about *him.* About what she could have, should have done to save him. The guilt for still being alive while he was dead gnawed at her, especially in the dark hours of the night when Michael's hands reached for her instead of his. But through the work, and because of Michael's constant reinforcement, she was finally becoming Abigail Quinn. Her past self was doggedly being sealed off, layer of brick over layer of brick, never to be seen again.

Perhaps her visitor was simply a thief who had watched Michael leave with Pongo, his Rottweiler, for their daily run to the lake. However, no casual burglar could have made it past the posted guard at the gate or the home's eleven-thousand-dollar security system.

Michael's pillow was still warm where his head had been minutes earlier. Her hand wrapped slowly around the hidden Beretta 92F 9-mm stored there and she felt the thrill of the hunted turned hunter. People underestimated her because she was a woman and because her characteristic quietness was often taken for ignorance.

It was always their mistake.

Julia willed her heart not to pump out of her chest as she eased the safety off the gun. It really didn't matter who the intruder was...he was in for a big surprise.

Chapter Two

Michael Stone stopped at the edge of the lake, watching the first rays of sun brightening the eastern sky and glisten off the gray water. Pongo ran ahead, pouncing in and out of the water as small waves sloshed around his paws. A light breeze cooled the sweat running down Stone's back and he raised the bottom of his blue T-shirt to wipe more out of his eyes.

This early morning run was the least complicated thirty minutes of his typical twelve-to-fourteen-hour day. No ringing phones interrupting his thoughts, no political agendas manipulating his people, no strategic actions, timelines or security briefs to worry about. Most days the run was thirty minutes of unadulterated freedom and he relished every second of it.

This morning, however, his mind was troubled by a piece of information that on the surface appeared to solve a serious problem that had plagued the CIA for months. There was a mole in the Agency, one that had been irritating and choking his human assets in the field for the past year and a half as effectively as the required office dress-code tie irritated and choked his thick neck every day. Now, because of a simple airport security tape from two days ago, the mole's identity was revealed...at least to those who were looking for an easy solution to cover their own asses if and when a congressional investigation was called.

Turning south, Stone resumed jogging easily along the lake's edge, his mind stewing about what the day would bring. Once he and Abigail reached the office everything would change between them. The past night he had spent with her was possibly the last. Dread squeezed its fingers around his chest.

Michael Stone was a swift and accurate judge of people because of his uncanny ability to figure out what motivated them. He was rarely wrong and his gut instincts had carried him far. That's why at thirty-eight, he was one of the youngest Director of Operations the CIA had ever known. He had trusted Julia Torrison from the first moment he met her but had been disappointed with her pairing with Conrad Flynn. Flynn was a cowboy, cocky and reckless and running one step ahead of the devil at every turn. As DO, Michael didn't like cowboys in his group of spies, but Flynn produced results where others couldn't.

Unfortunately after his death, Julia had arrived on Michael's doorstep at Langley a basket case. "Tormented" was the word stamped on his mental file of her the minute she walked in. He knew the devil had finally caught up with Flynn, knew it was the cowboy's own fault he was dead. But there stood Julia—her long brown hair pinned on top of her head, her beautiful eyes bloodshot from lack of sleep and too much crying, her black linen suit outlining her figure perfectly as she crossed the room to shake his hand—blaming herself. Stone had debriefed her, put her through a lie detector and sent her to the company shrink, knowing the whole time she was innocent of everything except being in love with a cowboy. He had set her up with a false identity and taken her under his wing at Langley, never once doubting her intentions or her motives.

However, a shift in his thinking had occurred the previous day the instant he recognized the face on the tape. He didn't trust easy solutions any more than he trusted rogue agents, but now he had to figure out where Abigail's loyalties lay. Her reaction to the tape would tell him all he needed to know.

Michael shook his head, frowning as he turned west, away from the lake and back toward his home. He whistled at Pongo and the dog reached his side in seconds, falling into an easy run with his master.

In one swift movement, Julia rolled onto her back, raising her shoulders and gripping the Beretta with both hands. She brought the gun to bear on the shadowed figure in the corner of the room and without hesitation squeezed the trigger twice. The silencer coughed as the bullets were sent speeding across the room toward the man's head.

A millisecond before her fingers released the bullets, he moved, dropping his upper body to the right and down. The bullets missed him and embedded themselves in the wall as he lunged at the bed.

The edge on Julia's reaction time was dulled from too many months of sitting in an office. She felt a spurt of fear as she attempted to realign her gun with her assailant, but she wasn't fast enough. As his body pushed hers back down on the bed, he deflected the gun and pinned her wrists up over her head. His thumbs bore into the center of each wrist, crippling her hands, and the gun dropped to the carpeted floor with a muffled thud. She refused to cry out but struggled beneath the weight of his body, kicking at him as best she could. He continued to hold both of her arms over her head, shifting them into his left hand while wrapping his right around her neck.

"You missed." He chuckled softly in her ear.

Her body went utterly still at the sound of his voice. She drew a sharp breath as her gaze snapped to his. Confusion and then crystal clarity made her swallow hard. He took a deep breath, as though immersing himself in her scent. Releasing his grip of her neck, he stroked her jaw line with the tip of his finger. "Julia," he murmured, the husky voice caressing her.

Julia held her breath, refusing to blink as she stared at the apparition hanging an inch from her face. Was this another of her horrible dreams? She automatically did a mental inventory of his face—the short dark hair, the eyebrows so soft to the touch, the fringe of dark lashes around his eyes, the straight line of his lips...

"Who are you?"

Another quiet chuckle from him. "The man who would love to kiss you."

Oh God, those words. She had brought Conrad to his knees over those words. She closed her eyes and tried to clear her head of the images that flooded her memory, trying to clear the nightmare she was experiencing now. But when she opened her eyes again, the apparition hadn't disappeared. It was no ghost. The man she was staring at was alive.

Her heart definitely pounding too hard, she whispered, "The price of a kiss is your life."

He released her arms and gently touched her lips with his.

"I'll gladly pay it."

Conrad glanced at his watch and back to Julia's face. Light was seeping into the room, lifting the shadows as the sun rose higher. He had five minutes before Stone would return. The timer on his watch gave him three to clear the house.

Julia's face was unreadable, her previous pain and shock veiled behind her unwavering gaze. She was sitting on the edge of the bed now, knees drawn up to her chest, hair spilling between her breasts and thighs as she hugged her legs. She was wearing a tight-fitting white T-shirt and a loose pair of men's boxer briefs that looked vaguely familiar.

Conrad raised an eyebrow. "You're wearing my underwear?"

"I didn't think you'd care since you were *dead*. Apparently, I was wrong on all counts. However, if you don't explain yourself this minute—and it better be one *hell* of an explanation—I will kill you right where you stand."

"Sheba, you've never killed anyone."

"First time for everything, Solomon."

He locked eyes with her, his humor fading. "I'll explain my actions later. I know you're confused right now, but I need you to trust me. I need your help."

Her full lips parted to let a bitter laugh escape. "Trust you? Trust is a gray area with you. I don't work in gray areas anymore. Put it in black and white. I want a clear-cut explanation." She dropped her legs and sat forward. "Why did you do it? Where have you been? And how in the world did you manage to get into Michael's house without alerting security?"

He smiled at her interrogation. She always, *always* had more questions than he was willing to answer. Glancing at his watch again, he rose from the chair. "You need to stay at your place tonight." He reached out to touch her, but let his hand drop to his side when she narrowed her eyes at him. "Expect me sometime after midnight. I'll explain everything then." He turned away from her, skirting the bed and heading for the door.

Her voice, barely more than an accusatory whisper, stopped him. "How could you? How could you do this to me?"

He hesitated for a moment as he stood in the doorway. That question he could easily answer. *Because I'm a mean son of a bitch.* Turning to look at her over his shoulder, he said, "This is bigger than you and me, Julia. You know I wouldn't have left you if it wasn't."

He reached inside his black leather jacket and pulled out a slim CD case. "I brought this for you." He tossed the case on the bed next to her. "Don't let anyone know you've seen me. Especially Stone."

Julia refused to acknowledge the gift or the demand. She watched Flynn's back pass through the doorway, and continued to stare at the empty space for several seconds. Her ears strained to hear his retreat from the second floor. There was nothing. *Confused?* That was too mild for what she was feeling.

Hurt, devastated, mad as hell.

Relieved. *He's alive.*

Oh yes, overwhelming relief. Dropping her head into her hands, she began to cry softly. A minute later she ran into the bathroom and retched over the sink.

Chapter Three

Michael carefully balanced a full mug of steaming Starbuck's French Roast in each hand as he climbed the carpeted stairs to the second floor. Thanks to the new Krups coffeemaker with a timer Abby had bought him, the coffee was freshly brewed every morning the minute he was ready for his shot of caffeine. This morning, he'd cut his shower short, shutting off the constant stream of unwanted thoughts about her, but the coffeepot was full enough he could still tweak out two cups. For now, he would force his mind to focus only on the next few minutes—coffee and the paper. *The Washington Post* and *The Wall Street Journal* were tucked neatly under his left arm.

He paused at the top of the stairs and listened for the sound of the shower in the master bath. Not hearing it, he continued down the hallway to the bedroom. Maybe Abby was still asleep. A smile touched his lips. Maybe he could slide between the sheets and wake her up before dealing with the reality waiting for both of them.

As he approached the room, his nose picked up a familiar but out-of-place smell over the scent of the coffee. He would have dwelled on it if the sight of the room's French doors, opened to admit the morning light, hadn't distracted him. Abby was sitting on the balcony, her back to him, her white shirt accenting the graceful arch of her shoulders above the black wrought-iron chair. Her lime green Sony Walkman laid on the matching glass and iron table, its ear buds lost under her brown hair. Abby and her music. She took it everywhere, usually with her iPod. Running, target practice, in bed at night, her iPod was as much a part of her as her right arm.

Michael paused for a moment at the threshold, enjoying the sight of her relaxing in the open air. He had worked hard to get her there. In his mind, he remembered the first time he'd led her to the balcony.

"Come look at the moonlight reflecting on the hills," he'd cajoled. It was a beautiful night and he had planned his seduction carefully. She had finally accepted an invitation to his house, but he knew she was only intrigued by that, by him. She was there because he'd been her friend, not because she wanted him as her lover.

"No." Shying away from him into the shadows of the bedroom, she saw the confusion on his face, and tried to explain. "I would be an easy target. *We* would be an easy target."

He'd mentally kicked himself for forgetting. Because of her past, she would never walk out on a second-story balcony to simply enjoy the moonlight. Not even in America. Not even with the security guard at the gate, the laser tripwires and motion detectors. And not even with the CIA's Director of Operations holding her. After what happened to her partner, it could be suicide.

Months later, even after Abby was reading his books, helping herself to his best wine and sharing his bed every night, she still avoided the balcony like a child avoiding an unlit hallway. Only in the past few weeks had she begun sitting outside with him, enjoying coffee and the paper in the fresh spring mornings, a shot of brandy or a quiet dance in the shadows of the Virginia nights. She had finally relaxed into the security of his house and the protectiveness of his arms.

He set the coffee cups down on the table and studied Abigail's face for a moment in the soft light. Her green eyes were closed, her focus tuned to the music she was listening to. She was pale this morning, and distracted. He couldn't remember one time in their relationship he'd entered a room without her knowledge.

He quietly slid a cup toward her and laid the *Post* next to it. Almost absently he noticed her bare arm under the glass top, her gun hanging loosely from her hand. His eyes did a double take. Snapping his head up, he stared past the open French doors and into his bedroom.

The smell. Abigail had fired her gun.

Julia knew the song Conrad had circled by heart. A year ago, she had listened to Sting's *A Thousand Years* echo inside her head long after she had taken the headphones off and thrown the CD in the trash.

In many ways, Julia was a prisoner of her mind. She had always been absorbed by thought. Analyzing details most people overlooked. The idiosyncrasy made her crazy sometimes—mystery novels, Clue, any Who Done It puzzle, was solved in a matter of minutes—but it also made her great at her job, whether behind a desk or in the field. She was good at troubleshooting, good at finding a common link and putting the pieces together. Good at figuring out who the bad guys were and more importantly how to nail them. She loved her job and had never sat back and watched the world go by.

But once in awhile, she needed to escape her left brain and enjoy her right. Music was the key in the lock that opened the door and freed her from overanalyzing everything—normal things other people didn't worry about.

She had ached for Conrad in the days and months after the explosion. She had begged the powers that existed to bring him back. Offered her soul to any devil who could raise him from the dead. *Just let me watch him sleep again. Hear him laugh. See his eyes peek at me over a hand of cards. Please.*

Wish granted. Conrad Flynn was alive. But he had betrayed her. Not a simple lie or a regrettable indiscretion. Those things she could forgive. No, Conrad's betrayal had sent her to hell.

And now Michael was sitting three feet away. She'd felt the slight tremor of the balcony as he'd approached the table and sat down. Keeping her eyes closed, she wondered how she could face him. The man who had reached down into hell and pulled her out. The man who had created a safe, relatively normal world for her. Michael's world. Comfortable and predictable, it was a fairytale world that offered vestiges of hope.

Under Julia's closed lids, Michael's face blurred into Con's.

Chapter Four

Scanning the sloping green hillside, Julia watched robins fluttering and hopping over the grass in search of their breakfast. The air was sweet with spring. Bringing her hand up, she laid the gun on the glass tabletop and pulled the ear buds out of her ears. Michael was sitting at the other end of the table, his newspaper and coffee untouched.

"What happened, Abby?" His blue-gray eyes watched her intently. He was always so calm, so rock-steady. Handsome. Kind. Patient. Everything she wanted in a man.

She shrugged and stared at the horizon. "Nightmare. When I woke up I thought someone was in the room. Remnants of the dream I guess. I apologize for the holes in the wall. I'll have them fixed immediately."

She glanced at him to see his reaction. He nodded, but his brow creased with a frown. "Are you all right?"

Am I? "I'm a little spooked." She stood and forced a smile. "I haven't had one like that in a long time."

Walking over to the balcony's railing, she rubbed the goose bumps on her arms before leaning her stomach against the parapet. She knew this would be the last morning she spent here.

What a shame. I was just starting to believe in Michael's world. She took a deep breath and closed her eyes, imprinting the beauty of the morning on her brain.

"Anything I can do for you?" Michael asked.

She turned and faced him. Concern etched his handsome face, a face that would still be handsome ten years down the road when Abigail Quinn was nothing more than a beautiful regret to him. God, he had done so much for her. She swallowed hard.

The balcony's tiles felt cool under her feet as she crossed to where he sat, crawling into his lap. She kissed him on the cheek and the clean scent of his aftershave filled her nose. "I'm all right," she whispered, laying her head on his shoulder.

Part of her actually meant it.

CIA Headquarters, Langley

Two hours later, the phone on her desk buzzed softly, interrupting her thoughts but not her concentration. Julia ignored it as she continued translating a satellite intercept of a phone conversation in French that had been picked up in the previous night's intelligence chatter. She was fluent in both Italian and French. Her German was passable, enough to buy a beer and find a public toilet. The phone conversation in her hands had been brief and on the surface made little sense, but was directly linked to the terrorist group she knew well. Translating the language was easy. The challenge lay in reading between the lines, peeling layers off the words. If Julia was right, Dr. Jean-Paul Bousset was back in business. He was producing and distributing biological agents to the Algerian GIA, the Armed Islamic Group, as well as another internationally wanted terrorist she'd been watching, Fayez Raissi.

The phone buzzed again. Her focus never leaving the paper, she pulled one ear bud out of her ear, pressed a button and picked it up. Susan Richmond, the CTC's director, was on the other end. "Abby, meet me in Director Stone's office, please."

Susan had been with the CIA for thirty-some years, working both in the field and at Langley in the intelligence and operations departments. She was one of the few people in the CTC who knew the story behind Abigail Quinn.

"I'll be right there."

Julia dropped the ear buds, stuck the transcript in her desk and started down the hall, the heels of her shoes soundless on the commercial blue carpet. Like most professionals, she could effectively compartmentalize her brain. On the balcony at Michael's house she had split off and shut down the part that wanted to dwell on Conrad. For today, she was Abigail Quinn and Abby had work to do. Julia Torrison would deal with Flynn tonight.

The door to Michael's office was closed. Knowing they were expecting her, Julia knocked softly and stuck her head in. The room was quiet except for the faint hum of the notebook computer sitting on the broad top of Michael's mahogany desk. He sat studying it, several files scattered nearby in front of him. His suit coat, discarded, Julia knew, the minute he'd walked through the door, hung nearby on a coat rack. The sleeves of his white shirt were rolled up to his elbows.

Susan was standing behind the desk, gazing out the window at the Agency's campus below. A tall woman at five foot ten inches, the CTC director was known for using her height to her advantage and always wore heels with her well-tailored suits. To level the playing field, she routinely told Julia with a wink. Her graying hair was cut in a short bob with bangs that accentuated her square face. It was a face Julia admired. This woman understood her, understood the seduction of playing spy. Susan had recruited her, had taken her through the Farm—the CIA's training camp—and sent her on her first tour in Paris.

Julia hesitated inside the doorway, the tension in the room prickling the hairs on the back of her neck. Michael glanced up and motioned her in.

"Abigail, have a seat." He stood and pointed to a chair facing his desk. His voice was neutral, his face expressionless. The two of them had agreed from the beginning to keep their personal relationship behind closed doors. Pragmatic discretion, Michael called it. There were rumors about them floating up and down the halls of the CIA headquarters, but they didn't lend credibility to them. They arrived at the office separately and left separately. There were no stolen moments together in his office, no shared lunches in the cafeteria. Everything here was strictly business.

Julia sat in the proffered chair and glanced from Michael to Susan. Something was off. Did they somehow know about Conrad? *This might be it,* she thought, taking a deep breath. *Time to decide which side of the fence I want to land on.*

Susan moved toward the desk and gave her a brief smile as she picked up a remote from Michael's desk. "Abby, we have digital video of a surveillance tape from Dulles Airport we want you to look at." She walked toward a TV/DVR unit on the room's west wall and pushed a button.

Julia let her gaze rest on Michael's face while Susan's back was turned. He avoided her look and resumed his seat. Julia turned toward the TV.

Susan stood off to the side. "This footage was taken two days ago as passengers were disembarking from an international flight that originated in London."

The footage was shot from an overhead camera angled down at a gate inside the airport. A solid stream of men and women with briefcases and carry-on luggage emerged from the gate and passed under the camera. Most seemed lost in thought and haggard from the flight. A few were impatient, pushing their way through the crowd but making little progress.

"What exactly am I looking for?" Julia asked.

Michael was watching her. "See if you recognize any of the passengers."

She stood and walked around to the end of the desk to get a closer look. She could feel Michael's gaze on her back. *Yep, they've caught him.*

In amongst the mostly British and American group, there was a smattering of other nationalities, although few were obvious. Turbans, veils or other distinguishing head coverings were all but absent. Fallout from 9/11.

Julia watched as a heavily bearded man tried to push forward with his sari-wrapped wife. Then she caught sight of another man's face weaving in and out behind them. Maybe it was the tilt of his head or the angle of his jaw that struck her as familiar. She leaned forward slightly, trying to pull the image in closer...

It wasn't Conrad. "Freeze it there, please."

Susan hit the pause button and the picture stopped. Julia frowned and studied the digital image of the man's profile. His sandy brown hair was longer than the last time she'd seen him and his eyes were covered with sunglasses, but there was little doubt in Julia's mind who he was. She almost let out an audible sigh of relief. "Smitty," she said under her breath.

Susan glanced at her and back to the paused picture. "Ryan Smith, your Chief of Station in Paris. If you remember, he disappeared four months ago, right after he took over as Chief of Operations/Europe."

Julia touched the face on the screen, a faint smile on her face. "Thank God he's alive."

Smitty had been much more than just her field coordinator when she was stationed in Paris. He had been her friend. During her first tour in Paris with Conrad, Smitty had been a junior case officer too. The three of them had sat in Smitty's small flat, playing poker and laughing for hours, sharing *corniottes,* warm cheese pastries and cognac. Three years later, when she and Con went back to Paris, Smitty had been given the COS position. There had still been evenings spent at Smitty's flat with a bottle of cognac between them, but things had changed. Smitty and Con were distant with each other, the easy camaraderie they had shared before strained. Ryan Smith was now the boss, the one enforcing the rules. Conrad didn't like rules.

On her last tour, the fatal one in Germany, Smitty left his post and flew to Luxembourg to pick her up. Instead of simply hustling her off on a plane for the States, he bought a ticket for himself as well and held her hand all the way back. That was it, just his hand over hers that gave her the lifeline she had so desperately needed to hold on to.

Julia dropped her hand to her side. "Has he made contact?"

"No." Michael let the word hang like a challenge in the silence of the room. "He hasn't made contact and we still have no explanation for his disappearance. He entered the country under an alias. We are assuming at this point he's AWOL."

Julia's stomach did a little flip. Ryan Smith AWOL from the CIA? Something was definitely off with that picture. Shaking her head, she looked at Michael. "I wouldn't jump to that conclusion." She turned back to the paused picture and squinted at it. "Look at him. Ryan Smith is a trained CIA operative. If he were AWOL and trying to avoid being seen, he would disguise himself. Sunglasses and a baseball cap isn't a disguise. Plus, he wouldn't enter the country via Dulles, which he knows is always under heavy surveillance. He doesn't care if you know he's here."

Susan and Michael exchanged a glance. "So why didn't he enter the country under his own name?" Michael countered. "Why wasn't he standing on my doorstep yesterday afternoon?"

Julia's mind was clicking through possibilities. "What was the last assignment he worked on? Could he be undercover?"

Michael let out a derisive laugh. "Undercover? For what?

27

He was Chief of Operations. He wasn't supposed to be working assignments, only overseeing the European COS operatives."

Julia's back stiffened instinctively in her friend's defense. *Smitty,* Conrad would have said, *always preferred to have his fingers in the pie.* What were the two of them up to? "Maybe one of his officers was involved in something too difficult," she offered. "Maybe Smitty was infiltrating or recruiting within an organization himself."

Michael shook his head. "We can't know for sure what he's up to at this point, but there's still too many unanswered questions. He's been out of contact with me for four months. He's now entered the States, unharmed and of his own free will, but fails to come in and tell me what's going on. In my book, that makes him a rogue agent."

Julia let out a sigh and resumed her seat. Susan was staring at the frozen picture. "We think it's possible he may contact you, Abby."

He better. If he doesn't, I'll hunt him down. "Why?"

"You tell us." Michael steepled his fingers under his chin. "You know him as well, if not better, than we do."

She held Michael's gaze, unnerved by the look on his face. Was her previous relationship with Smitty now suspect? *Michael thinks I'm the Agency mole.* The thought struck her mind with such force she felt like she'd been physically slapped. Her voice was harsh. "Ryan Smith is one of the best chiefs you've had in Europe over the past ten years. You owe him the benefit of the doubt to believe for now that his intentions are true to the Agency." She paused, scanning Michael's face. "As for me, if you think I'm the mole in your department, then say it straight out."

Michael leaned back in his chair and crossed his arms over his chest, studying her. Susan stepped forward. "Our European operations have been severely compromised, Abby. Probably from within Langley and quite possibly in conjunction with a field officer such as Agent Smith. Michael and I aren't accusing you of anything..." *yet* hung in her pause, "...but the timing of your return to this office and your past working relationship with him may suggest collusion to people outside this room."

Julia shifted her attention to the desk but otherwise remained completely still. It was part of the drill. Show no emotion, even when your pulse was racing. Underneath the façade, her mind was spinning and her feelings were hurt. She had whored herself for her country for the better part of eight years and basically no one knew or cared. The average American citizen took his liberties for granted and rarely wondered who exactly was keeping those liberties available. Now the two people she thought did care, the two she trusted and whom she believed trusted her, were accusing her of turning traitor.

Susan shot a look at her boss before continuing. "You'll have to take a polygraph, Abby," she said softly, "and then we'll go from there." Michael nodded his consent.

Julia continued to stare at the desktop. What they had proposed was completely logical. Reasonable. But how could Michael, after all they had shared, even suggest she was a mole? That she had committed treason? She looked up, searching his eyes, his face for a sign. Anything that would tell her he knew her, knew she'd never betray him.

The eyes she loved, gone steel gray now, refused to offer her comfort. "Susan, would you give me a minute alone with Abigail, please?"

The CTC chief hesitated, and then laying the remote on Michael's desk, she nodded and exited the room. Julia listened for the soft click of the door before gripping the arms of the chair and leaning forward. "Are you serious, *Director*? After everything I've done for this Agency and my country, you think a freaking polygraph is going to prove anything?"

He didn't move, refused to back down. "The polygraph is to cover your ass. Ryan Smith was your friend as well as your immediate supervisor. You are suddenly a convenient solution to the identity of the CIA's mole because of that. Everyone from the Director of Central Intelligence on down is looking for a scapegoat before this situation comes before Congress and the President. If we don't immediately eliminate you as a suspect, you will be crucified."

"I don't care what anyone else thinks, how could *you* believe I was the mole? My car and my apartment are bugged, my phone is tapped." Her voice was brittle with exasperation. "How could I secretly give out information when you keep me under your thumb day *and night*?"

The emphasis on the last two words weren't lost on Michael, but her meaning was. "Who's bugged your apartment and car?"

The corners of her eyes narrowed a millimeter. "You. The CIA. You've been listening to me for the past year and a half."

"I've never given any directive to have your residence or car bugged."

Sitting back in her chair, she was silent for a moment. "Who else besides the Agency would want to know what I was up to?"

"Ryan Smith possibly?" he asked, and then shook his head. "I don't know, Ab, but we'll find out. Why would you think it was me?"

"Come on, Michael, suspicion is part of your job. What you knew about me when I came out of the field was summarized in a couple of paragraphs in my Agency bio. I had to prove myself to you. I figured you were nervous about me so you had my place bugged. I left it all alone, hoping, I guess, that you would realize I was trustworthy."

"Any idea who might have done it?"

"If it isn't the Agency, I have no clue. I figured it was all part of your plan for Abigail Quinn..."

Michael frowned and pointed a finger at her. "I've never kept you under my thumb. Your work requires you to be in my department. You sleep in my bed because you want to."

The words stung, but they were true. Pushing herself out of the chair, Julia walked over to the TV and stared at Ryan Smith's frozen face again. His last warning resounded in her head. "Don't let Stone get close to you. He's a user, Julia. He's dangerous. Watch your back around him."

She'd held on to him, in essence clinging to her last link with Conrad. Smitty had pulled away and given her cheek a gentle pat. "You're going to be okay," he whispered, smiling his best lopsided grin. Then he was gone, disappearing into the menagerie of travelers in the crowded airport.

Julia heeded Smitty's words for nearly a year. She hadn't wanted a relationship with anyone, much less the Director of Operations. She had ignored his gazes that lingered a few seconds too long, turned away his casual offers of dinner or coffee, and kept herself in the background of the CTC office, doing her damnedest to imitate wallpaper.

But she had been so lonely after the grief had run its course. Michael had been the one to convince her that she wasn't the cause of Conrad's death. That she was no longer a target. That she could quit hiding in the shadows of her past. Piece by piece he worked his magic, putting the broken pieces of her world back together and making it solid again.

She started to believe him and found herself hungry for human touch. She looked forward to seeing him at work, began returning his gaze even when it sent a shiver down her spine. She sought him out to discuss information that came across her desk and he listened because he knew her time in the field with Conrad gave her an edge over the other analysts. She didn't just analyze the terrorists. She had walked where they walked, slept where they slept, watched their every move.

But now he was accusing her of being one.

The wave of her past crushed her under its weight. Michael sat in silence, watching her. *Let it go,* she told herself. *Stop feeling. Analyze, like Susan taught you to.*

Something was missing. Random pieces of the puzzle were there but nothing fit. Con was alive, Smitty had returned, and an unknown entity was eavesdropping on her. The picture wasn't complete...

She looked Michael in the eye. "Can I see the rest of this video?"

He nodded and she started the video rolling again. She scanned every face, watched every mannerism that could be picked up in the few seconds each passenger was on the screen.

Third from the last passenger, her breath caught in her throat. He was there and gone in an instant, his head tilted away from the camera. The disguise was good, but she had seen it before in Paris when he was recruiting a field asset. Just like then, his hair was dyed a rich black, his skin bronzed by tanning cream, and the beard and mustache were trimmed close to his jaw.

"Shit." The word was out of her mouth before she could stop it.

Susan Richmond picked up the telephone receiver at Abigail's desk and punched in a seven-digit code. She remembered the rage she'd seen in her top analyst's stiff posture. In a way it was difficult for her to push Abigail. She had once held strong feelings for her fledgling pupil and Susan knew she was innocent of betraying the Agency. But there was too much at stake these days. Any misguided feelings for Abigail could ruin her own position in the Agency and all that she had worked for. Abby was a pawn, just like a handful of others. Nothing more, nothing less.

When she heard the dial tone signaling she had reached an outside line, Susan carefully entered the number of a pager. Once connected to the paging service, she entered another seven-digit code comprised only of successive number threes, a simple signal to another pawn in her game: Operation Sheba was in motion.

A decoy. Con had used Smitty to take away any scrutiny of himself from those doing surveillance of the international flights. Julia felt like slapping her forehead. It was just the kind of thing he would do. *Insurance*, he would have said, *just in case the disguise isn't quite enough.*

The insurance policy had worked. Someone was on their toes enough to pick out Smitty and pass the tape along to Susan and Michael. With everyone's attention focused on Ryan, Conrad had passed right under their noses.

"What is it, Abby?"

Michael's voice made her jump. *Not what, Michael. Who.* She took a breath and forced her fingers to release their grip on the edge of his desk. Should she give Conrad up? After the hell he had put her through, it would serve him right...but what about Smitty? By giving Con up, would she somehow endanger Smitty too? She couldn't take the chance. At this point, she didn't know who was holding the cards.

And no matter what the two agents were up to, she still cared about both of them. She couldn't give them up.

"It's nothing." She refused to meet Michael's gaze. "I was hoping the video might offer something more, some explanation for this, but it doesn't."

"Do you have any idea what Smith is up to?"

Julia paced the floor of Michael's office for a minute, buying herself time, buying them all a little time. "All of the operatives and agents who were compromised in the past couple of years were in the European directorate, right?"

Michael nodded and began doodling on a piece of paper in front of him.

"So, counting Flynn, Ryan Smith lost five human assets in

less than two years, probably all due to the Agency's mole." Hands on her hips, she paced back to the office door where she paused. "Honestly, Michael, Smitty is one of the most dedicated operatives I've ever known. Dedicated to the cause and dedicated to his people. I'm sure he would take every loss as a personal hit against him. And I know he would never do anything to compromise his assets in the field. In fact he'd do just the opposite." She turned back to face Michael.

He raised his gaze to her. "Best guess?"

"Ryan Smith is tracking down your mole."

Chapter Five

Arlington

"I don't know, Conman. Do you really think this is going to work?" Smitty eyed Flynn with a mixture of humor and apprehension as they stood together in the hallway studying their handiwork. Artfully arranging flowers in a vase was more difficult than either man had imagined.

"Hell no," Conrad said, plucking at the drooping head of a tulip. "I'm going to spend the rest of my life making it up to her, but maybe flowers and dinner will take the edge off her anger so she'll at least listen to us tonight."

"She loves us, and besides, Julia doesn't hold grudges."

"Are we talking about the same woman? About five-four." Conrad held his hand up to his chin. "Hardheaded, fanatical about right and wrong. Thinks Martha Stewart should run for President?"

"It's Oprah for President. And, politics aside, she does love us."

Conrad patted Smitty's back. "You go with that. But I got a bottle of Glenlivet that says she'll hold this one against us until we die."

Julia's one-bedroom apartment was on the ground floor of the building complex. The rooms were small and tidy. Nothing in the sink besides her "I'd rather be in Paris" coffee mug. No dust on the furniture. A couple of power suits in the closet next to an array of brightly colored T-shirts and skirts, a collection of jeans. There was a flat-screen TV in the living room, but only one framed picture on her nightstand by the bed of her and her younger brother. There were cans of diet Pepsi in the refrigerator alongside a half-empty bottle of Pinot Grigio and a selection of expensive cheeses.

To Flynn the small apartment exuded Julia: a bottle of *Le Jardin* lotion in the bathroom and a collection of lipsticks from all over Europe lined up like army soldiers on the vanity, a book of Rumi poetry beside her bed, her red duffel bag—a survival kit of sorts—packed and ready to go in the bottom of her closet next to an assortment of Prada high heels and Puma sneakers.

"I'll be glad to see her. What time do you think she'll get here?" Smitty glanced at his watch. It was nearing five o'clock.

Flynn gave up on the flowers and shrugged. "She may not show at all, but she isn't expecting me until after midnight." He started down the hallway toward the kitchen.

"She'll show." Smitty followed him. "If for no other reason than to kick your ass."

Flynn stopped and placed a hand over the crotch of his button-fly jeans. "It's not my ass I'm worried about."

The two men exchanged a grin.

Julia pulled the pearl white Audi into the parking lot of the Borderline Bar and Grill and tapped her fingers on the steering wheel. She'd been toying with the idea ever since she'd left Michael's office that morning.

There was little doubt that even if Susan and Michael believed that she wasn't conspiring with Ryan Smith, they were having her followed and watched by the CIA's Office of Security. If Smitty or Conrad attempted to contact her tonight, they would be arrested. She didn't want that. Not before she knew why Con had faked his death only to show up again on her doorstep and why Smitty was helping him.

Then there was the issue of the other guys, the ones who had bugged her apartment. She had yet to tip her hand where they were concerned. For the time being she wanted to leave the bugs alone, so it would not be wise for her and Con to discuss anything inside her apartment.

Julia watched her rearview mirror for signs she was being followed. Checking over her shoulder had been second nature for years, but she had become less vigilant about it since returning to America. In the Land of the Free, she'd become one of the brave, or careless, as Con would say, again.

Assured no one was following her, Julia stepped out of the car and locked it before entering the bar.

Smoke hung lazily above the patrons' heads as their voices buzzed over the voice of Kenny Chesney crooning from a jukebox in the corner. The after-five crowd, wearing faded jeans, ratty T-shirts and leather boots, was off to a good start on the evening's drunkfest. Julia scanned the male faces that turned her way as she walked to the back of the bar. No one looked familiar and, outside of a few who ogled her, none appeared particularly threatening. She stuck her hand inside her purse looking for coins and felt the cool handle of her SIG Sauer P229R. Lighter than the Beretta, it was easier to carry and it could still do significant damage to anyone who got too close wanting to do her harm.

Of course, Conrad was right, she'd never killed anyone and she prayed she never had to. But she was CIA trained and still completed five hours of firearm training every week out of diligence to her previous life. She was more likely to shoot to injure but she could kill if necessary.

Two pay phones hung on the wall near the restroom doors. A stained and tattered piece of paper was taped to one of the phones, announcing it was out of order. No doubt had been for years. She would have used her cell phone, but couldn't take the chance anyone might pick up her conversation. Standing off to the side of the working phone, Julia glanced again at the men at the bar. Most had gone back to their glasses of beer, complaining about their wives or discussing sports. Dropping two coins in the phone, Julia dialed a number she had last used a lifetime ago.

Two rings and she was connected. "Ace's Mortuary," answered one of Conrad's favorite access agents. "You stab 'em, we'll slab 'em."

"Did you know he was alive?" she asked over the background noise. Her pulse was pounding viciously as she waited for the answer she didn't actually want to hear. There was a long pause and she knew Ace was trying to place her voice and put what she was asking in context.

"I take it you've seen him?" His question answering hers.

She grazed a finger over the buttons of the phone and tried to keep her voice from giving away the ecstatic relief and unbelievable hurt swirling around inside her heart. "He paid me a casual visit this morning."

"Casual?" Ace chuckled in her ear. "You ask me, wasn't

ever anything casual between Solomon and his queen."

Julia turned slightly and partially covered her mouth with a hand, keeping the bar patrons in her peripheral vision while blocking any spying eyes from reading her lips. "Can you get a message to him?"

"No guarantees, but for you, Sheba, I'll give it my best shot."

Julia knew Ace would dial Conrad's number the moment she hung up. If there was anything about Ace that Conrad loved more than his ability to land Knicks tickets on a moment's notice, it was his unquestioning loyalty. "The Queen of Sheba is being guarded closely. He should not, I repeat *not*, pay her a visit tonight."

A long pause. "Nothing else?"

She took a deep breath and let it out slowly. Oh yes, there was so much else. *Tell him I hate him for his lie. That I'll never forgive him. That I...that I missed him. That, God help me, I'm so glad he's still alive...*

"No. Nothing else." She surveyed the room again. A different man had slipped into the room and bellied up to the bar, his silver hair and crisp blue jeans looking oddly out of place with the rest of the patrons. Julia felt a twitch of fear in her gut. "Take care, Ace," she said into the phone.

"Ditto, Queen."

She hung up and stood for a moment watching the silver-haired man. He didn't look her way, but she could sense his hyperawareness. Was he a tail? Only one way to find out.

Several men at the bar leered at her as she walked past, offering a beer or a pinch on her ass. The silver-haired man continued to ignore her. Pushing through the bar's door, Julia fought the urge to run. Even if he was a tail from the Office of Security, he presented no real danger to her. She hadn't done anything wrong. All she had to do was act normal.

She slid behind the wheel of the Audi, locked her doors and started the engine. Taking a deep breath, she let it out slowly to calm her nerves and tried to recall the way the parking lot had looked before she went into the bar. Which car or truck was new? The red Honda? The Chevy Bronco? She scanned the area, but no matter how hard she tried, she couldn't remember. *Your apprentice has lost her edge, Con. Slipping big time.*

Shaking her head, she put the car in drive and bumped her

way out of the parking lot, watching her rearview mirror. It wasn't until she was on the highway that she noticed the Audi's hood bobbing slightly. Julia slapped the steering wheel. The Audi was nearing 180,000 miles and the metal release latch hidden in the grill had been loose for several months. An errant pothole or train track sometimes shook the latch enough to spring the hood.

Julia took the first off-ramp and pulled into the parking lot of a gas station. She sat for several minutes scanning the traffic passing by. When there was no sign of a tail, she got out of the car and raised the hood, keeping one eye on the cars entering the parking lot. There was no such thing as being a little paranoid and all of Julia's senses were on alert. She did a thorough check of the engine, and once she deemed it was clean, she slammed the lid and dropped to her hands and knees to examine the underbelly of the car. Again, nothing unusual. Standing up, she walked around the car, running her hands in the wheel wells and the undersides of the bumpers looking for tracking devices. All she came up with was a dirty hand. Sinking back into the Audi's driver seat, she found her antiseptic hand gel and cleaned up as best she could. Then she let out a deep sigh. *What a way to live,* she thought. And then, *This is all Con's fault, the dirty rotten sneak.*

The message light was blinking. Conrad pushed the play button.

"An old and dear friend of yours asked me to give you a message," Ace's voice said. "It goes like this: The Queen of Sheba is being guarded closely. You should not, repeat *not*, pay her a visit tonight. End of message." There was a slight pause. "Man, she's pissed. I wish you luck, bro."

The line went dead and Flynn stood staring at the phone with his hands on his hips.

Nice try, Jules. Like the Great Conrad Flynn couldn't outsmart whatever surveillance and security the Agency could throw at him.

He left his apartment, locking the door, and sauntered down the hall to Julia's place.

Hell, he smiled to himself, he already had.

She couldn't believe she was standing here. Keys out,

poised to unlock the door. What the devil was she thinking?

Oh, come on, Julia, her inner voice cajoled. *You loved him, still love him, why wouldn't you stay at your apartment tonight and wait for him just in case he does show up?*

She leaned her forehead against the door. *Because by faking his own death, he nearly killed me too. Because if he could do that to me, I don't want to be with him.* She racked her brain for more. *Because now there's Michael.*

Michael. Conrad. Two very different men, and yet, on some level, the same. Both were puzzles she couldn't completely figure out. Both were men she loved, respected.

Just not the same way.

Julia slid the key into the lock and let herself into the apartment.

She stopped short at the sight of her favorite flowers, red and white tulips, overflowing from a glass vase on the diminutive entryway table. She was confused and alert at the same time. Assassins and terrorists rarely announced their presence with flowers, but then again some were very resourceful...

Ex-lovers, even more.

Considering her options, she brought out the SIG. It wouldn't hurt to be prepared. And it certainly wouldn't hurt to scare the heck out of whomever it was—*the dirty rotten sneak—* just for good measure.

Slipping her heels off, she dropped her purse quietly to the floor. Standing motionless, her back against the wall, she slowed her uneven breathing and listened. The unobtrusive clink of silverware met her ears. The aroma of sautéing onions wafted past her nose.

Yep, ex-lover.

Gun at her side, she walked soundlessly down the hall feeling pissed off and relieved at the same time. She passed the living room and bedroom. It didn't surprise her Con had gotten in—he'd gotten into Michael's house without so much as breaking a sweat and she had to find out how he did that—but she hoped he'd been diligent enough to scan the apartment for bugs before he'd announced his presence.

She stopped in the kitchen doorway, scanning the room. Place settings for three had been squeezed onto her small dinette table. A single red tulip sat spotlighted under the low-hanging lamp. Con was at the stove, pushing chopped onion and mushrooms around in a frying pan. The blood red color of his Iowa State University sweatshirt matched the New York strips lying on the counter nearby.

Ryan Smith, in his standard polo shirt and chinos, was standing across from the sink, pouring wine into glasses. He looked up when she took a hesitant step forward and flashed her a big smile. "Welcome home, Sheba." He walked toward her, offering one of the glasses. "How was your day at work? Kick any terrorist butt?"

And just like that, Julia Torrison was back.

Chapter Six

Langley

Michael closed Smith's personnel file and threw it on top of Flynn's. He rubbed his eyes and swiveled his chair to look outside. Darkness was falling and he wished he could to say to hell with it all and go home. Branches of the nearby pin oaks bowed effortlessly with the wind as if waving him away.

He didn't really want to go home though—Abby wouldn't be there. Funny how fast he'd gotten used to her presence, how fast she had turned his home into hers. Unlike the other women he'd known, Abigail hadn't forced herself into his life. She hadn't been looking for the perfect man to hang on her arm and show off to her friends while she privately criticized his long hours at the office and nagged him relentlessly to give up confidential information on his network of spies.

Spies, always a double-edged sword. He turned back to his desk, his fingers toying with the manila file folder still unopened. Julia Torrison, aka Abigail Quinn. He knew the information contained in the file by heart, but he opened and scanned the highlights of her Agency bio again.

JULIA MARIE TORRISON
SEX/F
RAC/W
POB/ILLINOIS
DOB/060177
HGT/5'4"
WGT/125
EYE/GRE

HAI/BROWN
LV/APT
TWN/ARLING
ST/VA
EDU/BA-SYR UNIV
LANG/FLUENT ITAL-FREN
POSTGRAD/NO
OCC/INTELANALYST-CIA

A more reader-friendly report, updated the previous year, followed...

Torrison is single with no children. Lives alone. Psychological profile is negative, but shows she is prone to taking risks and harbors resentment toward those in authority. Agency indicators reveal that Torrison is a high analytic and excels working with ideas and data, but forms strong attachments to those few she does befriend.

Father is unknown. Mother Valerie (Torrison) Valhuis died in 1995 due to breast cancer. Stepfather James Valhuis remarried in 1997 and currently resides in Austin, TX. Brother Eric Valhuis currently resides in Baltimore, MD with his wife and two children.

Her career with the CIA was revealed in general terms. *Beginning as an intelligence analyst out of college, Torrison requested and was granted a transfer to field operations several years later. Torrison received multiple commendations for work in the field under COS Ryan Smith.*

Minute details concerning her level of involvement in operations were scant. *Torrison served in Europe between 2001-2006, working legitimately as a translator at three different U.S. embassies while also conducting surveillance and other covert operations with Conrad Flynn.*

Besides her proficient language abilities, Torrison is highly skilled in computer technology and bomb making.

Michael smiled to himself. Bomb making was indeed an interesting skill to have on your résumé.

Her last official tour as a case officer ended in Berlin, Germany, in September 2006, when Flynn's cover was blown and he was killed in a job-related accident.

Deputy Director of Operations, Michael Stone, requested

Torrison to return to the U.S. and resume duties at CIA headquarters in Langley in the Counterterrorism Center. Due to the circumstances surrounding her last assignment, a change of identity was initiated.

Between him and Susan, they had transformed Julia Torrison into Abigail Quinn. And since that time, they'd lost four more agents. There was no doubt in Michael's mind they were as dead as Flynn.

Rubbing his eyes, he closed the file and quietly thanked God Susan had had the foresight to pull Julia out of the field. Swiveling his chair, he watched the trees bend in the wind again. Images of Conrad and Julia swirled in his brain.

"What are you thinking about?" he'd asked her as they shared a lounge chair on the back deck of his house. The day was Abby's thirtieth birthday and that was how she wanted to end it, there, alone with him, enjoying the fading colors of the sunset. Several birch logs popped and cracked in the fire kettle while the songs of crickets and frogs rose and fell in the night.

She hadn't answered immediately, sifting carefully, he was sure, through the memory in her head. She'd stared down at their legs, his perfectly outlining hers, and traced the edge where skin met skin. Her face was partially hidden from his view.

"Isolation," she murmured.

He'd taken his turn at being quiet. Agency interpreters long ago had classified the woman in his arms as a high analytic with a corresponding high level of introversion. She craved solitude, preferred to work alone, and sought companionship on a one-on-one basis. A lone wolf to whom isolation was comfortable. Even then, Michael knew their conversation was somehow linked to a past that hung in the shadows of their relationship. He'd rested a hand on her stomach and waited for her to continue.

"Isolation and Interrogation is where it really started for me," she told him. "My training leader at the Farm thought he would get me to confess to the usual list of false crimes, conspiracy and espionage particularly, the way he had everyone else in the class up to that point."

She'd paused for a moment and he'd felt her sadness enveloping them. "The first twenty-four hours he left me in a cell with nothing but a pot to pee in. Isolation, however, didn't bother me. When he came back after the first day and told me to confess, I laughed at him.

"But of course, he was smart. He went back and read my file more thoroughly and figured out the way to break me was to overwhelm me with social interaction instead. So he began sending small groups of soldiers into the cell to verbally accost me. Every few hours a fresh set would enter the room, corner me and get in my face. They screamed at me, sang to me, told me vulgar jokes. Another twenty-four hours passed without a moment's peace."

She'd sighed and he'd caressed strands of her hair lying on his chest, sending her silent encouragement through the stroke of his fingertips.

"About four o'clock in the morning, my leader sent the last group of soldiers out of the cell and went for the confession again."

Sitting up, she'd pulled away from Michael and brought her knees to her chest. "He'd broken me, but he didn't know it. When he told me to confess, I didn't react at all. So he moved in closer.

"I didn't acknowledge he was there, mostly because my brain was fried. He decided to force a confession out of me. He pushed me up against the wall, pinned my arms at my sides, and whispered in my ear..."

Leaning forward, Michael slipped his arms around her waist and buried his face in her hair. "What did he say?"

She'd struggled to keep emotion out of her voice, but Michael heard it anyway. "He said, 'I would love to kiss you.'"

He couldn't miss the humor, but he still had stiffened at the inappropriate behavior of the trainer. "He made a pass at you?"

Abby had nodded. "Since he was in such close proximity to me, he left himself open to my knee and I drove his balls about six inches into his body. His sudden physical contact had sent me right over the edge. The proverbial straw that broke the camel's back, I suppose. He stayed standing for a couple of seconds, but then went down to his knees, and as he did, I pulled his gun out of his waistband and pointed it at his head.

"'The price of a kiss is your life,' I told him. I honestly thought about pulling that trigger too, but at the last second I threw the gun on the ground instead. I like to believe I never would have pulled the trigger, no matter how strung out I was."

Her fingers had combed through her hair. "Of course, that effectively ended the training session and landed me a thorough psych evaluation."

Michael hadn't tried to stop the slow rumble of laughter erupting from deep in his stomach. "Jesus, I bet he was pissed."

Abigail had laughed too. "He was and I knew enough about him to be scared shitless once my brain was functioning normally again. He had been a Navy SEAL, an SAS trainer for the Agency and a CIA operator in Germany for a year before they rotated him back to the Farm to train recruits. Susan said he was the best and she liked pulling him in to train whenever she could. Embarrassing him like that in front of his fellow trainers and the class wasn't my best move. He passed me anyway."

"Did you ever grant him his wish, let him kiss you?"

She'd nodded and understanding dawned on him. He couldn't help but ask, "Who was it?"

A spark from the fire had caught Michael's attention as it was lifted into the dark by the wind. "Conrad Flynn," she'd answered.

"You had no right to screw with my life, Flynn."

Conrad watched her carefully, felt his pulse beating a tad faster than he wanted it to as his gaze slid over her in a quick inventory. God, he just wanted to stand there and soak her up. Wisps of chestnut brown curls framed her face and lay on the shoulders of her double-breasted jacket. The blush-pink suit accentuated the delicate curves of her body. Her toenails sported deep bubble gum pink polish. He swallowed hard, forcing his gaze back to hers.

The words had been said with no emotion, just a statement of fact from the Queen of Reason. Her face was expressionless, her eyes guarded. As always, an excellent poker player.

But she was holding her gun, finger on the trigger. A personal tic that betrayed her feelings. Flynn shifted his weight, fought the urge to step back. *At least the gun isn't pointed at me...yet.*

He turned the stove burner off and took a deep breath. "You're right, Julia. It was a terrible thing to do to you, and I've regretted it from the minute I set off the detonator. But then it was too late. Smitty and I had set the plan in motion and I had to follow through. Now we're here to explain what happened, what *is* happening." He pleaded with her. "Give me a chance. Then you can decide whether or not to forgive me."

Belying the anger Conrad knew was boiling in her veins, Julia took a casual sip of the merlot from her glass and set the glass on the counter. "I assume you found and neutralized the bugs."

"Actually," Smitty said sheepishly behind her, "we're the ones who did the bugging."

Flynn saw her cool slip a notch, saw the slight narrowing of her eyes, the almost imperceptible twitch of her hand. Shit, she was going to shoot them both...

"Okay." She turned away and paused for a moment to let her attention sweep over the carefully dressed table. "I'm going to my room to change clothes and decide whether or not I'm going to listen to your explanation." She glanced back over her shoulder at Conrad. "Don't overcook my steak."

Julia sat on the bed in her underwear and bra staring at the open closet. A T-shirt and a pair of faded blue jeans lay in her lap but she made no move to put them on. Her fingers played with the frayed fabric of one of the pant cuffs as her mind attempted to sort through the implications of the day's events.

Conrad and Smitty had set up an elaborate scheme, one that had effectively ripped her world apart and set her on a reactionary course. She had run, with Smitty's help, back to the safety of America, back to the CIA, and had adjusted to a new life. Only now, Con and Smitty had reappeared to rip this world apart too.

They had accessed her apartment, bugged it and her car, wired her phone, and probably even followed her around whenever it suited their purpose—whatever that was. They knew everything she'd done in the past year and a half.

Man, talk about slipping, I never knew they were here.

Having grown up with an abusive stepfather, Julia had learned at a young age the cost of showing emotion. Emotions were not to be trusted. Emotions got you another punch from a hard fist. Instead she learned to tap down the emotions so she could analyze and control the situation in her favor. She tried to focus on outcomes. She always had a choice. It just depended on what outcome she wanted.

The red duffel bag on the closet floor was packed. She could grab it and run. Running away always appealed to the ten-year-old inside her. The seduction of becoming someone else, living someone else's life. Unfortunately she was on that path now, pretending to be Abigail Quinn. Abby had a comfortable life, but the truth was Julia wasn't sure she wanted to be Abby anymore, and she definitely didn't want to be on the run for the rest of her life.

She looked at the phone on her nightstand. She could end this before it went any further. Offer up Flynn and Smith like a sacrifice at the altar of Michael Stone to prove her worthiness. She actually owed the rogue agents nothing—they had used her, of that she was certain. They hadn't trusted her with the details of their scheme, and now they were jeopardizing her place in the Agency, her relationship with a man who respected her and cared about her. Were they truly her friends? It didn't seem like it.

And if Michael was right, it was possible she would be used as a scapegoat for the CIA. All her passion and devotion to her country easily reduced to dust and swept under the rug while she was made an example of what the CIA did to traitors in the post 9/11 world.

A shiver ran up her spine. She lifted the handset off the base and hit the first speed dial button.

Chapter Seven

Smith saw the tiny green in-use button light up out of the corner of his eye. He moved toward the phone hanging on the wall by the refrigerator. "Darn it." He slapped the wall next to the phone and looked at Conrad. "I knew I should have disabled the phones."

Conrad shook his head and eyed the steaks. "You watch these and I'll handle it."

"Who do you think she's calling?"

"Who else?" He sprinted toward the front door.

Michael answered the phone. "Director Stone."

"It's me," Julia said.

There was a pause. "What's up? You okay?"

Julia slumped down on the floor near the nightstand, resting her back against the wall. "No. Not really. I left things kind of...up in the air with you today. I want to apologize. I know you're doing what you think is right. Trusting me has to be hard for you."

A longer pause. "Abby, you must know by now that I trust you. I wouldn't be involved with you if I didn't."

Julia shook her head at the empty room. "I don't deserve your trust, Michael."

A heavy sigh. "We've been down this road before. We've both done things in our past we aren't proud of. Quit beating yourself up and worrying about stuff that happened before you came back to the States. Today counts. Our future together counts. This is just a bump in the road. We'll get past it."

Cradling the phone between her ear and shoulder, Julia

twisted the wide silver band around the middle finger of her right hand. A future with Michael. That was an enticing dream, wasn't it? A nice, normal life with a man who loved her. A man who knew about her past and wanted her anyway.

If only it could be that simple. If only she wasn't still in love with her ex-partner.

"Don't you remember last summer at the lake with Tom and Liz?" Defiance masked her fear. Bravado was such a nice defense. "That's what life with me is like, Michael. You don't want that kind of future."

Tom and Liz Scofield were friends of Michael's. He and Tom had known each other since their Corps days. Tom had become a family practitioner, meeting Liz along the way to conquering the American dream.

Now in their late thirties, Michael and Tom enjoyed sharing a drink and a cigar while they idealized Marine recon stories on board Tom's boat. Michael had brought Julia to meet Tom and Liz and take a sail around the lake the previous July.

She had dodged Liz's questions about her past and her relationship with Michael. She'd even managed to sound knowledgeable about HMOs and pharmaceutical companies during the hour-long ride. But when Liz pulled out a camera and began snapping pictures of her, she'd balked and abruptly left them all standing in an awkward silence.

Michael had sought her out below deck in the tiny galley. Julia remembered his words. "You aren't Julia Torrison anymore. You don't have to hide. No one is going to see those pictures besides the four of us. You're not in any danger from my friends."

That's when she realized Michael would never understand. Paranoia had been drilled in her by the best spy in the business. No pictures, period. The point was non-negotiable.

Julia twisted the ring again and scanned the bedroom with unseeing eyes. Poor Michael. Nothing like having your girlfriend freak out in front of your friends over having her picture taken. But he was always willing to exonerate her, even at his own expense.

Movement by the door caught her attention and she looked up to find Conrad standing in the doorway with her purse and shoes in his hands. Their eyes locked for a second and then he let his gaze roam over her nearly naked body. She felt herself blush, even as her heart ached for him.

Conrad tore his ogling gaze away and walked into the room. Holy God, he hadn't expected her to be sitting on the floor in nothing but a lacy bra and matching panties. Pink, no less, just like her suit and toenails. And he hadn't expected to have to tamp down the flood of testosterone suddenly coursing through his body.

He dropped the purse on the bed and sauntered over to set the shoes inside the closet next to her signature red duffel. He knew she was keeping some of her clothes at Stone's house these days, but she'd always left the duffel. She didn't take that with her because she felt safe with Stone.

Why not? he asked himself. What had he thought? That Julia would simply stop living, turn into a nun, if he wasn't around anymore? That she wouldn't find someone else— someone who appeared honest and trustworthy—to take his place? Christ, he couldn't stand the thought of her with Stone. To Julia and the rest of the world, the man's picture was next to *valor, honor* and *hero* in the dictionary. Only Conrad and Smitty knew the truth.

He turned away from the closet.

Julia's gaze, naked now with pain and longing, was on him. He walked over to her and held out his hand.

"I take it you haven't heard from Ryan Smith." Michael's voice sounded distant as blood roared in Julia's ears.

She reached out and put her hand in Con's, the familiar rough warmth sending electrical pulses up her arm. He pulled her to her feet. "No," she lied, the words spilling easily out of her lips as she searched Con's eyes. "I haven't heard from him."

"I'll be leaving here in about twenty minutes. Are you sure you don't want me to swing by and pick you up? It would give us a chance to talk about all this and come up with some ideas."

Conrad was touching her now. His fingers in her hair, caressing her shoulder, touching her hip. Even though she longed to give in, she pulled back instead, dragging in a shuddering breath and shaking her head at him.

"Not tonight, Michael. If I think of anything important, I'll call you."

She could feel his disappointment through the phone line. "All right. I'm here if you need me, Abby."

"Good night," she said as Conrad lifted the phone out of her hand and placed it back in the base. He pulled her into his arms, bringing his lips down to hers, and this time she didn't pull away.

The plates were pushed aside and they were starting the second bottle of wine. A Dave Matthews Band CD played in the background as the three kept their voices low over the dimly lit table.

Julia cut her gaze from one man to the other. "Well?"

Con refilled her glass. "Espionage against the CIA."

She raised her eyebrows. "*That's* what this is all about? Espionage against the CIA? Big whoop. In case you guys don't know your history, that's been going on since day one. Even our current administration's dipped their fingers into it."

"But this isn't a simple case of direct sellout, Julia." Smitty drained the last of the wine into his glass. "This is a multilayered, highly organized group working within the organization."

"A shadow CIA. An evil twin, working to destroy it from the inside out," Conrad added.

"You have proof of this?"

Smitty nodded. "Yes."

"And here Michael and Susan thought it was all you." Julia tipped her glass at Smitty. "With a little insider information from me of course. They showed me the tape of you entering the country on Tuesday to see what my reaction would be."

Conrad raised his gaze from the swirling wine in his glass. "Did Stone recognize me?"

"Your disguise fooled him. At this point, I'm the only one you have to worry about." She let the words hang in the air for a moment, before shooting Smitty a hard look. "You however are now on Michael's Most Wanted List, right behind bin Laden. You'd best lay low...or go see him tomorrow with a damned good explanation for your disappearance."

"We are not going to Stone," Conrad said.

"Then I don't know what you expect me to do. Michael trusts me, and I'm not going to blow that because you decided to run out on me and play maverick."

Her ex-partner focused on his wine, and Julia could see the muscle in his jaw jump. His voice came out softly, confirming her own suspicion. "If he really trusted you, he wouldn't be questioning your loyalty to the Agency."

"Right." Julia snorted. "You're a good one to talk about trust. If you trusted me why didn't you tell me what you were up to?"

"I was protecting you."

"Oh, well thank you very much. I *so* appreciate how you waited for me to start living a normal life with another man before you waltzed in here with flowers and dinner, and expected me to welcome you with open arms. That's bullshit, Con, and you know it." She pushed her chair back. "Who the hell do you think you are, anyway, to judge Michael Stone?"

He looked at her over the rim of his wineglass. "I'm the man who gave up his life to save yours, Jules."

"Everything we have is on here." Smitty showed the CD to Julia before placing it in the disc drive. They were in apartment 1C, one apartment down and across the hall from hers.

She glanced around at the vanilla-colored walls and beige carpet, exact replicas of her walls and carpet. *How could I have failed to see them living right under my nose?*

The floor plan was almost identical to her apartment as well, but lacked furnishings and personal effects. A small table with two non-matching chairs in the kitchen, a futon and portable TV in the living room, a twin-size bed and trunk in the bedroom.

Unlike Julia's place, a hub of computers and peripheral equipment dominated one corner of the living room. Scanners, a DVD read/write drive, listening devices, video equipment, a small fax/copy machine and a box of files covered the floor and nearby table.

"The shadow CIA has been giving out information that is crippling U.S. intelligence sources in Europe and putting our country in grave straits. We have uncovered a large portion of this network. Contacts, e-mail correspondence, a limited amount of money transfers." Smitty's long, slender fingers typed in a password and accessed a file on the disc. Ten seconds later Julia was staring at a database of names, cryptonyms, locations and operator contacts spread across multiple countries.

Smitty paged through the database. "However we don't have the big man, the leader of the shadow organization. Not yet, anyway." He turned to her. "That's where you come in."

"I can't wait to hear this," Julia murmured. Although her tone was sarcastic, the statement was completely true. Her adrenaline was starting to pump. It occurred to her the past year and half had been like suspended animation, predictable and comfortable. The lack of challenges giving her a false sense of security. While logic ruled Julia's brain, she still loved adventure. A challenge. An unpredictable outcome.

Her brain was now reasoning, her heart now hoping, that Conrad and Smitty were actually going to produce a credible excuse for putting her through the previous seventeen months of hell.

She chanced a look at Con, who had been completely quiet since leaving her apartment. His eyes were shuttered as he returned her stare.

"I'm listening." She crossed her arms over her chest. "Start from the beginning."

Chapter Eight

Arlington

Senator Daniel King filled his oversized leather chair to capacity, his size thirteen feet on the matching ottoman in front of him. Taking a sip of his ice-cold Scotch, he savored the tingle it left in his throat as he watched the ten o'clock newscaster embellish the day's top story on Capitol Hill.

It was King's favorite time of day. He could put his charming persona to bed, have a shot or two of his favorite Scotch and relax. The senator muted the TV's volume so he could reflect on his current state of affairs. Things were going well for him. In a time of economic recession, his portfolio was growing. The president's continuing war on terrorism had him nicely spotlighted as the chairman of the Senate Select Committee on Intelligence. Wife number two was still looking astonishingly appealing to him even after five years. His handicap on the golf course was a lucky seven.

Better than all of that was the fact that he was on the road to becoming President of the United States. Before he turned sixty, he would be calling the shots from the Oval Office, answering press questions in the West Wing's Cabinet Room and flying to Camp David for the weekend.

It had been a long, mostly rocky road up to this point and he was almost surprised at the tenacity he'd shown to get where he was.

Almost.

After thirty-one years in Washington, from freshman congressman to chairman of the SSCI, nothing surprised him much anymore. He had found that few people had the guts to pull off the things he had without alienating their constituents or fellow politicians.

Playing his role of a generous Democratic senator from Illinois, he scratched backs and offered generous assistance to anyone who could pay the favor back down the road. Both Democrats and Republicans found him genuinely likable and had the tendency to downplay any indebtedness they owed him. It was Washington, after all. Politics as usual.

Unfortunately for King, there was a problem looming over the horizon. It wasn't serious yet, but in the months prior to his bid for the presidency things would get nasty as his enemies—although there were few—and the press looked to crucify him. Better to quietly handle any potential problems now before they became the nails in his hands.

He sipped his Scotch and let out a sigh of regret. The problem to be dealt with was the simple result of bad timing. He had been young and, as was the trademark of youth, had errantly thought of himself as impervious to self-destruction. Even though he was married and making his first run at the Senate, he'd let himself fall for a beautiful, intelligent and completely power-obsessed CIA agent. The intrigue, the sexiness of having an affair with such an elusive woman had made him stupid. Off and on for a year, they met in secret at various hotels outside Washington and even once when he was on the campaign trail in Illinois. Even then, Susan Richmond had been a tireless campaigner for him in the tight-knit Washington circles of power.

He had known about his illegitimate child almost from the moment she was conceived. Susan ended their affair abruptly, transferring to some godforsaken hole in Russia, and went about quietly having the child and putting her up for private adoption. He'd offered her money for an abortion, but she refused it. Her determination to take care of the problem in such a moral way had surprised him then and still did. She claimed it was her Catholic upbringing. Still, he admired her. Her time in Europe was well spent, increasing her standing in the CIA.

Over the years, King had revisited his fear of the indiscretion being exposed to the public every time reelection rolled around. However, no reporter or adversary to date had unearthed the information, and Susan was a strong ally in his bid for the presidency. He could trust her to keep her mouth shut. The woman was as greedy as he was and King was most certainly her best bet for the appointment she craved. But unfortunately, the way things were these days, he couldn't be certain no one else would obtain the information, and he wasn't willing to chance anything when he was running for the most powerful job in the world. An illegitimate child emerging from the depths of his past would stop his campaign cold.

The senator rested the tumbler of Scotch on the table next to him and ran a hand through his hair. Susan was as strong an asset to his team as he could want. The CIA's CTC chief knew a bevy of influential people in and around Washington. With him, she had been a true friend as well as political ally and he wanted to keep her that way. Her willingness to share information with him about his fellow congressmen would continue to make his life easier. Her influence with potential political backers was paramount to his future career move. Their illicit past and youthful indiscretion had already cinched the deal.

As a veteran of the Senate Intelligence Committee, King knew all the dirty laundry Susan and her bosses were trying to cover up. The Central Intelligence Agency had experienced a great deal of conflict and problems over the past few years. Internally the loss of five case officers and a chief of operations in Europe had crippled foreign operations. Along with that, there had been limited success infiltrating the terrorist groups in the Middle East. If something wasn't done soon to stop the hemorrhaging, heads at the CIA were going to roll. It wasn't out of the question to suggest the organization might be gutted and the remains simply swallowed up by Homeland Security.

Externally, the public had lost faith in the spy agency and the current administration because of the terrorist assaults on the homeland and the outing of Valerie Plame. Suspicion and fear of abuse of power had always hovered like a shadow over the CIA in the public's mind, but now even the atmosphere in Washington regarding the CIA had turned frigid.

The President and Congress had given the CIA a substantial increase in authority and status in recent years as well as increasing the organization's budget by a billion dollars. But as Susan had been quick to point out to King on the golf course a week ago, those measures were simply a quick fix to try and address the current problems. The long-term problems couldn't and wouldn't be fixed by such simple, if expensive, measures.

The revolving door of directors over the last dozen years and the lack of integration between the nation's thirteen different intelligence agencies had definitely left the CIA in a critical position. Director Allen, the current CIA mogul, had not succeeded in asserting control over the operations inside the CIA, much less over the entire intelligence community. Homeland Security was just another layer of bureaucratic oversight, spending millions of hours and dollars every year on illegal immigration and other subjects best left to the lesser organizations.

The CIA had simply experienced too many failures in the past few years and needed a stronger leader, someone who had the skills to bring it back around to a world-renowned intelligence agency, as well as a presidential administration that understood the business of spying.

Susan had proposed a partnership that would do exactly that and benefit them both. Just that day she had called his beeper to let him know her plan was in motion. King knew she had sensitive information that could solve a multitude of the Agency's internal problems. In the right hands, that information could be used to refocus the CIA and its mission.

And the person who eradicated the CIA's problems and set it back on track would win bipartisan support from those on Capitol Hill and would be seen as a competent leader by the American people. Enter the chairman of the Senate Intelligence Committee and future president.

Susan could make King's dream to occupy the White House in a few years a reality for him. As president, he would want a director of Central Intelligence he could trust and who would work aggressively to complement his administration. Susan Richmond was the blue superhero suit that would turn King from Clark Kent into Superman. Their partnership could out distance any bullet, jump any hurdle. Tomorrow, he would call her—no, visit her—and find out how her stratagem for revamping the internal workings of the CIA was coming. He would also confirm his youthful indiscretion would be handled if it came out of hiding.

The senator glanced up just in time to see the blonde weather announcer flash her flawless smile at him from the television. He turned up the volume.

Tomorrow's weather would be sunny and seasonal. High in the upper-60s.

Perfect, he thought. Another perfect day for golf.

"Manny DeSmet was a CIA operator in Germany in the early '90s." Conrad laid a file on the coffee table in front of Julia. "He infiltrated a group run by a couple of good ol' German boys, Heinrich and Gustav Kramer, who dealt in black-market weapons acquired from American and Russian contacts.

"DeSmet cultivated an asset inside of the operation who acquired an extensive list of those contacts and enough information about the operation to take it down. The Kramer brothers were imprisoned and a large number of their suppliers and buyers were put out of business overnight.

"A few years later, along comes Heinrich's twenty-three-year-old son, Henry Junior, who decided to pick up where Dad left off. Only his operation was bigger and better. Junior didn't limit himself to selling simple munitions like AK-47s and SAMs, he was running anything he could get his hands on—drugs, biological weapons, chemicals, diamonds, you name it. And along the way, he decided to take a little revenge. He started gathering information on Americans, specifically CIA operatives and military folks he could burn down the road."

Julia leafed through the file's contents. A picture of Heinrich Kramer II with his arms wrapped around a woman caught her attention. The woman's eyes were hidden behind John Lennon specs, long dark hair blowing out behind her. "Who's this with him?"

"Cari Von Motz, his girlfriend, who just happened to be a foreign asset on the Director of Operations' payroll."

"She was feeding Kramer information about CIA operations?"

"At first it wasn't clear what was happening," Smitty answered. "Cari's chief of station was so happy to have someone inside Kramer's organization that he conveniently overlooked any possibility she was selling us out. According to him, she was following procedure and turning over important documentation about Kramer's operation. He repeatedly cautioned her against becoming involved with Henry, but she assured him she was simply *enjoying* her assignment."

Julia looked at Conrad. "This is the group you were infiltrating when you went to Berlin?"

"Yes." He leaned against the wall and crossed his arms over his chest. "In Paris I had hooked up with Pierre LeMont, the small-time arms dealer you and I did surveillance on."

"I remember."

"Through him, I was put in touch with Henry Jr.'s partner, Georges Durand. My cover was as a buyer for a private entity. As a test, Cari's station chief left her in the dark about my affiliation with the CIA. After negotiating a couple of deals with Durand, he hired me to do some independent contracting for him and Kramer. In the process I figured out Cari's romance with Henry was not an act. She was giving classified information to him and feeding mostly false information back to her COS."

Smitty swiveled in his chair and put his feet on the coffee table. "The topper was that the Kramer clan is kissing cousins to Germany's chancellor, Wilhelm Ruger. The information young Kramer received was being passed on to the German government. I decided to keep Con undercover there until we could determine what to do with Cari. We were hoping to find out more about Kramer's operation before we terminated her employment."

Julia sank back into the futon. "The warehouse we blew up in Berlin—was that part of your independent contracting?"

Conrad nodded. "Kramer and Durand needed some competition put out of business. Of course, that part of my contracting was never officially reported to the Agency."

Pushing off the wall, he leaned over the table. He rifled through the file until he found several papers. "Cari was receiving e-mail correspondence from someone at Langley." Handing the papers to Julia, he continued. "They were bypassing the European Chief of Op and her station chief with information a person in her capacity shouldn't have had access to."

Julia sat forward and studied the copies of e-mail correspondence. Names were in code, but the messages provided a cache of information ranging from the itineraries of dignitaries to the logistics of packages containing gray arms entering the country.

"Was Kramer paying for this information?"

Conrad shrugged. "Not that we could track, which was odd. It would have made more sense if someone was selling the info to him, but it appeared they weren't. Smitty and I decided we had to find out who was giving up the info and why. Since I was already inside, I continued to shadow Cari and intercept as much as possible in order to find out the identity of the mole. Her COS agreed to the arrangement.

"After you and I blew up that warehouse, I was sitting around getting Durand drunk one night when he showed me this." Conrad pulled a piece of paper out of his back pocket and handed it to Julia.

Folded down into a small rectangle, the paper was creased and worn at the edges. Julia's skin prickled with foreboding. If Con was carrying it on him, the link written on that piece of paper was crucial to the operation.

"Apparently Cari's friend in the Agency got bold enough to hand over names of operators in Europe—just the thing Kramer wanted. His plan was to expose the agents to the underground world and then sit back and watch. It wouldn't take long for the terrorists, organized crime lords or drug czars to eliminate the CIA operators, effectively crippling the European operations with no direct involvement on his part."

"And exacting the revenge he wanted for his father and uncle," Julia murmured, still holding the small piece of paper. Unfolding it, she began to read.

The heading was the same as the previous e-mail, but the body of the message contained a list of six people's names. She knew every person on the list, including the last one.

Hers.

Her breath stuck in her throat as she stared at her name. She dropped the paper on the table. "Holy Jesus." She searched Conrad's face. "Why didn't you tell me?"

Reaching out, he took her hands in his. "It was too late for me to stop the information from going out over Kramer's network, Jules. Even if I had, you and the others were still compromised. I had to get you out of Europe and secured back here where you'd be safe. And I had to find out who sold you and the others out."

She stared at him in disbelief. "How could I be safe here if the traitor was in Langley?"

"Your sellout wasn't to fulfill a personal vendetta." Smitty sat next to her on the couch. "Five other people were on that list as well. If the conspirators inside Langley had wanted to take only you out, they would have. An episode of misconduct could have been inflated to fire you, or, if they wanted you dead, they would have arranged an accident to end your life, and your life only, which would have been easy to set up while you were working in Europe."

"But messy to pull off with you right under their noses," Con added. "You were safer here than anywhere else we could put you. Plus, with you inside headquarters, we had a better chance of uncovering the person responsible."

Julia sat immobile for a minute, questions bombarding her mind. She lowered her voice in an effort to control it. "Why was my name on the list and not yours, Con?"

Conrad exchanged a glance with Smitty. "I have no idea, but it would have only been a matter of time before my cover was blown too. The best thing for me to do was make everyone, including those inside the CIA, believe it *was* blown and I was dead because of it. I could then watch your back and continue pursuing the people who sold you out."

Julia's mind raced, trying to make sense of everything. A part of her wanted to throw herself into Con's arms, tuck herself into his body for comfort, for the consoling protection only he could provide. But it had been too long since she'd found comfort in his arms. So much had happened in the last year, the last twelve hours even, that she felt out of sync, her mind and heart struggling to catch up. After squeezing his hands lightly, she pulled hers out of them, stood and walked away from him, trying to sort out the tangled logic. Love for him making the impossible choices he had made competed with the anger she felt over his arrogant manner of manipulation. Exasperated, her voice came out stronger now. "I understand what you did and why you did it, but I still don't like it. In fact, I hate it."

Conrad huffed out a sigh, but nodded once in acknowledgment.

Moving to the doorway, she leaned on the frame, ran a hand over her face. "Germany. Now I finally understand why you were always running off to that hellhole. God, I hated that country. Do you know how many nights I laid awake in our bed in Paris wondering what you were doing? I imagined you sleeping with a beautiful young *fräulein* or, worse, lying dead in an alley somewhere."

Conrad still said nothing, but his eyes were sad, watchful.

"Then came the bomb," Julia went on. "Synchronized watches and an explosion that happened two minutes sooner than planned." She shook her head. "Me, sitting helplessly inside the car, my body in shock, my mind totally unsure of what had happened. I prayed that night, Conrad. I prayed you'd come running around the corner any second and I could breathe again." She took a deep breath and blinked back tears. "But I knew, deep in my gut, you were never coming back. And it was my fault. I built that bomb and it went off early." She steeled her attention on him. "I thought I killed you."

Julia could see him visibly struggling with shame and guilt. His gaze went down to the floor, came back up to hers. Was it a silent plea for forgiveness she saw in them or only weariness? Before he could speak, she cut him off. "Only, my bomb didn't kill you, just my *life* with you." She wiped an errant tear off her cheek. "I want to be angry with you and this wicked deception you pulled on me, but all I can feel is sadness and regret lodged right here." She tapped her chest with a fist. "You sacrificed your career and your life to save me, so it's hard to feel self-righteous after that, but your betrayal has still broken my heart all over again."

Conrad moved for her then and she held out a hand to keep him back, but it didn't work. As soon as he grabbed her, the fight in her dissolved. She stiffened only slightly as his arms went around her and his grip tightened. He kissed her forehead and stroked her hair. Tears fell from her eyes and soaked into his shirt.

"I'm sorry," he whispered.

If she tilted her head up, she could kiss him. For a moment, Julia actually considered it. The kiss they'd shared that morning in Michael's bed had been surreal, weird, almost frightening. The kiss earlier in the evening in her bedroom had been shy and left her with a miserable ache of need. Miserable but desirable at the same time...she wanted to feel his lips again, wanted to suck the heat from his body and the tongue out of his mouth...and...

In the background, Smitty cleared his throat. Loudly. Julia moved back and drew in a ragged breath. Conrad looked down at her, his eyes grave and watchful again. And maybe a little heated, but now was so *not* the time to be thinking about kissing Conrad.

Smitty shuffled papers on the coffee table and tried to look like he hadn't been watching them. Julia stepped away from Conrad and set her focus on Smitty instead. It was easier to control her emotions if she wasn't looking at Con. It was easier to think. And she definitely needed to think.

"So, Michael was right when he told me Con's death was not my fault." She was pleased at the matter-of-factness in her voice as she spoke to Smitty. "But he was wrong about me being safe. Someone, possibly an intricately woven group within the Agency, sold me and four other case officers out. I survived, but that doesn't mean I'm not still a target. Why? Why would someone give five case officers up to a sure death sentence?"

"Power, money, vengeance." Smitty shrugged. His neck was slightly pink and he kept his gaze on a paper he was holding. "There are endless motivations, but we think power is the key here." He chanced a glance at her.

"Not money? They usually go hand-in-hand."

Smitty shook his head. "My money tracers have found no significant exchanges of money by the key players. No red flags in offshore accounts."

Conrad crossed to the futon. "Everything we've found, all the evidence we've gathered supports an eloquent power play, orchestrated by someone deep inside the Agency."

Power. A freaking power-grabber had done all this damage. Sudden anger flared in the pit of Julia's stomach. She wasn't good at playing the casual victim, had already done her time in that role. Ditto for turning the other cheek.

Her anger morphed into steel-edged resolve. "How do you know there's more than one person involved?"

Both Conrad and Smitty looked at her, measured hope in their eyes.

Smitty pointed to the computer. "We have evidence showing the S&T and INTEL directorates have been involved along with Operations. It's minimal but there." Science and Technology and Intelligence were the other two main directorates of the CIA.

"How did you obtain that information?"

Smitty glanced at Con and back to her. "I was running the

European operations long before I officially received the title. Since I knew what to look for, I kept a close watch on all the agents and operators, and used all of my assets in the field to figure out how far this operation went. I uncovered a cache of info from several reliable sources outside of the Agency."

Conrad cleared his throat. "And some of it came from a source on the inside who's been helping us."

She drilled him a look. "You already have someone inside Langley helping you?" She knew the answer to her next question, but she asked it anyway. "Then why do you need me?"

Her ex-partner's gaze was back on the coffee table. "Because you're the one sleeping with Michael Stone."

Silence hung between the three friends with crushing weight. So now she had the truth. Julia swallowed the lump tightening her throat and persisted. "Who's your source on the inside?"

Smitty smiled at her as if reasoning with an irritable toddler. "Julia, you'll be more effective to us if that person remains anonymous to you. Think about it. If you'd known about our operation, known that Con was alive, you wouldn't have penetrated the Agency as well as you have."

Penetrated the Agency. Julia stared at a spot on the far wall. *What a polite way to say shagging the boss.* She crossed her arms over her chest and put a hand over her mouth. There she was not a minute ago thinking about kissing Conrad and completely forgetting about Michael. What was wrong with her?

It was getting harder and harder to keep things straight. Once again, she reached for the safety of logic. "Why not take the information you have and give it to the DCI?"

Titus Xavier Allen had been the charismatic Director of Central Intelligence for a brief five years. A former spy once in love with the clandestine side of the CIA, he was now the sixty-five-year-old DCI in love with the Hollywood side of government. Tailored suits, dinner parties and vacations in the Keys held more seduction these days than running agents.

"Not until we have absolute proof about who's in charge of the rogue operation." Conrad vacated the futon and went to sit in front of the computer. His fingers poked awkwardly at the keys. "We have incriminating evidence, but if we take it to Allen right now, he'll sweep it under the rug. The last thing the DCI wants is to face a congressional committee or the Justice Department over improper conduct by the agency that has made him into the man he is. Plus, his buddy, the president, might get a little miffed if anything further damages his popularity poll ratings. Titus is one of the prez's favorite cronies."

A nearby HP laser printer began to hum. "Once we get the last bit of proof we need, we'll give it to the DCI, along with the president, the Inspector General, and, of course, the press." Conrad paused and looked at her. "We're going to burn this bastard's ass and everyone helping him."

Fear, like an icy finger, ran across the back of her neck. Conrad already knew who had put her life on the line, she was sure of it. "Who do you think the bastard is?"

He picked up the paper the printer had spit out and sat looking at it. She could see him struggle with the impending disclosure. "Is it that bad?"

"Just remember, you wanted the facts, Jules." He refused to meet her eyes. "Here's the facts, in black and white, just the way you asked for them." He pushed the paper he was holding across the table to her.

Unable to resist the magnetic draw of the answer, Julia grabbed it. Thirty or more CIA employee names were listed with their corresponding code names. There, in amongst the benign, was the identical code name on the e-mail that had changed the course of her life.

Director of Operations, Michael J. Stone. Her knees buckled.

Chapter Nine

"Would it help," Conrad said quietly from behind her, "if I said I was sorry? Again?" His silhouette reflected in the glass as lightning ripped through the black sky.

The wind chimes outside the patio doors clanged gustily in the wind. Julia sat on the floor, arms wrapped around her bent legs, watching the wind blow sheets of rain across the cracked concrete patio.

She had sought solace in her apartment, locking the door behind her and leaving the lights off. An attempt, Flynn knew, to keep him out so she could hang her head and lose the control she had been fighting so hard to keep after learning of Michael Stone's betrayal.

"No. It wouldn't help." Her voice sounded steady and yet still smart with emotion. "You'd be lying. You're not sorry it's Michael."

"But I am sorry the asshole did a number on you."

Julia's eyebrows rose as she calmly accused him. "The pot calling the kettle black."

Conrad clenched his jaw to fight back a response that would only get him in deeper shit. He couldn't win this argument. No sense trying.

Julia, sensing his refusal to argue, shook her head mildly and ignored him again. A crack of lightning, the follow-up roll of thunder a few seconds later. Long minutes of silence.

Conrad shifted his weight from one foot to the other. Damn this sucked. He wanted her to lash out at him, yell, slam a door, cry in his arms again—like that hadn't freaked him out a little, she never cried, but even that was preferable to this sudden silence—do something to blow off her anger and hurt.

Then he could help her. But this...this withdrawal wasn't healthy. The emotions would detonate inside her.

Maybe he should get in her face, argue with her until she broke. Tell her why he wasn't like Stone. She would break, he knew that, and he damn sure would be there to pick up the pieces this time. "You have to talk to me, Jules."

"No, actually, I don't. Leave me alone. I need some time to think."

"I have more information, more proof, if you want to see it."

Julia cut her gaze to him as the rain continued to pelt the concrete. "I've seen and heard enough. The less I know, the more...how did Smitty put it? Effective? Yes that's the word. The less I know the more *effective* I'll be in your little sting operation."

"So you're going to help us?"

She snorted. "Do I have a choice?"

No, he wanted to say, his need for her help almost as bad as his need for her forgiveness. At the same time he felt compelled after what he'd put her through to give her an out. "You always have a choice. I can't force you to do this, to work with me."

Her body tensed and he knew he'd said the wrong thing, although he wasn't sure why it was wrong. Her help was critical to the success of the operation, but he didn't want to push her into a corner. It would only backfire on him.

Her attention went back to the night outside the door. "What if," she said, her voice controlled, deliberate, "the roles had been reversed seventeen months ago? What if you thought I was dead, Con, and it was your fault?"

Taking a step back, he let his back slide down the wall on the west side of the patio doors. He let himself think about it for a moment, but a moment was all it took. "I'd have gone crazy."

Her response was just as quick. "But you'd have survived, just like I did." And accurate.

Lightning flickered, illuminating Julia's body with a blinking, strobe-like effect. The green eyes were black, her lips set in a grim line. Behind her set face, he knew she was coming to grips with Stone's betrayal. With her current situation. With his request for her help. He watched as she continued to stare out at the night. She was right, they were survivors. Whatever the outcome of this operation, they would both survive.

He waited for her to tell him that. To assert that she would be fine. But silence was all he got.

That's all right, he thought. *Take all the time you need, love. I'm not going anywhere. I'm never leaving you again...*

She was gone.

Cursing himself, Conrad bolted upright and blinked, forcing his eyes to focus in the deeply shadowed kitchen. He shouldn't have fallen asleep, but Christ, his body needed more than the five hours he'd had over the last two days.

Skirting the table still clogged with dishes from the evening's dinner, he made his way down the hall toward her bedroom. His heart was thumping, adrenaline lifting the sleep-induced stupor that fogged his half-dead senses.

Thunder echoed in the distance.

Please, God, don't let her be gone.

The bedroom door was ajar. Slipping his fingers around it, he held his breath and edged it open. Like the kitchen, the bedroom was nearly black but he found her form shrouded on the bed under the sheets. She was sleeping. He silently exhaled and rubbed a hand over his face.

Life with Julia had never been easy, but then he had never opted for easy in his life. To him, nothing easy was worth having. Challenge was what made his blood flow, his pulse pound.

Conrad Flynn had a superior operational mind and the balls to put his ideas into action. Intelligence mixed with cool logic and hyperawareness made him excel at everything from running agents to troubleshooting tickets for a sold-out game. Always ready for the next opportunity, he was an artful and cunning risk-taker. He loved the game and he loved to win.

In the *007* version of the Intelligence world, Flynn was an outstandingly good spy.

The problem was he had fallen in love with Julia Torrison, his opposite in ways the Myers-Briggs assessment test couldn't begin to measure. And although her scope of assignments had been more limited than his, she was operationally his equal. That had caused just a few problems.

Being a good spook was the antithesis of being a normal person. Those who excelled at flirting with terrorists, assassins, drug dealers and the rest of the Earth's scum usually sucked in the everyday departments of spouse, parent or friend.

When Julia had arrived at the Farm for case officer training, Conrad felt a pull toward her like a primitive force driving him to distraction even when she was out of his sight. He tried to convince himself his obsession with her was nothing more than physical attraction, but over the six months she was a student in his care, she became more than just a wicked form of Venus seducing him nightly in his dreams. She thrived on risk, stared down the impossible with confidence. Even through the paramilitary training he wrongly believed would break her, she was charismatic and fearless. Tough as nails.

A combination he found unable to resist.

The seduction was mutual, and when the moment finally came, Conrad found that possession of Julia's sweet body had nearly made him weep. The smell of her hair. The taste of her skin. The curve of her hip. The feel of her heart pounding in rhythm with his. Every piece of her took him to his own version of heaven.

Sex momentarily satisfied his physical need for her, but he realized immediately after the act was done that making love to her body wasn't enough. He wanted to tease and caress her mind as well. For the first time in his life, he'd found a woman he liked talking to. A woman he liked listening to. He couldn't get enough of her.

They'd both finished with what the Farm offered and Julia was graduating the next day to begin her career as a CIA case officer. Conrad was returning to Europe to deep cover. "I'm leaving for Paris in two days," he told her as they'd walked the footpath along the river. He'd stopped her forward motion with a hand and when she'd looked at him, he'd been struck again by the strength he saw in her eyes.

"There's an opening at the Embassy for someone with your skills." He hesitated, searching her face, for what he wasn't sure. "What do you say? Do you want to come with me?" After the question was out, he was afraid to breathe, afraid her answer would destroy him. She took her time, her gaze raking over his face as though she was memorizing every detail and choosing her words carefully.

As she'd leaned in close, her smile was full of smug satisfaction. "I'm already packed." She'd pulled his head down and kissed him.

Conrad rubbed the kink in his neck. No, life with Julia had never been easy, but life without her was like filling his lungs with water instead of oxygen. Drowning in the murky depths of the ocean, while watching the life preserver float just out of his reach.

He wanted, needed, to breathe her brand of oxygen again. It didn't matter that his gut, his mind and his best friend told him he had to eliminate the rogue leader of the CIA. He needed his ex-partner to tell him. Needed her to confirm what he was doing was right.

Her voice floated quietly across the dark divide between them. "Do you know what Hell is like?"

He stood motionless, considering the question, unable to come up with a suitable answer. What he knew about Hell was SEAL training, BUD/S to be exact. Followed by the Agency's Special Activities Service. Further down the road and the worst hell of all, was Julia sobbing from the exact spot she occupied now, grieving over him while he sat listening, unable to console her, two doors away...

The shrouded figure moved, shifted into a sitting position. "Sister Marjorie—she was my Sunday school teacher—she told us Hell was hot, that it would burn our skin and our souls for eternity. But she was wrong. Hell isn't hot. It's cold. Absolutely, mind-numbingly cold."

God, he couldn't stand not touching her. He took a chance and moved toward the bed. When she didn't tell him to stop and didn't bolt away from him, he squatted down next to her.

"I know you're hurting, Julia, and I know it's partly my fault." He reached out and ran two fingers across her cheek. Silently praying for a second chance, he let his hand sweep under her ear and into her hair, enjoying the soft feel of the dark tendrils. The round of her skull fit like a puzzle piece into his cupped hand. God, it had been too long. "I'm sorry I screwed things up between us, but I swear, if you'll let me, this asshole will do whatever it takes to make it right. I'll swear to it on a hundred Bibles."

Julia stared at him in the dark for several heartbeats. "Technically, swearing on a hundred Bibles is no different than swearing on one."

Conrad dropped his hand. "Why do you always do that?"

"Do what?"

"I'm pouring my heart out here—which I'd rather cut off my left nut than do—but I owe you big time, so I'm trying to be..."— he fought his brain for the right word—"sensitive." A shiver ran through him. Jesus, this woman could un*man* him faster than Dr. Phil. "And you completely blow it off to point out some philosophical technicality that makes me look like a dumb ass."

He saw the flash of her teeth in the dark. She was laughing at him. "You're kind of cute when you're mad."

Cute? *Cute?* "Julia."

"Shut up and kiss me, you sensitive dumb ass."

That stopped him. But only for a microsecond. His lips found hers like a heat-seeking missile. She was pulling him to her and he sat on the bed, his hands on either side of her bracing them both up. Her hands were under his T-shirt the next second, and, *Jesus*, the feel of those soft, slender, cool hands combined with her wet, hot tongue in his mouth after all these months...*bam*, flashpoint. He wanted her—needed her—now.

Hugging her to him, he started to press her down on the bed, but she pulled back, lips, hands, everything. He tried to follow her lips with his, but she stopped him with her hands on his chest. Pushed him back.

"That was..." She drew in a deep breath and let it out. "Nice."

Nice? Conrad sat up and tried to get his brain back on track. *Nice?* "What's wrong?"

"I need some sleep. You need some sleep." She patted his cheek. "I'll see you in the morning."

Conrad sat farther back and eyed her with suspicion. He didn't understand what had just happened. One minute she was sucking his lungs out and the next she's telling him his kiss was nice—*nice? there was absolutely nothing* nice *about that kiss*—and then she came up with she needed some sleep? Conrad rubbed his face with a hand and tried to slow his pulse. Julia was dicking with him. Pulling his chain. Jesus, he *was* a dumb ass. First-class.

Okay, score one for Julia. He could deal. No problem. "Sleep's good," he muttered, setting his hands on his thighs so he wouldn't grab her and kiss her again.

"We'll talk more tomorrow." She sounded a little too cheerful.

He sat there for a minute, purposely slowing his breathing. Julia would be going back to work tomorrow. Back to Stone. He turned his face to look at her again. "You do forgive me though, right?"

She sighed, with unusual dramatic flair. But then she leaned forward and pointedly stared at his mouth. He moved in, ready for the kiss that was coming...

Her breath fell lightly on his face. "I'll think about it."

She flashed him a grin and he knew he was had. She sat back, tugged at the covers and practically tossed him off the bed as she slipped down into it. "Now get out, Flynn. Go do good somewhere else, and let me get some sleep."

He could hear her giggling into her pillow as he walked out of the bedroom.

Chapter Ten

Alexandria

Susan Richmond pushed her lover's arm off her stomach and swung her long legs over the edge of the bed. Her head was pounding. She needed some Motrin and she needed it now.

The red digital letters of the bedside clock glowed 5:13 a.m. White sheers blew out elegantly from the bedroom window as she wrapped her silk robe around her and rubbed her head. The storm had brought rain and left behind cool air and a blinding headache.

In the bathroom she downed three pills with water from her cupped hand, relieved her bladder and started back toward the bedroom.

I wonder how Julia's doing. The thought caught her mid-stride and she stopped, her eyes fixed on nothing but empty hall space.

Abigail. She's Abigail Quinn now, remember? You have to stop thinking about her as Julia. You could blow everything.

Oh no. She would not blow it this late in the game.

Turning on her heel, she strode down the hall and made her way into the study. Her worn leather desk chair squeaked as she eased into it, and she gritted her teeth. Forcing herself to ignore the throbbing in her head, Susan mentally reviewed her game plan again.

The carefully thought-out strategy had taken years to put into action. She had handpicked each of the players, coached them to their full potential, and occasionally carried the ball for them when things got dicey. It was working. One day at a time, one play at a time, everything was coming together quite nicely.

Toying with the small gold-plated globe on her desk, she let herself envision what the future would be like. Even if things didn't go exactly as she had planned, she would still get what she wanted. With all of the troublesome players eliminated by one means or another, she had a straight shot to the top. To the dream she had been harboring for thirty years as she rose slowly through the bullshit bureaucracy of the CIA.

From analyst to field operator and back to Langley, Susan Richmond had done it all. She had been the CIA's most successful recruiter of case officers and topnotch analysts. She had done her tour of duty at the Office of Russian and European Analysis and returned home to serve on the National Intelligence Council for three years. Along the way she had received her master's degree in Military History. By and large, she was fully capable of running the CIA, if not the entire intelligence community.

And here she sat.

Directorship of the CTC was an important job that called on most of her skills, but she wanted more. She wanted what she couldn't have.

Because, even in the politically correct environment of the new millennium, the male-dominated clique of the intelligence world was opposed to accepting a woman as DCI. The public even more so, no matter what opinion polls said. Television and Hollywood could throw as many female actors as they wanted into Presidential-type roles, but the well-known and self-evident truth in the United States was that someone of great stature was needed to run the intelligence community and no woman had the right anatomy to do the job.

The CTC Chief snorted. When her plan finally came together, the men who controlled her career were going to get their balls pulled right out their noses and then some. From the Deputy Director of Operations to the Director of Central Intelligence himself, heads would roll as one after the other was exposed for the worthless, inefficient leader he was, all thanks to her diligent work. Once they were out of the way, Susan would rise to the position due her.

Out of the corner of her eye, she saw movement. Expecting to find her lover, she was surprised to see another pawn in her game emerging from the shadows of the hallway.

Cari Von Motz ran a gloved finger along the edge of Susan's desk. "Do you know what I love about America?" Her feminine voice was accented with the slightest hint of German.

Susan gripped the arms of her office chair and then forced herself to relax as Cari's musky perfume filled her nostrils. Some designer fragrance, she was sure. The woman's long hair had been cut into a short bob, a bold fringe of bangs lying across her forehead and squaring off her cheekbones. Cheekbones she had given her. "Why are you here?" Susan said. "How did you bypass my security?"

Cari touched the spines of the books shelved in layers on the south wall. "America truly is the Land of Opportunity. Look at all the choices you Americans have, all the places you can go, all the doors that are open to you just because of the country you live in."

Susan watched as Cari examined the bottles of liquor on the nearby antique buffet. Picking up a bottle of brandy, Cari poured some into a snifter and held the bottle up to Susan. Susan shook her head, feeling her headache returning in full force. Cari Von Motz was the last person she wanted to deal with right now, but she held her silence and waited for the young woman to make her move.

Cari carried her glass of brandy to one of the red damask-covered Queen Anne chairs across from Susan and sat down, propping her booted feet on the edge of Susan's desk. "It's payday for me." She sipped the amber liquid, "I delivered Flynn and Smith back to you, and carried my cover with Fayez. Now I want my money. Time for me to take advantage of a few opportunities."

"Your payment will be delivered into your Swiss account when the deal is done, Cari, just like we agreed."

Cari eyed her over the rim of the snifter. "But you have what you need to make the house of cards fall now and my work for you is done. I gave the information on Michael Stone's spies to Heinrich, led Flynn on a wild goose chase and got Smith to leave his position in Europe. I even delivered a nasty terrorist to your doorstep. You have no more use for me, and you owe me more than my fee. Pay up now and I'll be out of your life. For good this time."

Susan fingered the globe again and calculated the odds of that happening. If only she hadn't been young and stupid once. If only she hadn't fallen in love with a married man. "Half will be paid to your account by the close of business tomorrow."

Susan knew the money would never be enough, no matter how high the sum. "The other half will be paid upon completion of the operation."

Licking her lips, Cari studied the globe. "I still think killing Agent Flynn is a waste. Surely I could entice him into the black-market world."

Susan rubbed her forehead. "You'll never entice him into our world. He may cross the line into it once in awhile, but for him that's a means to an end. He is, unfortunately, one of the good guys through and through."

"Everyone has a price."

Susan shook her head. "Money has never been a driving factor with Conrad Flynn. Only loyalty."

"Loyalty?" Cari snorted. "There is no such thing."

This is a dig for the mistakes I made thirty years ago. But her "if only's" could change nothing, only remind her not to screw up now. "For Flynn there is such a thing as loyalty. His country, his friends and his family all garner his loyalty. It's nearly impossible to gain Flynn's trust, but once you have, he's your guardian angel. There isn't anything he won't do for you. On the other hand, if you threaten him, or he brands you a traitor, you're history."

"And you have used that to your advantage."

Susan let her mouth curve in a smile. "Exploiting his friendship with me and his loyalty to the CIA was easy. If anyone could bring down Michael Stone and Director Allen for me, it's Flynn. All I had to do was plant the seed in his head and place his partner in danger."

"What if this backfires and he figures out you are the CIA's traitor?"

Still smiling, Susan rocked her chair slightly. "If you were the DCI, who would you believe? A rogue agent, with multiple episodes of misconduct noted in his personnel file, a man who faked his own death and went AWOL from the CIA? Or the director of the Counterterrorism Center who's been a loyal and dedicated employee for over thirty years?"

Cari tapped the glass against her lips. "Still, it's a shame to waste such an incredible male specimen."

Susan sighed, struck by the idea that Cari and Julia were opposite sides of the same coin. Too bad they both would have to be disposed of. "It's time for you to be going."

Standing up, Cari drank the last of the brandy and set the glass down. "I expect full payment in my Swiss account by close of business tomorrow."

"Then you'll be disappointed. The best deal I'll give you is half now and half later."

She smiled coolly. "What a shame. Guess I better find myself another benefactor."

Susan returned the smile. "Be my guest, but I doubt you'll have any success."

Cari moved toward the study's door. "The Land of Opportunity, remember, Mother? America is the Land of Opportunity."

The older woman watched the younger version of herself slip out the door and let out a deep sigh. Julia Torrison? Who cared how she was doing. Susan Richmond was in full-court press in the final game of her season.

Oh no. She would not. Blow. It.

Julia sat in the rocking chair, staring at Conrad's back.

His muscular naked back. Stripped down to his black boxer briefs and white socks, he was flopped on her sofa, deep in sleep. She watched him breathe, stomach down, head turned toward the back of the sofa, feet dangling over the end. His right arm hung down, fingers resting on the butt of his gun that was lying on the floor. The other arm, complete with his classic sailor boy anchor tattoo, was snugged up under his head.

She let her focus wander over his olive-colored skin, allowed them to stop briefly on the two scars she could see. He had received both injuries during his SEAL days. One, on his right shoulder, he had received from a bullet and the subsequent surgeon's knife needed to extract it. The other one, about two inches long and located just above the band of his underwear, was the result of a knife wound. *Reminders*, he would say. *Never rely on others to get your back.*

Julia wanted to reach out and run her fingers across the tattoo, press her lips to the scars. She wanted to feel the heat Conrad's body gave off. Feel the sweat of his body mixed with hers.

She closed her eyes. God, this wasn't fair. This was *so* not fair.

She'd been able to think only about Conrad last night when

she fell asleep, but with the morning light came thoughts of Michael. Normally, she would have been on the veranda at his house about now, sipping coffee and reading the paper. Instead she was here, suddenly leading a double life again. Not only was she secretly cavorting with her supposedly dead ex-lover and an AWOL CIA chief, she'd kissed her ex-lover without any thought of her current one. She'd gone to sleep fantasizing about way more than a kiss too. *I can't decide,* she mused, *whether I'm crazy or just slutty.*

But now it was morning. Fantasy time was over. Hello real life.

Opening her eyes, Julia curled her legs into the chair and watched Con's back again.

Rise. Fall.

Rise. Fall.

Instead of retreating to the apartment down the hall, he'd spent the last few hours of the night on her sofa. Even after she had rejected him and told him to get lost.

Passive aggressive, he would say, *wins the war, Julia.* Wear the opponent down by waiting him...or her...out.

He knew what he was talking about. Conrad excelled in HUMINT—the clandestine term for human intelligence collection. He had no qualms about using violence when necessary, but enjoyed equal success in stillness. In relentless study of his target until he located the weak spot that would bring the target down. In patient, unwavering pursuit of whomever and whatever he wanted. Once assured of his success, Conrad Flynn hit with stealth and accuracy.

His kisses were lethal.

Julia hugged herself. She had been his target before, but she had wanted him just as badly as he'd wanted her. This game was different. This time Michael was the ultimate target. With or without her help, Conrad was going to take him and the rogue organization down. Her stomach rolled at the thought it could be Michael orchestrating the espionage and betrayal of his own spies. But it was worse to contemplate that he could have manipulated and seduced her after failing to terminate her life in Europe. That she could have been used and betrayed again by someone she loved and trusted with the core of her soul.

It's not Michael.

Conrad stirred, even in his exhausted state struggling to find a comfortable arrangement for his arms. Giving up, his right armed flopped back to the floor. A minute later, soft snores escaped from his lips.

Julia watched, feeling Michael's presence hovering in the background. Years of experience in Conrad's spy world had honed her gut instincts to a sharp point. She knew Michael was innocent and she had to prove it. She owed him that much. But how? Help Conrad and Smitty? Strike out on her own to find out who was setting them all up? Confront Michael?

She rubbed her temples where the beginning of a headache stirred.

Too many pieces of the puzzle are missing. I have to go back to step one and start filling them in.

Rising, she stretched and started a mental list of To Dos as she walked to the bathroom.

One: put Mariah Carey on the bathroom CD player and take a long, hot shower.

Two: makeup and hair.

Three: fat jeans (Michael was always feeding her and she'd gained seven pounds in the past year) and red cashmere sweater for casual Friday at work, topped off with her three-and-a-half-inch Prada's.

Four: take on the shadow CIA.

All in a day's work.

Chapter Eleven

Julia watched steam rise from the coffee cup setting on the vanity top and mingle with the steam from her shower.

God, he's good. Moves around just like a cat on silent feet, bringing me coffee in his continuing quest for my help.

Conrad's voice whispered through her memory. *Passive aggressive wins the war.*

Smiling, she wrapped her hair in one towel and dried her body with another. She heard dishes clang against the kitchen sink. *He's even washing the dishes. Next he'll be making my bed and offering to pick up my clothes from the cleaners.*

Hanging up her damp towel, Julia took a sip of the black coffee and then began rubbing lotion on her arms and legs. The memory of Conrad's hands doing the same thing sent a jolt of heat to her face.

Precious time had slipped by since she'd stepped out of the shower in her Paris flat to find him sitting on the window seat, a beer in hand, his dark eyes like melted chocolate as they skimmed her wet, naked body.

He had set the beer down, taken the towel from her hands and patted her skin dry. Then grabbing the bottle of her lavender-scented lotion, he'd smoothed it over her body in long, gentle strokes, letting his fingers linger in certain spots until she could no longer stand it. She'd pulled him into her bedroom, his husky laughter over her impatience like velvet on her bare skin.

A pan banged in the sink in the other room, jarring her from her reverie. She looked at her blurry reflection in the steamy mirror. Damn, she had to quit thinking about the past or she'd jump his bones before she even started her own secret investigation of the shadow CIA.

Pulling open her cosmetic drawer, she applied a touch of taupe eye shadow and a couple coats of mascara to her eyes. She dried her hair and pinned the bulk of it on top of her head. To the strands that fell around her face, she added a few curls from her curling iron. Then she set it all with hairspray. Last, she added her lip gloss and smoothed it into a perfect pout.

Throwing on her terrycloth robe, she opened the bathroom door to peek out. The apartment was silent. She stepped out into the hallway. Still nothing. She padded down to the kitchen.

The dishes were washed and stacked to dry in the dish drainer. The table and countertops were clean. Two pieces of dry toast sat on a plate next to the full coffeepot.

Conrad was gone. She felt keen disappointment swell inside her. Even though her past relationship with him had been an exercise in emotional bungee jumping, she had always respected him, always loved him to her core. He had pushed her to meet his expectations, both in their personal relationship and in their jobs because he expected only the best from her.

And she gave it to him, because she expected no less from herself. She always gave one hundred and ten percent.

Sitting in a kitchen chair, Julia stared at the tulip still in its vase on the table and sighed. This wasn't going to be easy. There was so much at risk, all of it mired in emotions. She was in love with two men and, without a doubt, she was going to have to choose between them somewhere down the road.

Before that, she had to prove Michael was innocent even though the best spy in the business had a ton of evidence proving he was guilty.

But she still had to help that spy and his current partner-in-crime. Conrad and Smitty had been, were still, her friends. Friends who had put their lives on the line for her. They were good men and even if they were wrong about Michael, they were right about the shadow organization. It had to be stopped. Those involved had to be brought to justice.

Unfortunately, Conrad and Smitty were now rogue agents who would probably end up in prison if the CIA's mole and his associates weren't revealed. Julia too, if she was caught helping them.

Deal with the shadow organization first, Julia. Then deal with your feelings for Conrad and Michael. Keep your poker face on and don't give anything away to either side yet. Be Miss Mary Sunshine on the outside and Mata Hari underneath.

Julia smiled to herself. Playing Mata Hari was certainly more fun than playing Abigail Quinn. She just had to be sure she didn't end up in front of a firing squad.

"Well?" Smitty asked, slicing a banana over his bowl of Wheaties.

"Well what?" Conrad stared vacantly at the contents of the refrigerator before snagging a gallon of milk.

Smitty watched as he poured a glass of milk and drank it down. "What you mean, 'well what'? Is she going to help us or not?"

"Hell, I don't know." Conrad set the glass on the counter and ran his hand through the disarray of hair on top of his head. "She's playing games with me. I guess she's still pissed."

Smitty took the gallon of milk and poured some of it over his cereal. "Did you apologize?"

"Of course I apologized. Weren't you listening? She told me to get out."

Smitty was grinning and shaking his head. "I shut off the receiver and went to bed as soon as you left. I assumed she'd forgiven you when you didn't come home." He walked past Conrad and set the milk in the refrigerator.

"Yeah, well, you can wipe that shit-eating grin off your face, Smith. If Julia refuses to help us, I'm sending *you* in to bug Stone's house."

Genuine fear showed on Smitty's face. "You know I suck at that cloak-and-dagger stuff. You're the overachiever in the covert operations department. I'm the behind-the-scenes guy who makes you look good."

Conrad rolled his eyes. "Right. How could I forget?"

Picking up his bowl and a cup of coffee, Smitty walked to the table and sat down. "Maybe you should let me talk to Julia. She might feel less defensive with me."

Before Conrad could answer, there was a soft knock on the door. Pulling the HK from his waistband, he edged down the hall. Smitty concealed himself by the kitchen doorway, motionless.

Conrad looked through the peephole and visibly relaxed.

"Speak of the devil," he said under his breath as he unlocked and opened the door.

"Good morning, Conrad." Julia shot him a warm smile, breezing by him in jeans and a loose-fitting red leather jacket.

Her fresh-from-the-shower lavender scent followed her, wrapping itself coyly around Conrad's head. He caught himself inhaling and had to force his voice to sound normal.

"Morning." Closing the door, he returned the gun to its spot in his waistband. Good was questionable.

Julia followed the smell of coffee into the kitchen. She nodded at Smitty, and he smiled at her as he resumed his seat at the table. "Cups are in the second cabinet." He pointed with his spoon before dipping it into his cereal.

She pulled a clean cup down and poured coffee into it, catching sight of Conrad in her peripheral vision. He was scowling at her from the end of the counter. *I'm Miss Sunshine,* she told herself. *I'm here to follow orders.*

Of course, she was always better at giving them than following them.

Turning around, she leaned casually against the counter, resting her focus for a moment on the tiled floor. "So what's on my to-do list today?" she asked, glancing up at Smitty.

He stopped in mid-chew and looked at Con, then back to Julia. Swallowing his food, he frowned. "You mean in terms of helping us?"

She smiled at him over the coffee cup. "Unless you've suddenly realized how asinine this plan is and have decided to go to Michael with your information."

Conrad snorted. "God*damn*. You are amazing, girl. After all the evidence we've shown you"—he rapped the countertop with his knuckles—"you have the balls to stand here and tell us our plan is asinine? Suggest we pay Stone a visit? Michael Stone—remember who he is? The man who gave you up, Julia. *The man who sold you out.*"

Julia straightened on an inhale, and she cut her eyes to him. *I will not let you get to me. I'm Mary Find-the-Mole Sunshine.*

Forcing her eyes away from Con's scowling face, she returned her gaze to Smitty. Smiled again. Then she repeated the question with exaggerated politeness. *"Please* explain to me what I'm supposed to do to help you."

Smitty grabbed his coffee cup and stood up. "Let's head into the living room." He motioned her forward and shot Flynn a look. "Con was just heading to the shower, so I'll go over the plan with you."

Conrad placed his hands on the counter and kept his head down as Julia walked past him. She knew he wanted to reach out and grab her, shake some sense into her, or maybe just kiss her again like last night, and the thought of him wrestling with himself made her smile. Pushing her, trying to force her to do and think the way he wanted wouldn't do any good. The harder people pushed her, the harder she pushed back. The people in her past who'd been stupid enough to tell her she couldn't win, wouldn't succeed, never saw what hit them.

Conrad knew from experience that under the soft sweaters and sweet perfume Julia was a pit bull, just like him.

And pit bulls went for the jugular.

Chapter Twelve

Someone was watching him.

The hairs on the back of Michael's neck were standing straight up. His stomach was tense. The easy gait he'd usually affected by this point in his run was absent. His legs were feeling a push of adrenaline. He tried to ignore the flight response his brain was sending them.

Jesus, Stone, you're getting paranoid.

He glanced at the Rottweiler running a few paces ahead of him. No paranoia there. Pongo was in full dog-mode, sniffing and spreading his scent on every bush and rock within shooting distance.

But he felt it. Someone *was* watching him. They weren't nearby or Pongo would have picked up the scent. That meant they were probably using a scope.

Holy Mother. Scopes usually came attached to rifles. Was there someone out there who wanted him dead?

At one point in his life, Michael had been trained to expect and react to such a scenario with the calm and self-assured manner of a U.S. Marine. However, those days were long gone, and right now he felt more like a sitting duck than a trained solider. He was stupid not to have his assigned security guard running with him these days, but a running partner cramped his freedom, his morning peace.

So, what was he going to do? Hide?

Trees sparsely populated the path to the lake, not one of them big enough to conceal his six-foot-three, two-hundred-and-twenty-pound frame.

Scratch that idea.

He casually scanned the area, eyes and ears on full alert.

There was nothing beyond the birds and the sound of his running shoes on the path and a rustle of grass as Pongo zeroed in on another tree. He attempted to reassure himself that if someone was really out there and wanted to kill him, he'd already be dead. Whoever it was was simply watching him.

But should he run, *really* run?

Don't overreact, Stone. Stay cool.

Why would someone be watching him?

Because of Julia. Ryan Smith warned you they might come for her.

Michael frowned. If the group Flynn had infiltrated had wanted Julia's head on a platter, they would have found her long before now. It had been close to a year and a half and even with her name change and the other security precautions they had taken, a determined party could have found her within a few weeks, maybe a month or two tops.

On the other hand, *he* had previously been the director of the CIA's Counterterrorism Center and now was the DO in charge of the CIA's spies. *That* would be the obvious reason someone might be watching him. Terrorists, mercenary vigilantes, Republicans—there was always someone who wanted to get his nuts in a sling.

Unh-uh. It's Julia.

Ah, Christ.

Michael double-timed his pace.

Conrad rocked slowly in the chair and stared at the far wall, feeling Julia's presence in the room even though she was miles away, zooming up the George Washington Parkway to another day of work at CIA Headquarters.

Conrad Flynn was scared. Scared shitless to be more precise.

It wasn't an easy thing for him to admit, but it was hard to ignore when it was slapping him in the face. He'd felt fear plenty of times before, but this time he was unprepared for it. Not that he was unprepared for what he was doing. He was mercenary-trained, had more field experiences than even he cared to admit, and pegged the top rung of physical and psychological fitness. He was confident about his skills and about the mission he was on. There was no doubt in his mind who the responsible party was and he was only days, maybe hours, away from getting the proof he needed. He could feel it in his gut. Stone was the man it would end with.

And Julia was obviously in love with him.

God*damn*. Didn't that just frost his balls? In his overall master plan, he'd somehow missed that contingency.

That's what had him scared shitless.

He stopped rocking.

But if Julia was in love with Stone, why was she willing to go after him? She'd agreed to bug Stone's house and was going to attempt to bypass his laptop's security and download any files and e-mail correspondence that confirmed or even hinted at his involvement in the shadow operation. It was dangerous for her, but she could handle it. She'd performed similar operations before.

It was her sudden cooperation that was bugging the crap out of him. After her reckoning with him the night before, he was completely surprised at the morning's change of tune. Julia was not a Jeykll and Hyde personality. If she really believed Stone was innocent, she would have told Conrad to go to hell without batting an eye.

In the beginning, when Conrad had first learned about the sellout, he had given hard consideration to the idea of following the trail on his own and simply putting a bullet in the head of whoever was responsible. He'd been furious and dangerously close to losing control. However, Smitty's common sense brought him back from the edge. They had to be clever and thorough, Smitty advised, to make sure they flushed out everyone involved.

It had never been part of their original plan to involve Julia. They had figured it would take them less than six months. Then they would walk in, reveal the rogue operation and bring the traitors to justice. But the trail was not as easy to follow as they had expected. It had taken months longer to track all the evidence back to its source.

And they'd never planned for Julia's involvement with Michael Stone.

Operationally, it was a gold mine to have her so close to the source. Like having an agent on the inside of a terrorist cell, it should have made his job easier.

Yeah, right. He should have stuck with his original plan. Put a bullet in the responsible party's head. Maybe not as thorough, but definitely more satisfying.

There was a faint noise behind him. The click of the door handle. Conrad was out of the rocking chair, stilling it with a hand and concealing himself against the near wall in one fluid movement.

"Con!" Smitty called, barely above a whisper.

"I'm here." He pushed off the wall and strode into the hallway.

"You better come quickly." The shit-eating grin was back in place. "She's talking to you from the car."

Traffic was horrible, inching along in spurts, thanks in part to an early morning accident. Julia hit the brakes yet again and lowered the volume of the Audi's CD player.

"Hope you enjoyed that selection from Creed," she said to the invisible ears of the car. "It's called 'Who's Got My Back Now', which brings up an appropriate subject for us to discuss this morning. So, get yourself a cup of coffee, Con, and take a comfortable seat. I have a few things to say to you.

"I appreciate how you've been watching my back since your, uh...pseudo death. And I'm considering accepting your apology, however"—she slapped the steering wheel with her hand—"I'm still mad as a hornet that you lied to me. That you left me behind, ignorant of your game, so you could use me down the road for this sting operation. You had no right to play God with me, Conrad, but as usual, you're too busy trying to save the world to care about the consequences of your actions. Did it ever occur to you the world is too screwed up even for the Great Conrad Flynn to save?"

Julia could feel eyes on her and she glanced to her right across the passenger seat. Stopped next to her in a hearse was a young black man, a red and white striped knit cap pulled down over his rowdy hair. After meeting her gaze for the briefest of seconds, he looked away, a faint smile on his lips.

Yeah, I'm talking to myself. Big whoop.

She returned her attention to the car in front of her and continued her lecture. "I know what you're saying to me right now. I know how you're trying to justify your actions."

She lowered her voice, doing her best imitation of him. "Jules, you know I couldn't turn my back on what was happening and let this group of traitors ruin what you and I and dozens of others have worked for. Traitors are cut from the same cloth as terrorists and murderers. You know I have to fight them, Jules. *We* have to fight them. If we don't, who will?

"Well, I guess on an intellectual level I understand that, even agree with it. But right now, I don't give a rat's fat ass about the *logic* behind your actions. For all your integrity and honor, you still suck. You let me down, Conrad.

"And, from here on out, I don't want to hear any more justifications, and I don't want you bristling around with anger at me for refusing to jump on the Let's-Crucify-Michael-Stone bandwagon. I'll make my own decisions and draw my own conclusions as soon as I have all of the evidence. But let me be clear about one thing. Even with what you've shown me, I'm not convinced Michael is responsible. I know him. He's..." Her voice trailed off and she smiled to herself imagining how her next words would send Con straight up out of his chair. "He's a lot like you."

She let the words hang in the silence for a moment before continuing. "So for now, I'm going to help you and Smitty, but I want you to know I really hate..." *you.* Damn it, she couldn't bring herself to say it.

"I hate this whole big, fat lie." Okay, not quite as effective, but... "I hate what you did to me and I hate what you're making me do to Michael. If he finds out I've helped you, he'll never forgive me. And by the way, I have a polygraph test this morning. You'd better pray I don't fail it. If I do, Michael's going to be asking questions and I swear to God, if my butt ends up on the line, I'm going to tell him everything. *I will not take the fall for you, Flynn.*"

She felt the eyes watching again and let out a sigh. Pulling her sunglasses down on her nose, she flipped her head to the right to look at the man, shooting her eyebrows up.

What?

This time he held her gaze for a moment longer and she experienced a twinge of recognition. His face was an open book and he looked at her as though she was familiar to him.

He glanced away again and she studied his profile for a second as she pushed the sunglasses back up on her nose. Damn, was that...? No. Couldn't be. Conrad wouldn't have Ace Harmon tailing her, would he? The man was a mortician for heaven's sake. Access agent or not, Ace wouldn't know the first thing about tailing someone.

Traffic began to move and Julia watched the hearse pull into her lane several cars back. Shaking her head, she chuckled to herself. *That's a first. I'm being followed by a freaking mortician.* Absently, she turned her focus back to driving and eased the Audi forward.

Now where was I?

"So, having said all of that, I also want you to know…" She took a deep breath and lowered her voice. "I'm glad you're still alive."

There. It was out.

She released the rest of her breath.

Accelerating as the traffic in front of her moved forward, she kept an eye on the hearse moving behind her.

"Oh, and one more thing, Flynn." She glanced in her rearview mirror as she opened the Audi up. "I really hate it when you call me 'girl'."

She reached for the volume knob, "And now back to our regularly scheduled program."

I'm glad you're still alive…

Conrad closed his eyes and leaned back in the chair, bringing his hands behind his head.

While it wasn't exactly an admission of her undying love, it was good enough. Julia was glad he was alive.

Life was good.

Chapter Thirteen

Langley

Julia was pulling a file when Michael approached her from behind. She felt her stomach tighten. Abigail Quinn was supposed to be laboring through the stacks of communications and news updates about the latest military recruiting and outfitting in Iran as well as a conflict developing again between Israel and Palestine. Titus Allen was in Florida of all places and Michael was to have a briefing with the Senate and House Select Intelligence Committees in two hours to bring them up to date on the CIA's related intelligence gathering.

Analyst Chuck Atwater, the CTC's official Middle East expert, was undergoing gallbladder surgery, and Susan had asked Abigail to have the important information culled for Michael in time for his meeting.

But Julia was struggling with nagging doubts about Michael's possible involvement with the shadow CIA. Her gut told her he was innocent, but now that the seed of doubt had been planted, she couldn't keep from thinking about it. Her brain kept replaying the last few months of their relationship over in her head as she looked for any hint of betrayal or manipulation on his part. She couldn't come up with anything solid, but it was still easier to hide from him while she tried to figure things out than face him.

So she was sort of hiding, but still doing her job. After another round of morning intel analysis, she was picking up the trail of a known terrorist. One whom she was convinced was on his way to America.

Keeping her back to Michael, she pretended to be deep in concentration as she fought the butterflies in her stomach. *He's innocent, Julia. You know he is. Just relax.*

Loosening his tie a notch, Michael stopped to watch Abigail. Surrounded by the towering gray metal shelves that held rows of terrorist biographies, Abby was, Michael thought, the polar opposite of the fanatics she studied.

At one end of the spectrum were men focused on ideological and secular hatred, attempting to control the world through fear and violence. On the other, Abigail Quinn, a woman who they would perceive as weak and would expect to be submissive, fighting them and their fanaticism with every breath she took.

Watching Abby pull out another file, the male part of his brain admired the snug jeans and high heels that came bundled with her incredible intellect and integrity. Lucky for him *and* the United States of America, Abby was on their side.

Without turning, she addressed him. "Good morning, Director Stone."

He smiled. "Good morning, Ms. Quinn. Finding anything of interest?"

Facing him, she pulled a file from the stack in her hand and tapped it against the others. "I think our long-lost friend Fayez Raissi is up to no good."

"A hunch of yours?"

"He dropped off the radar after 9/11, but three months ago a field operator spotted him in Paris. Susan asked me to keep an eye on him, see if he was stirring anything up. Last week, a state department cable stated he was recruiting for Takfi-wal-Hijra in London at the Finsbury Park mosque. That group is a hard-line Islamist movement founded in Egypt as a splinter group from the Muslim Brotherhood."

"I thought he was with the Armed Islamic Group."

Abigail nodded. "He was, and before that he was with an extremely radical group in Kazbekistan. He joined them as a teenager to fight the K-stani Army whom he believed was responsible for the death of his two brothers."

"Refresh my mind on his MO."

"Charismatic and intelligent, Raissi is an expert in explosives and weapons. He is an excellent sharpshooter, has done some assassination work, but prefers taking out his targets in more spectacular ways, such as car bombs. He has no trouble finding young Muslims to do his dirty work and has orchestrated more than a few suicide bombings."

"Hmm, builds bombs and jumps from one extremist group to another. Sounds like your kind of guy."

A smile played on her lips. "The Takfi organization is under bin Laden's umbrella of fanatic Islamic groups. They have received financial and material support from him, but Takfi is even more puritanical with their beliefs than bin Laden. Even Muslims who don't adhere to their views are regarded as infidels and are targets in their holy war. Raissi has point-blank executed several Muslims himself."

"What do you think our boy is up to?"

Abby shrugged. "His usual motive for anything is to bring attention to his homeland and destroy infidels. If he's traveling and recruiting again, he's up to something bad, probably involving a target that gets him some attention. From the trail he's leaving, I'd say he's moving fast and heading our way. I'll do some more digging and type up a report for you and Susan later today."

Michael had learned over the past year and a half to never underestimate the CTC's top analyst. "I'd like to discuss this in further detail, but right now I need you to bring me up to date on the Israeli situation." His attention wandered to her legs again. "Why don't you bring those files"—he brought his gaze back up to meet hers—"with you to my office?"

Michael left Langley at 10:36 for his briefing with the Intelligence committees. He took Susan with him. Five minutes later, Julia shut off her computer, turned her voice mail on and took off for D.C. too. Only she was visiting a much smaller, much less conspicuous part of town.

The listing inside the door of Ace's Mortuary informed Julia the funeral of R. J. Bellingham was in progress. It was the first time she'd ever been inside the converted Victorian. Ace was one of the few trusted contacts Conrad cultivated and used in the Washington D.C. and Arlington areas. A civilian who unknowingly provided useful information to Con on occasion and scored tickets for sold-out Knicks games regularly. Julia had never actually met him, only seen him from a distance years ago. She and Con had been home on a short leave at Christmastime and Ace had scored prized front-row tickets for

Con. Julia had no idea the extent of Ace's services, but she was determined to find out.

Organ music and singing voices filtered through the closed doors off to her left. She passed the doors and looked for Ace's office. At the end of a long hallway she found a kitchen and mudroom, but no office. Retracing her steps, she climbed the carpeted stairs across from the front door. The upstairs held three bedrooms. One had been converted into an office. Ace had his worn desk chair tipped back, his feet on the window ledge behind the desk. He was talking on a cell phone.

Julia walked into the room, took a seat across from him in a barrel chair with gaudy red velvet upholstery. She cleared her throat and watched as Ace jumped. His feet hit the floor and he jerked around to see who was in the room with him. Julia smiled and gave him a little wave and almost laughed when his jaw dropped open.

"Hey, man, I gotta call you back." He snapped the cell phone shut before the person on the other end could reply.

"You really should have a bell on your front door," Julia said, still smiling. "Or an electronic buzzer to let you know someone's downstairs. Less chance of them sneaking up on you."

Ace, still standing, stared at her. "That's what Con—" He stopped, wiped a hand across his forehead. "Security system's down. Buzzer don't fly right now."

"Conrad could fix that for you."

"Shit." Ace slipped the cell phone in the side pocket of his cargo jeans. "He all right?"

"Conrad's fine," Julia said, studying the younger man. "Relatively speaking, anyway." She sat forward. "How deep are you into this operation, Ace?"

Ace seemed to consider sitting down in his office chair, but a glance at Julia and he chose to stand. "Don't know what you're talking about."

"But you know who I am."

"I know who you are. You're Sheba."

"And you know what Conrad's done to me."

Ace eyed her with suspicion. "I didn't have nothing to do with that. All these years, I just delivered Solomon's messages for him. To you. To Smitty, and back to him sometimes. That's it." Ace moved his hands in gesture. "Just a messenger."

Julia watched him for a moment, enjoying the fact he was so nervous. No telling what Con had told Ace about her. "You were following me this morning. I'd say you're a lot more than just a messenger service."

Shaking his head, Ace swore under his breath. "I ain't done nothin' wrong."

Technically that was true and Julia found no value in threatening Ace, scaring him into helping her. It wasn't her best option. Hearing the organ music below rise in a crescendo, Julia decided on a different approach. "It's kind of fun, isn't it?" She fixed her best smile on him again. "Playing *007?*"

Ace crossed his arms, but his posture relaxed a smidgen. He slouched against the wall behind him.

She went on. "Conrad's good at all that covert stuff. You could learn a lot from him. I did." She shifted in her chair, crossed her legs and tried to look nonthreatening. "He trusts you and that's nothing to sneeze at. Next he'll have you tapping phones and videotaping suspects. And if you're not careful"— she chuckled under her breath—"he'll be signing you up for The Farm. You'll be a legitimate employee of the CIA before you know it."

Dropping his arms, Ace eyed his chair. Thought for a moment. Looked back at her. "The Farm? That's that place where they teach you spy mumbo jumbo, right?"

Julia nodded, dropped her smile. "I bet being a mortician is hard, isn't it? Long hours, sad people. Not a lot of excitement. Sort of a dead-end job. No pun intended."

One side of Ace's mouth quirked up. He let himself sit in his chair. "It's a community service for my brothers here, you know? My daddy did it, now I do it. Funerals are important in my community. Everybody wants to go out with a bang, even if their life wasn't so good. But some days..." He shook his head and slid down in the chair. "Dead-end job is right."

Julia noticed Ace had dropped the casual vernacular he'd been using. She sympathized with a nod. "It's a good cover, though. You might want to think about keeping it as your day job. Do a little spying on the side, like you did today."

Ace looked up at the ceiling. Scratched his chin. "Might not be so bad."

Julia let him think it over for a minute. "I've got something you could help me with," she said offhandedly. She saw interest spark in his eyes as he dropped his gaze to her face. "That is, if you're not too busy working for Solomon."

"I might have some free time." Sitting up, Ace rocked his chair. "What do I have to do?"

"I just need a little information. All you have to do is ask a certain person a few questions and feed the answers back to me. Without him knowing, of course. This is strictly top secret. And, you can be sure he'll never even know why you're asking. Think you can handle it?"

"Sure." Ace nodded. They shared a smile and were conspirators. "Who's the person?"

Julia leaned forward, her smile turning wicked. "Guess."

"You failed the polygraph."

For the second time that day, Abby sat across from Michael in his office. It was the end of another twelve-hour day and Michael was tired. He dangled his pen between his fingers and tried to gauge Abigail's reaction to his news.

There was no surprise, just an edginess that had been with her all day. She studied him with guarded eyes. "I've failed them before," she said with forced neutrality. "You know they are less than sixty-percent accurate."

He scanned the sheet of paper in front of him for a moment before leaning back in his chair, feeling like the professor about to give his failing student a stern lecture. "I have to tell you I'm disappointed."

She shrugged indifference. He knew it wasn't the first time she'd heard those words in her life, but it was the first time from him. "You failed a very serious question, Abby."

Refusing to meet his gaze, she remained detached. He waited for her denial. At the very least, he'd thought her analytical brain would want the complete picture and she would quiz him about what questions she had failed.

Silence was all he got.

"Let's see." He looked down at the paper again for reference and struggled to keep the smile off his face. "The question you failed was 'Is your name Abigail Quinn?'"

Silence again enveloped the room. She arched an eyebrow at him in disbelief. "I failed because I lied about my name?"

"Dr. Passarti thought it was odd, which under normal

circumstances it would be. He suggested I follow up with you." This time Michael let his smile break free, and that seemed to coax a faint smile from her.

"The polygraph machine is only as good as the operator running it," she said. "In my professional opinion, Dr. Passarti is an idiot. Why don't you hook him up to the box and let *me* ask *him* a few questions? I could start with his cross-dressing and work up from there."

"A little testy, are we?" he teased.

Abigail folded her hands in her lap and worried the silver band with a fingertip. "I'm not being testy. It's just..."

"Just what?"

A twist of the ring. "You know for years I lied about everything. I mean my whole life was a lie. And the psychologists and the polygraphers and everybody else around here would stroke out if they knew the things I did in that other life. Quite a few wouldn't be too happy if they knew what I'm doing in this life either, functioning under an assumed name, hiding in the bowels of CIA headquarters, sleeping with you." She looked up at him. "I don't like other people sitting in judgment of me, Michael, and, quite honestly, some days I'm not sure what's true and what isn't."

Michael frowned. Abby was stressed out and it had little to do with her polygraph. "I didn't think you gave a damn what other people thought and you shouldn't. Your intelligence and analytical skills are a huge asset to the counterterrorism department. No one needs to know the details of your past. As far at the polygraph goes, like I told you before, you needed it to cover your butt."

She shifted in the chair and stared past him out the window. Finally she met his eyes. "I think the truth is I needed it in order to keep your trust."

He pushed his shoulders back into the chair and mentally debated the merits of continuing the current thread of conversation. Deciding it was pointless to rehash the trust issue, he instead decided to tackle a more urgent issue. "Any more ideas about what Ryan Smith is doing since his return to the States on Tuesday?"

She looked away. "He's probably doing the same things you are," she said, her voice curt. "Eating, sleeping, working."

Abby's averted gaze made Michael check himself. Her body

language all day had been off. Something was definitely up and he wished he could read her mind. He studied her for a moment. "Working on what?" He kept his tone mild.

She shrugged. "I told you he's tracking the Agency's mole."

Leaning over, Michael rested his elbows heavily on the desktop, rubbing a finger around the rim of the blue ceramic mug sitting there. Imprinted with the CIA logo, it was a leftover from an early '90s administration. Did Abby know something about Smith that she wasn't telling him? He picked up his pen again, worked it between his fingers. Direct questions weren't getting him anywhere so he chose a different tactic. "I think someone was watching me with a scope this morning during my run."

Abigail's gaze came back to his face, her eyes now showing concern at the turn of the conversation. "Someone watching you? Are you sure?"

He nodded. Waited.

"Who?"

It was his turn to shrug. "Ryan Smith? Possibly the same person who's bugged your apartment?"

Abigail didn't move.

Michael stilled the pen. She knew something. Damn, why wasn't she telling him?

Loyalty. She wouldn't tell him out of loyalty to Smith. Apparently that carried more weight than loyalty to him. He threw his pen down. "It's unlikely," he continued, suddenly wanting to change the subject, "but there is a possibility someone from your past is looking for you."

Her expression showed mild surprise. "I thought we were presuming I was safe here."

He locked eyes with her. "I never presume anything, Abby."

Twisting her ring, she sat silent again.

"Up to this point," he went on, "we've had no reason to believe you were being sought. But you and I both know it pays to be cautious. I want you to watch your back and report anything out of the ordinary. I've ordered your apartment and my house swept for bugs and I've requested personal round-the-clock surveillance for me during the next forty-eight hours. I'll request it for you too if you want to be on your own this weekend or"—he watched her carefully—"you can spend the weekend with me."

She stopped twisting the ring and considered his offer. Then she narrowed her eyes slightly with challenge. "Why? Because you think you need to protect me, Stone?"

He couldn't miss the teasing tone and he felt himself relax. Maybe he was too tired, or too paranoid. Maybe Abby wasn't hiding a thing. His mouth quirked in a half-smile. "Actually, *Quinn*, I was hoping *you* would protect *me*."

She grinned. "No problem, boss."

Chapter Fourteen

Arlington

It was nearly dark. Julia killed the Audi's engine, grabbed the dry cleaning out of the back seat and entered the apartment building. She breathed a sigh of relief once she was behind the door of her apartment. All was quiet and she leaned against the interior wall of the entryway, letting her shoulders sag.

She'd gotten through a tough day without giving anything away. Now she needed to regroup before she headed to Michael's. He was suspicious and watchful. She knew he'd picked up on her uneasiness, but she'd been able to bluff through his questions well enough she thought he'd chalk it up to her stressful workday.

Spending the weekend with Michael would be another challenge but it would give her the opportunity she needed to hack into his computer and bug his house per Smitty's instructions. Meanwhile, she had Ace primed and ready to wheedle info out of Con. If everything fell into place like she hoped, by Monday Michael would be in the clear and she would know who the real traitor was.

Julia dropped her keys and iPod on the nightstand and hung the dry cleaning in her closet, turning around to find Conrad in the doorway. Her hand flew to her chest. "Jesus, you scared me. Sneaking up on people is a bad idea, you know. Could get you killed."

He ignored her jest, his intense gaze regarding her warily. "You're late. I, *we*, were beginning to get worried about you."

"Yeah, well, I'm tired, but fine." She shrugged off her jacket, avoiding his eyes. The memory of what had happened in her bedroom the previous night flashed through her mind. All she wanted to do was get changed, get the bugs from Smitty and get out of there. She needed to stay away from Con and his lips.

"I take it you passed the polygraph."

"Actually, I failed one very important question. I lied about my name." She snapped her fingers. "Dr. Passarti caught me on that one."

"Dr. Piss Ant is still there, huh?"

She nodded and walked to her chest of drawers. "Who did you have watching Michael during his run to the lake this morning?"

"Shit. Did Stone see him?"

Taking out a T-shirt, she threw it on the bed and pulled the sweater off. She was in a hurry, Flynn or no. "He didn't see anybody, but he knew someone was there. He thinks it was Smitty. Who was it?"

"Ace."

She dropped the sweater on the bed and shot Conrad an incredulous look. "You let *Ace* do surveillance on Michael for you? What, are you nuts?"

"I was busy this morning and I had to be sure Stone wasn't rendezvousing with anyone."

"Has Michael ever rendezvoused with anyone on his runs?"

"No."

No wonder Ace had been so nervous when she accused him of spying. He really had been. "You are nuts. Ace is not exactly stealth about his surveillance. I had no trouble spotting him following me this morning. The hearse was a dead giveaway."

"So he's not a stealth machine. He is trustworthy and loyal, and he doesn't ask questions. Right now, I don't have too many loyal friends to pick from when I need help."

Julia averted her gaze and undid the top button of her jeans. "Why were you and Smitty in London earlier this week?"

Conrad watched Julia's delicate fingers slip the button of her jeans open and felt his blood begin to pump faster. Jesus Christ, she was going to undress right in front of him. This was good.

"We were watching Cari Von Motz." He scratched the back of his head. "Are you going somewhere?"

She rubbed her forehead with her fingertips. "Ace's

surveillance has Michael on alert, and before I knew you were living down the hall, I told him about the bugs in the apartment and car. He's ordered the Office of Security to sweep this place and his so you better sanitize everything. He also called in the Keystone Kops for himself this weekend and offered me two choices: entertain one of them here or spend the weekend at his house. I'm going to his house so I can plant the bugs." She pulled her camisole out of the waistband of her jeans. "Cari Von Motz?"

He kept his focus locked on her face, but his brain still registered the rest of her. The choker that dangled a pearl between the tiny bones at the base of her throat. The white bra under the plain, pedestrian camisole. The form-fitting jeans she was now unzipping...

Okay, maybe this wasn't so good. He dropped his gaze to the floor, crossed his arms in front of his chest and leaned against the doorjamb.

"Kramer and Durand were there that night. The night I officially died. I concocted a story to get them both there at that abandoned building and I blew them away with it. But I let Cari live. She was my link to Langley.

"Smitty helped you get back to the States and under Langley's protective wing. I had already set up a post here when you arrived. Smitty went back to Europe to start tracking down Cari. We thought we'd be able to get the evidence we needed from her, but she dropped out of sight. Five months ago, she turned up in London trying to get a job with the German embassy. Smitty disappeared from his position so he could shadow her constantly. We believed she was still in touch with her source from Langley and we didn't want to lose her again."

Julia walked to the closet to kick off her high heels. "And?"

"Last week, Smitty thought she was gearing up to meet with her source. He was afraid she might disappear again so he asked me to come and help him. We decided we'd follow her 24/7 and check out anyone she so much as looked twice at, but she jumped on a plane and flew to America late Monday night before we realized she was leaving the country. Smitty and I followed on the next international flight out Tuesday morning, but we haven't been able to locate her yet. We know she has to be somewhere close."

Julia was back on the other side of the bed. She didn't

move and he looked up to find her staring at him with her hands on her hips. "You know you went about this all wrong. If you had kept me in the game, I could have buddied up to Cari Von Motz at the very beginning and solved this for you months ago." She pulled the camisole off and threw it on the bed. "Now you've got a major mess on your hands."

"Cari would've figured out who you were and put a bullet between your eyes," he challenged.

Julia glared at him. "Why don't you go get the listening devices from Smitty for Michael's house so I can get going?"

Damn, his stomach hurt. Julia was spending the weekend with Stone. And that's exactly what he needed her to do. Get in the house, set up the bugs and extract any damning evidence she could get her hands on. But it wasn't what he *wanted* her to do. No, he wanted her to spend the weekend, the rest of her life, with him.

"I'll get them in a minute. Did Smitty go over with you where to plant the bugs?"

She pulled the clip out of her hair and ran a hand through the dark tresses. "He told me to use my best judgment."

Conrad shifted his focus away from her again, but his peripheral vision was taking in everything and his stomach wasn't feeling any better. She was challenging him in her bra and low-rise jeans. Her unbuttoned, unzipped low-rise jeans.

He cleared his throat. "I want one by each phone in the house and one in—"

"Why didn't you plant them yourself when you were there yesterday morning?" she interrupted as she drew the T-shirt over her head.

"It was too risky. There wasn't enough time." He chanced a glance at her face. "My mission yesterday was to see you, not plant bugs."

Julia hesitated before tucking her shirt in and then deciding against it, pulled it back out. She slid one foot into a Puma. He knew she was wrestling with something. She velcroed the strap and put the other sneaker on. Then she turned her poker face on him. "All the phones? You know there's one in the bedroom."

And just about every other room we do it in. The unsaid words hung between them. He watched as she zipped and buttoned the pants before looking up at him again.

Conrad turned his focus to her open closet, made his mind log the clothes hanging there so he could keep control of the jealousy burning his stomach. He didn't want her to see it on his face. Didn't want her to know just how bad he hurt.

As if the previous seventeen months hadn't been hard enough...watching and listening to her day in and day out without being able to touch her, talk to her, occupy space in the same room with her.

Now, he *was* in the same room with her, but she wasn't welcoming him with open arms. The passionate kisses and this undressing scene were all part of some whacko plan to make him suffer. It was working too.

Especially when she was bluntly warning him she'd be getting naked with Stone this weekend. Of course he could turn off the receiver, *would definitely* turn off the receiver when that happened. Imagining her with the bastard was hard enough. Hearing her sigh and moan and call his name in the heat of passion would send Conrad over the edge.

Taking a minute to control his emotions, he ran a familiar mental drill of cleaning his gun. He wasn't the only one who could bluff. "Well, Jules dear, you can put your mind at ease. I'm quite familiar with your screwing preferences." His voice lowered in pitch. "I don't need an audio replay."

She froze, her eyes widening a fraction before she turned away. "You are a tactless son of a bitch." Returning to her closet, she hung up the cashmere sweater, then crossed back to the bed and slid a short purple v-neck shirt over her head, refusing to look at him.

Christ, now what had he done? He hadn't come here to hurt her, alienate her even more. He'd just wanted to talk to her, wanted to try and mend the rift he'd caused between them...but he was never good at this kind of war. In the war of words, jealousy made him say stupid things. Especially when he knew she was playing him for a horny idiot.

"Poor Julia." He laughed without humor. "Stuck between a traitor and a tactless son of a bitch."

Her gaze came up to meet his, anger burning bright. Taking a step toward the bed, he stared back at her. "I feel real sorry for you, sweetheart, but guess what? We're all getting fucked on this merry-go-round. One way or the other every one of us is taking it in the shorts. Why should you be the exception?"

He saw her hands clench and then she forcibly relaxed them. Her voice came out low and controlled. "Why are you being an asshole to me? I agreed to help you, *even after what you did to me.* I'm sacrificing my loyalty to Michael to help you. Why are you treating me this way?"

"Just like I told you last night. You always have a choice. You don't have to help me. You're free to walk away."

"Free?" Her voice rose with anger. She pointed a finger at him. "You forced me into this, and until it's over, I won't be free of it or you. Oh no, I'll see it through, thank you. I'm going to be right there when you nail this guy. That's what you want, isn't it? You want me there when you nail Michael? Prove to me you're a better man than he is?"

Conrad held his breath and counted to ten. She'd called his bluff. He couldn't stand fighting with her. "What I want is you, Jules." His voice was sincere, reasonable. "I want you here with me, not at Stone's mansion on the hill."

"Stop it."

"You don't belong with—"

"Shut up, Flynn."

"—him. You belong with me." He jabbed a thumb into his chest, hating himself for always pushing her, but unable to stop. "I want your tongue in *my* mouth and your legs wrapped around *my* waist. I want you—"

"*Shut up!*"

"—totally, completely here with *me.*"

She jumped up on the bed, crossed it in one step and came at him, pushing him up against the wall with unbelievable force for someone he outweighed by seventy pounds.

"You have no right." She slammed her hands into his chest again. "You have no goddamn right to me anymore!"

Conrad stood still, looking into her eyes and hating himself. Hating the whole damn mess he'd gotten both of them into. "You're right," he said softly. He grabbed her arms and gently pushed her back a step. "I'll go get those listening devices for you."

She deflated like a balloon and dropped her hands to her sides. The green eyes he would die for looked at him unflinchingly. "It's not him, Con," she said, almost pleading. "Michael is no traitor."

Chapter Fifteen

When Michael entered his bedroom after midnight, Israel was on his mind. Safe rooms had been a standard feature in newly constructed homes there for years. A safe room, with its metal doors, could be sealed off to keep out poisonous gasses, a constant threat from Iraq.

This is my safe room, he thought, pulling off his suit jacket and throwing it on the bed. The room wouldn't keep him safe from chemical or biological weapons, but it did offer him something less tangible and every bit as important when he left the CIA behind. It was the one place where he could find peace and happiness, no matter what was happening outside its walls.

Abigail must have given up her vigil of waiting for him. The room was dark except for moonlight shining through the western window. His eyes adjusted to the darkness and he snapped his fingers at Pongo to lie down on his dog bed. The dog obeyed with a heavy sigh and Michael glanced casually at Abby's side of the bed. No Abigail, just an open book of Rumi poetry she had been reading. He shifted his gaze to the nearby chair. Her leather jacket was strewn haphazardly across the back.

Setting his briefcase on the floor, he looked around. The security alarm's usual green light was red, meaning it was off. He stood still and listened, noting that Pongo was not at all distressed, but still feeling a strange sense of unease. Something was off, and Michael was not one to ignore his internal warning system. A noise outside brought his attention to the French doors. On the balcony stood a figure dressed in black from head to toe...

Michael picked up his remote security device and put his back to the wall. Before he could push the alert button, the figure shifted and something about the way it moved seemed familiar. Another second passed as he continued to watch the figure's face become illuminated by the moon.

What the...?

Michael threw open the doors and the figure startled. Abby turned, her face opening up in a smile for him. "Michael," she breathed on a hard exhale. "I didn't know you were home."

"What in God's name are you doing, Abby?"

When Michael entered his bedroom after midnight, Julia was pulling herself up over the balcony's side railing. Ace, her new partner in crime, had come through for her. Conrad had gotten in to Michael's house by bypassing security with a few simple tricks involving Pongo's outside dog kennel.

Using night-vision goggles, the spy had slipped between the infrared tripwires near the dog kennel which sat almost directly under the balcony. The kennel itself was directly connected to the house with a doggy door Pongo used daily. The motion detector in that sector was set at thirty-six inches off the ground because the dog was constantly tripping it. No motion detector, no alarm. And when Con entered the kennel, Pongo was off for his daily run with Michael. No dog, no problem.

Julia had had to try it for herself. So she'd shut off the motion detector for that quadrant just like Michael did whenever they were going to sit on the balcony. Then she snuck out by way of the balcony, dropped down to the kennel area below and—*voilà!*—entered the house through the doggy door, Pongo her eager sidekick in the game. Reversing the route, she'd gone out through the kennel, to double check. Unfortunately she'd heard the sound of the garage door opening and Michael's car zooming in when she was still outside. Pongo took off to greet him and Julia stood for half a second holding her breath. The doggie door entered the kitchen, right off the mudroom that tied the garage to the house.

Trying not to panic, she'd considered her choices. One, she could go back into the house via the doggy door and make up some story about playing with the dog that would sound totally lame, or, two, she could climb back up the balcony and try to sneak into the bedroom, throw off her black turtleneck and jeans and jump into bed.

Option two seemed viable. Michael usually stopped off in his home office to unload his briefcase and check his messages before he came upstairs to the bedroom. Scrambling to the top of the kennel, Julia jumped and climbed hand-over-hand up one of the balcony's posts and hauled herself over the railing.

But, surprise, Michael had bypassed the routine stop in his office and was entering his room a few seconds later.

Catching her breath, Julia held on to the railing and racked her brain for a good story. When Michael opened the patio doors, she still didn't have one. So she smiled and silently begged her right brain to get creative. "Michael," she breathed on a hard exhale. "I didn't know you were home."

"What in God's name are you doing, Abby?"

Reaching out for him, she pulled him to the railing, stalling for the briefest of seconds, desperate to dodge what was coming. What was the best way to handle this? A full-blown lie? A half-truth? "Waiting for you," she said cheerfully. *Score one for truth.*

His gaze slid over her clothes. "Why are you dressed like that? You look like *Mission Impossible* trying to break into my house."

Julia glanced down at her clothes and gave a dismissive wave. "I wanted to see the moon, stargaze a little, and after everything that's been going on, I wasn't sure who might be watching me or your house, so I threw on some black clothes. You know, to camouflage myself. You told me to be careful, remember? Isn't it beautiful tonight?" She pointed up at the moon, cringing inside at her rambling half-truth and inane attempt at changing the subject.

Michael ignored the night sky and took her in, processing her words, her clothes, her too cheerful explanations, Julia knew, which made her acutely aware of two things. One, Michael didn't believe her, not totally anyway, and two, she had definitely lost her ability to lie successfully under pressure. She was sure she could blame Conrad for that.

Michael leaned his hip against the railing and crossed his arms. Waiting. Patiently.

For the truth.

As she took a deep breath, Julia flipped on the bravado switch. *Truth or Consequences* was always a tough game, but sometimes a little truth mixed with a lot of confidence would carry it off. "I was playing spy." She looked him squarely in the eyes, hoping the act to follow was more believable. "And checking out your security system. The bugs in my apartment and car, the fact someone might be watching us, following us. The fact that we still don't know who disposed of Conrad and the others..." She let her voice trail off before she continued. "I'm a little freaked. I needed to double check things here myself. To feel safe again."

Michael's posture didn't change, but Julia felt a subtle drop in tension. His voice was smooth, calm and assuring instead of accusatory, when he commented. "That's understandable. Do you feel safer now that you've checked things out?"

A flush of relief spread through Julia's body and for a second she almost told him the truth—that any decent criminal could slip through his expensive security system. But something—that little spy voice Con had planted in her head—made her stop before she spilled the beans.

Staring at Michael's dark gaze and knowing what a crappy day he'd had and yet he was still able to understand her paranoia, she felt a little flip in her stomach. It *was* a beautiful night and any other time she would have enjoyed seductively wiggling her way into Michael's arms and pushing a few of his testosterone buttons. He was smart and intuitive, but he was still of the male species and sex was always the fastest and most fun way to pull him out of a bad mood.

But the instant she thought about laying Michael, naked and needy, out on the patio table under the full moon, Conrad and his damned lips popped into her head. And then a memory of the two of them lying on the floor of a small walled balcony outside of Paris, rain falling on a canopy of potted palms and ferns that circled the stone walls and dripping off onto their naked bodies. Con kissing her wherever a drop fell. She felt a shiver and the flip in her stomach again, but this time it made her lightheaded. She grabbed the balcony railing and looked out into the night.

"We need to talk, Abby."

Uh-oh. Still not off the hook, and sex was out of the question. From somewhere deep inside her brain, a thought sprang forth. She faced him. "Say my name."

Michael raised his eyebrows. "Abigail," he responded.

Julia shook her head. "I want to hear you say my real

name."

The air between them seemed to fuzz out as Michael hesitated. He rubbed his eyes and dropped one hand to the railing.

"Please." A true ache of longing had lodged in her chest. This wasn't just about getting Michael off track or buying herself a few more minutes to think. She really wanted to hear him say her real name. To see her, not as Abigail Quinn, but as Julia Torrison. Not the Julia he'd picked up and put back together, but the Julia who stood before him, confident and able to take care of herself.

Michael closed his eyes for a moment and seemed to resign himself to her lead. "Julia," he said, his voice hoarse.

She smiled. "Again."

"Julia." This time it came out stronger.

Letting out a sigh, she slid into his body, her back to his stomach as she looked out over the dark landscape lit softly by the moon. "It's late," she said, drawing his arms around her. "You've had a long day. Let's save the talk until morning."

After a second, she felt his chin rest on the top of her head, felt the release of his breath, and she knew she'd won this round of *Truth or Consequences*. At the very least, delayed it.

A few hours later, just before sunrise, Julia awoke with Michael's arm thrown over her. Before she could think, she scanned the room, looking for Conrad. Assured he wasn't there, she snuggled down under the covers and tried to go back to sleep, but her brain wouldn't let her. While she'd been sleeping, her subconscious had seized on a thought. Now awake, her brain spit it out and it seemed reasonable. Fleshing out the details, Julia let the idea float around for awhile while she listened to Michael's solid deep breathing. She knew how to take his doubts away and still get out from under his watchful eye while she tracked down the real traitor.

Pleased she still had some deviousness left in her and satisfied her plan wouldn't hurt Michael in any way, she relaxed and fell asleep again as the room began to lighten with the first bars of sunlight.

Chapter Sixteen

Fayez Raissi lay on the damp grass and hugged the butt end of the Russian-made SVD sniper rifle to his shoulder. Dressed in black from head to toe, his face smeared with camouflage makeup, the terrorist blended into the canopy of trees and bushes around him as he lay on his stomach. The sun was clearing the horizon, spotlighting his target nicely.

Allahu Akbar. God is great.

He shifted his arm slightly and drew in a steadying breath. Looking through the PSO 1x4 scope attached to the top of the rifle, he slowly followed the perimeter of the large property two hundred yards downhill from his post. There was a gated entrance but no fence in the rear, only the double set of infrared laser tripwires that enclosed the half acre lot in the back where it sloped downhill. Raissi had found the tripwires on a previous scouting trip as well as the location of every motion detector and security camera posted around the house.

To the average criminal looking for a place to rob, the house's security was a deterrent. To a trained terrorist who had been observing the place and gathering intelligence, the simplistic security was almost insulting in its lack of challenge.

Raissi was no average criminal.

The house was dark, no one up yet. The terrorist scoped the woodsy area beyond the flowerbeds and the perimeter of the yard and mentally scoffed at Americans. Even with their heightened paranoia about terrorism in their homeland, they were still amateurs in comparison to security standards of officials in the Middle East. Their lack of security measures was not surprising, even for a CIA director. Americans were still arrogant in their belief they were safe on their home turf, especially because no attacks had taken place since 9/11. This arrogance made them easy targets. Stupidly, they were more concerned about their personal freedoms than their very lives. America's throat was fat and soft and that made Raissi and his comrades' job so much easier.

God is great.

Of course, this part of his job was made easier by his current benefactor. She was the reason he had made it to America and now stood on the threshold of destroying key leaders of the CIA. It galled him to think he was taking orders from a woman, but the means to the end was sanctioned by more than his own personal glory. His people would attain respect, and maybe, Raissi thought, some peace from his act of global revenge.

Raising his eye from the scope, he swung the rifle underneath his shoulder and onto his back. Rising to his feet, he glided smoothly from tree to tree and made his way down the side of the hill on the vacant lot adjacent to the target's property. As he neared a hedge that ran between the property lines, he dropped to his stomach and crawled the last few yards, never leaving the shadows.

Raissi squinted at the house but there was still no change in its dark façade. Rising up on one knee, he pulled a night-vision scope from his cargo pants and traced the infrared beams again. They wouldn't be a problem.

God is great.

After replacing the night-vision scope, he climbed snake-like back up the hill, stopping now and then to watch the sun continue to push the edges of night back. He also wanted to keep the woman at the top waiting. He knew her patience with him was measured out in small, controlled chunks. Making her wait gave him a minute or two of control, a reminder to her of his importance in her plan.

The number of sunrises he would witness was dwindling swiftly. If he stopped to notice this last one, so be it. At forty years of age, Raissi had seen more than his share of life and figured he'd already used up his allotment of days on the earth. He was battle-hardened from watching the land and the people he loved beaten again and again. The dreams of his youth had been beaten along with them. Now he was simply a messenger. One more messenger bringing war to the West.

Raissi scratched at the thick stubble on his jaw and ran a finger across the scar on his cheekbone. He had one more day. When the call from his benefactor came, Raissi and his comrades would be ready to move. They would deliver their message and strike another blow into the soft throat of America for their beloved Islam.

Allah's will be done.

In the shadows of the tree line, Raissi gave Susan Richmond a nod of commitment as he passed her by.

"Ace's Body Snatchers. Rack 'em, pack 'em and stack 'em. What can I do for you?"

"You've been made," Conrad said into the phone. "Did it ever occur to you to not drive the freakin' hearse?"

There was a short silence on the other end. "The Jeep had a flat, Connie. It's gettin' fixed today. And, come on, who'd suspect my body wagon?"

Conrad rubbed his forehead. "Stone also made you. No more surveillance for you, Ace."

"Aw, don't pull me yet. I needed a little practice, that's all. C'mon, bro. I'm down with this. I can do it."

"I'll get back to you." Conrad hung up and then paced the living room floor for the hundredth time.

"You look like a tiger in a cage, Con," Smitty said. "You're wearing a hole in the carpet."

"Go to hell."

Smitty toyed with a zip drive. "Why don't you do something constructive? Take your mind off her?"

The tiger's pace slowed but he didn't stop. "I don't need to take my mind off her. I'm fine."

"Really? Since when is 'fine' defined as aggressive, hostile and confrontational?"

Conrad stopped and blew a sharp breath out between his lips. "Stone has already informed Security about the bugs, so we can't remove them without throwing suspicion on Julia. When they do their sweep and find those bugs, they won't stop with her apartment. They'll sweep and search the whole building and then we're screwed."

"They can't search the other apartments without a warrant or permission from the renters."

"Hello. We're talking CIA here, Smith. They'll do whatever they want. Once they uncover the bugs in Julia's apartment, they won't have trouble getting permission from a judge or the other renters to search for more."

Smitty scratched his head. "So what do you want to do?"

"Do you still have the extra keys you lifted from the super's office in the basement?"

"I made copies and returned the originals."

"Good. Get them out. We're going to spread a few more listening devices around and plant a receiver in the basement."

"What about this stuff?" Smitty swept his hand across the computer hub. "You said we couldn't risk moving all of this in the middle of the day."

"Changed my mind. We need to break camp and get out of here."

Smitty let out a sigh and swiveled in the office chair toward the computer screen, shaking his head. "Okay, suggestions for a new home base of operation?" He moved the mouse and began shutting down the system.

"We're going mobile."

"How do we let Julia know where we're going to be? You can't exactly call her at Stone's."

Flynn actually toyed with the idea for a minute before discarding it. "I'll think of something," he said and headed out the door.

Conrad found the iPod he was looking for on Julia's nightstand beside the clock radio. It was surprising she hadn't taken it with her, but then again, she'd been distracted by their fight when she left.

Slipping it out of the leather case, he flattened the paper with his cell phone and pager numbers on top of the menu pad and slid the whole works back into the case. His fingers played with the cord from the ear buds, rolling it between his fingers as he wondered what Julia was doing. Was she at Stone's now, sitting out on the balcony? Reading a book in his study? Working out in his private gym in the basement?

Jesus, Flynn. You're losing it. Big time.

Not his mind or his insatiable drive. *It* as in his edge.

Yes, he was definitely losing his edge.

He figured he could blame his age. Chronologically, he was only thirty-two, but physically he was too old to deal with this crap. Mentally too. After years of living undercover, running agents and messing around with the worst of the worst, he was burning out. He'd done his damnedest, but the dictators, the religious zealots and the drug czars were still out there.

Terrorists were still terrorizing the innocent.

Special interest groups were still running the government.

Now on top of everything else, traitors were running the CIA.

It was getting harder and harder to convince himself he'd made any difference in the world at all. When it all came down to it, the changes he had brought about were unnoticeable in the Big Picture. He was feeling more like George Bailey these days than Conrad Flynn. Before he knew it, he'd be contemplating jumping off a bridge and find himself talking to his guardian angel.

He was giving serious consideration to walking away. If he'd really lost his edge, his guardian angel was a moot point. He was destined to meet with a bullet.

It wouldn't be difficult for him to disappear for good. He already had two separate identities established for himself that no one, not even Langley, knew about, and he had plenty of money, courtesy of the government and Smitty's investment proficiency, securely stashed in a bank in the Caymans.

All he had to do was walk.

He tossed the cord back on the nightstand and ran his hand over Julia's pillow.

But not yet.

Because there was Smitty, who was counting on him to finish this sting. Smitty, who had put his career aspirations aside and gone bad to help Conrad eradicate the shadow CIA. Smitty, who had worked side-by-side with him to protect Julia.

Ah yes, then there was Julia.

Conrad stared at her white camisole lying on the crumpled bedspread. Could he really walk away from her again? He played with the idea for a moment, remembering her outburst at him the night before...

You have no right to me anymore.

He'd never had any right to her, period. None. No one, not

even the Great Conrad Flynn as she liked to call him in bed, could ever own a piece of Julia Torrison. She was too independent to let them.

The best thing he could do for her, as well as himself, was to walk away. Disappear for good when this was all over.

Don't kid yourself, Flynn. Walking away from the CIA is child's play. Walking away from Julia Torrison is suicide.

Chapter Seventeen

Calculated risk. That's what it all came down to.

Daniel King finished his sandwich and lit a cigar as he sat on the patio just outside his home office. The estate was awash in bright green. Six massive oak trees, three on each side, lined the property, their spring leaves a perfect match to the normally well-manicured lawn.

However, today was not normal. An ugly line of rich black dirt bisected the once beautiful carpet of grass, and at the end of the trail, a small skid loader and a smattering of tools, hoses and pipes littered the ground. The part-time groundskeeper was working diligently to install a water fountain in the center of the property. Wife number two had insisted it was exactly what the place *needed*.

King blew smoke out of his mouth as he continued to watch. What *he* needed was to find the weak link in the proposal Susan Richmond had spelled out for him in detail yesterday to deal with the CIA's problems.

He had to admit, the way she had it laid out, it was damn near flawless. She had evidence showing a conspiracy in the CIA spearheaded by the Deputy Director of Operations, Michael Stone.

His motive? Revenge. Stone's father, William, had left the Marine Corps after ten years of service and was recruited as an intelligence officer for the United States. He took his family to Germany while under cover as a security consultant to a German diplomat. After two years, the elder Stone had extracted a good deal of compromising information from his foreign employer, all of which he had routinely fed back to the United States. However, the diplomat's wife had figured it out and turned William Stone over to the local authorities. Because his nonofficial cover did not afford him diplomatic immunity, William was arrested and imprisoned for spying.

While the American and German governments were negotiating his release, William Stone was beaten to death by a group of fellow prisoners. Michael was ten when his father died. His mother returned to the United States, disgraced and devastated, with her family of six children.

While Michael had grown up to follow in his father's footsteps, he was not suspected of harboring any ill will toward the CIA or the U.S. government. His psych evals and polygraphs were negative. His commitment to his country had been demonstrated in the field as a U.S. Marine, Force Recon, and later in the CIA's counterintelligence and counterterrorism departments before he became the Operations director. He was currently in line for the Director of Central Intelligence's spot.

But according to Susan, whether Stone showed it or not, somewhere along the line he had cracked.

The web Stone had weaved was intricate and Susan claimed she had detailed it down to the last strand. Stone of course had connections spanning all of the directorates of the CIA, but he also had a highly placed source within the National Intelligence Council.

To top it off, Stone's current girlfriend, an analyst and former spy in Susan's department, sat at the heart of the conspiracy. King knew the details of Julia Torrison's CIA career. Her former partner had not been killed in the line of duty, as everyone believed. According to Susan, he was actively working with Torrison and another defunct operator, Ryan Smith, to assist Stone. Disgruntled employees all four, they were systematically wreaking havoc with the CIA.

The senator took a long drag on his cigar. Susan, after watching them all for years, clearly knew the modus operandi of each of the four players like the back of her hand. She believed if any one of the rogue employees suspected they had been found out, the whole operation would shut down and the participants would disappear. If the plug was pulled on their operation, she was positive they would resist apprehension and therefore cause a unique situation, one that might call for lethal force. Lethal force would lead to a formidable and exhaustive investigation.

In an effort to avoid that, King and Richmond had agreed the best way to handle the group was to neutralize them in a calculated manner. Torrison was the group's weak link. Susan would use her to draw the others out. Conrad Flynn was the most dangerous of the group. His SEAL training had been honed to a steely efficiency for the CIA and his field skills used to quietly cripple countless terrorist organizations.

While Susan had left King in the dark about many of the specifics, he knew she had planned every step down to the smallest detail. The CTC chief had assured him she had analyzed every possible contingency and devised a strategy to handle each one. All she wanted now was a little help from him.

Because in the end, Susan Richmond still needed a safety net. Director Allen was at best an ineffectual leader who could not be trusted and therefore had to remain out of the loop. Nor did Susan know exactly how high the NIC source was in the food chain. If she delivered her information to the wrong person, Torrison and the others would not only disappear, the CTC chief herself would no doubt meet with a convenient death. She needed someone functioning outside the tainted halls of the CIA and the NIC to sign off on her operation and give her authorization to clean house. And because of the sensitive nature of the operation, national security issues had to be weighed against Congressional Notification.

In return for her allegiance, Susan Richmond wanted the DCI position when King became president. It was not an uncomplicated request nor was it an unreasonable one. He was sure there would be little blowback on him. She would have to be confirmed by the Senate, but with Michael Stone out of the picture and the fact she was more than qualified, she was assured serious consideration. He could make it happen.

For Senator King it all came down to calculated risk. Would Susan's plan work in his favor so he gained the bipartisan and constituent support that he needed? He would definitely have to stand up to intense scrutiny, but fulfilling his end of the bargain would be easy enough. If indeed he were elected President of the United States, he would offer Susan up as a good DCI candidate and let the congressional wolves tear her apart as they saw fit. She would have to survive the confirmation hearings on her own two feet.

If, however, King refused to help her, he knew she would

take her proposal to someone even higher in the government, possibly President Jeffries himself. The shit would definitely hit the fan, but the president would come out smelling like a rose. Jeffries would take full credit for cleaning up the CIA and, with his Homeland Security Director, would rebuild it from the top down to reassure the American people his administration had national security well under control. The voting public would sign him up for another four years without batting an eye.

King stubbed out the cigar and entered his office. Picking up his secure phone, he dialed Susan Richmond's home number.

Julia picked up Michael's briefcase off the bedroom floor and studied the digital keypad secured on it. "Piece of cake," she muttered to herself. Michael and Pongo, along with Michael's security detail, were out for a run. The only day Michael didn't run was Sundays. She had approximately forty minutes to open the case and copy the contents to a memory stick Smitty had supplied. The previous night, before her midnight foray outside, she'd managed to copy the files from Michael's laptop in his home office, including some encrypted files that had caused her problems. They were set up with special recognition software that wouldn't allow them to be copied. Running diagnostics on them, however, she'd found a way to hack into the software, disable it and make her copy.

Now computer number two. Julia set the timer on her watch for thirty minutes and snapped a pair of latex gloves on her hands. A little more time-consuming because of the lock, but probably no more complicated.

Michael was organized and had an excellent memory, but he also dealt with layers of passwords and secret codes with multifarious letter and number combinations. Julia had already found several of these hidden in different spots in his office—inside his favorite Tom Clancy novel, underneath the encased American flag given to his mother at his father's burial, a couple taped on the back of a framed shot of him and Tom onboard Tom's boat, cigars and beers raised in salute. One of them had been for his home laptop. She pulled a piece of paper from her jean pocket and stared at the three combinations she had left. One happened to be a set of numbers.

Taking her time, Julia typed the numbers into the lock.

Two seconds later, Julia let out a whispered "oh yeah" as the case opened.

Her joy was short lived. Every file on the computer was encrypted with a range of security levels. Disabling each level, copying the information and enabling the security codes again would take longer than the twenty-eight minutes she had left.

She started disabling anyway.

One hour later

"Have you seen my briefcase?"

Michael was standing in the office doorway, glowering, but on him Julia thought it was sexy. Pongo bounded in, carrying the large rawhide bone she'd brought him, and dropped it at her feet to begin chewing on it.

Michael was fresh from the shower, his blond hair still wet, and he was sporting a dark blue T-shirt and sport pants, looking every bit the weekend warrior ready for a backyard game of football. Unfortunately, she couldn't enjoy his GQ looks, since the laptop that was supposed to be in the briefcase in question was under the couch where she was sitting, still in mid-download. She'd slid it there when she heard his footsteps on the stairs, picking up the remote and flipping the widescreen TV on. A rerun of *Get Smart* was filling the room. Julia hoped the doofus spy show wasn't some sort of cosmic comment on her current situation.

"I brought it down," she said, pointing casually to the briefcase sitting next to Michael's desk and praying he wouldn't open it.

Of course, he went right for it. Julia shut off the TV and jumped up. "You're not going to start work already, are you?"

Michael picked up the briefcase and set it on the desk. Good thing she'd stuck a heavy coffee table book in it to weight it just in case. "I have a lot of work to do, Abby." He dropped into his leather desk chair. "This thing with Iran is getting serious."

So they were back to using her alias. Julia sighed inwardly. Before Michael could key in his security code on the briefcase's pad, she inserted herself between him and the desk, and pushed the case back, planting her butt where the briefcase had been. "It's Saturday and you haven't even had breakfast or a cup of coffee yet. You need to get a life, Stone."

Sitting back in his chair, he met her gaze with defiance, but his voice held little. "Watch it, Quinn. You're starting to sound like my last girlfriend."

She shot him a wide grin and used his own words against him. "Are you being testy, Michael?"

"I'm too tired to be testy, Ab."

She planted her bare feet in his chair, one on each side of his lap. "What exactly happened to your last girlfriend?"

She was still wearing her capri pajama bottoms and Michael ran his hands over the smooth skin of her calves. "I admitted my darkest secret to her," he said, "and then I had to kill her."

Julia quirked an eyebrow at him. "Michael Stone has deep, dark secrets worth killing for?"

"Don't we all?"

Regarding him for a long moment, she leaned forward. Putting her face down next to his, she whispered, "Tell me yours and I'll tell you mine."

The humor that had been in his eyes disappeared. "Don't tempt me. There's a lot about you I still don't know. Huge gaps I can't fill. Questions I should ask, but don't because I'm not sure I want to know what you're hiding."

Julia pulled back, feeling slapped and wishing she'd kept her mouth shut. Before she could try to change the subject, Michael sat up. "If I ask about your childhood, you change the subject. If I bring up a family story, like a favorite Christmas or a pet I had, you listen and ask questions, but never offer your own family version."

"My childhood isn't full of fond memories. You know that. I never knew my real father. James liked to drink and knock us around. My mother died when I was still a teenager. That about sums it up."

Michael nodded, seemingly in understanding, but didn't stop badgering her. "How about your past adult life? Drunken college forays? Waitressing jobs? How Susan found you? The only time you volunteer information about your time in the field is when it's directly linked to your current CTC work. Why is that?"

Julia studied him carefully for a moment, wondering which direction to take this conversation in. The laptop was still working away under the couch and she estimated it needed another few minutes to complete the file transfers to the jump drive plugged into its USB port. Then she needed another five to reestablish the security fields. And then she had to get the laptop back in the briefcase without Michael knowing.

And at some point, she had to feed her growling stomach. She was starving.

Go get 'em, Mata, she told herself and took a deep breath. "That's not exactly true. I've told you personal things about me and my life on several occasions, but I could tell you didn't really want to know more details about my life with Conrad."

Michael removed his hands from her ankles. "The Great Conrad Flynn." His laugh lacked humor. "Isn't that what you called him?"

Julia drew herself up a little, putting space between them. Sharing that piece of info probably hadn't been her best move, but she couldn't deny the female part of her kind of liked that Michael was jealous of Con. Conrad was definitely jealous of Michael. Having two good men in love with her wasn't the worse thing in the world. However, she knew it was definitely time to get off this track with boyfriend number one. She needed Michael in a better mood before she could get him out of the room and hit him up with her plan.

"Michael, I have never respected any man as much as I do you." On cue, she saw his jaw unclench. Good. She leaned forward, kept her eyes locked on his. "What you do for this country every day, the millions of people you help keep safe whether we're at war or at peace...it blows my mind you could be such a good guy, through and through. There aren't many like you. Not in Washington, not in the whole country." She paused, searching his face. "I don't talk about my past, because I try hard to live in the present. My present is so much nicer than my past. Every day I spend with you is like a dream. You make me happy and you make me feel safe. In case you didn't realize it, those are two pretty cool accomplishments."

Michael softened, reached up and patted her thigh. "Are you brown-nosing, Quinn?"

Julia grabbed her chest in mock indignation. "Me? Brown-nose? Never."

"You're up to something. Mind telling me what?"

Julia smiled at his astuteness and his directness, two qualities she'd always admired in him. "Not so fast, big guy. You need coffee and breakfast." *She* needed coffee and breakfast. She stood and pulled him out of his chair.

He started to argue, but Julia cut him off. "The world will not end if Michael Stone takes half an hour for himself. Come with me."

"Okay, okay," he relinquished, following her to the kitchen. Pongo tagged along. "But there's a new conflict brewing in the Middle East with Iran, and terrorists are about to wipe out the G5 summit in Geneva. When Titus calls this morning and wants to know what I'm doing about all of that, what do you suggest I tell him?"

"Tell him I forced you at gunpoint to eat breakfast." She filled a large white mug with hot coffee and pushed it into one of his hands. Then she grabbed the *Post* off the counter and put that in his other hand. "Tell him I seduced you with my tantalizingly delicious French toast."

One of Michael's eyebrows rose. "You made French toast?"

"I'm going to make some right now. You go upstairs and relax on the balcony. It's a beautiful morning. Drink your coffee, read the paper. Breakfast will be ready in about twenty minutes."

Michael studied her for a moment and took a sip of his coffee. "And then we'll talk."

Filling a second mug for herself, she nodded. "Then we'll talk." As Michael turned to go, she added, "I want to know about that girlfriend you mentioned."

He shot her a *yeah, right* look over his shoulder and was gone.

Letting out her breath, Julia found herself looking down at Pongo. Never one to ignore the possibility of food finding its way to the floor when she was cooking, he wagged his stubby tail in anticipation. "How do I get myself into these messes?" she asked him. His mouth opened slightly and he panted.

"Thanks for the insight." Without wasting more time, she went to work starting breakfast and finishing her traitorous spying.

Chapter Eighteen

"Eat," Julia demanded.

Michael didn't need to be told twice. He poured maple syrup on his French toast and dug in. The first bite was enough to make the Middle East conflict and his worries about impending doom in Europe suddenly seem less important.

"Do you know," he said, looking at her, "that you are the best thing that's ever happened to me?"

He saw something flicker in her eyes...sadness? Regret? She diverted them to her own stack of French toast and sprinkled powdered sugar on it. Pongo sat at her feet, gaze never leaving the table.

Michael willed her to look at him. She obliged and gave him a halting smile. "Now who's brown-nosing? Trying to get me to forget about that past girlfriend?"

From experience, Michael knew that a current lover asking about an ex meant she was thinking about a future with him. He smiled and feasted on some more of his breakfast. For a few moments they ate in peace, Abby slipping Pongo small bites of toast under the table.

"Pongo's trained to never take food from anyone but me," Michael said.

"My cooking's hard to resist."

Michael agreed. Finishing off the last few bites, he took a long drink of coffee and pushed his chair back a few inches. He sat watching Abby. After a minute, she stopped chewing and raised her eyebrows.

Michael just waited. He knew she knew what he was waiting for. She kept struggling to act and sound casual when she was anything but. Her body armor was back in place and it made him damn frustrated. Up until Ryan Smith had made his appearance, Michael was sure he had been making progress at destroying that armor. He'd thought Abigail was finally allowing him into her inner world. In the past few days though she'd been distant at times, almost confrontational at others, and the next minute she was working him over with charm and teasing. Was it really all because of that damned polygraph test? Or the memories of her past life that Smith resurrected?

She still thinks you don't trust her.

Michael met her eyes. "Talk to me."

Abigail threw her last bite of French toast into Pongo's waiting mouth and pushed her plate back. She grabbed her glass of milk and took a sip. "I pulled the listening device out of my car. Has Security debugged my apartment yet?"

He nodded. "Ben Raines called while you were fixing breakfast. He personally swept your place and found three bugs and the wiretap on your phone. Along with some of his security officers, he then swept the rest of the building and found six more bugs located in two other apartments. Looks like your landlord might have been doing a little eavesdropping."

Abby coughed, choking on the milk she was swallowing. She reached for the napkin in her lap and wiped her mouth with it. Setting the milk down, she gave him a confused, somewhat horrified look. "Do we know why?"

"Raines ran a background check on him and found a prior arrest record for taking photos and video of women unbeknownst to them and posting it on a website. All misdemeanor stuff, but apparently the guy likes to look up women's skirts."

"God, did he have hidden video cameras too?"

That brought a smile from Michael. "Raines didn't report any. Why? Got something to hide?"

She laughed and cleared her throat a couple of times. "Just me running around in the buff, I guess."

"Well, maybe I better call Raines back and ask him to install a few surveillance pieces for me then."

Rolling her eyes, she scratched Pongo's chin. "Is Raines tracking Ryan Smith?"

Michael raised an eyebrow at her.

"What? Is that confidential or something?"

"Yes."

"Yes, that's confidential? Or yes, Raines is tracking Smith?"

"Both," he answered matter-of-factly.

Her face lit up and she grinned. "You're so easy, Stone. I make breakfast for you and I have you eating out of my hands."

"Anything else you want to know while I'm so gullible?"

The grin left her face. She went right for the kill. "Do you really trust me?"

He didn't hesitate, didn't even blink. "You know I do."

"Then let *me* track Smitty."

"What?"

She leaned on the table. "Ben Raines is never going to find him. But I can. I know how Smitty thinks, how he works. I'm your ace in the hole on this one."

He shook his head. "No way. We don't know what he's up to. It's too dangerous."

"Too dangerous?" She straightened up and frowned at him. "My God, Michael, I was a field operator for five years, tracking everything from terrorists to gunrunners. Ryan is the CIA's version of Mr. Rogers. I think I can handle him." She pointed a finger at him. "Plus, Smitty and I were close. He trusts me, and that can work to your advantage. I'm probably the only person who can bring him back in."

Michael crossed his arms over his chest and stared at her for a moment. "I don't like it."

"But you know I'm right."

Damn, she *was* right, Michael stewed. She *was* his ace in the hole. He'd actually already given the idea consideration. If only he wasn't so tied up with the current state of foreign affairs, he'd work it with her just so he could cover her back.

"I'll authorize you to work on the case on one condition." He held up his finger. "You work with Raines. That way if anything serious goes down, you've got experienced backup."

She crossed her arms, mimicking him with dogged determination. "No way, Stone. I don't do that partner shit anymore."

"Take it or leave it, *Quinn*. You either do the partner *shit* or you don't work the case."

Abigail sat back and let out a seemingly disgusted sigh. Pongo moved closer, laying his head on her thigh and staring up at her with his big brown dog eyes.

She patted the dog's head. "It's not a good move. Raines won't like being pushed into working with me, an analyst, and he'll want to know why I'm qualified to track Smitty. If he figures out who I really am, my cover will be blown at headquarters."

He'd already considered this. "It's still the best arrangement I can give you. Raines doesn't have to know anything about your past. If I give him the order to work with you, he'll do it, no questions asked."

She was silent for a several heartbeats, her analytical brain in overdrive. Michael could see her weighing her desire to go after Smitty with having this undesirable partner. "I'll have to take a leave of absence from the CTC."

He shook his head. "Susan won't go along with losing her head analyst. You might get away with partial leave though if I tell her what you're working on. She'll need to know anyway, you'll need her help with this."

"I'll need her to give me everything she's got on Smitty and I'll use her as my source if I need assistance. Besides you, she's the only one I trust."

"You aren't authorized to read Ryan Smith's file, but Susan will give you the unclassified material. Raines is on his way here to check for listening devices. You can meet him then and we'll go over your plan."

"What's his background?"

"He's ex-FBI. Plenty of citations in his file and he'll probably take over the CTC Director slot when Susan moves on. I've known him for a lot of years. Always found him professional and easy to work with."

"What makes you so sure I have a plan?"

Michael looked at her in mock disbelief. "Abigail Quinn without a plan?" He made a dismissive gesture with his hand. "You've been thinking up a plan from the moment you saw that tape."

She rose out of her chair, Pongo moving out of the way, and wrapped her arms around his neck. "Think you're pretty smart, don't you?"

He parted his legs and pulled her close. "Smart enough to keep you under my thumb day *and night*," he said, mimicking her.

She laughed. "So which is better, the sex or my cooking?"

"Hmmm." He rubbed his chin. "That's a tough one."

She smacked his arm and he tickled her ribs, Pongo barking and jumping at him in fun. After a moment, Abby pushed off him and started clearing the table. He started to help.

"I'll do it," she said, taking his plate out of his hands. "I know you need to get to work."

Michael kissed the top of her head. "You really are good for me."

She smiled and he saw the flicker of sadness pass over her face again before she walked away.

As soon as the door to Michael's office closed, Julia breathed a sigh of relief. The two memory sticks were tucked inside her bra, the laptop with its security system back in place was sitting safely inside Michael's briefcase. On top of that, she'd gotten Michael to okay her plan to go after Smitty. Now she could get to work.

Only she wasn't working with Ben Raines. No way. No how. Not in this lifetime.

After sticking all the dishes in the dishwasher, she filled the soap dispenser and turned it on. Then she high-tailed it upstairs, grabbed her purse and her jacket and came back down. She stuck a short note on the door telling Michael she'd forgotten an appointment and would be back later. He was on the phone. She could hear his voice filtering through the door. It would be awhile before he even missed her. She kissed the top of Pongo's head and headed for the door.

As she pulled the Audi out of the garage stall, she plugged her cell phone into the battery charger and turned J. Lo up on the CD player. Her heart was pounding a little faster than normal as she gave the guard at the gate a big smile and a flirty wave. He tipped his hat at her and motioned her through.

Chapter Nineteen

Just drive, Julia told herself. *Don't look back, just drive.*

It was no surprise someone was following her. She'd been expecting it for the last three days, although now she was sure the order hadn't come from Michael. However she wasn't sure who the driver was behind the wheel of the rusty Ford Econoline van that stayed three to four cars behind her. Raines? Conrad? Good grief, even Ace was in on surveillance these days. At least the car wasn't a hearse this time. The thought of that following her around conjured up weird vibes, like someone was just waiting for her to keel over dead.

Julia slipped off the highway and began crisscrossing smaller roads, casually weaving her way around Arlington while circling closer to her apartment. She needed to drop the memory sticks off to Smitty and tell him and Con about her plan and how she now had Michael's official okay to track Smitty down. She'd have more time to help them—that part they'd like. The rest...well, she'd probably have to call Ben Raines, turn Smitty in and explain the rest of her plan afterwards...

Julia glanced in her rearview and noticed the tail had disappeared. She slowed the car by a few miles an hour and divided her gaze between the road in front of her and the road behind while she drove. If she'd lost her tail that easily, it had to be Ace or someone else equally unqualified.

Or she was just being overly paranoid.

Julia checked the mirror again after another mile. Nothing.

She increased her speed and headed back toward Interstate 66. Within minutes she exited the interstate and headed home with still no sign of her tail. She scanned the parking lot outside her apartment building and saw nothing out of the ordinary.

Just inside the building's main door, she waited at the window, hidden behind what was once a white gauzy curtain now gone yellow with age. After ten minutes, she was rewarded for her patience as the Ford van pulled slowly up to the curb about fifty yards away. It looked right at home parked behind a neighbor's woody-sided Plymouth station wagon.

Fact: Conrad Flynn wouldn't be caught dead in a Ford.

Julia went directly to Con and Smitty's door. There was no answer. She considered picking the lock and letting herself in. No doubt they'd packed up the computer equipment, wiped the place clean of prints and taken off before Raines and his group had canvassed the place. But Conrad would be in contact...he might even be in her apartment at that moment, so she left the lock alone and went to her apartment instead.

She was shocked to discover her apartment was a mess. Couch cushions were askew. Her measly amount of silverware was dumped in the kitchen sink. Her bed had been stripped. Drawers of clothes had been dumped on the floor. The place looked like professional criminals had tossed it.

The CIA had handheld instruments that could scan a room or car for listening devices without ever touching a thing. There was no reason for this destruction of her personal property. Michael had only requested Security check for bugs. Julia felt a wave of uneasiness wash over her.

What was Raines really looking for? Numbered bank account books? Classified documents? *The name and number of my bookie?*

Conrad's voice whispered in her ear. *Access is power, Julia. Whoever did this is trying to scare you, show you who's in control.*

Julia shook her head to remove that thought and fixed the cushions on the couch. She moved on to the bedroom and felt her blood begin to boil as she picked up her bras and panties and returned them to the dresser drawer. She couldn't stop the fleeting image of male security officers enjoying themselves slingshotting her thongs around the room. The image didn't fit with her impression of Benito Raines, but then she didn't really know him.

Benny, my boy, you are in deep shit when I get hold of you.

As she continued returning her apartment to normal, she

contemplated marching out to the van and shooting its tires out if it were Agency goons in it. That would certainly get her message across to Ben but rob her of real satisfaction. Michael would no doubt pull her off Smitty's case to chastise her. No, she'd have to hold her anger in check for now. As long as she was in charge of tracking down Smitty, she could buy him and Con, and herself, a few more days to figure everything out.

Julia had just picked up her iPod, when she heard a noise behind her. Expecting to find Con, she took a step back when it was a woman standing in the doorway instead.

"What a mess," the woman said, her leer scanning the room's dishevelment. "You should think about hiring a housekeeper."

She was tall, dark-haired and her words were crisp and accented ever so slightly. Warning bells were going off in Julia's head—she knew she knew this woman, but she couldn't place her. Slipping the iPod casually into her purse, Julia let her hand rest on the SIG hidden there. "And you should think about knocking before entering someone's home."

"Touché," the woman acknowledged with a glance at Julia's purse.

"You're the one following me?"

The woman's hair moved with her nod.

"Do I know you?"

The woman brushed her red fingernails across a neat row of bangs and smiled coyly. "Not exactly." Her accent was definitely German. "You and I are going to help each other out, Ms. Torrison."

Letting the purse slid out of her hands and to the bed, Julia pulled out the gun and crossed her arms, leaving it showing. She raised her eyebrows, doing her best to imitate Michael, and waited.

The woman took the hint. "I have information that will save Conrad Flynn's life. Yours too."

Julia studied the woman's face and felt another twinge of familiarity. She remembered the picture Con had shown her of Heinrich Kramer and his girlfriend. Her pulse, already pounding out a pretty good tempo, kicked up another notch. "I'm listening."

"The person you are looking for is Susan Richmond."

Julia sat at the kitchen table and watched Cari Von Motz carefully. Cari was doing the same to her—their eyes were locked in a stare down. It was hard to gauge her truthfulness, Julia decided, but not her confidence. Or defiance.

She immediately liked her.

"First of all," Julia said, "how do you know I'm looking for someone?"

"I know Flynn is alive and Smith is AWOL from the CIA, and I know why," Cari answered with forced patience, as if explaining to a three-year-old. "I know you are sleeping with Michael Stone and helping Flynn and Smith. I know a few other things as well. Things that are—how do you say it? Sensitive in nature?" She spread a well-manicured hand. "How do you think I know these things?"

Julia felt her morning's breakfast twisting in her stomach. "Susan." Her gut rejected the idea, but her brain was snapping pieces into place at the speed of light. Susan, her boss. Long-term, loyal employee of the CIA. Conrad's trusted friend. A traitor?

It was hard to wrap her mind around it.

Julia chewed the inside of her cheek. The gun was still in her hand, the memory sticks still in her bra, and they were starting to dig in just above her underwires. Her body was humming with a discomfiting energy that made her want to jump up, find Con, call Michael and hunt Susan down and demand an explanation all at the same time. And she positively had to get those darn silicone jump drives out of her bra in the next minute or she was going to scream. Instead, she took a breath and considered her options.

Nope, the memory sticks were going to have to stay put. She had to get the full story.

The listening devices Con had given her to distribute at Michael's house were in the pocket of her coat. Because Raines hadn't swept the house for bugs yet, she'd kept them on her, planning to distribute them tonight. Now, she set the gun on the table to distract Cari while she slipped her left hand in her pocket, brought out a bug under the table, ran a finger over it to turn it on and stuck it to the wood. *Please, Con, be listening.*

"Okay, Cari," she said, smoothing her hand over the black SIG, "Susan's told you about Conrad Flynn, Ryan Smith and myself. How do you know she's the person we're looking for?"

Cari brought her eyes up from the gun. "Because I'm the one who has been helping her all along to lead Flynn and Smith on a wild goose chase ending here in America. She is the CIA's traitor. She used me to set all of you up."

"Why you?"

Clicking her nails on the table, Cari flipped her hair back and sighed. "It is a long and complicated story."

"Give me the Cliff Notes."

"The what?"

"The condensed version."

Cari studied her for a long minute. "I was given up for adoption at birth. It was a private adoption. The records were sealed in Geneva. As a teenager, I began looking for my birth mother but I only found dead ends. When I hooked up with Heinrich Kramer, he had various connections who helped me find her. When I found out who she was, Heinrich and I decided to blackmail her."

Julia was momentarily baffled. "You're telling me Susan Richmond is your mother?"

Cari nodded. "I wanted a life here in America. A life of privilege, like she enjoys. She owes me that. But when I contacted her, told her I would out her if she didn't bring me to America, she turned the tables on me. She told me I had to do something for her first, and then she would bring me here and set me up with a trust fund of sorts."

Julia weighed the story judiciously. On a cellular level, she was relieved Cari was pointing a finger at someone other than Michael, but she needed more evidence to believe Susan was in any way connected to the shadow CIA. "Give me concrete details, Cari. I'm finding it very difficult to picture Susan as the CIA's mole."

Resignation spread across Cari's features. "My mother's top analyst, I knew you would ask for proof." She reached into an inside coat pocket and Julia's hand closed over the butt of the gun. Cari stopped, eyed the gun and shot a look at Julia. Julia nodded for her to bring her hand out. She did so slowly. "A disc." She laid it on the table. "It contains a diary of sorts of the past five years. Flynn and Smith will corroborate much of what's on here. They'll recognize their own parts in my mother's great scheme."

Julia clenched her jaw, took the disc and fingered it. There was only one way to find out if Cari's story was true. She needed a look at that disc. "Why is Susan doing this?"

Again, Cari struggled to be patient. "You know very well she is an aggressive career woman. She has an agenda. A timeline. Her career has not progressed as quickly as she thought it would." She paused. "Even though she refused to marry my father, and she gave me up, she has never made it to the top of the CIA like she expected."

Fingering the gun, Julia thought of Conrad and Smitty's "inside" person. It had to be Susan.

Cari shifted in her chair. "Susan has a partner outside the CIA, but I don't know who he is. Someone high up who has promised her advancement if she makes the CIA look strong again."

Meeting Cari's gaze across the table, Julia asked, "Why are you here, Cari, telling me all of this? What do you want?"

"Revenge, and a new life." Sitting forward, she rested her arms on the table. "America is where I want to be, but I've realized my mother will never allow me to live here. I'm a mistake she does not want to think about. She has already refused to fulfill her end of our bargain until you, Flynn, Smith and her bosses at the CIA are out of the way. I do not believe she will fulfill it even if her plan works. And where does that leave me? Back in Germany, broke and out of work. Heinrich is dead. I have nothing to go back to." She tapped one nail firmly on the table. "I want to stay here."

"Get a green card, get a job, become a citizen. It's not that hard."

"You don't understand," she hissed. "I have a criminal record in my country. It is not so easy anymore to become an American with a background like mine. That's why I needed Susan to help me. She could erase my past and give me a nice, comfortable future."

Julia decided to skip informing Cari that by participating in Susan's treason, she was a criminal in this country as well. It was hard to feel sympathy for her, but in some ways she did. "Why are you bringing this information to me?"

"I want you to take it to Michael Stone. He will believe you, and he will help me. My mother will be arrested and I will testify against her. The CIA's problems will be solved." She quirked an eyebrow. "And so will yours and Flynn's. Susan is planning to eliminate all of you, you understand."

She understood. No need to know if Cari's definition of *eliminate* was the same as hers. She could see it on the younger woman's face. "How?"

"I do not know the details. But I do know if Plan A fails, she has Plan B."

"And what does Plan B involve?"

Smiling indulgently, Cari rose from her seat. "I've given you enough for now. You give that disc to Director Stone and tell him what I told you. If he agrees to give me immunity, I will testify against Susan." She pushed in her chair. "Then I will tell you what I know about Plan B."

As she made her way down the hallway, Julia followed. "You're in as much danger as Flynn and I are, Cari. Susan will eliminate you too, if she believes you are a threat. Why don't you come with me right now and we'll go see Director Stone. You can tell him in person what's going on and walk him through the information on this disc."

Cari stopped at the door, shook her head. "No. Not yet."

"Why not?"

Cari gave Julia a defiant look. "Sorry, Ms. Torrison, but I do not trust you. Not completely, anyway. You are my mother's protégée. If you follow my directions, and help me, then I will help you in return. I'll be in touch."

Julia watched her go, her nerves tingling with anticipation. She half expected for a car to come whizzing around the corner and run Cari down, or a bullet to drop her in the street. But the woman made it to the rusty van and disappeared a few seconds later.

As Julia locked the apartment door, her phone rang. Caller ID told her it was private caller. Debating whether to pick it up, she unceremoniously pulled the memory sticks out of her bra, breathed a sigh of relief and stuck them in her coat pocket. The phone rang again and she relented.

"Hello?"

"Where the hell did you find Cari Von Motz?" Conrad's voice rumbled in her ear.

"She found me."

"Are you at home?"

"Yes."

"Doors and windows locked?"

"Yes."

"Gun loaded?"

"Conrad—" Julia started, but he cut her off.

"Gun loaded and in your hand, Torrison?"

Julia quick scooped the gun up off the table, but she wasn't intimidated by his gruffness. "Yes," she said levelly.

"Don't open the door to anyone but me."

"I wouldn't dream of it."

"I'm on my way."

The phone went dead in her hand.

Chapter Twenty

Julia paced, eyeing the disc. She knew she should wait for Con before she looked at it, but she was seriously thinking about discarding that idea. Cari had given the disc to her. It only made sense she be the first one to look it over.

But on the other hand, confirming Susan's traitorous actions alone wasn't all that appealing. She felt the same sickening feeling she'd felt after the explosion when she thought Con had died. Feeling like someone had just gutted her. She wanted Conrad there when she looked at the contents of the disc. He and Smitty were really the only ones who would know for sure if Cari was telling the truth or not.

Relief washed over her at the thought of Conrad. Funny how after months of living without him, she had welcomed his presence back into her life again so easily, and after the past two days of knowing he was near, she missed him.

Glancing at the disc as she passed the kitchen table again, she decided to boot up her computer and just take a peek at the files. She was too antsy to sit and wait while the computer was opening Windows, so she grabbed her backpack from the closet floor in her bedroom, threw some underwear and other essentials in it and set it on the bed.

Just in case, she told herself.

Back at the computer, she put the disc in and started to read. It was a mixture of German and English, mostly German, and Julia swore under her breath. Ten minutes later, she was rubbing her temples where a headache was brewing when Conrad and Smitty came sweeping into her small den.

"How do you do that?" she asked. "Turn into ghosts and float through the walls or something?"

Smitty held up a key as Conrad blew past him to look at the computer screen. "Keys are easier."

Julia rolled her eyes and vacated the seat. Conrad plopped into it, reading before his butt hit the upholstery.

He closed the file Julia had up and hit several keystrokes. The hard drive hummed. Without taking his attention off the screen, he held out his hand and snapped his fingers. "Disc."

Smitty opened a slim case and exchanged the disc with the one in the tower. A few seconds later, the original had a copy. Conrad pulled up the files and began to read again. Smitty unzipped a briefcase and opened up a laptop. Using the copy, he began to read as well.

Julia went to the kitchen and started the coffeepot. Waiting for it to brew, she paced between the kitchen and the den, trying to read over Con's shoulder, but not able to keep up with his good German. As he flew through the typed pages, Julia's headache kicked up a notch.

"Goddamn," Conrad muttered several times under his breath in the space of about five minutes. Smitty said nothing, but Julia noted the way he kept running a hand through his hair. Pretty soon he'd have it standing straight up.

It took over an hour for the two men to read through everything. Another hour to discuss and analyze the information contained in Cari's diary entries. Julia listened and analyzed, filled coffee mugs and asked questions until she was exhausted. Cari had been a busy woman. So had Susan, apparently.

Since none of them had eaten lunch and Julia's cupboards were bare, she called Ace and ordered him to pick up groceries and come over. When he arrived, she put him to work in the kitchen with her. Pulling out a wok, she heated olive oil, and made Ace sauté onions, peppers and mushrooms. She put several cups of rice in her rice cooker with a bouillon cube and turned it on. Next she added precooked chicken strips and teriyaki sauce to the wok. While the chicken was heating, she called Michael, got his voice mail and left him a message that she was staying at her apartment again. Throwing snow peas and carrots into the wok, she concentrated on cooking and tried not to think about how irritated he would be with her.

The smells drew the hungry men from the den. Smitty set the table and Con set out beers for all of them. During the meal, cramped around Julia's small table even with the leaf in it, Ace made light conversation, but Con sat staring at his beer, moving the bottle in slow circles with one hand while devouring his food in silence with the other.

When the last grain of rice was gone, Ace cleared the table and Julia loaded the dishwasher. It was growing dark outside and Smitty took Ace to help unload computer hardware from the van he and Con were using. He wanted to set up their base center again in their apartment.

Con sat at the table. His jaw was clenched so hard Julia feared he'd shear off enamel. Sadness welled up in her for all of them to lose such a trusted and respected friend, but especially for Conrad.

Susan had recruited him to be a special counterterrorism expert in Europe, placed him in the jobs he wanted and had given him enough lead to do just about anything he deemed necessary in those jobs. She had trusted him to carry out his work with little interference and he knew she'd claim deniability if he was caught taking care of business outside the normal parameters established by the U.S. government and the CIA. Not at all how Michael ran things, but Susan and Conrad had formed a bond over the years that was nearly unbreachable. Susan was one of a handful of people Conrad had trusted with his life.

Now, she had betrayed him.

Julia knew exactly how that felt.

She sat at the table, took the beer bottle from his hand. "Sucks, doesn't it?"

Con looked at her, looked away. "Yeah."

For a few minutes, they said nothing. Then Julia got up, brought Con a fresh beer. "I wonder who Cari's dad is."

Con took a drink, eyed her over the bottle. "Why?"

Julia gave a shrug, got herself a beer. "I never knew my dad, either."

"So now you're feeling sorry for her?"

On some level, Julia did feel sorry for her. "I was just wondering. I wish I'd have asked her."

Con rolled his eyes, twisted the beer bottle around. "We can't know for sure she's even telling the truth, Julia."

Julia stared at him in disbelief. "Five-plus-years of diary

entries is a pretty elaborate lie."

"Cari may be working for Stone, trying to throw us off his trail and onto Susan's."

Words eluded her for a moment. "Have you lost your mind? You still think Michael is behind all of this?"

When he didn't answer, Julia felt a fissure crack inside of her, white-hot anger born of exhaustion and frustration reaching for the surface. "You need to get a grip, Flynn. Cari Von Motz just handed us the Titanic on a platter and you're still questioning whether the ship actually existed."

"All the evidence Smitty and I have points to Stone."

"Because Susan set it up that way!"

For the second time that day, Julia found herself locked in a stare down. Con was more intimidating than Cari, but Julia was not, nor ever had been, scared of him. "I know this requires a big shift in your thinking, but you have to look at the facts. Susan Richmond is using you to destroy Michael's career so she can further hers. She set us all up, Con, including her own *daughter* to pull this off. She's a coldhearted bitch who will stop at nothing to get what she wants."

Con pushed his chair back, left the table to stare out her patio door. His arms crossed over his chest, his back to her, Julia remembered the definition she'd seen in his back yesterday morning when he was lying asleep on her couch. She closed her eyes for a minute to remember it fully. Then took a deep breath and plunged back into the present. "Your dislike of Michael is clouding your judgment," she said quietly.

He turned on her, his eyebrows drawn down, a nerve in his cheek dancing. "And your schoolgirl crush on him is clouding yours."

Schoolgirl crush? Julia sat speechless for a moment. Thinking about it, she decided arguing with Conrad, throwing down a gauntlet, wasn't going to resolve their disagreement. "Okay." She struggled to keep her voice steady. "Maybe you're right. But I'm right too. We have to look at this with logic, not emotion. We'll get it figured out tonight and tomorrow we'll decide what to do with the information, who we'll take it to. Agreed?"

Smitty and Ace came breezing in, but they stopped at the visible tension in the room and looked from Conrad to her and back to him. Con shrugged. "I'm not agreeing to anything at this point."

Julia felt her anger rise again. "It's the right thing to do."

"Maybe for you."

"What does that mean?"

Con scrubbed his face with both hands and looked at his feet. "I want you off this operation. You can go back to Stone's tonight. Smitty and I will figure this out."

Julia got up and stood by her chair, gripping the back tightly. "I risked life and limb to copy Michael's computer files and risked my career to protect you, to help you." She pointed at the chair. "I sat here and got Cari to tell me how and why she's been helping Susan create this whole mess, and now you think you're going to kick me off this operation?" She paused. "You better think again."

Con crossed his arms again. His next words came out firmly, distinctly, and cut Julia to the quick. "I can't trust you, Jules."

"*What*? Why you dirty rotten—"

Before she could reach out and slap him, Smitty grabbed her arm and steered her into the den. "Let me talk to him," he said in a low voice. "He's barely slept in a week and he's already on emotional overload because of you. This thing with Susan—gosh—the guy's skin has been peeled back and his guts are hanging out, you know? He's mad as hell and he doesn't know what to do with all of that. He doesn't trust anyone right now, probably not even me. We have to cut him some slack. By tomorrow we'll have this figured out and Con will feel in control again. That's all he needs. To feel in control."

Tears stung the back of her eyelids even as anger bubbled inside her like a hot springs. "I'm not going back to Michael's tonight. I don't care what he says. I'm staying here and helping you figure out what is going on. So decide what you want me to do because I'm staying."

Smitty gave her a lopsided smile, and ruffled her hair. "All right, I can use you. The first thing on our agenda is to set up a timeline using Cari's journal entries and our notes and see if it all jibes. You can help with that. You'll notice details I won't. But hang tight for a few minutes and let me talk to Con."

Julia nodded and let Smitty push her down onto the couch before he went back to the kitchen. Tears slid down her cheeks as she listened to the muffled conversation in the other room.

Ace came in, sat down beside her without a word. After reaching into his back pocket, he brought out a clean cotton hankie and offered it to her. She took it, blew her nose and gave him a thankful look.

Ace shook his head slowly and clicked his tongue against his teeth. "Man, this spy shit is crazy stuff."

Julia sniffed. "You haven't seen anything yet."

Chapter Twenty-One

Thoroughness was a hallmark of Conrad Flynn. Ryan Smith too. At one a.m., Julia left the two of them in their apartment with the computers and the timeline and dragged herself to her bedroom and collapsed. She stuck the SIG under her pillow.

The room was still dark when she woke around five thirty with all her senses on alert. There was no noise, but she knew someone was in her room. Had Cari come back? Slowly, she reached under her pillow, wrapped her hand around the gun...

"It's me, Jules." Conrad's voice came to her from the corner. As Julia's eyes adjusted, she could make him out, sitting on a chair. "I'd rather not be target practice today, so don't shoot at me. I'm too tired to move."

Julia withdrew her hand and sat up, pushing hair out of her face. "What are you doing in here, sitting in the dark?"

"Watching you sleep." He paused, let out a sigh. "Making sure you're safe."

Julia yawned. "This may come as a shock to you, but I can take care of myself."

"Yes," he said, surprising her. "You can."

She waited. Heard him shift in the chair.

"You were right. Looks like Stone's been set up by Susan, just like we have."

Julia's breath caught in her throat. "You matched it all up then?"

"Smitty's verified ninety-nine percent of the information Cari gave you. We also went through the files you brought us from Stone's computers. He's clean."

Julia let out a little whoop of joy. "Yes! I knew it."

Conrad leaned forward, resting his elbows on his knees and dropping his forehead into his hands. Julia's elation turned to concern. "Have you slept at all?"

"No." He pushed himself out of the chair. "I wanted to tell you about Stone before I went to bed. I may not get up for awhile."

Even in the darkness, Julia could see his shoulders were stooped, his posture one of resignation as well as exhaustion. "Thank you."

He moved to the side of the bed and held out his hand. "Truce?"

Julia took his hand in hers and that wonderful spark for him that always lay right under her skin jumped to life. "The Great Conrad Flynn saves the world again."

His hand gripped hers firmly. "Yeah." His chuckle held only sadness. "And here I was only trying to save you."

Her heart beating a fast and familiar rhythm, Julia pulled him down to sit beside her. His face was inches from hers and shadowed, but in her mind she could see it clearly. She released his hand and touched his face, running her fingers over his eyebrows, his cheekbones and stopping at his lips. She breathed in his Conrad smell. "I would love to kiss you," she half-whispered to him.

He leaned forward a micron, but stopped and then pulled back. "Don't play with my head, Jules. You want to make me pay for betraying you? I get it, and I've said I'm sorry, and I'd do anything to get you back because I'll love you until they bury me six feet under, but I know you're in love with Stone. I get that too. So even though it's killing me, I'll leave you alone. Let you have him. After this is done, after we've caught Susan and righted all the wrongs, I'll go away, and you and Stone can live happily ever after in that big mansion of his on the hill."

He started to rise, but Julia caught his arm, jerked him back hard. He fell nearly on top of her. "Shut up," she said, pulling his face to hers, "and kiss me, you dirty rotten sneak."

She kissed him before he could say anything, slowly and thoroughly. And then he kissed her back, just as slowly and thoroughly. For a few minutes, all they did was kiss each other. It melted her bones and made her heart ache with relief. He was here, he was alive and he loved her. The ache in her heart spread through her muscles and pulsed in her veins and she felt tears sting her eyes.

"You're crying, Jules." He drew back. "This isn't what you want—"

She cradled his face with her hands. "It is what I want, Conrad. I want you."

A few beats of her heart went by. "If this is a test," he whispered, "I'm about to fail it."

"It's not a test."

He pulled her to him. This time their lips came together harder, seeking the familiar and yet new terrain of the other's. Julia wrapped her arms around his neck and inhaled him. She pulled at his T-shirt as he pulled at hers. In seconds they were both naked from the waist up. His hands were on her breasts, cupping them, brushing his thumbs over the tight nipples until she moaned. Arching her back, she clasped his head with both hands and brought his mouth down to her breasts. He eased her back onto the mattress, his wet tongue working one and then the other breast over with just as much thoroughness as he'd applied to her lips.

God, she needed him so bad. Needed a release only he could give her. *He's alive,* her mind and heart sang in unison. We're *alive.*

She tugged at his jeans, unzipped them, watched as he struggled out of them. Then he threw back the covers and yanked her pajama bottoms off in one fell swoop. She was wearing another pair of his old boxer briefs. He stopped, and she saw the flash of his teeth as he grinned at her.

She giggled. "God, I've missed you."

Conrad descended on her again, kissing a hot trail down her chest, over her navel and to the edge of his underwear, several days' worth of stubble scratching her skin. He planted his hands on either side of her hips and tongued her through the cotton material. Julia's hips rose and she tore at the underwear to remove it. Conrad helped her, took his mouth to her and just like that, just from the touch of his tongue against her naked, wet self, she came apart, crying his name in one long sob of release.

He let her rest for a minute, and she drifted, boneless and happy.

Laying kisses on her thighs, he touched her with his

fingers, and a whole new current of desire rushed through her. He fed her with soft, sure strokes, but before she reached her climax, she drew away from him and pushed him down on the bed. In seconds, she had stripped his underwear off and taken him in her hands. He sucked in his breath and grabbed her hips with his hands, maneuvering her on top. Guiding each other, they came together in a forceful impact.

With her need burning deep and raw, Julia came apart on top of him in two strokes. She threw her head back and gave voice to the explosion inside her. Conrad laughed softly, roughly, under her, and in the growing light, she saw the ownership in his eyes, but she didn't care. She planted her hands on his chest and pumped her hips. A few strokes later, it was Conrad who lost control and Julia who smiled down at him and laughed under her breath.

The descent was slower and quieter. Julia sagged on Conrad's chest and he held her close. Her heart felt like it would beat out of her body, but soon it slowed and kept time with his. Morning dawned, but still neither of them moved.

Conrad fell asleep before her, his arms still holding her. Julia stretched her body the length of his and felt herself relax, really relax, for the first time in days.

Listening to his deep, steady breathing, she closed her mind off to everything else and joined him in sleep.

Chapter Twenty-Two

"From Cari, we know Susan has a Plan A and a Plan B," Smitty said, handing Julia a gallon of milk. She measured out two cups, dumping them into the flour mix and stirring.

She and Smitty were in the kitchen whipping up pancakes. Ace was heating syrup in the microwave. Con was still sleeping. A part of Julia wanted to be nestled in bed with him, but she was hungry and a sense of foreboding hung over her. What Con had said last night about Cari had stuck in her head.

"You've got the goods on her," Ace said. "Why do you care what her plans are? Give Big Mike the low down, and she's in the state pen."

Conrad said, swaggering into the kitchen, barefoot and shirtless, only his jeans on, "It's not enough." He still looked tired, but Julia could see immediately there was less frenetic energy pouring out of him. The sleep had helped.

And possibly the sex too. She smiled smugly at him as she dropped chopped pecans into the batter.

He pinned her with his dark brown stare, smiled back and the next thing she knew, he had her in a full-body embrace with her back up against the counter. He kissed her, leaning her back slightly. Even with an audience, she couldn't resist him. She opened her mouth and kissed him back.

Breaking the kiss, he patted her *derrière* and sent her a silent message with his eyes. He was happy.

Julia felt a rush of desire and her own happiness heat her cheeks. She avoided Smitty and Ace's stares and went back to stirring the pancake batter, trying to bring her train of thought back on track. *O-kay, what were we talking about? Susan, right.*

"We don't know who Susan has helping her besides Cari,"

Smitty said, "and Cari's last journal entry mentions another player she was escorting to America for Susan, but it doesn't say who it was or what role this player has in bringing down Stone and Titus Allen. Cari must know why Susan wanted that person here, but she left out who it is and why they're here to insure our cooperation."

Julia considered this, adding cinnamon and vanilla extract, then a few spoonfuls of brown sugar to her batter. Smitty had the griddle warmed and ready. "There's also a slim chance Cari's confession is still part of Susan's plan." She poured rounds of batter onto the griddle and watched them start to bubble. "Maybe Cari is Plan A."

Conrad poured himself a cup of coffee. "It's a good possibility. If we take our information to Stone and Allen and Cari conveniently turns on us, we're screwed. It's simply our word against Susan's and that, my friends, is a sure ticket to prison for us. No one, especially Stone, will take my word over hers."

Julia flipped the pancakes over. "So we have to trap Susan. Either get a confession right from her mouth, or catch her in the act, preferably on video so we have visual proof."

Smitty nodded, eyed the pancakes. "Tough to get either way."

Con pulled another mug from the cabinet and filled it with coffee, topped it with milk and handed it to Julia. She accepted it and sipped at it, grinning to herself that he remembered how she liked it. When the first stack of pancakes was done, she loaded them on a platter, poured more rounds on the griddle and set the platter on the table.

Butter and syrup were passed between the four friends. "I can do it," she said after a minute.

Conrad stopped chewing and looked up at her. "Do what?"

"Get Susan to confess."

Shooting Smitty a sideways glance, he wiped his fingers on a napkin. "This ought to be good."

"Oooh, I know," Ace said, chewing a mouth full of breakfast. "We kidnap her, rough her up a little." He made punching motions in the air, and then made a gun with his hand. "Julia can hold the gun to her head, force a confession."

Conrad rolled his eyes, got up and flipped the second round of pancakes on the griddle. Returning to his chair, he patted

Julia's back. "While giving Susan a little pain appeals to me, Ace, it's ineffective and could put us in even deeper trouble."

Ace dropped his boxing/shooting routine and looked disappointed. "It works on *The Sopranos*, bro."

Smitty passed Ace the platter with one pancake left on it and he perked up. "Torture is duress of the worst kind," Smitty told Ace. "People will say and do anything to stop the pain—sign confessions that aren't true, accuse innocent people of horrible crimes, betray their own mother if it means no more pain. No matter what the movies lead you to believe, it's ineffective and it's inhumane."

Ace shook his head. "You guys are no fun."

Smitty took the empty platter, retrieved the fresh pancakes from the griddle. "I'd like to hear Julia's idea."

Con smiled, a wicked grin that made Julia's heart pick up speed. "Me too."

Julia picked up her coffee cup and held it between her hands. "The missing piece with Cari is her biological father, but I know after years of trying to track down my own father, that finding that piece might be impossible. However Susan had an affair twenty-six years ago that culminated in her pregnancy. I was on the Internet this morning and it just so happens Susan put in for a transfer to the Russian office at about that time. I figure she got pregnant, decided to have the child for whatever reason and transferred to Russia in the hopes of hiding her pregnancy and giving the child up for adoption as secretively as possible."

Conrad spoke between bites. "So?"

"Susan's career is on the Internet?" Smitty said.

"If you know where to look," Julia answered. After all the years trying to locate her real dad, she knew a lot of places to look. "But trying to blackmail Susan about that affair obviously won't work if we don't know who the guy was."

"Could've been a nobody," Ace offered. "A truck driver, or the mail man or some loser she picked up at a bar for a one-night stand."

Julia frowned, shook her head. "I think Susan is too Machiavellian to have a one-night stand with a loser. It was probably someone she was in love with. It had to be someone politically important to her as well. Maybe someone in the CIA or at least in her political circles. That may be why she chose not to have an abortion, but still hid the pregnancy and kept Cari a secret."

The three men were silent for a moment. Con got up, brought the coffeepot back and refilled their mugs. "That makes sense, but I'm still saying, so what? How does that help us?"

"Maybe it doesn't," Julia said, "but you're the one who always says, 'information is a bargaining chip in the game of life'." Smitty snickered. He'd heard Con's wisdom dispersed as many times as Julia had. "I think we should keep working to figure that out. Cari's father could be a very important bargaining chip."

She pushed her plate back and set her coffee mug down. "In the meantime, if I call Susan and tell her I know everything, and I'm pissed as hell at you two for lying to me"—she motioned to Con and Smitty—"and that I'm going to Michael and turn you all in, she'll make her move. I'll tell her I'm after her job so she either cuts me in for a piece of her rising star, or I'll blow her out of water with you two."

Smitty's eyes lit up. "And because of your illicit affair with Stone, she'll think he'll be more inclined to listen to you than her."

Julia avoided Con's gaze. "There is nothing criminal or unlawful about my affair."

Smitty held up his hands. "Illicit's the wrong word, I apologize. Forbidden, maybe or...unethical."

Julia raised an eyebrow. "I work for the CIA. So does Michael. There's technically nothing forbidden or unethical about our relationship."

"*Technically,*" Conrad said, his jaw set, "you no longer *have* a *relationship* with Stone, am I right?"

Pressing the palms of her hands into her forehead, Julia sighed. "Yes, but he doesn't know that yet and neither does Susan."

Smitty was still thinking about her idea. The light bulb behind his eyes was glowing brighter and a smile was spreading across his face. "At the very least, Susan knows Stone would start an investigation of her. No way can she afford for that to happen, even if she believes she's set us up for the fall. An investigation of any kind into her activities could stop her career goals dead."

"Exactly," Julia said. "It's time for the Wicked Witch to get a dose of her own medicine."

Con leaned forward and rested his crossed arms on the table. "What if you blackmail her and she tries to kill you?"

"I'm the brains in this operation, Con. You're the muscle. She tries to kill me? You run in with that scowl on your face and wave your gun around." Julia waved a finger in the air. "You know, save the day like always."

He stared at her for a long moment before a tiny grin tugged at one corner of his mouth. "I could do that."

"Of course you can." Smitty winked at Julia as he rose. "And since I'm apparently not the brains or the muscle, I'll be the supervisor. Which is what I do best." He stared into space for a half a second and then nodded at them. "I know how we're going to do this. Let's get to work."

"What about me?" Ace asked.

Julia handed him her dirty plate. "Clean off the table and wash the dishes."

Smitty and Conrad handed him their plates as well.

Ace's face fell. "So I'm the grunt?"

"You're the grunt," the other three replied in unison, walking out and leaving Ace with the mess.

"Man," he mumbled to himself, "this spy shit sucks."

Chapter Twenty-Three

"These are transmitters with a GPS chip in them that will let us know where you are at all times." Smitty handed two small flat pieces of silicone and plastic to her. "Keep both on your person so we can track you."

Julia threw one in her tote bag and stuck the other in her bra. Smitty raised one eyebrow. Ace's eyes widened. Con didn't even blink.

"Next, more listening devices." Smitty gave her three tiny plastic bugs. They really did look like bugs in a way. Ladybug-size, they were round with skinny, sticky legs and a single antenna. "Just like the last ones, brush your thumb over the sensor to activate them and then stick them to something with texture. Draperies, upholstery, that sort of thing. Not metal or finished wood. The only reason the last device stuck to your table is because the underside was unstained. Avoid carpets for the obvious reason."

"Right." Julia was due to be at Michael's in half an hour. He'd called, asked her to come for lunch. He'd sounded strange, and she was worried. He was pissed about her no-show last night, but there was something else in his voice she couldn't place. All she knew was that she had to go, act as normal as possible, and hope her Mata Hari skills would carry her through. She wanted to see him again anyway before she placed the call to Susan that would put her plan in motion. She needed to say good-bye to him in her head, take one more look around his house and remember the good times she'd shared with him.

"If you have the opportunity," Smitty continued, "get one of these in Susan's personal effects. Her briefcase, her purse, her office."

It was Julia who raised an eyebrow this time. "You want to me to bug the CIA's counterterrorism chief's office?"

"Headquarters is swept for bugs every couple of weeks," Con said. "So be careful. Don't leave any telltale fingerprints on the bug or the site."

Smitty tapped his chin. "As far as I know, CIA technicians have never found a listening device inside the buildings. It would be interesting to see how security would react to such a thing."

Julia knew how they'd react. "I'll be running mostly on instinct. I'll try to keep you guys in the loop at all times, but Michael's already suspicious so don't freak if I don't make contact every five minutes, okay?"

Smitty nodded. Conrad ignored her. Julia continued to walk through the plan. "As soon as I'm ready to place the call to Susan, I'll let you know so you can tail her."

"At that point, one of us"—Con pointed a finger at his chest and then at Smitty—"will be on your tail at all times as well, except, of course, when you enter CIA headquarters."

"Do you really think Susan might try to kill me?"

He answered without hesitation. "Yes. If she's guilty, she's spent the better part of the last ten years putting this plan together, and she won't let you or me or Smitty screw it up for her. If we're alive, we can talk, and even if Stone and Allen don't believe us, our stories will throw doubt on hers. Like Smitty said, Susan's career can't risk a criminal investigation and she knows that. The easiest way to avoid that is to take all of us out. I'm not sure how she'll try to do it, but she will."

Julia suppressed a shudder and picked up her big black tote bag—she'd switched from her purse to the larger bag to carry everything she needed, including both the Beretta and SIG Sauer, concealed. She checked her cell phone and both guns. Everything was ready.

She turned to Smitty. "In the meantime, you'll work on finding out who Cari's father is, right?"

"Will do." He patted her cheek and nodded. "Go get her, Sheba. We've got your back." He gave her a smile and walked out of the room, forcing Ace to go with him. Ace gave her a thumbs-up sign over his shoulder.

Julia looked at Conrad. Her heart hurt at the thought of

leaving him. He reached out and drew her into his arms. They stood that way for long minutes, and Julia rested her head against his shoulder.

"I don't want you to do this." Con spoke into the top of her head.

"I know." She laid her fingers at the base of his throat, felt his pulse beating under them. "But I'm the only one who can make this happen. We have to stop Susan, and when it's all done, if Cari's kept her part of the deal with me, I want to help her if I can."

Con laughed in disbelief. "Why would you want to help her?"

"We've both been used and hurt by Susan. I know Cari's made some bad choices, but I think she deserves a second chance. If she comes through and testifies against Susan, then I'll talk to Michael and whoever else I have to and see if they can help her stay in the States. Get her a job. I really believe she deserves another chance."

Con pulled back and looked down at Julia. "Damn, you're a better person than I am."

"This is just dawning on you?"

The side of Con's mouth quirked, and then fell again. "Susan's the most cunning and devious person I've ever met. Don't take any unnecessary chances, Jules. Be prepared."

She understood the message behind those words: *I just got you back, I can't lose you again.*

"There's a part of me that still can't believe the Susan Richmond I know would turn against her country or betray the people she worked side-by-side with."

Con nodded in understanding as Julia went on. "That part of me still hopes she's innocent. That she's at Langley poring over the latest briefings out of the Middle East, itching to find a germ cell of information that might warn us about a terrorist strike. It believes she's too damn dedicated to value us so little, and there's no way she could be the CIA's mole."

"I know."

"But the other part of me..." Julia shook her head, blinked back a stray tear. "The other part of me knows it's her. I think about how she set you up, how she gave up those other operators, how she used her own daughter to further her career, how she's setting Michael up to clear the way for herself." Her voice had risen and now she took a deep breath and let it out slowly. "I want to tear the limbs from her body. She's not going to get away with it. I won't let her."

Con rubbed her arms. "Just be careful."

She pulled on her jacket and slid the strap of her bag over her shoulder. "I love you too," she said, giving him a kiss.

"You've got my cell number?"

"I memorized it and programmed my phone with it."

He scratched the back of his neck. "What are going to do if Stone, you know, tries to, um..."

Julia smiled, enjoying Con's discomfort. "Kiss me?"

"Well, yeah, that, but more than that..."

Julia reached into her tote and brought out a box of tampons and flashed them at him. "I set these on the bathroom counter. Works every time."

"Right." Con avoided looking at the box. "Good one."

Dropping the tampons back into her tote, she threw her arms around him. "Don't. Worry."

"Sorry, kiddo. That's my job."

She kissed him once more, long and deep, and then she left for Michael's.

Chapter Twenty-Four

Langley

A vague sense of relief washed over Julia as she absentmindedly walked around the room's nerve center filled with computer screens, faxes and phones, and breathed in the familiar stale office air. A smattering of dedicated men and women from the CIA, the FBI and the Secret Service were bent over various electronic equipment and piles of paper, all giving up a weekend afternoon to work toward a common goal. Keep America safe.

It had been her goal too for all these years. CIA Headquarters was a place that had offered refuge to her, and up to now, had provided reinforcement in her psyche that her country *was* a safer place because of these quiet but extraordinary guards.

But now she wondered as she passed the cubicles partitioned off for bin Laden and Hezbollah, what harm was coming out of these walls? The shadow CIA was effectively crippling the United States' intelligence community and no one but a couple of men, highly skilled yes, but ordinary men nonetheless, knew the specifics of what was happening.

Throwing her backpack on her desk, Julia ignored the weekend's dump of intelligence information on it. She was already late for lunch with Michael, and she knew Con was probably wondering what the hell she was doing, but she needed to check her desk and get a personal item out of it before she started the whole charade to expose Susan. If she didn't, she would not most likely get it back.

Julia bent down and shuffled through the contents of her bottom desk drawer. Under the miscellaneous files and tech manuals lay a picture. She stared at it for a second, a snapshot of her previous life.

April in Paris. She'd been so happy. Con had been happy then too, but there he was in the picture, angry with her for taking it, all dark and forbidding and looking like the Devil himself. But she'd won out over his anger, took the picture, and had kept the only picture she had of him all these years.

April in Paris. Long walks in the dead of night. Words of love and commitment filling her ears while her heart seemed to expand until it would burst.

April in Paris. Cherry blossoms falling from the trees in Luxembourg Gardens as she and Conrad hid underneath the canopy in the darkness and made up a fantasy life for themselves that didn't involve the CIA. Back at her flat, he laughed at her as she lay on the bed with cherry blossoms still stuck in her hair. God, she loved making the Great Conrad Flynn laugh.

She had known at that moment that she was living a life many women dreamed about but never experienced. She was attractive, intelligent and successful, but it wasn't enough. She wanted more. She wanted to be the woman with cherry blossoms stuck in her hair, making Conrad laugh for the rest of his life.

It hadn't happened. Her future with him had been ripped away shortly after that by the unseen force manipulating the CIA. All her dreams, all her success, reduced to ashes.

Julia swallowed the lump in her throat. She had to draw Susan out and turn her over to Michael and Titus Allen as soon as possible. She couldn't, *wouldn't*, let Susan win. Shoving the picture in her jacket pocket, Julia closed the desk drawer and stood up.

When she, Conrad and Smitty exposed Susan, Julia knew she'd have a lot of explaining to do. She might even be asked to leave the CIA and she certainly would have to switch departments because of Michael. She wouldn't be able to face him every day once all her secrets were out on the table. He truly would never trust her again and her status as top analyst would be forfeited. Julia's heart sank at the thought. She stood for a long minute, looking at her desk, all the puzzles piled on it, and wondered for the first time what she would do after this was all over. She'd been so wrapped up in her happiness with

Con and so determined to figure out how to bring Susan to justice, she hadn't really considered what would be left of her career.

Susan has successfully managed to ruin my relationship with Michael and cripple my career. She shoved her hands in her pockets, felt the listening devices still in them and remembered Smitty's advice. Suddenly the thought of bugging Susan's office was overwhelmingly appealing.

Susan's Cadillac was in the below-ground parking garage and Julia knew that running into her right now could blow her only chance to play her cards successfully. But if this was her last time in the halls of the CIA, she figured she might as well make it worthwhile.

Behind the glass walls of Susan's office, Julia could see evidence the CTC chief had been in her room and was planning to return. The lights were on. A bottle of Evian was sweating on the desktop. A stack of papers on the desk rustled lightly from the breeze generated by a small fan positioned on a filing cabinet in the corner of the room.

Julia stopped outside the closed door and forced herself not to look up at the security camera in the corner of the hallway. Susan was probably running down information somewhere else in the building. She could be back in minutes or it could be hours.

Julia's heart hammered. A tickling urgency was tightening the muscles in her stomach. She didn't have hours, that she was sure of. And she didn't want to run into Susan if she could avoid her.

As she stared at the doorknob, Julia's fingers toyed with a listening device in the pocket of her jacket. She knew the code to open Susan's door. She had figured out the code to Michael's too. It had been nothing more than a game to her before today, and she'd never seriously considered using the codes. They changed them every few months, and it didn't take a member of the Geek Squad to figure it out. Shifting her feet, Julia let her gaze go up and down the hallway, acting as if she were simply waiting for Susan to return. Could she bug the CIA's counterterrorism director's office and get away with it?

Of course she *could* bug Susan's office, the real question was, *should* she bug Susan's office? No matter what the reason behind it, bugging any office in this agency was a serious breach of conduct, sure to earn her an immediate dismissal...

Taking a deep breath, Julia cut her eyes left and then right to check again if anyone was nearby. Seeing the coast was clear, she pressed her fingers to the coded key entry. The doorknob turned free and Julia felt cool air from the fan touch her face as she entered the office.

Chapter Twenty-Five

Here there be dragons, Julia thought, remembering the warning of ancient maps, as she opened the file drawer of Susan's desk. Scanning the tab headings, she pulled out four folders and spread them on the desktop.

Two were bulky, their dull camouflage-green covers worn and nearly falling apart. They were labeled as the official personnel files of Ryan Smith and Conrad Flynn. After a moment's hesitation, she decided she dared not open either for fear of losing herself in information. The other two folders were slim and had nice, new covers. One was labeled *Julia Torrison/Abigail Quinn*, the other *Operation: Sheba*.

Her hands shook as she slipped the listening device from her pocket and secured it under Susan's desk. After activating it, she returned her attention to the file with her name on it and used a fingernail to carefully lift the cover. The first page was her bio and a black and white headshot of her. She flipped to the next page. Scanning the text, she realized it was a greatly edited version of her career in the CIA. No mention of the official covert operations she'd worked in Europe or her partnership with Conrad. In two brief pages, her time as an employee at the American Embassy in Paris and her return to Langley was summarized in cold, bureaucratic language.

Behind the last page was a collection of memos stuffed in the file folder's back pocket. Julia scanned the first one dated October 2006, a month after Flynn's death and her return to CIA Headquarters. It was from Susan Richardson to Benito Raines.

Initiate random surveillance checks on Abigail Quinn immediately. Currently appears emotionally unstable. May reach out to family or close friends. I am concerned about breaches of security...

Benito's reply was dated three weeks later.

Chief/CTC: No security breaches witnessed. Subject sticks to routine between work and apartment. Has not contacted anyone outside of headquarters with exception of brother, Eric. Discussion centered around his two children...

The next memo came again from Richmond, five months later.

Quinn has begun relationship with DO. National security issues at risk. Per DDCI's request, investigate discreetly and advise me of improper conduct by either party.

The papers trembled in Julia's shaking hand and a chill ran over her body. Damn. Jurgen Damgaard, the Deputy Director of the CIA, and Ben Raines knew about her relationship with Michael. Worse, Susan had them suspecting her of pumping him for classified information.

Plan A, Julia told herself.

She flipped to the next memo, this one again from Raines.

Chief/CTC: DO continues to be discreet with operational matters when Torrison visits. There is occasional pillow talk, but nothing damaging to the Agency or national security. Audio is available for your review.

Pillow talk? Audio is available? Was Raines listening to her and Michael in bed? Nice. While it was doubtful Raines could have bugged Michael's house, he did have access to directional microphones and had had Jurgen Damgaard's okay to use them. Wait 'til Michael found out about that.

Julia pulled the memos out, rolled them and stuck them in the back of her waistband. As long as she was burning bridges by illegally bugging her boss's office, she might as well steal a few pieces of classified material as well.

She carefully pushed the folder over and looked at the cover of the next one. *Operation: Sheba.* Julia felt the hair on the back of her neck rise. Was this more of Plan A?

Again using a well-manicured fingernail, she opened the folder and began to read.

The chill of trepidation froze her blood.

Ace's Mortuary

"Still nothing?"

Smitty shook his head and cracked his knuckles. "Nothing. All I get is static. Either she hasn't installed any of the listening devices yet or she installed them incorrectly."

Conrad started pacing again, but this time it was across cold, hard linoleum. The basement of Ace's Mortuary was not exactly the Taj Mahal, but it worked better than the back of a van for cover and it was closer to CIA headquarters and Stone's house than Julia's apartment building. The only thing he couldn't stand was the smell.

"Julia knows how to plant a bug." Conrad wished he had a cigarette to burn and block the smell of antiseptic and embalming fluid. Wished he hadn't let the woman he loved take off on her own. Wished that just *one* of the freakin' bugs would start transmitting so he didn't have to say out loud and confirm what they all were thinking. Julia wasn't following through with her part of the plan.

She'd said she was going to Stone's place and then she'd gone to Langley. Conrad didn't know what she was doing and when he called her cell phone all he got was her voice mail. Her phone was off. She hadn't performed an undercover operation for years and while part of him believed she could handle anything that went down, another was totally freaking out that she was in danger.

And he was the person who'd put her there after spending the last seventeen months trying to keep her safe.

"Y'know what I don't get, Connie?" Ace said, spinning himself around on one the ancient medical stools he had managed to steal somewhere along the line. "Doesn't Big Mike think it's weird his girlfriend sleeps in your underwear?" He stopped to shoot an inquisitive look at Flynn.

Conrad let his head fall back on his shoulders and wished he'd never shared that bit of trivia with his newest partner. He gave careful consideration to yelling, *I don't give a damn what Big Mike thinks*, but realized, as he looked over at the twenty-eight-year-old mortician, that he wasn't joking or teasing with Conrad. As always, he was totally sincere.

Conrad swallowed the yell and shrugged. Now that he thought about it, it was kind of weird. But what struck him as even weirder was that his underwear had actually fit Julia. Sure it had seemed a little loose around the waist, but... *She must have shrunk them.*

He walked over to look out the ground-level window, wishing again he'd followed her. Wishing he'd hid himself in the car with her. Wishing she hadn't changed the game plan without telling him why.

The receiver popped behind Smitty and all three men jumped, turning to look at it. In the dead silence of the mortuary's basement, they heard the sound of a small motor and then the quiet shuffling of papers. Smitty hit the Record button on the nearby tape deck and turned to Conrad with a lifted eyebrow.

That's my girl, Conrad thought with relief. She'd bugged an office at Langley. Susan's office, no doubt. He felt a stab of pride and then the fear for her returned. *Now get the hell out of there, Jules, before I stroke out.*

There was no absentmindedness this time as Julia sped by the cubicles of her coworkers, exited the CTC department and hurried through the rest of the building.

Taking the stairs down to the parking garage two at a time, she hit the heavy door, throwing it open.

A minute later, as she wheeled the Audi out of the main level, Julia didn't see Susan Richmond's level gaze following her from the basement door.

Chapter Twenty-Six

Senator King accepted the blue Central Intelligence Agency mug full of hot coffee from Susan Richmond and followed her statuesque form across the lobby and down the hallway. Even though the area was empty, conversation between them was sparse and dealt with the usual benign issues such as the weather and their latest round of golf. While it certainly appeared that no one was within earshot, Daniel couldn't get over the feeling of being watched and listened to, and it wouldn't do for someone to overhear the reason he was paying CIA Headquarters a visit today.

While he had walked the building's hallways many times over the past few years, Daniel had never stopped feeling the edge of disquiet that existed here. Even now, acid sat in the pit of his stomach and he knew he didn't need the jolt of caffeine from the coffee he was carrying to jumpstart his nerves. The building itself was as normal as any he'd been in, but there was no mistaking the eerie feel of Spookville.

King mentally chastised himself over his unease as he and Susan entered the CTC and nodded to a few of its employees as they passed the sterile cubicles. He had every right to be here, was a part of it in his own way. But just like his first day as a freshman senator, he stood watching from the fringes in awe, like a foreigner who didn't quite speak the language or understand the customs.

Running his left hand through his hair, he tried to bring his mental focus back to the task at hand. He had to admit to himself it wasn't just the surroundings making him uneasy. He was about to sign off on the biggest operation of his career.

As usual, the Senator was going to have to negotiate to

effect the outcome of the operation in his favor. In this case, as with many of the favors he had extended in the past, he needed the ability to take credit if the operation was a success while maintaining distance and anonymity if the operation failed.

It was an almost impossible feat to pull off.

Almost.

"Please come in and have a seat," Susan said as she held the door open to her office and gestured Daniel through.

"Thank you, Susan." He set his coffee on the only clear spot near the edge of her desk and unbuttoned his sport coat before sitting down.

Switching the fan on the file cabinet off, Susan pulled out her chair and sat at her desk. She looked at the man across from her, feeling a surge of excitement. Her goal was so close she could almost reach out and touch it. "This is an unexpected visit. I assume it has to do with our plan?"

The Senator nodded, steepling his fingers in front of him. His voice was firm but non-aggressive. "Your plan is sound, but there is one small..." he paused, searching for the right term, "...*adjustment* to it I need before I can give you the go ahead."

Susan smiled. Of course. Daniel King was the supreme negotiator and she had learned a lot from studying him over the years. Everything was negotiable according to the good senator and she agreed. Everything *was* negotiable, especially when she held the trump card.

Conrad was listening to Susan Richmond talk to the Democratic senator, Daniel King, but it took him a minute to figure out what they were talking about.

Ace and Smitty were staring at him. He stared intently at the receiver. "Don't ask me." He shook his head at his partners. "Just be sure you're getting everything on tape."

Smitty nodded and both he and Ace returned their gazes to the receiver as they heard Susan's voice again. "Adjustment? You said you were ready to sign off on Operation: Sheba."

Conrad sat up a little straighter and frowned. What the *hell?*

His friends' stares turned to him again, curiosity mingled with the first inklings of fear. Something here wasn't right and

Chapter Twenty-Seven

Arlington

Lunch was over. The remnants of grilled butterfly pork chops, baked potatoes and spinach salad decorated their plates. Julia tossed a section of trimmed fat to Pongo. The dog snapped it out of the air and sucked it down in a gulp.

"I could use a walk," she said to Michael, unsnapping her jeans. "As usual, you overfed me, but I enjoyed every bite."

He'd been on the quiet side, but hadn't said or done anything to make Julia think he was suspicious of her recent actions or mad because she'd run out on her meeting with Ben Raines. Over lunch, they'd talked about normal things...the latest e-mail virus, a gossipy scandal involving a senator and his aide, and a trip Michael was scheduled to make to London in the fall. "We could walk to the lake."

"A walk to the lake sounds wonderful," Julia said.

They left the dishes on the table, and Michael pulled an old Marine sweatshirt of his off a hook in the mudroom for Julia to wear. He threw on one that matched, right down to the faded letters and the holey pockets. They set off with Pongo running ahead and Michael's security detail keeping some distance behind.

"Did Raines find something here yesterday when he searched your house?" Julia asked as they followed the trail Michael ran six days a week.

"No, the house was clean."

"But you're still keeping extra security?"

Michael shrugged indifferently. "I'm supposed to have them around the clock. Usually I choose not to."

"So why is Brutus following us?"

"His name is Brad." Another shrug. "Things still feel off."

Julia understood that feeling quite well.

They walked in silence for a mile or so and Julia tried to enjoy the fresh spring day. The grass was green again and pink blossoms on the wild apple trees dotted the area.

Michael threw a stick for Pongo to fetch. "You know about the journalist the insurgents took hostage three days ago in Iraq?"

Julia had seen the information on a daily brief that had passed over her desk. She summarized what she remembered. "Female, works for CNBC, covering Iraq war in Baghdad. She went out on her own instead of sticking with the army unit she was covering and got nabbed. Insurgents want two prisoners released in the next forty-eight hours or they'll behead her."

Michael watched Pongo. "She's not a journalist. She's one of ours."

She kicked at a clump of grass. "Damn. Are we going after her?"

"We're in negotiations but Jeffries won't give the presidential okay to go after her. They're afraid she'll be exposed as a CIA operator and we'll get blowback from it."

"So you've technically lost another agent."

He rubbed his forehead as if he had a headache. "Titus is on his way back from Florida. He wants to meet with me this evening." He glanced at her. "I think I'm about to be fired."

Julia stopped in her tracks. "What?"

"This was the last straw." He stopped too, but kept his gaze on Pongo. "Losing all these operators not only makes the U.S. look bad, it makes Titus look bad. He needs to put blame somewhere and I'm it."

"But it's not your fault."

Michael shot her a look. "Isn't it?"

"No," she said. "It's not."

"Then who's to blame, Abby, if not me? I'm the Director of Operations. I'm the man in charge."

He started walking again and Julia wrestled with her conscious. She wanted to tell him, wanted to hand him the disc and papers she had stolen, but she had to start the ball rolling with Susan if she was going to make her case airtight.

So she shoved her hands in the pockets of Michael's jacket

and followed him to the lake in silence. Now she knew why he had sounded weird on the phone and had been exceptionally moody the past few days. It wasn't all due to the fact Smitty had reappeared or her own odd behavior. This made her breathe easier, and at the same time, knowing Michael was about to be fired for Susan's tricks, her breath seemed too thick inside her chest.

The air around the lake was chilly and Julia was grateful for the bulky warmth of the sweatshirt. She pulled its hood up over her head. Clouds were moving in from the west and it looked like a spring rain might be on the way. She watched Michael chase Pongo in and out of the water a few times, but she could see his heart wasn't in it. They turned back to the house without walking the perimeter of the deep lake.

"If you leave the CIA," she asked when they were halfway back to the house, "what will you do?"

Michael ran a hand through his hair and looked at the clouds gathering on the horizon. "A few months ago, the NSA offered me a job. I might look into it."

"The National Security Agency offered you a job and you didn't tell me?"

"When it came up, I wasn't interested. I like what I do, you know that. Since I've been at the CIA, I've never considered anything else. Now, I may have to."

"Who will take your place?" She already knew the answer.

"Susan most likely." A nerve jumped above his temple. "She's been with the Agency longer than I have and has quite a lot of experience recruiting and placing operators. She's always wanted my job, and she's the best candidate."

Julia refrained from comment even though anger was spreading through her veins.

"Director Stone," the security officer called to Michael. As Julia turned, she saw Brad picking up his pace to reach them. She instinctively moved closer to Michael and scanned the area nearby looking for a threat.

Michael had tensed too at the man's call. "What is it?"

Brad held up his walkie-talkie. "Front gate says Susan Richmond is asking for admission."

Michael glanced at Julia, and she felt her stomach tighten. It was as if the mention of Susan's name had conjured her out of thin air.

Not knowing the danger she represented, Michael relaxed. He glanced at the house, fifty yards away. "Tell them to let her in."

"She has Ben Raines and several security officers with her, sir."

Michael's eyes narrowed. "Why?"

Brad glanced at Julia and back to Michael. "She claims she has an arrest warrant."

Julia's heart slammed into her ribs. She instinctively took a step back. "For who?"

Brad watched Michael this time. "She's here to supervise the arrest of Abigail Quinn."

"*What?*" Michael drew up to his full height and looked at Julia, a frown pulling his eyebrows down. He searched her face, questioning her with his gaze.

Julia took another step back and saw his gaze turn accusatory.

"Good God, Abby," he said. "What have you done?"

Julia turned on her heel and started a swift pace for the house. In a few steps Michael was next to her. His hand touched her elbow, but she refused to look at him or slow down. She could hear Brad's footsteps behind her. "I need to give you something, and then I have to go."

His hand tightened on her elbow. His voice was low and demanding. "Tell me what's going on."

"I don't have time to explain everything, but I have a disc that will explain most of it."

They reached the back door and Julia shot through it, Pongo cutting in front of her. Michael was right behind her, protesting and insisting she stop and tell him what was going on. She ignored him, running through the kitchen and up the stairs to the bedroom where she'd left her tote bag.

"Here." She grasped the disc and jabbed it at him when he caught up with her. Brad had followed and was standing directly behind Michael, eyeing her over Michael's shoulder like a cat ready to pounce. She had no doubts he would tackle her to the floor if she tried to run.

Drawing in a quick breath, she decided she needed to tell Michael a condensed version of the truth. "Susan Richmond is the CIA's traitor," she said, removing the papers she'd stolen from Susan's files from her bag. "She's set all of us up in an attempt to undermine Titus and become the next director of Central Intelligence. Con and Smitty thought you were the mole and Susan led them on, planting evidence of her own misdeeds and linking it back to you for them to trace. She was using them and me to help her get rid of you." She handed him the papers.

"*Con* and Smitty?" Michael's voice fell a notch as he accepted the papers. He stilled completely. "What are you talking about?"

Truth or consequences. Only this time it wasn't *or* consequences, it was *and*. "Conrad Flynn is alive, Michael."

Julia saw the enormity of what she said reflected in his face. Disbelief, confusion, anger. *Been there*, she thought. Biting the inside of her cheek, she pushed on. "He faked his death and Smitty went AWOL to help him track down the mole. Only they thought it was you. They came to me and asked for my help. I knew it wasn't you so I only agreed because—"

"Flynn's alive," Michael echoed, his voice deadly soft. It wasn't a question. Julia saw the pieces in his head snap together and flinched when his eyes narrowed at her. Anger trumped the other emotions. His voice rose, hard and unforgiving. "Conrad Flynn is fucking alive?"

Willing herself not to shrink back, Julia only nodded. It was not from fear of Michael's anger that made her want to step back, but from what she knew would come next.

"And you knew?" He glared down at her. "You knew, and you didn't tell me?"

Brad's walkie-talkie buzzed. "Sir," he interrupted. "What should I tell the guard at the gate? Ms. Richmond is pressing to come in."

Michael ignored the security officer, his accusatory gaze burning through Julia's skin. She tried to shut down her emotions, knowing Susan was but a few paces away from arresting her and throwing her in jail for some bogus charge. She couldn't let her guard down and get tangled up trying to sort things out with Michael.

Yanking her Beretta out of her bag, she slid it into the waistband of her pants, and didn't miss that Brad moved his free hand to cover his own weapon. Next she reached for her cell phone and fumbled with the buttons to turn it on.

"That's where you've been the past few days and nights when you haven't been here with me." Michael's voice was filled with hurt. "You've been with Flynn."

Brad's walkie-talkie buzzed again while Julia's cell phone played its opening ring tone. The security guard stepped forward and addressed Michael again, and Julia felt her ire rise at him. She and Michael were having one of the most important conversations of their relationship and Brad was hanging on every word.

She blocked his interruption. "Tell Susan Richmond the Director is on his way back from the lake and he will meet her at the gate as soon as he returns."

Brad drew back, a little nonplussed, and waited for Michael's instructions.

Michael just continued to stare at her. She dropped her cell phone into her bag. "Listen, Michael," she said, wishing her heart wasn't breaking. She could feel it literally hurting in her chest, but she couldn't stop to think about it. Not now. "Don't get hung up about the Conrad thing. What he did was wrong and he knows it but he had a good reason. My name was on the list of operators Susan was having killed off. Conrad was trying to protect me, not screw you over."

"Not screw me over?" Anger turned his face hard. "*Not screw me over?* He faked his death, and you're telling me he didn't screw me over?" He took a breath and paced to the balcony's edge and back. "You lied to me."

Julia paused and tried again to take the heat off Conrad. "This is important. That *disc* is important. Read what's on it, but don't tell Susan you have it. There's a detailed log on it from a woman who's been helping her all along. Cari Von Motz. She's Susan's illegitimate daughter."

Michael's eyebrows rose and he started to say something, but the sound of someone banging on the front door downstairs stopped him. A man yelled out his name and demanded Michael let him in.

Julia's cell phone rang. She reached for it, but didn't open the flap. "I have to go. I'm sorry." She stood on her toes and kissed him softly on the mouth. His lips were granite. "I'm really sorry, Michael."

"Abigail." He reached for her, but she stepped toward the balcony. She flipped open the phone and heard Con's voice in her ear. "Get the hell out of there. Susan's coming for you."

"Thanks for the update," she answered, but before she could say more, Brad grabbed her from behind, wheeling her around.

The cell phone flew out of her hand, skidded on the balcony, hit the railing and dropped off to the ground below.

She clocked the security agent on the ear with her open palm and kicked him in the shin at the same time. He shifted, trying to move both left and right from the double assault, and she threw her body weight into him with all the strength she could muster, making him stumble backwards. Her hand flew to the Beretta and before the guard could draw a breath, she had the end of the gun buried in his gut. Pongo came to stand beside her, a low growl coming from his throat.

"Get your hands off me," she said, staring up at Brad.

He let her go, stepping back with his hands up. Julia stepped to the railing, her gun still on him. Downstairs, the front door banged open and Julia could hear Susan's group pouring into the house. Susan's voice called out to Michael.

"Abigail." He stepped in front of Brad, as if to take the bullet Julia was threatening him with. "What the hell are you doing?"

It happened so fast and furiously, Julia's hand twitched. Frustration overtook heartbreak and fear. "My name is Julia." She now looked down her gun at Michael. "Julia Torrison. Abigail Quinn doesn't exist. Not anymore. But I do, and I'm trying to save your career. Read the papers and look at that disc. I'll be in touch."

Feet pounded up the stairs. Sticking the gun in her waistband, Julia dropped her bag over the balcony and let it fall to the ground below. "Tell Susan I know who Cari's father is," she said as she straddled the railing. "I'm going to him next." She flipped herself over the edge and wrapped her legs around a post. Just as she began sliding down it, she heard a man call to her, demand she stop.

She hit the ground and rolled, grabbing her bag as she regained her feet. She snatched her cell phone off the ground, flipped it closed and took off running to the sounds of more shouting. She heard Michael's voice yelling at the officers to put their guns away. Pongo was barking furiously.

Clearing the tripwires, Julia set off the house's security

alarm. The floodlights came on and she heard the buzz of the alarm inside the house before another command for her to stop came from the balcony. She jumped the small ravine and heard the retort of a gun. The bullet smacked a low-hanging branch of a tree on her left, and Michael's voice rang out across the clearing, a booming, "*No!*"

She dodged, stumbled over her own feet, but ran on, ignoring more hanging branches that smacked at her face as she reached the cover of the woods. Her cell phone rang inside her tote, but she ignored it.

Chapter Twenty-Eight

She'd dropped her phone. "Julia!" Conrad yelled.

Smitty and Ace were on their feet, staring at him.

He'd heard her voice, far away, and he'd jammed the phone tighter against his ear. Stone's voice had mixed with Julia's voice and then a thud, the unmistakable sound of a body hitting the ground had sent chills down Conrad's spine.

"Julia!"

But yelling didn't help. The connection was dead.

"Goddamn it!" He punched buttons to call her phone again. While it rang, he held out his hand to Ace. "Give me the keys to your car."

"No way, bro," Ace said, but he dug into the front pocket of his baggy cargo pants for the keys anyway. "You're going after her? I'll be your wheel guy."

Conrad started to say no, it was too dangerous, but Smitty interrupted him. "I'm going too."

Julia's phone continued to ring. Seeing his own fear mirrored in his best friend's face, Conrad checked himself. How ironic it was that with all their differences, the years of walking side-by-side between the rocks and the hard places with Ryan Smith had bound him in a loyalty that surpassed any he'd ever known. Even with his own brothers. "No. Smitty, you're not going this round. I'll take care of Julia. You take care of the files and all this stuff. Make a backup of all the information, especially the networks and liaison contacts worldwide, and secure it in one of Ace's vaults. And then"—Conrad wished he could squeeze the life out of Susan's throat—"you go see Stone and tell him everything. We have to stop Susan. Now."

Smitty nodded sullenly. "It won't be hard to find Julia." He reached underneath the counter and pulled out a briefcase. He unzipped it and handed Conrad a Toshiba portable satellite computer. "This baby will dial up the satellite and find her for you."

Conrad took the computer and jerked his head at Ace to get moving. "Thanks."

Smitty followed them to the door. "If Stone throws my butt in jail, you'll break me out, right?"

Conrad slapped him on the shoulder. "Damn straight, Smith."

"Man, I dig this 007-shit, Connie. Flirting with danger, dressing incognito." Ace touched the brim of his baseball cap. "Rescuing nicely stacked damsels in distress. This is some life you lead. Where do I sign up?"

Conrad kept his eyes glued to the tiny computer screen in his lap as the unit tried to acquire the satellite uplink it needed to track the GPS chip in Julia's bra. "You already signed up, Ace. You're the wheelman, remember? But you should understand the most important rule of this partnership. I get first pick of the nicely stacked damsels, distressed or not."

Ace laughed into the wind roaring through the CJ. "You're my hero, bro."

Conrad reached down to check his cell phone while the computer continued trying to find the satellite signal. *Come on, Jules, call me.*

"Hey, what was that *indiscretion* stuff Susan was threatening King with?" Ace asked.

Raising his head, Conrad answered, "Daniel King is Cari Von Motz's real father. Susan is using their affair and Cari as a trump card to get King to back her up on this operation."

Ace nodded and Conrad returned his focus to the computer. A second later, the satellite zeroed in on Julia's location. "Yes! She's still in the woods west of Stone's house. Looks like she's following a north-south road that parallels Highway 65."

"I'm on it."

Conrad felt a stab of relief, pulled his hat farther down on his head and watched the image on the screen continue southwest.

Come on, Jules, call me.

Julia was still moving, but had slowed her pace. She was sure security officers were following her, but she couldn't hear anyone moving through the woods when she stopped to listen. Hugging the tree line beside the gravel road, she watched a pair of horses on the other side of a white fence across the road. Nervous energy from the approaching storm was eating at them. Their tails swished viciously, their heads up and ears pricking forward as they watched her pass from tree to tree.

A few fat drops of rain fell on the leaves around her. Shifting her attention back to herself, Julia stilled again and listened. Still no telltale noises. She shifted her Beretta to her left hand, shook some feeling into her right and pulled out her cell phone.

While the phone tried to connect, Julia held it to her ear with her shoulder and took the picture from her bag.

She was shivering from head to toe. Her face was scratched and her feet hurt like hell after running several miles through the woods. Somehow she'd managed to step in something that smelled awful. Her body ached from the drop off Michael's balcony and the cool spring air seeped through his sweatshirt and made her teeth chatter. The first rush of adrenaline had worn off, and as she pushed on through the tangle of fallen branches and decaying forest, her mind kept swimming with Michael's face. She put the picture of Con in front of her and silently pleaded with him to answer his phone.

"Go faster," Flynn yelled to Ace over the whine of the Jeep's tires.

"Jesus, Connie, I'm doing ninety! My tires will blow out if I push it any faster!"

Conrad pointed ahead. "Turn there."

Ace slowed and bounced the CJ onto the gravel road. "Now this is better. Baby loves rocks."

Ace shifted and the Jeep picked up speed. Conrad surveyed the growing storm system moving in their direction. Rain would kill the Toshiba and Smith would kill him if he let the computer get wet, but with the top off the Jeep, he had little choice. There was no way he was stopping now to reattach the soft roof, even if it meant saving the precious computer. An impelling force was pushing him to get to Julia. They were less than two miles from her and if the rain would just hold out another five minutes...

The cell phone vibrated in his hand. He flipped the case open. "Jules, are you all right?"

"Not exactly," came her reply. She sounded a little shaky. "Your queen has managed to step in shit, and I mean that in the most literal and technical way imaginable."

He chuckled, grateful to hear the professional reference to their past working relationship. "I'm here to serve. Want some help?"

"I'm on foot, on some backwoods country road southwest of Michael's house, and Susan's Agency officers are looking for me."

"That happens when you play with bad guys." He forced his voice to sound calm although he was spitting mad and scared for her safety to boot. "Ace and I are on our way to pick you up. We're approximately two miles south of your location."

Relief relaxed her voice. "Thank goodness for Smitty and his computer gadgets."

"Yeah, the one-man geek squad adds something to our team, doesn't he?"

"What if the Agency men find me before you do? Any suggestions?"

Conrad glanced at Ace and did a circling motion with his finger, signaling him to pick up speed. Ace nodded and pressed the Jeep's accelerator harder. "They mean business, Jules. Susan may have given them the okay to shoot to kill. You have to fight dirty. No fighting like a girl."

"I'm *not* a girl, Flynn."

Conrad smiled to himself. "Got your gun, sweetheart?"

"In my hand and fully loaded."

That's my girl. "Use it. Understand?"

Julia returned the picture to her tote bag. Her mind swerved as Conrad's current advice merged with the past...

Survival, Julia. You do whatever it takes to stay alive. Steal the food, pull the trigger, hot-wire the car. It's all the same. It means you live and someone else dies, but you do it anyway. Understand?

Tidewater, Virginia. Training camp. By day, crawling on her

belly like a snake in the Farm's underbrush while Flynn and his soldiers hunted her and the other students from the air. By night, crawling into her bed exhausted, only to have Flynn wake her two hours later and lecture her about staying alive in the field. *If shooting the guy in the head means you walk away and he doesn't, you shoot him. Understand?*

She could clearly remember dark eyes snapping at her, the voice demanding, *Understand?*

Julia heard a sound in the distance behind her, a man's feet crunching fallen leaves? She wasn't sure. The rain was picking up, clattering on the tree leaves all around her like marbles falling on a tile floor, and the light between the trees was fading. She crouched behind a bush and watched the area behind her, straining her ears to pick up more sounds.

Her right hand, holding tightly to the Beretta, twitched. Fight dirty. Survive. "Yeah, I understand," she said softly, struggling to keep her teeth from chattering. "Just hurry, Con."

Chapter Twenty-Nine

"You let her get away." Susan's face was pinched with anger as she stood accusing Michael.

Raising his attention from the warrant in his hand, he took a step toward her and stared her down. "You forced your way into my house, Susan. You ordered Ben Raines to shoot at the woman I love. Don't stand there and expect *me* to justify *my* actions." He paused and pointed a finger at her. "You're lucky I don't toss you over that railing."

Susan stood indignant, but Michael saw the quick glance she gave to the balcony's edge. Below them, Raines's men were spread out, watching, he supposed, for Abigail—*Julia*—to return. Yeah, like that would happen in a million years. A more likely reason they were spread out along the perimeter of his yard was to make sure he didn't take off with her.

His head was spinning from it all. Flynn was alive. The ramifications of that alone made his head pound with anger. He didn't know what the hell was going on, but he did know Susan and her officers had invaded his most personal space and, warrant or not, had attacked Julia. That was unacceptable in his book.

"Raines will track her down," Susan said, more to herself than him as she scanned the tree line. "He'll find her before she gets too far."

Michael threw the warrant down on the patio's table, covering the papers Julia had given him. She was being accused of treason, along with Flynn and Smith. Her face swam in front of him, and he took a deep breath and closed his eyes for a moment, wishing she hadn't run off like a guilty criminal.

But she had. "Tell Raines he is not to shoot her under any

circumstances."

"I won't," Susan responded. "She's resisting arrest and she's armed. Raines's life could be in danger."

Michael balled his hands into fists. He would go after Julia himself, but Raines had a good head start on him and was by far a better tracker. The only way he could insure Julia's safety at this point was to give the order not to harm her. "Julia would never hurt anyone unless she was threatened. Now call Raines on your portable radio"—he pointed at the one Susan was holding—"and tell him I order him not to shoot."

Susan studied him with a critical eye. "Your judgment is clouded, Director. I'll give no such order."

It was a standoff and Michael called on all his willpower not to follow through with his threat and throw Susan off the balcony. Julia had said her name had been on the list of candidates to take out. If Susan was the CIA's mole, then she was still looking for a way to eliminate Julia Torrison, especially if Julia, Flynn and Smitty had uncovered her secret dealings.

Michael fingered the disc stuck in the pocket of his sweatshirt. Then he looked Susan in the eye. He'd always found directness to be an efficient tool. "Are you setting me up, Susan? Are you the insider undermining everything I do?"

She started, but checked herself. He saw the lie pass through her mind before her dark eyes returned his stare as blank as steel. "You've been sleeping with a traitor, Director Stone. I believe you're the one now under the microscope."

"Does the name Cari ring a bell?" He saw Susan blanch and lifted his eyebrows. "I suggest you radio Raines and call the search off. It seems you and I have some talking to do."

Susan skirted past him and walked through his bedroom as if she would run away. Michael grabbed the papers off the table and followed her. "Julia gave me a message to pass on to you," he said, trying to stop her.

It worked.

Susan, her back to him, stopped on the stairs.

"She said to tell you she knows who Cari's father is." He moved up behind her. "And she's going to him next."

The enraged look Susan turned on him was startling. Michael could see Julia's words had hit their mark, and he wondered who the man Susan was hiding was. But Susan said nothing, only turned her back on him and continued down the stairs and out the front door which she left open.

Following behind her, Michael closed the door and rested his hand on it.

"She's either extremely gutsy or extremely stupid," Brad said from behind him.

Michael had forgotten his security officer was even still in the house. "Who is? Susan?"

The young ex-Marine pointed a thumb over his shoulder. "No, Abigail, or Julia. Whatever her name is. I can't believe she just did that."

Me either, Michael thought and went into his office where his desk phone was ringing. As he answered it, he set the papers on his desk and pulled the disc out of his pocket. "Stone."

"Hello, Director." The voice was quite familiar. It was Ryan Smith. "I need to talk to you immediately."

Michael drew a deep breath and willed his voice to sound unemotional, unconfused. "This better be damn good, Smith. You are two breaths away from finding my foot buried up your ass so far you'll never be able to sit down again. Start talking."

The rain had stopped but the clouds were still threatening. Julia sat quietly, wrapping her arms around her knees and trying to conserve heat. She'd buried her bag under leaves and brush beneath a bush across from her, taking only her guns, her phone and the picture of Paris, hidden in Michael's sweatshirt, up to her hiding place.

She saw Ben Raines before she heard his footsteps and mentally swore. He was a good tracker and she knew he would eventually look up and see her crouched in the branches of the hundred-year-old oak tree, but she held her breath and prayed something would distract him.

The tree was next to the gravel road and Conrad was only minutes from picking her up. She glanced at the distant hill and willed him to come charging over it. He did not.

Her fingers gripped the SIG Sauer tightly. She'd had to switch to the lighter gun because her hand and wrist were exhausted from carrying the Beretta. Now she wished she had the more familiar gun back in her hand, but didn't want to risk digging for it. Movement of any kind would attract Raines's attention.

He moved to the left and stood almost directly under her. Her teeth started to chatter and she carefully pulled the sleeve of Michael's sweatshirt over the heel of her left hand and shoved it in her mouth, keeping her right hand with the gun trained on Raines's head.

Again she glanced at the distant hill and willed Conrad to come. All she saw was an empty dirt road and layers of dark clouds.

Below she heard Raines snap the safety off his gun. She looked down and found herself staring at the dark hole of a .40 caliber Glock. Forty-caliber weapons offered more takedown punch and better penetration than the popular 9-mms, and Julia had no doubt the Glock had already sent a bullet her direction earlier. She shivered thinking about the damage it could have done, could still do.

"Drop your weapon." Raines backed out from under her. "And come down slowly. One wrong move and I have orders to shoot."

Julia swallowed hard and released the SiG. Raines retrieved it, emptied it of bullets and motioned at her to come down. She gripped the tree branch she was sitting on and swung down, dropping the last few feet to the ground.

Her feet and legs cried out in pain. It was easy to let her body fall to the ground and roll down the ditch. As she did, she grabbed the Beretta hidden in Michael's sweatshirt pocket. Coming to her feet, she raised the gun with both hands and pointed it at the black Glock.

Raines smiled.

"You're not really going to shoot them, are you, Con?" Ace asked over the roar of the wind. He cast a nervous glance at Flynn's drawn Heckler & Koch as he brought the Jeep up over yet another rolling Virginia hill.

Conrad shoved a full clip into the gun. "If necessary." He raised his head to look up the road. "There she is."

Ace's focus followed his, locking on Julia only a hundred yards ahead of them. Her gun was drawn on a man—a decent-sized brother who had one hell of a big gun pointed at her head. A Mexican standoff.

"I think I changed my mind about wanting to be your wheel guy," Ace said, even as he continued to press the accelerator.

"Too late." Flynn grinned at him before fastening his attention on the scene in front of him again. "Think of it as a rite of passage, brother. You do good on this one"—he patted Ace on the shoulder—"and I'll hire you to be my full-time wheelman."

"Fuckin' A," Ace muttered.

The only thing Raines had moved since finding a gun pointed at his head was his mouth, which was still quirked in a smile at her. Julia knew that smile. She'd seen it before. It said, *yeah, right.* The man didn't believe for one minute she was going to shoot him.

"Drop. The. Gun. Or. I. Will. Shoot. You." Each word received equal stress in a voice that said she meant business. And she did.

But he didn't drop the gun.

Julia sensed more than heard one of Raines's men a few feet away. If he were smart, he'd come at her and distract her. Working as a team to divide and conquer. That's what good partners did. It had been an early lesson in Conrad's school of spy survival.

Julia backed up a step toward the road. Out of the corner of her eye, she saw the Jeep, like a rock hurling itself in her direction. Finally. Good partner to the rescue.

Taking another step back, Julia returned Raines's smile.

As thunder boomed in the distance, he moved toward the edge of the ravine, towering over her. The smile on his face faded as his eyes took on the look of a hunter. In the echo of the thunder, she heard the muffled sound of footsteps in the rustling grass off to the left. She saw a shadow move.

Fight dirty, Julia.

Raines cleared the tree line and registered the Jeep, his focus flickering to the road and back to her so fast she might have missed it. But she was expecting it. With a sudden but accurate shift of the Beretta, Julia dropped to her knees and pulled the trigger without hesitation.

The heavy black gun Raines had been holding thudded on the ground and he cried out, falling to his own knees in pain and holding what was left of his right hand with his left. As he fell, Julia fired a second round at the trees where Raines's man was moving and saw him duck for cover. He fired his gun, but the shot went over her head.

Back on her feet, Julia jumped out of the ditch and ran for her life. She continued to send bullets at the woods as she ran to meet the Jeep.

Chapter Thirty

Ace couldn't believe his eyes. She'd actually pulled the trigger.

Julia Torrison had never been real to him until she showed up at the mortuary. Even then—even after the last few days of helping her and Flynn and Smitty—she was simply the Queen of Sheba to Flynn's Solomon. He was playing a fun, silly spy game with them, he, himself, tucked safely away in obscurity.

Watching her shoot the brother, roll, come to her feet and shoot some more as she ran toward him changed his mind. *O-kay*, he thought, *not a game.*

So much for obscurity. So much for safety. Now he was smack-ass in the middle of something *big*. It scared the bejesus out of him, but was intoxicating all the same.

Julia was running all out now, looking every bit like a movie star in an action scene. But even twenty yards away, Ace could see the fear in her face, and he felt a surge of protectiveness in his gut. She wasn't just a player in a silly spy game. She was a real, live person. Not just *any* person, either. A person Conrad Flynn was willing to risk his life for.

Conrad Flynn: invincible, unstoppable and damn near God-like. What Flynn wanted, Flynn got. In this case, he wanted Julia Torrison and the world be damned if Ace wasn't going to help him.

Because in his book, Conrad Flynn walked on water.

"That's my girl." Conrad stood up and brought his gun to bear on the targets ahead. "Let's roadhouse!"

Add Army of One to that list, Ace thought as he jammed his foot into the brake pedal and jerked the steering wheel left. Conrad's baseball cap flew off into the air as the Jeep spun in a donut, its back end coming to rest three feet from Julia.

As the Jeep swung around in front of his partner, Conrad held on to the roll bar with his right hand and fired three shots at the tree line.

One bullet punched a tree and the others rained down around the security officer Julia had shot. Not bad considering he was standing up in a moving vehicle and firing with his left hand. After that rain of bullets, a smart man would think twice before leaving the protection of the woods, and that would buy him and Ace a few more seconds to get Julia out.

She bounded toward the Jeep as it stopped, throwing up her left arm. Flynn reached out and grabbed her. Swinging her up into the backseat, he yelled, "*Go!*" to his wheelman.

As Ace pressed the accelerator and shifted on the fly, Conrad caught sight of not one, but three Agency officers hauling out of the tree line to shoot at them.

Ballsy bastards.

He pushed Julia's head down and fired off another dozen of the 9-mm parabellum rounds near the ditch and the man still writhing on the ground. The bullets ricocheted off the ground, sending the others back into hiding.

Conrad ejected the spent clip and jammed a fresh one back in while continuing to balance himself as the Jeep jerked in acceleration. "Come on, Ace," he shouted, thinking he could run faster than the CJ was moving. His wheelman definitely needed a different car. A speedy getaway this was not.

Lightning struck in the distance and Conrad could see rain begin falling in sheets as the storm moved in and they moved out. He switched the HK to his right hand and kept it trained in the direction of the woods for another half-mile before he glanced down at Julia. She was lying on her back, errant drops of rain hitting her in the face as she shoved the closed Toshiba under a too-big sweatshirt.

Ignoring the faded Marines emblem emblazed on the sweatshirt and raising his head to sky, Conrad let out a whoop at the stormy heavens that echoed over the hills like thunder. He hadn't felt this alive in months.

God*damn*, even Smitty's precious computer was safe.

Michael listened as Smith walked him through the disc's

contents. Listened while Smith explained from beginning to end Susan Richmond's manipulation and calculated career moves. He listened as Smith laid everything out in a succinct and efficient time line.

And then he asked the question burning in his mind. "Why didn't you come to me in the beginning, Smith?"

Ryan Smith was silent for a moment on the other end. "With all due respect, sir, Conrad and I thought you were the mole."

Michael sat back in his chair, disgusted. "Flynn *wanted* me to be the mole."

"Susan led us to believe you were." Smith let out a tired breath. "She was the one who set this in motion and pointed us continually in your direction. It was nothing personal, Director."

"The hell it wasn't," Michael said, more to himself than to Smith. He dropped his hand to the arm of his chair. "And you never doubted her."

"No, sir. We've always believed her intentions were true."

That was certainly believable, but Michael's ego was still smarting from Smith's confession. "Explain Julia's part in this."

"We purposely left her out of the loop for as long as possible. She knew nothing about any of this until three days ago."

Three days. Three nights. Flynn and Julia together. "But she has been helping you and Flynn."

"Because of you," Smith said in defense. "She knew you weren't the mole, and she was determined to prove your innocence."

"And how did she do that?"

Smith was silent, as if gauging his answer. Michael shifted in his chair. "What did she do? Bug my house? Read my mail? Listen to my phone calls? Tell me, Smith. What did Julia do to prove to you and Flynn that I wasn't the mole?"

"Cari Von Motz shifted our attention to Susan. She came to Julia with her journal and that's what convinced us."

Michael knew Smith was holding something back, but he let it drop. "Titus Allen is on his way here, to my house, at this very moment. I expect you and Flynn on my doorstep within the hour with every scrap of evidence you have to present to the Director. Got it?"

Smith's answer came one beat too slow. "I will be there."

"Flynn too," Michael insisted.

"He's a little tied up right now, sir."

"You tell him to get his perfidious ass over here or I swear I'll come after him myself."

Smith assumed a soothing tone. "Director, Conrad is picking up Julia to remove her from harm's way. Susan and her Agency officers are a real threat to her at this moment."

Michael closed his eyes and rubbed them again with his fingers. Flynn to the rescue. *Goddamn son of a bitch.* "I'll call Director Kipfer in security and ask him to find Susan and put a tail on her."

"Aren't you going to seek a warrant for her arrest?"

"We're talking about the chief officer of the Counterterrorism Center, Smith. An employee who's dedicated her life to the CIA without so much as a reprimand in her file. Absolutely every duck you have has to be in a row, and if it is, Titus and I will take the necessary steps and have Susan arrested. We need absolute proof, do you understand?"

"Of course. What about Senator King? He's involved too."

"We'll deal with King in time. We have to tread lightly with him too. You have damning evidence from a black bag job, illegally entering and bugging Susan's office. Neither Susan nor King knew they were being recorded. The law in this area must be interpreted carefully by carefully selected judges on our side if you know what I mean."

"Susan got him to sign off on the operation. She has his signature."

"She may have already destroyed it."

"Right." Smith sighed.

"King is not much of a threat to us or Julia right now. Let's concentrate on Susan."

"Cari too. If we have her, we have the star witness."

"Any idea where she is?"

"No, but she said she would contact Julia to see if you'd agreed to her proposition."

"Okay, get your butt over here and make your case. We'll go from there."

"I'll be there in twenty minutes."

Chapter Thirty-One

Alexandria

Plan A had gone straight to hell. Susan sat in her home office in her desk chair and rocked it slowly, rubbing the glass globe between her fingertips. Cari was a first-class turncoat. Julia had escaped and disappeared with Flynn, alerting Michael before Susan could stop her. Ben Raines was in the hospital, and Susan was keenly aware of the security team watching her house from the street. Daniel had called to tell her Titus Allen was requesting a meeting with him at Michael's house. She warned him of Julia's threat.

Plan A was definitely shot. Within hours, if the damage was not controlled, Susan could find herself in jail, on the run, or worse.

Fortunately for Susan, not even Daniel or Cari knew all the details of her alternate plan.

Susan set the globe down and picked up her desk phone. In less time than it took for the globe to make a full rotation, she placed a call to a man as desperate as she was.

Instantly, Plan B was initiated.

Arlington

"Is Julia safe?" Smitty asked Conrad.

"She's fine." Con glanced over his shoulder at her in the backseat. She was staring out the Jeep's back window, but he knew she wasn't seeing the rain or the dark landscape they were passing by. They were on their way to a safe house Conrad knew was empty. A place Susan would never think to look for them. "The Queen shot Ben Raines."

"No kidding? Injured or dead?"

"He won't be using his gun hand ever again."

Smitty whistled under his breath. "Self-defense, right?"

"Of course. You should have seen her," Conrad continued, hoping he might bring Julia out of her melancholy. "Dropped Raines like a pro."

"Tell her she did well."

Conrad moved the phone and said to Julia. "Smitty says you done good."

Julia looked at him, tried a smile and then turned back to the window.

"Did you tell her about Cari's father?"

Conrad spoke to Julia again over his shoulder. "Cari's father is none other than Senator Daniel King."

Surprise registered on her face as she met his gaze. "I bluffed and told Michael to tell Susan I knew who it was just to throw her into a tailspin, but I never would have guessed it was King."

"Did you hear that?" Con asked Smitty, smiling at Julia's deviousness. What would Susan think about that?

Smitty confirmed he'd heard her. "She's been hanging around you too long."

"You say that as if it's a bad thing."

"I'm headed to Stone's house. I walked him through all our information. He wants me to present it to Titus."

Conrad rubbed the back of his neck. "Yeah? What did he say about it?"

"You mean, what did he say about you?"

"That too."

"He called you a perfidious ass."

This time Conrad whistled. "I can feel the love. Stone always was too huggy for me."

"He wanted you to come with me, but I explained your predicament with Julia and Susan. He said he'd put Susan under watch but he couldn't ask for an arrest warrant until we present everything to Titus."

"He's right," Conrad said.

"I'll let him know you concur."

"Just convince him, Smitty. Otherwise we're all in a world of hurt."

"No problem, Conman. This is my area of expertise,

remember?"

"Any thoughts about what Susan's doing right now?"

"Plan B, I assume."

"Exactly. Watch your back, partner."

"Ditto."

Conrad closed his cell phone and ignored Ace's look of inquiry. Julia spoke from the backseat. "What did he say?"

"He told Stone everything over the phone and now he's going to meet with him and Titus. They'll get a warrant for Susan once they have all the evidence."

"What did Michael say about me?"

Ah, Conrad thought, *that's what she really wants to know.* "Smitty didn't mention anything."

"Oh." She turned back to the window.

He racked his brain for something to distract her. "Stone did however call me a perfidious ass."

That worked. She raised an eyebrow at him and a small grin passed her lips. "That's it?"

"What do you mean, is that it? I just saved his career and the CIA from ruin and he calls *me* a perfidious ass."

"What's perfidious mean?" Ace asked from the driver's seat.

"You deceived him and stole his girlfriend out from under his nose," Julia said to Conrad. "I think technically 'ass' is a pretty mild revilement."

"Revilement?" Ace looked at one and then the other in his rearview. "This is some kind of spy talk, isn't it? Okay, I'm down with it. Just tell me what it means."

Conrad ignored Ace and turned his head away to look out the Jeep's window, but inside he was smiling to himself. It didn't matter what Stone called him. Julia was right.

I got the girl. Game, set, match, Conrad Flynn.

Michael handed Titus his requisite martini and sat behind his customized mahogany desk.

Titus took a sip and sucked the olive off the toothpick. "So my CTC chief is bringing down the house of cards, is that what you're telling me, Michael?"

Thunder sounded overhead. "Yes, sir. Looks like she was shooting for your job ultimately."

Titus was quiet for a long minute, savoring his martini and

staring at the wall. He sucked his lined cheeks in. "Never did trust that woman."

Michael let his surprise show. "Sir?"

"Always knew she was after my job." Titus finished off the martini and set the glass on Michael's desk with a flourish. "Had the hots for her once. Thank God she rejected me or she'd have busted my balls and taken over my job years ago. She was in love with Daniel King back then and couldn't see I was the better man." Titus winked at him.

At a loss for words, Michael just stared at his boss as the DCI went to the wet bar and mixed another drink. He came back to the chair and kicked his cowboy boots up on Michael's desk. "Don't look at me like that, young man. You're in quite a pickle yourself with a woman right now. Lust makes us do stupid things." He shrugged. "This Torrison, she worth damaging your career for?"

Michael sat back in his chair. "Is my career damaged?"

Titus waved him off. "Don't be stupid. Your career is just taking off. I've been priming you to take over when I retire." He pointed a weathered, but well-manicured finger at Michael. "Mind you, I'm in no hurry."

"I thought you were coming here to fire me."

"Fire you?" Titus laughed. "I was coming to tell you about Cari Von Motz."

Again Michael was at a loss. "You were coming to tell me about Cari Von Motz?"

"She contacted me yesterday down in the Keys. Damn if I know how she got my cell phone number, but she told me some interesting stuff about you and Torrison, Flynn, Smith and Susan. Confirmed what I suspected. I flew back today to tell you Susan was gunning for you and your girlfriend. I figured I was next in line."

"So you knew?"

Titus smiled at him. "This old spy ain't as stupid as he looks. I've had my suspicions about Susan over the years, but could never prove a damn thing. I was hoping you'd keep her in line. That's why I saddled you with her."

Michael stared in disbelief. "And did you know Flynn was alive before Cari told you?"

"Ah," Titus said, raising a finger. "Now that boy is an operative after my own heart. Can you believe him?" He shook his head and laughed. "A sac of steel, he's got! I was never that good."

Michael jabbed the end of his pencil into the top of the desk, noticing that Titus had not answered his question. "Flynn faked his death and misled all of us, Director. I hardly think he's a hero."

The old man dismissed his concerns with a wave of his hand. "Pull your shorts out, Michael. Flynn's the best spy you'll ever have working for you. Sometimes he's unconventional, but he gets the job done." He eyed Michael for a moment and then the boots came off the desk. "Wait, this is about Torrison, isn't it?" He snapped his fingers. "Now I remember. She was Flynn's partner in Europe, wasn't she? That's why you're so upset."

"I'm not upset," Michael lied.

Titus nodded with a *sure you're not* look on his face. "All right, I'll let you deal with the two of them." He sat back. "I invited Daniel King to talk to us here tonight. Thought we'd interrogate him a little and see if he gives anything up voluntarily. He should be here shortly."

Michael raised an eyebrow. "You think you can get information about Susan's schemes from King? He'll feign ignorance or deny it."

"He might, but it will be fun putting him on the hot seat." He rubbed his hands together with anticipation. "King wants to be President. He stands to lose more than Susan's ever dreamed about. He won't jeopardize that. If his ass is on the line, he'll give her up without blinking and that's worth more to us than Cari Von Motz's journal and Flynn and Smith's evidence."

Michael considered the old spy's reasoning. Having an esteemed leader of the senate come forward and testify against Susan would certainly solidify the others' stories. "Smith claims King signed off on Susan's operation to charge Julia and the rest of us with treason."

"She covered her backside. I'd have done the same thing. That way, if her plan doesn't succeed, she can put the blame on King. His name's on the line, not hers. She could conceivably make it look like it was his idea and exonerate herself."

"Why would he sign it then?"

Titus shrugged. "She's always been very acute at working every angle. She either blackmailed him with Cari or promised him something to further his career. Probably both, knowing her."

"Guess we'll find out." Michael tapped his pencil. "You want to be bad cop or good cop with King?"

It was Titus's turn to look surprised. He smiled at Michael and returned to the bar with his glass. "You're going to make a good DCI some day, Stone."

He stuck an extra olive in his dry martini and saluted Michael from across the room.

Chapter Thirty-Two

Houston, we have a problem. Ryan Smith watched the black Lincoln Town Car thirty yards ahead of him stop at the gate to Stone's house. The guard checked the driver's credentials and waved him through. The car's plates read SENKING.

Smitty drove on by. Michael Stone had not mentioned Senator King being in attendance for their meeting, and with his involvement with Susan and the afternoon's melee, Smitty was reluctant to venture into the gated property. Only a careless man would assume he was safe at this point, no matter what his boss said, and Smith was anything but careless.

Half a mile south of Stone's house, Smitty pulled the van over and killed the lights. He watched the rain run in rivulets down the windshield as he contemplated his next move. Lightning flashed in the valley and thunder followed a few seconds later. Zipping up his jacket and pulling on a cap, he wished begrudgingly Conrad were with him instead of with Julia. Sneaking around in the woods at night during a thunderstorm to do surveillance wasn't his idea of fun. Con's, yes. His, definitely no.

But Conrad wasn't there and Smitty was, and Stone and Allen were waiting for him. Pissing off his boss and his boss's boss by being late wasn't his best career move, especially while AWOL, but ending up dead or in jail was far worse. Even Conrad couldn't help him if he was dead, and he'd probably already damaged his career beyond fixing at this point anyway.

Grabbing his flashlight and night-vision binoculars, he locked up the van and backtracked along the road at a run until he was less than one hundred yards from Stone's property. The rain was coming down in sheets and he was already drenched. Ducking into the tree line, he felt the rain ease but the darkness, if possible, got darker.

He stood still for a moment, closed his eyes and willed the sudden rise of claustrophobia back down. It was just like camp—dark as hell, raining, bullies ready to jump out at you on all sides like a carnival funhouse. It was almost worth turning around and taking his chances with Stone, Allen and King.

But he didn't turn around. Following his flashlight's beam, he cut through the woods in an easterly direction, moving as quickly as the rough, muddy terrain would allow. He hunkered his shoulders under his jacket and wondered what his chances of getting a decent letter of recommendation from Stone were after this was over. From the annoyed tone in Stone's voice, Smitty guessed his chances were slim to none.

West Virginia

Conrad sloshed a half-inch of Chivas into the bottoms of the two glasses on the worn countertop in front of him. He'd found the bottle of whiskey in the pantry behind the cans of tomato sauce and mentally thanked the last guest of the CIA safe house for leaving it behind. It wasn't his brand, but it would do.

Setting the bottle down, he listened for the sound of movement in the old farmhouse...feet moving across the scratched and faded hardwood floors, the sound of the shower running, the groan of bedsprings or a squeak of hinges from a door swelled with oppressive humidity. Ace was gone, Smitty was at Stone's house, but Julia was somewhere above him, and his senses strained to pick up her presence.

Only the scratch of a maple tree branch against the window outside broke the silence in the deserted house. Spider webs and dust, which had accumulated exponentially over the months of inactivity, coated everything. A musty smell permeated the air. Conrad cracked open a window.

Set across the state line in West Virginia, the two-story farmhouse wasn't far from the Appalachian Trail, but it was far enough from the people who had equipped it to hold human assets.

Running surveillance on the house off and on for over two months, Conrad knew the house had not been used during that time. Non-perishable foods were stored neatly in the pantry, men and women's clothing hung in the bedroom closets, waiting for the next temporary houseguest. A secret room in the basement held a cache of communications equipment. A Honda Civic sat in the barn along with a backup generator, battery charger and a carefully hidden and highly efficient armory of weapons.

For tonight, he hoped he didn't need any of those things. He simply needed a safe house, one that would grant him a stiff drink, a shower, a soft bed and time to think.

The papers Julia had stolen were in Stone's hands along with the disc. Possession of those documents, Cari's journal and his and Smitty's evidence all provided Stone and Allen with a tidy and satisfying wrap-up to the problems plaguing the CIA for the past year and a half.

With what he knew from eavesdropping on Susan and the Senator, and from what Julia had garnered from the *Operation Sheba* documents, the overall picture was less puzzling, but no less dangerous. He could see what a fool he'd been, how he'd put his trust in the wrong person.

However, there was no benefit in dwelling on his mistake tonight. Time would balance the scale of right and wrong and an opportunity for revenge would present itself soon enough. He'd take it without hesitation after he was sure Julia and Smitty were safe.

Throwing a shot of the Scotch whiskey into the back of his throat, he swallowed it with a grimace and set the glass back on the counter. As he emptied his pockets of a handful of change, his wallet and his cell phone, his mind registered heat spreading in his stomach. He refilled the glass.

Unanswered questions about Susan's Plan B cycled through his brain, but now that he knew who his real opponent was, he could guess her next move with some degree of accuracy. While she probably didn't realize it, she was no longer in control of the playing deck. He was. And while he didn't always play exactly by the rules, he held himself to a high standard of integrity, despising cheaters whose actions were unjustified or self-serving. Susan Richmond's betrayal of her country and her honor for self-gain was unacceptable. Her actions had sacrificed countless operations and the lives of multiple CIA officers in the field as well as endangering her own countrymen. She had to be stopped.

On the surface, it was easy for him to calculate her downfall, but underneath the forced indifference of intellectual reasoning, Susan's betrayal scratched his soul as raw as the whiskey did his throat. All the years of cultivating trust, shattered into a jagged-edged pill he had to swallow.

You can only be betrayed by someone you trust, Flynn.

A second shot of whiskey cleared his throat and assaulted his intestines. This time he allowed himself a moment of emotional release. The empty glass flew through the air, exploding against the far wall and sending fragments flying over the kitchen table and under the chairs.

Turning his back on the broken glass, he grabbed a replacement from the cabinet, rinsed it in the sink and poured two fingers of Chivas again. He recapped the bottle, slipped it back into its hiding place in the pantry and listened to the house. Hearing nothing but the tree branch continue its grazing of the window, he slid his fingers around the two waiting glasses and went to find Julia.

She was standing in the bathroom in front of the mirror, twisting the ring on her finger. He handed her one of the glasses. "Drink," he commanded.

She did, shivering as the whiskey ripped down her throat. "Ugh." She stuck her tongue out. "That's awful."

"Strip. Clothes, shoes, everything."

Julia handed him the glass. "Your seduction technique could use some work."

Conrad snorted as he turned the shower on hot. "As you well know, my seduction technique is first rate. This is my survival technique and it's even better. You're going into shock, Julia. Now get your clothes off and get in the shower."

Julia shivered under Con's fingers, the stress of the past two hours bleeding off like a second skin. If she followed her usual pattern, the shakes would start soon. She needed to follow his advice and get warmed up, but she was still feeling hurt that Michael had not asked Smitty about her.

"Have you ever been hurt by someone you love, Con?"

The faintest of sighs escaped his lips and she saw him struggle with his next words. "I've only ever loved you, Jules. And, yes, sometimes you've hurt me."

"Not intentionally, though."

Conrad only shrugged. He started to help her out of her shirt. "Is this about me lying to you again?"

Julia shook her head as he tugged the shirt over it. "I thought Michael would have asked Smitty if I was okay. I thought he would..."

She left the thread of the sentence hanging, because she wasn't sure exactly what she thought. Conrad paused before dropping the wet shirt on the floor, but he didn't say anything. Instead he bent down and untied her muddy shoes.

She unbuttoned her pants. "I guess he's really pissed."

Between the two of them, they managed to peel off her wet jeans. Julia removed Smitty's GPS device from her bra and handed it to Con. The room was steaming up from the shower. "Michael knows we're back together," she said to him. "He knows I betrayed him. He probably doesn't care what happens to me now."

Conrad took a sudden interest in the GPS unit. "Did you know tracking devices can be as small as the head of a pin these days? They can be sewn into a shirt hem or stuck into the sole of a shoe. They can be planted in a piece of jewelry or a belt buckle. If Smitty had let me, I would have stuck one in each of your bras."

And if she hadn't been so tired, she would have rolled her eyes. "Been reading the *Encyclopedia of Espionage* again?"

That brought a tight smile from him. "Tom Clancy."

Goose bumps stood in rows on her arms. Julia unfastened her bra and dropped it on the pile of wet clothes. Then she pulled off her underwear. Conrad watched unabashed as she stood naked in front of him, but he only moved her into the shower.

Leaving her there, he picked up the clothes and walked out of the room. Julia rested her head against the tiled wall. The warm water was a welcome relief and she closed her eyes.

Dance in your blood. That was the line from a Rumi poem inscribed inside the band of silver on her middle finger. The ring had belonged to a woman who had done just that, living through years of abuse. Julia tried to remember more of the poem her mother had whispered to her in the dark...

Dance, when you're broken open.

Dance, if you've torn the bandage off.

Dance in the middle of the fighting.

Years, lifetimes ago, she had found love and happiness in her mother's lap, songs and poetry flowing from Valerie's mouth. While the young Julia struggled to grasp the meaning of it, she reveled in the passion she heard in her mother's voice and the security of her arms. At that moment in the shower, she wished she could feel that kind of security again.

Sagging against the tiled stall, Julia hugged herself. Her job was gone. Her friendship with Susan over. Her relationship with Michael unsalvageable. She was on the run with Conrad.

This wasn't how her life was supposed to play out. She'd never wanted fame and glory, but she'd never wanted to sit on the sidelines and watch the world go by either. All she wanted was to protect the innocent and find a minute's worth of peace for herself. She wanted to be loved, accepted, respected for who she was as much as for what she did. Yes, her job was unique and had satisfied her desire to protect her country while providing her with the challenges she longed for, but underneath it all, she was just like every other woman. She just wanted to be happy, safe, loved.

The last of the adrenaline left her and even her ferocious determination couldn't keep her legs from wobbling under the sudden weight of her situation.

Firm hands grabbed her as she slid down the wall and hauled her back up. Nose to nose with Conrad, he murmured, "Stay with me, Jules," and she felt the strength return to her legs.

He had stripped his own clothes off and joined her in the shower. His hands pulled her further into the spray and he wet her hair and washed it gently with shampoo.

He had been and still was the love of her life. There was no denying it. There was something between them, something that linked them together. If Julia had believed in soul mates, she knew Conrad would be hers.

In her mind, she saw him again that fateful night in Germany. Saw him moving with purpose, remembered the sound of his voice and the urgency behind his caress. He had sacrificed everything. To save her, to save the Agency, to protect his country. He was not an illusion. He was a tangible, verifiable, authentic hero.

The faintest smile touched her lips. The moment Conrad

had appeared in Michael's bedroom, rare and wild exhilaration had flooded her senses. He was the toughest, shrewdest, most magnanimous man she'd ever known. The flip side was just as extreme—noble, kind-hearted and considerate to those he cared about. Her previous anger and disappointment at his deception had been overshadowed by the precious gift of having him alive again.

"I was a good partner," she said to him, needing to confirm that he was there, that he was alive. "I never failed you. Never left you with your balls to the wall. You said, 'Do this, Julia' and I said, 'Yes, Conrad'. We were a good team, weren't we?"

Conrad paused while rinsing her hair. "You were a good field operator, but I don't remember there ever being many 'Yes, Conrads'. As I recall you were quite opinionated and your opinions rarely coincided with mine."

She wiped water from her face and narrowed her eyes at him.

"Not that there was anything wrong with that," he backpedaled. "I've always respected your opinions and appreciated the assertive way you've shared them with me."

A small laugh escaped from her throat. She studied him critically for a minute as he picked up the bar of soap and began washing himself. "I still don't really understand why you left me out of the loop," she said. "If I'd known what was going on, I would have never gotten involved with Michael. I wouldn't have hurt him like this. I wouldn't have spent all these months trying to get over you. Don't you feel the least bit guilty for all of that?"

Julia didn't want logical arguments this time around and somehow Con understood this. He shrugged and began rinsing. "Maybe I screwed up."

Her eyebrows hit her hairline. "My God, did you just admit to being wrong?"

Conrad grimaced. *Wrong* was an inflexible word. A word he hated when applied to him. Admitting he was wrong was like admitting he was weak, and he had little tolerance for weakness. "Not wrong, exactly. I probably could have made better choices in how I handled the situation, but—"

"Ugh!" She took the soap from him and started washing herself. "You are such a..." Her lips moved as she tried to think of a name bad enough to describe him. "Man! Why can't you admit you were wrong? Just once? You shouldn't have left me in the dark about the shadow CIA or the fact my cover was blown, and you know it. That was the most stupid, idiotic, asinine thing you've ever done, Flynn. I ought to shoot your balls off."

Conrad Flynn had been shot, knifed, beaten up and tortured to the brink of insanity. He'd taken the worst the world could hand him and used it to make himself stronger. But SEAL training and hunting terrorists from Britain to Indonesia had nothing on facing down Julia Torrison with a bad attitude, gun or no gun. He felt his precious jewels tuck themselves a little tighter into his body. "Crippling me in such a fashion would only give you short-term satisfaction."

She dropped her gaze to his lower half and quirked her head to the side. "Oh, well." She pursed her lips and casually waved the bar of Dial at his genitals. "I don't have much to live for these days. Short-term satisfaction sounds pretty good."

She was bluffing, but he enjoyed it. She'd had a really tough day, had to be exhausted and still she was making jokes and trying to take *his* mind off the mess they were in. He smiled at her. "I can think of more enjoyable ways to achieve short-term satisfaction with my..." he searched for a euphemistic term, "...equipment."

Julia let several antagonizing moments pass before she spoke. "And, again, I repeat, you are such a man." But she smiled at him and handed him the soap.

She did not however ask him for any satisfaction. As she finished washing herself, time stopped and started like a mouse moving through a snake and it became clear to Conrad, as the two of them moved through the common daily chore of showering, why he felt like he was losing his edge. It wasn't age or frustration level or job burnout. He had felt he was losing it because he had thought he'd lost the one person in the world, besides his mother, who believed in him and his cause. His brothers thought he was crazy. His father had always been disappointed in him for not following in his footsteps and making the Navy his career. His previous girlfriends had found his hyperawareness, paranoia and long stints out of town too hard to handle.

The hell of it was, losing Julia had been his own fault. She was right—he had set her on this course, pushed her into a major clusterfuck of espionage and betrayal, robbed her of her identity and a normal life with someone she loved. He'd taken away her royal flush and dealt her a pair of twos.

It's not about the cards you're dealt, Conrad reminded himself, *it's about the people you play with.*

Now she was his again and, as he watched her step out of the shower and dry off, he fought his own demons. He wanted her back in the shower with him, wanted her body slamming into his, but she was vulnerable right now and smarting after the long day, and he knew if she wanted to have sex, she would have jumped him already. He would be patient. He would be on his best behavior.

On his top ten least-favorite-things-to-do list, behaving himself ranked right up there with listening to opera and playing dead.

After a return to trip to the laundry room to retrieve their clothes from the dryer, Conrad found the bedroom adjacent to the bathroom and turned on the bedside lamp. Dropping the towel from around his waist, he laid his gun on the bedside table and pulled on his briefs. His cell phone was still downstairs and needed a recharge, but the thought of one more trip down and up was enough to make him groan. However, he was still waiting to hear from Smitty. So he made the run to the kitchen to retrieve the phone and brought it and Julia's upstairs with him. In his rush to rescue Sheba, he'd forgotten his charger. He checked the phone for messages, but found nothing. Either Ryan was still talking to Stone or Con's half-dead cell phone didn't like his choice of sleeping quarters. This area in West Virginia bordered the outer limits of tower range and was dotted with dead zones.

After propping himself on the bed in a half-sitting position, he rested his head in the crook of one arm and laid his gun on his stomach. A minute later, Julia came in with the Chivas and their shot glasses. She pulled on her shirt and underwear and climbed into bed next to him, pouring them both a round before setting the bottle on the floor. He tossed the whiskey into his mouth and let his thoughts drift.

Susan Richmond. Cari Von Motz. Michael Stone. Classified documents. Senator King.

But his mind kept turning in ever-tightening circles around the woman next to him. The way she'd outwitted Susan and defended herself against Raines. The way her body had moved against his two nights ago. Julia, wet and smiling, a few minutes ago, warm water and lots of soap mixed with her firm legs and...

And the combination of whiskey and exhaustion coupled with thoughts of her naked under the pouring water pushed his libido into overdrive.

He chanced a glance at her out of the corner of his eyes. Her head was on the pillow, her eyes closed. Goddamn, behaving was hell. He wasn't going to make it if he kept entertaining soap-and-water fantasies about her. Taking a couple of deep breaths, he shut down his libido by running his mental exercise of cleaning his gun. Within seconds, he was asleep.

He woke some time later to find his gun on the nightstand and Julia curled next to him on the bed. Instinctively he reached for her and pulled her body to his. She spooned into him naturally and he smoothed her still wet hair with his hand, breathed in her clean scent and relaxed for the first time in months.

She's mine, he thought before drifting back to sleep.

Chapter Thirty-Three

There was a knock on the door and Michael called to Brad to come in.

"Senator King is here, sir."

"Good," Michael said. "Send him in."

Titus pointed at a sleeping Pongo. "King doesn't like dogs."

Michael rose from his chair as Brad backed out of the room. "I'll kennel him."

"Hell of a night for a dog to be outside."

"Hell of a night, period." Michael found himself hoping Julia had found a safe, dry refuge somewhere. He refused to think about her with Flynn. Rousing Pongo from his dog bed, he said, "Come on, boy."

A few minutes later, Titus and Michael shook hands with Senator King and Michael invited him to sit on the couch. Titus set him and King up with martinis, Michael declined.

"You're probably wondering why I asked you here," Titus said.

King nodded and took a sip of his drink. "I assumed it was something important to call me out on a night like this."

Titus smiled at him and raised his glass in salute. "Daniel, this may be the most important night of your life. Yes"—he glanced at Michael—"I'm sure tonight will change everything for all of us."

Lightning cracked and twenty yards from where Fayez Raissi lay, one of his men cut the electrical power wire at the pole.

Michael Stone's house went dark.

The security officer at the gate stepped to the door of the small guard house, cigarette in hand, looking at the main house. Raissi took his time, lined the man's head in the sights of his scope and squeezed the trigger. He continued to watch through the scope as the man's head snapped back and his body went limp, falling to the floor of the guard house.

With calm movements, Raissi sat up, removed the scope from his weapon and gave a nod to the young man at his side. Muammar sent the word to the others stationed around the house. Inside the Director of Operations was entertaining the CIA's top man, Titus Allen. It was supposed to be a secret meeting, but what they were discussing was no secret to Raissi, although he didn't care what had brought them together that night. Senator Daniel King had just arrived to join them, and Susan's directive had been clear. No survivors were to leave the house.

Raissi moved the rifle to his back and snapped night-vision goggles over his eyes. For a moment, he enjoyed the feel of the cool rain on his face. The last rain he would feel.

Thunder boomed overhead and Muammar flinched. One of Raissi's team was already at the guard house, removing the body and donning the dead man's clothes. The terrorist would replace the guard for tonight. Tomorrow they would all die inside with the hostages.

Raissi motioned to Muammar and the two set off toward the house, melting into the darkness.

A peal of thunder shook the dark house.

"Damn weather," Titus swore under his breath. "Florida was the same. Storms, rain, wind. A man can't even have a decent vacation anymore."

Senator King chuckled, but it had a nervous edge to it. "Weather's been pretty good here the past few days, Titus, except for a minor storm the other night. I've been out golfing every day. You must have brought this rain back with you."

Letting his vision adjust to the darkness, Michael glanced at the video monitor. He hadn't been paying attention to it since Allen arrived with his squadron of security people. Now he felt a twinge of anxiety. The battery backup hummed to life and the screen showing the four quadrants around the house flickered. Everything looked normal. The guard was in the guard house, the grounds were empty. "I lose power once in awhile during storms." He moved toward the office's French doors. "Generator's in the basement. I'll have the lights back on in a minute."

Michael and Titus's security details were alert outside the doors. "Director?" Brad said as Michael emerged from the room. He and Tad Carmichael, Titus's favorite security officer, had been instructed not to interrupt the meeting for anything short of a nuclear explosion. The two other members of Titus's group were stationed at the front and back doors.

Michael grabbed a flashlight out of the antique buffet in the hall. "Storm's knocked out the power. I'm headed to the basement to turn on the generator. Let the other officers know so they don't panic and shoot each other or me."

"Yes, sir," Brad answered, and Michael heard the screech of the man's radio behind him as he made his way to the basement stairs.

"Is anyone watching your cameras, sir?" Carmichael called after him.

"The monitor's in the office. Keep an eye on it until I get back."

Michael automatically reached for the basement's light switch and then cursed himself down the carpeted stairs for forgetting. He found the generator, hardwired into the house's main electrical current, and flipped the switch. The engine buzzed to life. Light came on at the top of the stairs.

Before he could take a step toward those stairs, he heard what sounded like a shout, then running footsteps. Instinctively, he crouched and stared at the basement's ceiling, his ears on alert. Something was wrong.

After his years in the military and the subsequent career with the CIA, Michael was comfortable carrying a gun whenever he left his house. Inside it though, he left his favorite handgun in the gun safe in his office along with his hunting rifles that had barely seen use in the past five years. He had never felt the need to be armed inside his home. At that moment, however, he would have given anything to have his favorite S&W in his hand.

Still straining his ears, he flexed his hand on the Maglite he was carrying and crept on silent feet to the bottom of the stairs. The generator was buzzing along off to his right and he wondered if he dared turn it back off. He heard another loud voice—not familiar—and all the hairs on the back of his neck stood up. A man rushed past the landing above him and Michael drew back into the shadowed basement just as he heard three shots fired succinctly.

His pulse double-timing it, he hit the generator's switch, throwing the house into darkness again. Commotion over his head followed and then ceased. Silence enveloped him.

A minute later, a man's voice called to him from the top of the stairs. "Michael Stone." A Middle Eastern accent laced the syllables of Michael's name. "CIA Director of Operations. Am I correct?"

Michael didn't answer, his brain trying to figure out who had invaded his home and why.

The man tried again. "We have much work to do tonight, Director. Please come upstairs."

Michael stayed quiet.

The man disappeared. Michael wondered who the man was, what he was doing there and who was dead.

"Director Stone." The man was back. "I am holding a gun to your security agent's head. If you do not show yourself in the next five seconds, I will kill him."

Feeling like Tom Clancy's character Jack Ryan in *Air Force One*, Michael quickly and damnably considered his options. Stay hidden, which might be Titus and King's only chance of surviving, but killing his security guard, or giving himself up and, in the process, screwing them all over.

The logical answer was to stay hidden. Make the man at the head of the stairs come down to the dark basement and get him. But would the man stop at Brad? Were King and Allen already dead?

Michael knew the man at the top of the stairs meant business. Three people, probably the security guards at the doors and Tad, were already dead and Michael assumed the man was taking the DCI, a well-known senator and himself hostage. The terrorist was not a person to challenge, and Brad's life would not be the only life forfeited if Michael forced his hand.

In good conscience, Michael could not let the security guard die for him. Not when there was a slim chance he could save them all.

Ryan Smith was on his way. His unexpected arrival could give Michael and the others the slim chance they needed.

"I'm coming out," Michael announced clearly.

"Turn on your generator first," the man instructed.

Michael flipped the switch and climbed the stairs with the flashlight stuck down his pants.

The cut through the woods had been tedious, the forest more like a tropical jungle than a simple wooded acre or two. But once Stone's house came into view, Ryan had blocked out his soaked clothes, his muddy shoes and his scratched face. He'd laid down on his stomach and used his binoculars to watch the house and its occupants.

A moment later, the house had gone completely dark. Then the lights had flashed on. There was movement by the bay window, a man running by it, and Ryan had felt an uncomfortable twinge between his shoulder blades. Before he drew another breath, he'd heard three gunshots fired inside the house and a second later, like a door slamming shut, the house had gone dark again.

Ryan had instinctively jerked himself off the ground and backed farther into the tree line. The house was lit again but the sound of gunshots echoed in his mind. Digging out his cell phone, he wiped his wet fingers on his wet pants and swore as they slipped over the keypad. Conrad's phone rang on the other end.

And rang. "Come on. Come on," Ryan whispered. Finally, he heard Conrad's voice, but it wasn't live. He'd gotten Conrad's voice mail.

Swearing under his breath, he kept the binoculars trained on the house. Con's phone might be out of range, or it might be turned off or it could have fallen into someone else's hands. It didn't matter. Out of paranoia, Ryan wouldn't give specific names or details. Instead he kept his message short and to the point. "Big problem, Solomon. Call me as soon as you receive this message."

He sat tight and waited.

Chapter Thirty-Four

Arlington
Rule number one: Don't make eye contact.

Michael walked up the basement stairs, ignoring the first rule of being a hostage. His attention locked on the man holding a gun to Brad's head, noting his height, weight and dress. The terrorist was in green camouflage from head to toe and his face was smeared with grease paint, but he was clean-shaven and, Michael made another note, totally calm.

The man pulled Brad backwards as he made room for Michael to enter the hall. Brad glanced to Michael's left and, instinctively, he ducked, but a heavy object clocked him above his left ear and he went down on his knees, grabbing for the door, only to bounce off of it and drop face down on the floor. As he turned his head to the left to see who or what was attacking him, the butt of a gun smashed into his head and the room went black.

Safe house

She was running for her life. But as is the case with dreams, invisible quicksand sucked at her feet, rendering her legs sluggish and slow.

Julia fought her way through the crowd of people, searching for a familiar face, panic rising in her chest. She wanted to yell for help, but her voice was mute, stuck in her throat, so she just kept pushing past the people blocking her. The man was close behind her and she had to get away from him.

How could there be so many people in one place? She pushed herself through the throng, absently noting the Ferris wheel and the merry-go-round. A carnival. The hawkers called out to her, their laughter echoing in her ears as she continued to try and move forward.

She broke free and kicked her legs into high gear. It was dark and she was running down an alley. Where was she? Paris? Berlin? Arlington? She couldn't remember. Couldn't remember why the man was chasing her. Only that he had a gun and he wanted her dead.

She hit a door and it swung open and she continued to run, heavy footsteps reverberating down the long hall. Hers or his?

Up the stairs. Another door, a hallway, the last door at the end.

Poor choice, she saw at once, blood pounding in her ears. Nothing more than a restroom. A dead-end with only one way out. She whirled to find the man was now there, blocking her exit.

Sliding down the wall, she sat on the cold, grimy tile floor. *I'm going to die all alone,* she thought, and she raised her gaze to look into the black hole that would kill her. She felt nothing as she saw the man's finger pull the trigger, but raised her focus another notch to see his face.

Dark eyes under soft eyebrows met hers. She screamed.

Julia's body jerked upright, lifting her out of the dream with a pounding heart, her ears acutely aware of her fading scream. Was the noise real or only in her head?

She rubbed her face with a trembling hand and tried to get her bearings in the unfamiliar surroundings. *Where am I?*

A warm hand on her back made her flinch and she jerked around to see who was beside her in the early morning light.

Dark eyes under soft eyebrows met hers. "What is it, Julia?"

Conrad's sleep-roughened voice muffled the scream still echoing in her head, dulling the sharp edges of the nightmare. But suspicion lingered in her brain, the seed planted by her subconscious.

She shook her head and looked away from him, focusing on the hundred-year-old dresser across the room. She took a couple of deep breaths and ran her hands through her hair. Why would she dream Con was trying to kill her?

There's been too much betrayal, she thought, pulling her

hair over her left shoulder. She asked him in a shaky voice, "Have you ever thought about killing me?"

He moved, raising himself to sit beside her, their shoulders touching as he draped both arms over his bent knees. "I missed the left turn you just took there, Jules."

"What if when we were case officers in the field I had gone bad and you were instructed to bring me in, dead or alive. Would you have killed me if necessary?"

"How much whiskey did you drink?" He pulled her hair back from her face. She could feel more than see his frown. "If you'd have gone bad, I would have gone with you."

"What would we have done?"

He pushed some of her hair behind her ear. "Oh, I don't know. You'd have thought of something."

"Why me?"

"You're the brains of this operation, remember? I get us into deep shit, and you get us out. All great partnerships are that way. Tom and Huck, Bonnie and Clyde, Butch and Sundance..."

"Juveniles and outlaws. Perfect. We fit right in. You're a juvenile and I'm an outlaw."

"So what are we going to do, Bonnie?"

She punched him on the arm. Comfortable silence hung around them for several minutes. Julia's heartbeat returned to normal.

Or almost normal. The nearness of Conrad's body was doing funny things to her. Funny, familiar things to her stomach and her heart that messed up her equilibrium.

Julia turned her head to look at Conrad and her equilibrium swung in a one-eighty. There was heat and desire in his eyes and she felt her body respond just like it had every other time he'd looked at her that way. He made her feel wild and reckless because he was, but in a weird grounded sort of way. In the back of her mind, she knew if she grew too wild, too reckless, he would catch her when she fell.

Her attention fell to Con's lips, almost close enough to kiss. "You're incredibly good at making me feel safe." She leaned into his mouth. His lips were warm and his hands pulled her close.

"Damn." He broke the kiss. "Sometimes patience is a virtue."

"Since when have you exercised patience?" she asked and laughed low in her throat as Con's teeth bit softly into her bottom lip.

Arlington

Michael Stone gritted his teeth to fight off the throbbing pain in his head. A phone was ringing, its shrill cry piercing the room.

Someone answer the damn phone.

Fighting the fog around his brain, he tried to grope for the offending instrument, but found his arm wouldn't obey. After a second of concentration, he realized his arms and legs were tied to the chair he was sitting in. Grimacing, he fought a wave of nausea as he raised his head and tried to focus his vision. The room seemed to rise and fall as though he was drunk. He shut his eyes against the vertigo.

The phone stopped, the ringing replaced by the tick-tocking of a clock. *Better, but...where am I?* Struggling to remember what happened, he became aware of other people in the room, sensing their stares on him. Blinking several times, he tried again to bring something into focus.

Cold, detached eyes met his. The terrorist sat at his desk, blending in comfortably, Michael thought as recognition of his surroundings cleared his brain a little, with the dark wood and black leather chair. Michael registered a familiarity about the man staring back at him, but could not cultivate it into a definitive identity.

"Director Stone." The man stroked the butt of a gun. "Did you really think I would not notice your flashlight?"

Rule number two: Don't call attention to yourself. Not hard to do since he couldn't move. The synapses in Michael's brain began to fire through the pounding. He kept still, not liking the message they were sending.

The man smiled benignly. "You and your friends are part of my plan, Director." He moved his arm in a tight gesture to the right. Michael let his gaze follow, seeing Senator King and Titus similarly bound on a couch nearby. Brad as well. "My comrades and I came to the West on a simple but important mission, and you are a key player. Allah is great. We have accepted our calling from Allah."

Allah, my ass. Michael tallied information as fast as his

fuzzy brain would allow. *Terrorist, Middle East, probably one of bin Laden's, possibly Hezbollah, but which one?* His brain twisted and a memory of Julia's legs swam in front of him.

Jesus, Stone, focus here. A religious fanatic is holding you and a group of important people hostage. Now is not the time to...

Religious fanatic. Tight jeans and high heels. Julia's voice. *"I think Fayez Raissi is up to no good."*

Michael zeroed in on the man's face, the white scar now standing out like a neon sign. His top analyst was dead-on again.

Michael knew all about terrorists. There were those who martyred for a social agenda and those who acted for personal gain. In each category there were smart terrorists and dumb ones. The smart ones were highly trained and planned their missions with skill and intelligence. The dumb ones might be well trained but usually lacked leadership and effective intel.

With peripheral vision, he surveyed the other terrorist in the room. Clean-shaven and dressed in white Armani shirts and tan pants, the young man sitting at the video monitor did not look like the brand of terrorist the world was used to seeing on CNN. Except for the semi-automatic rifle he held in one hand, this man looked more like a Harvard grad student than a terrorist.

Fayez Raissi stood and walked around the desk toward him. "I now have in my possession a prestigious senator of the Democratic Party and the Director of CIA Operations." Raissi leaned against the desk, crossing his ankles. "Along with the Director of Central Intelligence, that makes a powerful group, would you not agree?"

"If he's traveling and recruiting again, he's up to something bad, probably involving a target that gets him some attention..."

A powerful group indeed. Raissi was holding the United States of America by the balls. All he had to do was give a yank and he would have everyone's attention.

Frustration burned inside Michael as he kept his face stoic. For all his and Titus's security, a terrorist had still managed to get through. And terrorist stereotypes be damned, these were radical Islamic fundamentalists. Any person willing to come after the Director of Central Intelligence of the United States of America was a soldiering martyr. Prepared to kill. Prepared to die.

The benign smile of the terrorist turned more genuine. "I am told you are a leader, Michael Stone."

Raissi wanted to make nice. Okay, two could play that game. It pained him to do it, but for now, Michael would play along. He thought of Julia smiling at him, purposely, to give his return smile some warmth. The terrorist seemed pleased.

"You and I," Raissi said, leaning toward him, but still maintaining a safe distance from the larger man, "we are warriors with passion in our bellies." He clasped his stomach to emphasize the point. Then his hand moved to his head. "But Allah called us to be leaders too. To control our passion with intelligence and move our peoples away from adversity and toward a better future. We each seek justice and peace for our countrymen but we accept that violence is the only proven method to achieve this. Yes?"

Michael couldn't sustain his smile, and he withheld comment. Raissi continued. "Yes, I think so. We are on opposite sides of this war, Michael Stone, but deep in my gut, I recognize you as a fellow leader, a brother. Because of that, Allah has chosen you to help me with my plan."

All the pistons were firing now in Michael's brain. The situation had all the makings of a Schwarzenegger movie, only with real bullets and an unhappy ending. Ignoring the sharp pain radiating down the left side of his head, he turned again and gave Titus and King another glance.

He turned his attention back to the terrorist leader while his peripheral vision logged two terrorists moving past the door of the study. They were carrying standard firearms, including AK-47s. There had to be more than four total, but how many and where were they? There had to be at least two on surveillance. What other weapons did they have?

"...Raissi is an expert in explosives..."

For the first time, Michael became aware of something strapped to his chest. He looked down and felt his worst nightmare pale with what he saw taped to his body. He twisted his hands, testing the cord for slack. There was none. Welcome to Survival 101.

The Director of Operations knew he had one thing on his side—time. The longer he kept Raissi talking, the better the hostages' chances of survival were. Ryan Smith would show and hopefully have enough sense to raise an alarm. Within minutes, a predetermined action plan would be put in place. A Hostage Rescue Team would be called in to evaluate the situation and a group of Special Forces commandos would no doubt be asked by the FBI to assist them. Negotiations would begin to buy them more time while the SEALs and the HRT decided how to eliminate the terrorists.

And maybe, just maybe, some of the people in the house would leave it alive.

Rule number three: Do whatever it takes to stay alive.

Michael addressed the terrorist leader. "So, tell me how I fit into your plan."

Chapter Thirty-Five

Safe house

Julia was in his lap, naked and warm in all the right places, and Conrad buried his face in the curve of her neck. Moving his mouth to the hollow of her shoulder, he felt her shudder as he licked her skin.

Amazing. Even after the rain and the mud and the Dial soap she'd used to wash it all away, she still smelled faintly of lavender. His hand found her breast and she opened her mouth with a sharp gasp. Leaving her collarbone, he claimed her lips, living in the wet heat of her kiss and wanting more.

Her hands were in his hair, her body pressing against his and he let her leverage him back in the bed, feeling faintly disappointed when her mouth broke free of his as she straddled him, and her upper body took her wonderful heat away.

But he did enjoy the view.

She slipped her tousled hair behind her ears. "Okay, here's the deal. If we're really going to work together again, we need to get the Rules of Partnership out on the table."

"Rules of what?"

She blew out a deep breath. "Think of it as Rules of Engagement for war, only this is about our partnership."

Forcing himself to raise his gaze from Julia's breasts, he looked in her eyes as she traced a finger over one of his eyebrows. Her expression was serious and he didn't want to mess up by not paying attention. "Our partnership?" he repeated, trying to catch his breath and shift out of sexual overdrive, although that didn't seem right. Was *definitely* not right.

"Yes." She flexed her legs, tilting her hips into him, and he strangled the moan in his throat. He was trying to concentrate on her voice, but it was hard. Everything was hard.

He ran his hands up her thighs and moved his mouth up toward her, licking a taut nipple. "Can we talk about that later?" He squeezed her breasts together and buried his head in her cleavage.

She pushed him back down with a hand. "Listen, this is important."

"This is important too," he said, massaging her breasts and moving underneath her, "and it's totally about our partnership as well."

Julia knocked his hands away and leaned over him, putting her face right in front of his. "Focus for a minute."

He *was* focused. Just on different topics than hers. "How, when you're sitting on top of me naked?"

Her grin was wicked, but her voice came out serious as she sat back up. "Rule number one: don't lie to your partner."

Conrad rubbed a hand over his face. "Okay, Jules. Whatever you want."

She raised an eyebrow.

"I mean it." He sort of did too. He'd compromise anything when she was straddling him. "From here on out we'll play it your way. You say 'Do this' and I'll say 'Okay, Julia.'"

She let out a disgusted sigh. "Come on, Conrad. I'm serious." She ran the tips of her fingers across his stomach and down to the elastic on his underwear. His breath caught in his throat right behind a moan as she tugged the garment off, grazing her cool fingers over him.

"So am I," he said in a strangled voice, not caring for one second about anything except burying himself between Julia's thighs. He would have sworn he was a nineteen-year-old sailor boy again who'd just got into port. If he wasn't careful, he'd lose control of his blatant erection and embarrass himself.

"Rule number two," Julia said. "Don't put your partner in emotionally compromising positions with her boss."

Doing his best Boy Scout salute, Conrad answered. "I swear I won't."

Keeping his touch light, he ran his fingers around to Julia's back and stroked her lower spine. She arched into him and he took that as an invitation to do more. He slid his fingers into the space between her legs.

She shifted her hips, pulling herself away from his touch. "Flynn! I have more rules to lay down."

"And I'm trying to lay *you* down. Give you a screaming-at-the-top-of-your-lungs orgasm. Now shut up and let me do it." Pulling her hips back down, he rocked up into her, and felt smug satisfaction as she threw her head back and gasped, "*Mon Dieux.*"

"I love it when you speak French." He moved higher with each thrust and enjoyed how her body countered his, pushing down hard. "Especially during sex."

"I think you're forgetting who's in charge already," she said, but she was laughing. It was a sweet sound.

Conrad's focus was solely on where their bodies were joined. "Believe me, sweetheart, when it comes to us having sex, you're always in charge. Whatever you want, you can have. As often as you want, you can have. Just say the word."

"We have a lot of time to make up." She ran her fingers over his chest.

"Years worth."

She looked down at him, her hair spilling over her breasts, and arched an eyebrow.

"I know, I know," he said. "That's my fault and I feel guilty as hell about that. I'm oozing guilt. There's guilt everywhere."

She punched him in the stomach, and he pulled her down, twisting his body to stay inside her. She rocked her hips up under him and he met her ferocity with his own. Her skin was flushed and damp in the pale moonlight filtering through the white sheers at the window. He took her mouth, licking into it, and felt a twinge of macho triumph at the low moan that came from her throat. Moving his mouth down, he kissed and licked the dampness at the base of her throat, then trailed his tongue down to her breasts.

She arched against him as he teased each nipple for long moments and then ran his hands over her ribs and down her sides. He began a slow descent, kissing his way down to her navel, but before he could go lower, her hands were in his hair, forcing him to raise his head and look at her face. "I want to see you. When I come, I want to know it's you inside me."

She pulled him back up and he slid hot on top of her. Their eyes locked as he pushed himself between her legs again. With each stroke, he whispered in her ear how beautiful she was and how much he wanted her, and his hands raised her hips up to meet his.

And then he deliberately pulled himself back from the edge, slowing his rhythm to match hers, slowing the pulse so they could tease out the vortex of pleasure building between them. When he looked in her eyes, the half-lidded green orbs pulled him into her soul and he knew she understood. She slowed her body with his, letting them both live in the moment, a parallel universe that wiped away an ugly reality.

Minutes, eons later, she tightened all around him. *"Please."*

Conrad bore down on her, rocking into her hard and fast until she broke, his name on her lips as she arched under his body.

Struggling to breathe, she went limp until an aftershock made her muscles tighten and she twitched, and Conrad felt himself go, shuddering on top of her and dropping his face into her pillow.

"Rule three, Con," she whispered in his ear. "Don't die."

Arlington

Raissi watched with the eye of a mentor as another of his recruits wired Stone's back door. The plastique explosives were being secured at all major entry points of the house. If any attempt were made to enter the structure through the conventional openings, the house would be reduced to rubble.

Originally Raissi had wanted to take the leaders hostage at CIA headquarters, but Susan Richmond had cut that plan down in one breath. He considered ignoring Susan's orders, moving them all to CIA headquarters and following through with his original plan, but the risk was too great they would be stopped, the mission blown. Raissi would not risk that. This was his last stand. He had to make it a strong one.

Touching the young man on the shoulder, Raissi offered a comment in their native language, *When dealing with explosives, don't rush.* The man nodded and took a deep breath before continuing, slowing his fingers and re-checking his work.

Leaving the young man to finish his work, Raissi walked the house. In the opulent dining room he stared at the crystal chandelier, the expensive china in the cabinet and the silver tea set on the buffet. He ran his hand along the backs of the intricately carved wooden chairs. He sat in one of them and savored the moment, imagined what it was like to live in this world of greed and riches. It was not an unpleasant thought.

Drawing himself out of that fantasy, he played out a different one instead. One where his countrymen would speak his name for centuries as the prophet who had crucified the great leaders of Evil. Sheik bin Laden was already receiving such acclaim, and Raissi now had the chance to claim some of that for himself. Fayez Raissi would be the next great leader to bring Islamic pride and vengeance to the West.

Raissi smiled. That fantasy was much more satisfying.

Chapter Thirty-Six

Three bodies were brought outside and left at the bottom of the front steps. Ryan Smith could not make out their identities because Titus Allen's and Senator King's cars in the circular drive were parked in front of the house, blocking his view, but he guessed they were security officers by their dark clothing. It was nearing midnight, and he had received no return call from Conrad. His best friend was either in trouble or out of cell tower range.

He drew out his cell phone and made three calls.

First, he called Ace, roused the wheelman out of bed and demanded he go get Con and Julia from the safe house and bring them to him.

Second, he called Stone's house. No answer.

Third, he called the FBI.

The phone rang in the background again. Raissi had considered disabling it, thus killing the annoying interruption, but decided the unanswered phone worked to his advantage, like the three dead security officers and the deserted automobiles outside the front door. Soon it would be time to talk, to play the game and offer the prize, but for now it was in Raissi's best interest to keep silent. Let the United States government hypothesize and analyze and live in their fear for awhile. Make them sweat.

The beeper went off at 12:02, waking FBI Special Agent Tim Buchanan as he dozed on his couch.

Pushing himself up on one elbow, he turned the TV off and read the pager's LCD screen. His heart, already tripping over itself from the rude interruption of sleep, started a quarter-mile all-out sprint as he dialed in to headquarters.

In less than five minutes, he was in step with his heart and driving through the rain to a meeting with FBI Director Lyle Banker and the FBI's East Coast Hostage Rescue Team.

Langley

A mere four hours had passed since Susan Richmond had left CIA headquarters. Paranoia had driven her there for the evening where she shredded certain documents and prepared one more alternate plan in case Raissi somehow failed. She now entered the conference room on the seventh floor and nodded at the two men and one woman already seated at the long table in the center of the room.

With the addition of Susan, all four directorates of the CIA were represented. As was typical of the group, no one spoke. There was no love lost between the separate deputy directors, each one chauvinistic about his directorate's importance in making the beast known as Central Intelligence function. And since the current DCI had cut his teeth on the clandestine side of the CIA, Science and Technology, Administration and Intelligence usually focused the brunt of their dissatisfaction with everything from paperclips to toilet paper on Operations.

Jurgen Damgaard, the Deputy Director of Central Intelligence, or DDCI, had told Susan little over the phone about the purpose of the meeting. As the second in charge of the Agency, Damgaard flaunted his position with flair but handled his knowledge with annoying secrecy. Though an outsider to the CIA, he was competent enough as DDCI. He had served for several years as director of the FBI, and before that as a judge. Unfortunately with that background, he often treated the spy group the same way several of his predecessors had—as a troubled teenager. Tough love was his motto when dealing with Operations.

The door to the director's office opened and Damgaard strode in with purpose. He spoke to his three deputy directors and nodded at Richmond. A deliberate shunning.

She ignored it and kept a neutral expression on her face. At this point she didn't give a damn about Jurgen and his over-inflated ego. She wanted to know what was happening at Michael Stone's house.

Dropping his notepad on the table, Damgaard glanced at his watch and cleared his throat. "At approximately midnight, I received a phone call from FBI Director Lyle Banker. One of his men, Agent Tim Buchanan, had an anonymous phone call from a man claiming to be outside the home of Michael Stone. He reported to Agent Buchanan that Director Allen and Senator Daniel King were inside, three shots had been fired and three bodies, supposedly security officers for Director Allen, were left outside the front door.

"Director Banker placed calls to Maime Allen and Lacy King. Neither has seen or heard from their respective husbands since late afternoon. Both men were believed to be meeting with Michael Stone at his home. Maime told Director Banker she has repeatedly called the house and gotten no answer. Lacy King, Senator King's wife, reports she cannot raise him on his cell phone."

The leaders of the three directorates around the table exchanged glances and shocked murmurs. Susan stared at the table.

So far Plan B was going perfectly. The anonymous caller was no doubt Flynn or Smith.

Damgaard continued. "The anonymous caller assured Agent Buchanan that there was movement inside the house. He has seen at least three different men with guns. One is stationed at the guard house and two others brought the security officers' bodies outside.

"We are assuming we have a hostage situation, probably terrorist-linked. From our caller's description of the men he's seen, our hostage takers are quite possibly Middle Eastern. My gut says Palestinian based on the U.S. stand on recent events in that area, but they could be associated with anyone. The FBI, the NSA and the Pentagon have been notified and an action plan has been initiated." He glanced at his watch again. "A hostage rescue team should be in place by now at Director Stone's house. They will monitor it and try to make contact with the hostage takers. We should have more answers shortly."

Susan's analytical brain was unconcerned with the specifics of the hostage situation except in relation to her plan. She knew there would be no hostage rescue. Everyone in that house was going to die. "Who will be assigned as acting Director of Operations, Jurgen?"

"You," he said without hesitation and Susan's heart leapt at her new role. One step closer to her final goal. "I want you out at the site as soon as this meeting is over and I expect your counterterrorism people to be available as well to assist the FBI. Director Banker wants every specialist you've got. Get your bin Laden, Hezbollah and GIA people on site to give the HRT whatever information it needs."

"Of course," Susan replied, calm as ever on the outside.

"Who's your head analyst?"

The question hit her like a sucker punch and she hesitated, clenching her hands on the arm of the chair. "Abigail Quinn."

The quirk of his eyebrow was subtle and then he nodded. "Good. See that Ms. Quinn is briefed and on site with you within the hour." He paused to look around the table. "Any further questions?"

Chapter Thirty-Seven

Safe house

"Julia! Connie!" Ace banged on the door of the old farmhouse. He was still on a rush from the afternoon's escapade and, like a junkie needing a fix, he wanted more. When he'd arrived back home at the mortuary, he'd thought he'd never calm down, but a few minutes in front of the TV and he'd fallen dead asleep. Then the phone rang.

When Smitty had called, he'd felt adrenaline flood his system again. He'd thrown his pants on and had his keys in hand before Smitty had given him all the details.

Unable to wait for Con to open the door, Ace ran to the garage door and punched the numbers Con had made him memorize into the keypad. The door went up and Ace did the same to the keypad inside, opening the door connected to the house.

Running through the laundry room, he took the stairs two at a time to the second story of the house. "Where you guys at?" he yelled again, drumming his fist on the wall as he cleared the top landing. All the upstairs doors were open and he could hear the shower running in the bathroom on his left.

He stepped into the bathroom, his hand going up to knock on the open door, and stopped short, Connie's name dying on his lips as he registered two naked bodies behind the frosted, but clear enough, shower curtain. Dazed, he took a step back but couldn't peel his gaze away from the fuzzy scene across the room.

And then he heard Julia cry out something in another language and he jumped, stumbling backwards and throwing a hand out to the doorframe to keep from falling on his ass.

Backing out the bathroom door, he continued to stumble downstairs and came to rest in the kitchen where he sat down hard at the table and stared wide-eyed at nothing in particular.

A second later, his brain clicked back to real life and he remembered his mission.

"Connie's going to kill me," he whispered to himself as he jumped up from the chair and paced the kitchen floor. He grabbed the phone receiver off the wall and dialed Smitty's cell phone. Before Smitty could say anything, Ace told him of his transgression.

Ryan Smith chuckled tiredly. "Way to go, Ace. Pull yourself together and make some coffee. The Great Conrad Flynn is more likely to grant leniency after he's had some caffeine, and it's going to be a long night. We're all going to need it. The FBI's all over the perimeter of Stone's place so the three of you better meet me at Julia's apartment." He yawned. "And bring me a gallon of that coffee when you come."

Ace looked down at the table, seeing it for the first time. "Good grief. There's glass on the table and floor. What happened here tonight?"

"Let's leave that to our imaginations. Now get Conrad out of the shower and bring me that coffee."

Ace nodded even though Smitty couldn't see him. "My imagination has had all the stimulation it can handle for one day."

Julia's eyes were still closed as the hot water pulsed on Conrad's shoulders. His legs were trembling from the sex and her weight. Nuzzling her earlobe, he asked, "Did you hear something?"

Her shoulders shrugged faintly in response as she unwrapped her legs from around his hips and let out a satisfied sigh. "Bats. Mice, maybe. Either that or *someone*, as in *human*, just witnessed you performing your Captain Nemo imitation on me in the shower." She wiped a hand over her eyes and face to rid them of water. "The good news is the guy didn't shoot us so he must be on our side. Someone like your *wheelman*, maybe?"

"What a shame." Conrad shook his head. "Now I'm going to have to kill him."

Five minutes later, Julia was ready to kill Flynn's

wheelman herself. "What do you mean"—she stared at Ace in disbelief while her stomach twisted in two different directions— "that Michael is being held hostage?"

Ace took a step back, holding out a cup of steaming coffee to her like a shield. "Ryan was staked out, watching Big Mike's. That senator guy showed up and then all hell broke loose. He's been calling your cell phones, but you were out of range or something."

Julia ignored the cup and swung her attention to Conrad.

He smacked the counter with one hand. "Goddamn it. Who's with him besides King? Is Allen there?"

Ace nodded and offered the cup to Conrad. Conrad took it and set it on the counter. "And who's got them? Does Smitty know that?"

Ace shook his head. "Some Mid-Eastern terrorist dudes he thinks from what he's seen. They shot three of the security men and dumped them outside the front door."

"Oh my God." Julia held her stomach and turned in a circle. She hadn't eaten since lunch but was grateful for her empty stomach. Its contents would be coming up at this news.

For a moment, all three of them were quiet, both men staring at her. Julia closed her eyes and felt guilt swim through her veins like ice. She'd been tucked away in the middle of nowhere sleeping and having great sex with Con while Michael was being held hostage in his home by a terrorist.

Her brain shifted and a thought popped into her head. "What if Susan did this? What if this is Plan B?"

Conrad crossed his arms over his chest and looked at her like she'd grown a second head. "Oh, come on, Jules. Recruiting a terrorist to take Stone and Allen hostage? That's crazy. Even Susan isn't that good."

"Isn't she?" Julia was sure Susan was exactly that adept. "By doing this, she can take out Director Allen, Michael, and Senator King with one fell swoop and if she's crafty enough, make herself look like a leader in the process. If Michael's out of commission, she's next in line to head up Operations."

Conrad stared at her for a long moment, considering her logic. "But she wants Allen's job."

"One step at a time and only Damgaard's in her way if Michael and Titus both die."

Ace started opening and closing cabinet doors, scanning

the shelves. "Ryan called some friend of his at the FBI and alerted them. He says the whole place is locked down now so we have to meet at Julia's apartment." He opened another cabinet, scanned the shelves and closed it again. "Don't you got any of those travel mug thingies for drinks?"

Conrad opened a cabinet above the microwave and handed two thermal coffee carriers to Ace, all the time his focus still on Julia. "Susan could be watching your apartment. I don't think it's safe for us to meet there."

"Don't kid yourself, Con." She shook her head. "Susan's right there at Michael's house with the FBI. Or she's making herself comfortable in Michael's office at Langley. She has bigger fish to fry right now than us. We can always be rounded up later."

"And with Stone, Allen and King all out of the way, no one will believe us."

Ace finished filling the travel mugs and turned off the coffeepot. Julia started for the stairs. "All I need are my shoes and my gun and I'm ready to go."

Conrad grabbed the cooling mug of coffee off the counter and downed it, rubbed his mouth with the back of his hand and motioned at Ace to get moving. "You heard the lady. Let's go."

Chapter Thirty-Eight

Arlington

Agent Tim Buchanan surveyed the scene before him.

When he'd first arrived, only a few people had been in the area, keeping their presence concealed as they garnered information about what had happened during the night at 9125 Thurman Lane. Now, sunrise only four hours away, blue box vans were arriving, bodies dressed in black Nomex jumpsuits piling out of them. Gone was the need to keep the counterassault a secret, but reasonable precaution dictated each person keep a low profile so as to not become the next target of whoever was in the house. Voices were hushed, movement was directed and purposeful.

And, finally, the rain had quit.

A base of operations for the Critical Incident Response Group and the FBI's Strategic Information Operations Center, or SIOC, had been set up using several vans and a massive black tent top. Three portable tables had been set up, men and women of the FBI manning laptops, phones, televisions and fax machines.

Two of the vans' cargo doors were open, revealing an impressive assortment of communications and electronic equipment which was being checked and tested by three of the FBI's best cyber geeks. Telephone transmissions into and out of the house were being controlled. Incoming calls would be intercepted. Outgoing calls would only ring to the secure phone under Tim Buchanan's watchful eye.

The nearest neighbors, who were a mile away on either side, had been evacuated. Traffic on the road was being diverted. Air space had been secured. The house itself sat quiet.

The three bodies of the fallen Secret Service men lay sprawled beside the porch in pools of their own blood...the only visible testament to the seriousness of the situation.

The HRT's best sniper, Agent Elaina Koburn, approached the table, nodding as she came to stand beside him. "What a way to start the day, huh, sir?"

Tim nodded. "Appears someone woke up on the wrong side of the world again and decided to take it out on us over-privileged Americans."

She scanned the area with a dark look in her eyes. "Do we know what group we're dealing with?"

"No contact with them yet, but probably a cell allied to bin Laden or another Middle East group according to my source." He motioned toward the house. "That's no group of everyday psychos in there. I'd say from the way the situation has proceeded up to this point, the attackers are intelligent and highly trained. Holy Warrior bad boys dispersing God's wrath on us is my guess. I just can't figure out why they haven't made contact."

"A mute entity is hard to negotiate with."

"Negotiate?" Tim's expression showed a spark of humor. "Why, Agent Koburn, you know the United States doesn't negotiate with terrorists."

Elaina smiled at him. "Of course it does, sir. That's why we're here."

Within minutes, the rest of the HRT was present and accounted for as well as a Special Op group of SEALs. Tim welcomed them to the table. "First let's start with what we know," he said, glancing at the digital watch on his arm. "Approximately six hours ago, between six and seven p.m., a group of people including Senator Daniel King and CIA Director Titus Allen entered Operations Director Michael Stone's house for a meeting between the three of them. None of these people have emerged from that meeting, nor can they be raised by phone. Neither the DCI's driver nor his security protection officer have responded to pages or made contact with anyone since that time and we are assuming without further ID their bodies are those out front. Senator King was traveling alone. Director Stone had two security officers on the property, one at the gate, the other inside the house. No unusual or suspicious activity was reported by any security detail."

Everyone was quiet. Tim continued. "The people in charge have not made contact with us at this point, but we are assuming they are terrorists. We do not know their demands and can only guess at their motive. I have been informed this is, so far, an isolated incident. The president and vice president are secured in their appropriate residences. All cabinet members and the other three CIA deputy directors are accounted for at this time. Susan Richmond, the CTC Chief, will be joining us shortly along with her top counterterrorism experts. All other congressional members have also checked in."

Unrolling a sheet of blueprints, Tim anchored the corners on the table for everyone to examine. "We have secured the perimeter of the Stone residence and are ready for our counterassault team to begin reconnaissance shortly."

Tim took a deep breath and rubbed his hands together. "Now, are there any questions?"

Chapter Thirty-Nine

Ryan Smith's cell phone rang. "Uh-oh," he said reading the small caller ID window and giving Conrad a look.

Their two a.m. breakfast of Hostess donuts and coffee in Julia's small kitchen had been full of analyzing and brainstorming, but the trepidation in Smitty's voice silenced them all.

"Uh-oh?" Ace spoke around a mouthful of powdered sugar donut, his eyes wide. "What 'uh-oh'?"

Conrad motioned to Smitty as the phone buzzed again. "Give it to me. I'll handle her."

Smitty passed the phone across the table to him and Julia dropped her half-eaten donut on the plate in front of her, appetite gone.

Letting the phone ring a third time, Conrad flipped open the cover and chose his words carefully. "I'd say I was sorry Plan A failed, but you'd know I was lying."

Julia smiled at him and he smiled back as he listened for Susan Richmond's response. There was none for a few seconds.

"I assume your ex-partner is with you," she said in a terse voice.

"Assume whatever you like."

"I need to talk to her. We have a..." she paused, searching for the right terminology that could be used in an open phone conversation, "...*situation* that requires her skills."

"Sure you do. And Osama bin Laden just confessed his sins to the Pope."

"This concerns her friend at the Agency. He's in serious danger."

If Susan wanted to flush Julia out of hiding, Stone was the perfect carrot to dangle in her face. Conrad decided to play dumb and see what Susan tried next. "What kind of danger?"

The CTC chief sighed. "It's just like you to need a visual aid, Solomon. Turn on CNN. I'll call you back in five minutes."

The call was terminated and Conrad threw the phone down on the table. He left the kitchen, his friends exchanging a glance between them before jumping up to follow.

In the living room, he flipped channels on the satellite dish receiver, landing on CNN. The female anchor was starting the hour's top breaking news story. Conrad turned up the volume as Ace camped on the floor. Julia and Smitty stood behind Ace.

"Sources inside the White House confirm there is a domestic terrorist situation at the home of CIA Director of Operations Michael Stone outside of Arlington, Virginia."

Julia sucked in a sharp breath and shot a glance at Conrad. "It's already on the national news? That's bad. This broadcast is going worldwide. The terrorist is getting exactly what he wants."

Conrad gave a curt nod. "And Susan along with him."

"...We go now to WQPX correspondent, Gus Schultz, who is on location. Gus, what can you tell us?"

A panoramic view of Virginia countryside appeared, eerily beautiful in the dark of night. Only an assortment of commercial vans and Ninja figures moving around marred the otherwise peaceful setting. As the camera zoomed in on the TV news reporter, orange barricades and law enforcement officials could be seen in the background. "I am standing here a few blocks away from the home of Michael Stone. He is the Director of Operations for the Central Intelligence Agency. In other words, he is the man in charge of the CIA's spy group. It is believed that along with Director Stone, there are several prominent members of the Washington political system being held hostage by a group of terrorists, including the CIA's top man, Titus Allen, and Senator Daniel King, a Democrat from Illinois and head of the Senate Intelligence Committee..."

"All thorns in Susan's side," Conrad murmured.

"I'm going to kill her," Julia said to no one in particular.

"...Inside sources tell me Senator Daniel King and CIA Director Titus Allen were in attendance at the Stone home last night when a group of men, whose affiliation and motive are unclear at this point, infiltrated the house and took them hostage."

Julia narrowed her eyes at the TV. "I will tear her limb from limb."

"We have confirmation at least two Secret Service officers are dead and several others missing."

"Three," Smitty corrected. "Three are dead."

The camera shifted away from the reporter and zoomed in at the area around the house. "The FBI has moved in a hostage rescue team and is being assisted by Special Operations commandos. I am told by an on-the-scene source that FBI negotiators are attempting to contact the terrorists now."

The cell phone on the kitchen table rang, breaking the intensity of the moment. Julia was on her feet and moving toward it in a split second. Conrad moved to catch her, but Smitty was already a step ahead of him, wrapping a lanky arm around Julia's slim waist and swinging her back in front of him.

She fought against his grip. "I'm going to claw her eyes out."

"Let Con handle Susan," Smitty said. "Then we'll figure out how to resolve this."

"*I* want to talk to her."

Smitty shook his head, held Julia firmly. "No, Julia. Not while you're this emotional. Let Con handle her this time. I promise you'll get your chance to kill her later." He nodded at Conrad.

Conrad walked into the kitchen, stared at the phone and took a deep breath. The situation was indeed serious, but Susan's request for Julia's assistance was out of line. Domestic terrorism was the FBI's jurisdiction since Americans had a healthy suspicion and dislike for the CIA operating on its home turf. And what value was one CIA analyst to a highly organized and trained conglomerate of counterterrorism and counterassault experts?

It had to be another of Susan's traps. Conrad ran a hand over his sandpaper beard before flipping the phone's cover open. "I wouldn't want to be you right now, Chief."

Susan's voice was more relaxed this time. "Oh, I don't know. This situation could work in my favor. In the meantime, Damgaard has requested your partner's presence at the site. Her knowledge about the people inside could be of great value to those in charge."

"You know who the hostage takers are?"

Her silence lasted one beat too long. "The FBI has identified several possibilities."

Conrad still wasn't totally convinced Susan was capable of orchestrating a hostage situation itself, but he knew she was definitely capable of manipulating the fallout from it. "And what guarantee does my partner have that you won't proceed with your previous plan?"

"No guarantees, but I'll allow you to come in with her."

Conrad snorted. "Way to dangle the carrot, Chief. The queen comes in after her friend and I come in after her. Aren't you going to invite Smitty too?"

Susan tsked at him. Her voice now held challenge. "Afraid of me, Solomon?"

Gripping the phone to keep from throwing it against the wall, Con forced himself back from the edge. His mind tripped through Julia's plan and another couple of scenarios, and he saw a kernel of opportunity sitting in his hand. He smiled as he spoke. "A piece of advice for you. If you're going to hang your collective balls out, you better damn well know how to protect them."

"My balls are in no danger from you, Solomon," Susan said, bemused. "There will be ID badges and a personal escort waiting for you and your partner at the north entrance to the site. I expect to see her within the hour."

She hung up and Flynn looked over to see Julia standing in the doorway, Smitty behind her.

"The web is strung." He leaned on the table. "The spider's waiting."

Julia pulled the Beretta out of the back of her waistband and checked its clip. "Good." She snapped it back in. "Then it's time for me to give her what she wants."

Chapter Forty

The doorbell rang and Julia jumped, drawing her gun instinctively and pointing it at the door.

Staring through the peephole, she relaxed, let out the breath she was holding and returned her gun to her waistband. She called to Con and Smitty, "It's Cari."

"Make sure she's alone," Con said from his hiding place behind the living room doorway.

Julia double-checked. "She's alone." She unlocked and opened the door.

Cari pushed by her. "I need a drink. What do you have?"

"Excuse me?"

Cari paused to look Conrad over as he emerged from hiding. "You again."

"Ditto," he replied.

Continuing on to the kitchen, Cari addressed Smitty who was standing by the back door. "Liquor." Her tone was demanding. "What do you have?"

Julia exchanged a look with Conrad, and he rolled his eyes.

Cari threw herself down in a chair across from Ace and rested her forehead in her hands. "What a night." Raising her head, she pointed at Smitty. "Why are you not getting me something to drink?"

"I'll drive you down to the liquor shop and buy you a case of the finest brandy they have," Conrad said, "as soon as you tell me what Plan B is."

Cari dropped her head slightly and gave him a wide-eyed look. "Raissi."

Julia's brain clicked with instant recognition. "Fayez

Raissi? The terrorist?"

Cari smoothed a section of her hair back. "You mean the great CIA analyst didn't know? Susan has been throwing him into your lap for the past week and you did not guess?"

Julia put her fingers to her mouth and looked up at the ceiling, feeling like a fool. Then she took a deep breath, drew out a chair and sat next to Cari. "Susan brought Raissi here to take Michael and the others hostage."

"No." Cari wagged a finger at her. "I brought Fayez here. He is a rude lout too. I almost gave him another scar to carry around."

Smitty leaned against the counter. "But Susan provided his papers, right? To get him in the country? She's using him as her backup plan."

"Of course. But, his plan and her plan..." Cari tipped her flat hand back and forth. "I don't think they were the same plan. Fayez, he wanted to blow something big up, not take hostages."

"Something big?" Smitty echoed. "Like what? A building? A bridge? A power plant?"

Cari smiled. "The Agency."

Conrad whistled under his breath. "So why did he end up at Stone's house with three hostages?"

Cari shrugged. "All I know is everybody is supposed to die."

"Jesus," Julia said softly. Her stomach felt like someone was wringing her insides out like a wet washcloth. She had to get to the hostage site and let the FBI know who they were dealing with and what his plans were.

She rose from the table. "I've got to go."

"I'm going too," Cari said. "With you."

"No," Con and Smitty said in unison.

Julia checked herself. "You can't come with me, Cari."

Cari smiled. "We are a team, now." She pointed to each of them and herself. "If Stone and Allen die, I have no one to protect me, except the three of you." She glanced at Ace. "And you, I guess."

Ace puffed out his chest and offered Cari his hand. "Ace Harmon, wheelman."

Cari shook his hand. "Nice to meet you, wheelman."

Conrad threw his hands in the air. "Un-fucking-believable."

"We're wasting time." Julia grabbed her jacket off the back of the chair. "Let's go."

Cari gave Conrad a look. "Don't forget, you owe me a case of brandy."

"Don't forget, I carry a big gun," he murmured as he grabbed his own jacket and followed Julia out the door.

It was almost time.

The terrorist leader watched reporter Gus Schultz end his commentary and felt a ripple of anticipation in his stomach. The news was out to the American people. Panic would be setting in as word spread. The West would again be gripped with fear, glued to their television sets in shock that yet another terrorist had invaded their sacred homeland. What destruction would he impart? What classified secrets would escape from the hostages' lips to endanger their safety even more? Arguments between the warmongers and the peace lovers would break out, slowing the behemoth government of the United States from making any decisions before the day was over.

The anchorwoman solemnly announced that CNN would run continual coverage of the hostage crisis in order to keep their viewers updated on the latest happenings. Raissi flipped through several other channels on the TV and saw the other networks were doing the same. Valid information was, as usual, scarce, but wild conjecture and equally wild opinions flourished as each network fought for top position in the ranks, interviewing anyone deemed an expert that they could get their hands on.

This pleased the terrorist. Keeping the politicians and the military analysts guessing served a valuable purpose in his plan. Strangling the people of the United States of America with fear was icing on his cake.

Raissi turned down the TV's volume and sat back in the recliner, steepling his fingers under his chin. His plan was morphing again. He and his compatriots had brought their *jihad* to the enemy, and instead of one spectacular at CIA headquarters, he had seized the opportunity from Susan Richmond to use the leaders in this house as a different, but just as powerful, spectacular against America. He planned no demands or negotiations, only a brutal lesson, execution-style, about interfering with the Arab world.

But now Raissi saw another opportunity. Before the executions, he could speak out for his family, his neighbors and his country in a way no other brother of Islam had been able to before him. Americans worshiped their televisions and believed the daily propaganda it imparted. What better resource to use to spread the truth about his people and their fight against the unholy West? He had already used specially prepared videos in his homeland to spread his doctrine there. What better way to immortalize his name in the history books with the vengeance he was bringing in the name of justice?

Smiling, Raissi rose from his seat and began calculating the risk of his new plan as he paced the floor. He could control the risks with a few simple demands and that would work in his favor. Having studied the counterterrorism tactics of the United States, Raissi knew the FBI negotiators would try to play with him, prolonging the hostage situation for the amount of time it took them to figure out who he was and how they could destroy him with minimal collateral damage. The game would begin with him stating his demands and then the FBI would dance around those demands, buying time for their commandos to form a plan to take him out and Congress to okay it.

In order to keep the FBI and the U.S. government feeling in control, he needed to make his first contact with the FBI short and simple. Give them a false sense of confidence and hope by making his first demand easy to fulfill.

Raissi felt the ripple again in his stomach. His smile widened. He was excited.

Collecting specific terrorist information and planning for every possible contingency was a superhuman feat, but in the middle of the controlled chaos of their hostage situation, someone, God bless them, had remembered to make coffee and score cinnamon rolls. Tim Buchanan, now seated at the table where all the planning was going on, sipped from a Styrofoam cup and ran different strategies and outcomes through his brain.

The rectangular table was organized but overflowing with telephones, blueprints and computer printouts. Around it were translators, counterterrorism *cognoscenti* and the senior chief, executive officer, and leader of the East Coast SEAL Team. Tim was leading the group in a discussion, prepping everyone for both negotiations and takedown if the need arose.

They all knew the need would arise. There was no such thing as a good hostage situation, but of all the ones Tim had witnessed, this one was by far the ugliest in terms of outcome scenarios. As he took another sip of coffee, he listened, not only to the words coming from those at the table, but also to the tone and other verbal nuances of his coworkers' voices. The atmosphere of a group like this under similar conditions was always charged with a super-sized amount of electric current. That current usually pulled the members of the group into a close, cohesive unit. Today, due to the fact the hostages included a senator and the head of the United States Intelligence community, there were extra people bringing their two cents, and a lot of current, to the table. The usual balance of egos and agendas was skewed. Everyone had an opinion and few of them agreed.

Tim scribbled a note to himself as he listened to several CIA analysts discuss a list of possible terrorists who could be responsible for the current hostage situation. When the group around the table fell silent, Tim looked up and then followed the group's attention to a spot over his shoulder.

A woman stood just inside the tent with a police escort. A CTC analyst, Tim had seen her before in the halls of Langley. Susan Richmond had been waiting for her.

He'd been waiting for her.

"Ms. Quinn," Susan said from the far end of the table. "You finally made it. Let me introduce you."

Everyone around the table stood as Abigail approached, and Tim saw her jaw was clenched. She disregarded Susan and addressed him with an outstretched hand. "Abigail Quinn, CIA Counterterrorism Center, sir."

Tim shook her hand. "Tim Buchanan, FBI."

"Yes, sir. I'm familiar with you and your team of specialists. I believe I have pertinent information on the identity of the terrorist inside Michael's house."

Although several of his comrades fidgeted and exchanged glances, Tim showed no surprise. Ryan Smith had already called him and told him about Julia, a.k.a. Abigail. Smiling at her, he motioned her to a chair across from him. "Please have a seat and tell us what you know."

"Fayez Raissi," Julia began, "is a professional terrorist who began his career at age fifteen in Kazbekistan. For the past twenty-five years, he has struck targets from Pakistan to Paris working with a variety of terrorist groups, including the GIA, and using a number of different names. He has also assassinated a string of Islamic moderates whom he accused of abandoning their faith, and he has served as a hit man for various Arab backers. Most recently he has been linked with the extremist group Takfi-wal-Hijra."

"I'm familiar with him." Agent Buchanan motioned to his left at Susan and the CIA's Middle East specialist, Chuck Atwater. "But your CIA counterparts here believe the group behind this hostage situation is one of bin Laden's sleeper cells. Why do you think Raissi is our man?"

It would have been so easy to tattle everything she knew about Susan and her plans right there and then, but Julia held herself back with tight control. Michael's life was on the line and if she came across sounding like a raving lunatic, turning on her boss in front of all these people, he might very well die. "I'm not ruling out the involvement of bin Laden," she said, and that was true. "Probably the men working with Raissi *are* from one of bin Laden's sleeper cells here in the States. But Raissi's been traveling in our direction for several months, starting in Paris, hitting London along the way, and recruiting as he went."

Susan tapped her pencil on a stack of papers in front of her. "Why would he come here?"

Julia chose her next words carefully. "An anonymous source has come forward to say Raissi planned a spectacular on American soil."

Susan raised one eyebrow at Julia. "Another anonymous source? How interesting. There sure are a lot of those running around tonight."

Agent Buchanan ignored Susan. "What kind of spectacular?"

"He was planning to blow up CIA headquarters in Langley," Julia said. "Instead, he had a change of plans and ended up here, holding Michael and the others hostage."

"CIA headquarters? That's pretty ambitious. You believe this hostage situation is something he would orchestrate instead?"

She nodded. "Raissi is extremely radical, but he is also

extremely intelligent. I have studied his attacks and assassinations all the way back to the embassy bombings he pulled off in Paris in 1997. Taking hostages is not part of his usual bag of tricks, but he does like attention-getting spectacles so this situation is not out of the realm of possibility. As far as Raissi himself, orchestrating this entire thing"—Julia looked directly at Susan—"who knows what kind of help he's had here in the States?"

Chuck Atwater, fresh out of the hospital, grimaced slightly as he shifted forward in his seat. "Since Raissi has been moving in this direction over the past couple of months, I believe Ms. Quinn may be right. He never does anything without a premeditated plan and he's been lying low since 9/11, probably laying the groundwork for something of this magnitude. His original plan may not have included taking hostages in this manner, but he was definitely after the DCI. Raissi is an explosives expert. I would guarantee he was and still is planning on making a statement we won't soon forget."

Buchanan nodded at Chuck and returned his focus to his newest advisor. "You agree?"

"Definitely." Julia shifted in her chair to look over her shoulder between the vans. The house sat in silence sixty yards away. "Are either of those vehicles Raissi's?"

"No," Buchanan said. "One's Allen's and the other King's."

"So Raissi and his men had to carry their explosives with them. That cuts down the amount by at least half of what a car or van could carry for them. Still..." she studied the house, "...C-4 bricks are light and easy to carry so at the very least, he's got every door and window wired to blow and has booby-trapped the hostages."

Lt. Brad Diamond, the direct and self-assured leader of the SEAL team spoke. "What kind of explosives does he usually use?"

"He favors Semtex or C-4, but will use anything handy."

"What kind of detonators? Tripwires? Motion sensors? Pressure pads?"

"Tripwires would be easiest for him to transport and set up," Julia responded, "and more effective for this type of situation."

"The HRT can bypass the doors and windows by making holes into the walls to get in," Agent Buchanan stated.

"That will work if Raissi hasn't strung wires across the walls," Julia countered. "But since he had to pack the explosives on his men, he probably didn't have enough to layer them throughout the house. If you successfully penetrate the outside layer, there may be others, but it's unlikely. However, he's been dealing biological weapons ever since he worked with the GIA, and those are light enough to transport easily. There is a possibility he has anthrax or smallpox with him."

Buchanan glanced at Chuck Atwater, who nodded his affirmation.

Julia glanced at the house again. "Have you cut power to the house?"

"Power was already cut at the pole," Buchanan answered, "but somehow they have electricity."

"Michael has a generator," Julia told him.

Lt. Diamond made a note on the paper in front of him. "Why do you think Raissi has refrained from contacting us with his demands, Ms. Quinn?"

Julia cleared her throat. "He doesn't have any."

"No demands?" Buchanan asked. "Why would he take hostages if he has no demands?"

"He's an anti-American Islamic fundamentalist who plans to use those hostages as an example. Bring retribution to the evil West. Like Chuck said, he wants to take out the DCI and the head of the spy group and blow something up to get the attention he wants."

Buchanan looked down at the papers in front of him while chewing on her words. Exasperation tightened the muscles in his face. "So everyone believes this is a suicide mission?"

Of course everyone nodded.

"Agreed," he said. "Options, anyone?" He looked at Lt. Diamond. "Lieutenant?"

Lt. Diamond looked at Senior Chief Leon Cassell. Cassell spoke. "The situation is currently stable, but obviously life expectancy for our hostages is down to days, maybe hours. Even with urban camouflage gear, the SEALs can't get close to the house during daylight hours without alerting Raissi and his crew. Sunrise is in"—he checked his watch—"approximately two hours. We either move shortly or we'll have to stall any plans he has until nightfall again. I don't recommend rushing this situation, but we may not be able to stall him that long. While it's dark, we can install microphones and possibly fiber-optic cameras at sites around the house so we can hear what's being said and get a look inside. We can also use IR thermal-imaging cameras to approximate where the hostages and the tangos are. But if Ms. Quinn is right about the explosives, overcoming them is damn near impossible to do without serious injury to our assets.

"We can't rule out a biological attack either. A bioterrorism group is here and ready with masks and suits.

"One more thing," the senior chief added. "If you're going with the theory that Raissi is our man, we need an updated picture of him. Recent pictures of all of the hostages as well. We don't want any mistakes when the shooting starts."

No one spoke for several long minutes, each contemplating the next few hours.

"All right," Buchanan said, "everybody take a break. I don't want any of you to stray far, but I do want everyone to stay fresh, so grab a cup of coffee and report back to this table in ten minutes."

The group rose reluctantly, all except Julia. Susan walked a few yards away to consult with an aide, but her gaze stayed on Julia. Julia followed Agent Buchanan and when she thought they were out of hearing range, she laid a hand on his arm. "Sir?"

"Yes, Miss Quinn." He poured himself a cup of coffee from a large stainless-steel drip machine.

"I know a way into the house that may help us rescue the hostages."

Buchanan eyed her intently. "I'm listening."

Julia took a deep breath and watched Susan watching her. "There's a dog kennel, sir, at the back of the house..."

Chapter Forty-One

Julia walked out from under the tent, feeling Susan's gaze on her. She didn't know where to wander to, didn't feel like making small talk with her coworkers. Conrad was somewhere nearby, but she couldn't look for him. She didn't want to anyway.

Agent Buchanan had listened intently to the information about the kennel entrance to the house, but he had vehemently rejected her reasoning that the only way to keep Pongo from raising the alert and blowing their one chance to save the hostages was for her to lead the rescue team.

Michael is going to die and it's my fault.

She couldn't keep the horrifying scenarios from running through her brain. Just like when Conrad had supposedly died in the bombing of the warehouse, the bad images just kept coming.

Leaning back against the rough bark of a tree, she tried to take a deep breath, but her lungs wouldn't fill. She'd blown Susan's primary plan, forcing Susan to deal her next set of cards. Michael and the others were being held hostage because Julia had forced Susan to call in Raissi.

But deep inside, Julia knew she wasn't to blame. Susan was the culprit here, not her. The supreme puppeteer was leading them all through each act as it suited her purpose.

And now Michael's going to die.

Julia bent at the waist, covered her face with her hands and tried to breathe.

"You look like hell." Susan's voice was soft as people milled around a few yards away. She leaned her shoulder against the tree and looked down at the back of Julia's head. "Rough night?"

Julia rose to face her. "You are unbelievable," she murmured, matching Susan's voice level. "I can't believe what you've done to all of us."

"You played your part well, my dear, and I appreciate that. You even put Raines in the hospital, adding another crime to your list. You're lucky I could even get you in here."

"The only reason you haven't had them arrest me is because Damgaard ordered you to bring me here. Where is he, by the way? Cari and I'd like to talk to him."

Susan glared at her. "Let's talk about Flynn. Where is he?"

Julia turned away from her and watched her counterparts filing back into the tent. Of course Conrad was the only one Susan was worried about. "Gone. Probably headed to Bermuda or the Caymans by now."

Susan snorted. "Not a chance. He wouldn't leave his precious queen with her back against the wall."

"You forget. He left me before without so much as a backwards glance."

Susan's impatience got the better of her. "Stop playing word games. Where is he?"

Running her fingers through her hair, Julia remained cool. "You didn't really think he'd be stupid enough to show his face here, did you?"

"He was stupid enough to let you come alone."

"He didn't *let* me do anything. Nobody controls me, Susan. Not Conrad and certainly not you. If you still want a piece of me, go ahead and try to get it. You've already failed once. This time you'll have quite an audience watching."

"Ah, Julia, you were always too cocky for your own good."

"I learned from the best."

"Your arrogant partner?" Susan snorted. "He's hardly the best."

"I was referring to you."

Susan studied her for a few seconds. "I do see myself in you at times. Smart, aggressive, not afraid to seize an opportunity when it presents itself. You're driven by the same forces that drive me so you must understand why I've used you and your friends to get what I want."

"What I understand, is that you're a manipulating bitch who has sold out her country and betrayed the people who trusted her."

Ignoring the comment, Susan looked away. "Just tell me where Flynn and Smith are."

"I don't know. Probably at CIA headquarters, ransacking your office."

"They shouldn't waste their time. I set your boyfriend up to take the fall, and now, with the current situation, my promotion to DCI is in the bag. No one is going to walk out of that house alive, especially not Director Allen or Michael Stone."

"I can't believe you were devious enough to set up a hostage situation to eliminate them."

Susan laughed. "A stroke of genius, isn't it? The terrorist gets what he wants and provides me with a valuable opportunity to seize what's rightfully mine."

"What about Jurgen Damgaard?" Julia asked. "If Titus dies, the deputy DCI is next in line."

"A minor problem." Susan dismissed the idea with a wave of her hand.

"When this is over, Susan," Julia whispered with detached calmness, "I'm personally taking you out."

Susan met her stare. "If I were you, I wouldn't be so sure about that. You're under Damgaard's protection right now because he's acting director and doesn't want anything but a positive outcome. But as soon as the hostage situation ends, Julia Torrison will be officially AWOL from the CIA and considered to be a felon. You will be taken into custody, or..." She let her voice trail off and shrugged.

Julia finished the sentence for her. "A stray bullet will find its way into my head during the counterassault."

"I'll talk to Damgaard and get you on Agent Buchanan's team." Susan smiled as she took a step back. "You want to play the hero, so be it. You'll die with Michael and Titus and Daniel.

"It will be a shame for our country to lose such a valuable counterterrorism specialist," she added with a false sigh, "but just think how proud your stepfather and brother will be when they learn you died in the line of duty." Turning her back on Julia, she walked away.

Julia bent over at the waist again and put her hands on her knees. She directed her words at the microphone taped to her stomach under her loose shirt. "I hope to hell you guys got that recorded. That's probably as close to a confession as I'll get out of her." Then she stopped talking at the sound of footsteps.

"You didn't want coffee," a man said. "So I brought you a Pepsi."

Julia looked up and accepted the icy bottle of pop from Agent Buchanan, even though she didn't want it. "Thank you, sir."

"I'm glad you're here. Until you showed up, Chief Richmond didn't even list Raissi in our top five subjects. You seem to know a lot about him."

Julia let out a disgusted sigh and raised her gaze to the canopy of leaves shading them. "If only I'd figured out what he was up to before this happened."

"Don't be so hard on yourself. My people didn't figure it out either. Your input about the explosives has already saved the lives of SEALs and my HRT group. With your knowledge assisting them, they can formulate a course of action that will result in fewer dead and injured if an assault is carried out. I told Lt. Diamond and Senior Chief about your idea regarding the dog kennel and they were actually quite grateful for it. But you will not be allowed to assist them."

Julia felt the cell phone on her hip vibrate. She ignored it. "But Pongo knows me. If I can get into the kennel with him, I can place a muzzle on him to keep him from barking at the lieutenant's men."

"They'll handle the dog. He won't be a problem."

"He's a guard dog, trained by Michael himself. He won't accept treats from anyone but Michael. And me," she added. "They'd have to shoot him to keep him from sounding an—" She broke off, understanding dawning on her. "You're going to shoot him, aren't you? You're going to kill Michael's dog."

"The dog's life is a small price to pay to rescue these four men."

Julia shut her eyes, squeezing back tears that were suddenly ready to fall. The image of Pongo dead on top of everything else made her want to punch the tree, but she knew she had to keep her emotions in check. She could hear Flynn's voice in her head, *No acting like a girl, Jules.*

Blocking the image of a dead Pongo, Julia steeled herself. "Pongo weighs one hundred twenty-five pounds. The kennel door is not big enough for most of Lt. Diamond's men." Technically that was a lie, because Conrad had somehow managed to squeeze through it, but if lying got her inside, she'd lie her butt off. "I fit perfectly."

Buchanan raised an eyebrow at her. "You've tried it?"

Julia straightened. "I've spent a lot of time in that house, sir. I know every possible way in or out, and I know how to get in without raising an alarm or showing up on camera."

Buchanan shifted his attention to look at his command center. "So the rumors are true about you and the director. That's one of the reasons I wanted to talk to you alone. If you can give us more details about the house and the security system, it would be helpful."

Hope sparked in Julia's chest. "I'm sure I can help. My relationship with the director is a plus for you. It raises the odds in your favor a hundred times over *if* you use me to gain access to his house. I know for a fact Raissi's plan does not allow for any of the three key hostages to walk away from this alive, no matter what he pretends to negotiate. When your teams approach that house and are detected, everybody dies instantly. Why risk that when I can get them in undetected?"

Buchanan cocked his head to the side and studied her. "I'm a human calculator, Ms. Quinn. I always prefer the odds of numbers over blanket statements of emotion, but you are not trained to lead a rescue team into a hostage situation."

"That may be true to an extent, but please give me credit where credit is due. I made it through the Farm and have five years of experience as a field operative in Europe with an ex-SEAL as a partner." Julia ticked her points off on her fingers. "I'm the expert in this group on Raissi, and I have an extensive background in explosives. I know my way around Michael Stone's house. I know how his alarm system works and how to disable it room-by-room. And his dog would never bark at me and raise an alarm." She took a deep breath. "My ex-partner taught me to think like the bad guys for my own survival, but he also taught me how to recognize an opportunity when I see one. You have an opportunity here, sir, to use me and save those hostages. My plan is the best one you've got."

Buchanan shook his head. "Fayez Raissi and half the

people here think he has the odds stacked in his favor, but I have the brightest and best hostage rescue team members ever to wear a badge. Combined with the SEALs you just sat with at that table, I have the ability to turn the tables on Raissi and lower his odds of a successful mission considerably. You'll have to forgive me if I refuse your offer and disagree with your assumption that my counterassault teams won't play God and work a miracle here today."

Julia struggled mentally to figure out a way to make Buchanan understand. Rumor around Langley had it that his single personnel file had more commendations in it than all of his HRT experts combined. From what she could see, he hadn't even broken into a sweat yet.

Confidence stemming from experience was a great asset in the field, but mistakes could still result. Especially when the playing field was skewed and the good guys had no idea who was working against them. "I know your team can and does work miracles," she said, acknowledging the abilities of his HRT and SEALs. "But you don't have the big picture here, Agent Buchanan. Trust me when I say I do, and the only way you're going to work a miracle here today is to use me."

The distinctive ring of a telephone blared from the tent, its echo vibrating off the vans around the base of operation's table and sending all those nearby into action. Buchanan shook his head and chuckled. "Ryan Smith warned me about you," he said and then he ran off to answer the phone.

Julia swore under her breath and ran after him.

Chapter Forty-Two

Conrad sat in a captain's chair bolted to the floor of the white van that said "Forever Flowers" on both sides and had an 800 number written underneath each sign. The cover on the van wasn't totally bogus. The company had been real but went out of business a few months after the last downturn on Wall Street. Conrad had purchased the van for a mere eleven hundred in cash, cleared out the inside and let Smitty go to town. The van now contained high-tech surveillance equipment and monitors rivaling just about anything the CIA or FBI had.

He replayed the audio they'd just received from Julia's microphone. "For God's sake, what the hell does she think she's doing, volunteering to take the SEAL team in?"

Smitty sat beside him in another captain's chair. "She wants to help."

"She better get the hell out of there."

"I think she's right. Tim and Lt. Diamond should use her."

"Have you lost your mind?"

"No," Smitty answered sincerely.

Conrad tapped his fingers on the counter. "How did she figure out the kennel trick?"

"Uh." Ace cleared his throat from the floor of the van where he was seated. "I told her."

Conrad sent him a look of frustration. "You couldn't keep a damn secret if I cut out your tongue and tied your lips shut." He turned to Smitty. "We can't protect her from Susan if she's at the hostage site, and we have a confession. She has to clear out of there before she ends up dead."

"You should have gone with her," Cari said from the front seat of the van.

"Too risky. Susan would have had me arrested the minute I stepped inside the barricades."

"What about you, Ry Guy?" Ace said. "Why didn't you go?"

"Same reason, Ace." Smitty adjusted a wire. "We're both AWOL from the CIA. Susan was waiting for us to come in with Julia so she could nab us. We couldn't take the chance she'd arrest all of us."

Conrad ran a hand over the two-day growth of beard on his face. "I don't like this. Julia has to get out of there," he repeated. "Now."

Smitty shook his head. "She won't leave until this is over."

Cari's eyes were wide. "How will she kill her?"

Conrad and Smitty exchanged a look. Con breathed impatience. "Kill who?"

"Julia said she was going to take Susan out when this is over," Ace answered. "Will she shoot her?"

"She's bullshitting. There's nothing she can do to help Stone anymore and she can't take Susan out."

"I wouldn't bet on that, bro." Ace shuddered visibly. "I saw what she did last night. She seems completely capable of taking just about anybody out."

"Of course, she's *capable* of doing it," Conrad said. "But she doesn't have the balls for it, Ace, trust me. Besides, I'm not done with Susan Richmond yet. I want her alive." He spoke to Smitty. "Call Julia and tell her to get out."

"I did. She didn't answer."

"Call her again."

"I've called her twice already, Conman. She's not answering."

"Dammit," Conrad huffed. "What am I going to do with that girl?"

Julia watched Tim Buchanan glance at the young woman in the van controlling the recording equipment and, after receiving her okay sign, pushed the speakerphone button. "Special Agent Tim Buchanan here."

Julia's knuckles were white as she gripped the back of a chair. People were still flooding into the tent, but all were quiet as they listened for what they hoped might be the voice of a terrorist ready to make a deal.

What they got instead was almost as good. "Agent Buchanan, it's good to hear your voice. This is Director of CIA Operations, Michael Stone."

Quiet cheers erupted from the group as renewed hope soared through them. Julia didn't cheer, but relaxed her grip and sent up a silent thank you to the heavens. Michael was alive.

It was a good indication the other hostages were alive as well.

"Director, it's good to hear your voice too," Buchanan answered. "Can you tell us what the situation is inside your house? We assume you are unable to leave on your own, that you and the others are being held against your will."

"That's correct, sir. I've been instructed by my captors to tell you a few things. First, as you probably have already deduced, there are four of us: Daniel King, Titus Allen, Brad Kinnick—my security officer—and myself, being held hostage. Secondly, none of us has been injured, yet, except for me, but I'm all right. However, any attempt to free us will result in the deaths of all of us. Do you understand, Agent Buchanan?"

"I understand, Director. Please go on."

"The men holding us are from the group Takfi-wal-Hijra, but they say they speak for all Islamic fundamentalists. The leader, who says his name is Frank, has but one demand..."

At the pause, Tim Buchanan said calmly, even as the makeshift room erupted with hopeful murmurings, "Go ahead, Director. We're listening and will do everything in our power to meet that demand."

"Frank requests that news reporter Thomas Heller from CNN visit him inside the house in order that he may appeal to the American people to change the United States' political stand in the Middle East. When Mr. Heller arrives on the porch, Frank will release one hostage."

Silence hung in the air for a few seconds. "Let me make sure I understand Frank's request." Buchanan motioned toward another of his agents to get on the phone to the news agency. "He wants an interview on national television with a news reporter from CNN in exchange for one hostage?"

"Not any news reporter. It has to be Thomas Heller. One cameraman will be allowed in with Mr. Heller, but that's it. No one else. Do not try and trick him or"—they heard Stone let out a deep breath—"I'll be the first to die."

Julia's hands gripped the chair again and she locked her knees to keep from swaying. Complete silence filled the space in the tent, the earlier elation gone.

Michael's voice broke the silence. "Agent Buchanan?"

"I'm here, Director. One of my agents is working on Frank's request as we speak. I don't know if Mr. Heller is even in the country, but we'll do our best to locate him and get him here as quickly as possible. Please advise Frank it may take several hours to meet his request."

"Frank has instructed me to tell you you have one hour."

Julia saw Tim Buchanan set the timer on his watch. She did the same to hers.

Chapter Forty-Three

The blueprints of Stone's house were back on the table. Six SEALs, with their lieutenant, executive officer and senior chief, hovered between them and a blackboard with various takedown scenarios that stood nearby. It was nearing four in the morning. Most of the CIA consultants had wandered off to find food and more coffee, but Julia couldn't eat or drink. She was waiting for word that Damgaard had ordered her participation in the rescue, knowing it was unlikely he could or would do such a thing. But she had permission to sit next to Agent Elaina Koburn from the HRT at the back of the tent and listen to the SEALs discuss their plan anyway.

CNN had been notified and Thomas Heller was on his way. He had already boarded a helicopter with a special CIA consultant who was briefing the extremely nervous news reporter on proper procedures for interviewing a terrorist on live TV. From what Julia was gathering from the SEALs, Heller didn't need to worry. Thermal-imaging cameras were already providing data to the HRT and SEALs. Odds were, there would be no interview.

"The laser trip sensors are set up here." Lt. Diamond pointed to a spot on the blueprints. "And here. Trees and undergrowth along the property line will conceal our approach, and we'll avoid the sensors as we cross the property line. The dog kennel is attached to the back of the house here."

"There's a Plexiglas door between two rubber curtains," Julia volunteered, "where the dog door attaches to the mudroom. The Plexiglas door opens and closes from the inside. Michael usually leaves it open during the day, but if he wants to keep Pongo out, he closes it. Since Pongo is outside, Raissi must have closed it. The second rubber curtain hangs inside the mudroom."

There was discussion between the SEALs. The rubber curtains would be simple to cut away, but they debated the most efficient and quietest way to deal with the Plexiglas.

"The dog door is not large," Julia continued. "As I told Agent Buchanan, Pongo weighs about one hundred and twenty-five pounds, which by dog standards is a decent size." She looked at the extremely fit, extremely muscled SEALs at the table. "However, any of you with more than a T-shirt on are going to struggle getting through it."

Several of the SEALs exchanged looks, but no one commented.

"Another option," Diamond continued, "is a chimney. The house has a large gas log fireplace"—he tapped his finger on the paper—"here in the living room. The chimney is big enough for a small human being to shimmy down."

"Just like Santa Claus, huh?" Buck Harris, the youngest of the group said, grinning.

"A skinny Santa Claus, but yeah." Diamond looked at Tony Belcini, his team's sniper and smallest man at five feet, six inches and one hundred forty pounds. "What do you think, Belly? Can you squeeze down the chimney and put coal in Raissi's stocking?"

"Would be my pleasure, sir, but I wonder if we could, y'know, get some actual dimensions of the chimney before I stick myself into it."

The Senior Chief patted Belcini on the back. "I'll get somebody on it." He walked out of the tent.

Julia jumped slightly when her cell phone vibrated again on her hip. She didn't need to read the caller ID to know what it said. *No way, guys. I'm not done here.*

Diamond addressed her from the table. "Raissi has booby-trapped the fireplace and kennel entrance?"

She considered his question for a moment before answering. "Tripwires maybe by the fireplace, but I doubt he'd put anything by the kennel door. Raissi wants his explosion to be big and set off by him at just the right moment, not a partial explosion set off accidentally by a dog scratching to come in. He might set up a wire to trip an alarm though just for security purposes."

"Seems like he would have killed the dog by now," Elaina murmured as the SEALs spoke again to each other.

"Raissi understands that a dog is a better security measure than any expensive system," Julia said. "Michael will be devastated when he finds out they killed Pongo."

"That will be my job." Elaina met Julia's gaze. "Sorry."

Diamond motioned to his men. "Harris and Worley cami up for insertion into the house through the kennel. Your job will be to gather intel and disable as many bombs as possible prior to the assault. Belcini, you prepare for a drop into the house via the chimney. The helicopter on the front lawn will provide the noise and distraction we need to drop you, Milford and Saville on the roof via a second helo. Milford and Saville will go in through the second story windows." He glanced at Agent Koburn. "We know Director Stone's surveillance and security network is contained in this room on the second floor." He pointed at the blueprints.

"That's wrong." Julia jumped up from her chair. "His video monitors are in his office on the first floor." She pointed to the exact location on the blueprints. "The main security panel is here in the mudroom just off the garage on the west wall."

Diamond thanked her. "That makes sense. Thermal imaging shows Raissi and the hostages are all in the office with single guards stationed at the front and back doors of the house."

"What about the balcony's French doors upstairs?" Julia asked.

"One man," Diamond answered. "Agent Koburn, you will be responsible for taking that man out from a position on the northwest side, here. Station yourself outside the tripwire perimeters on the elevated hillside and wait for my signal. We'll use Mr. Heller's entrance into the house as takedown time."

Elaina nodded once.

Thunder rolled above their heads. "The weather is our ally for the time being, but that may change again at any moment. Any questions?"

There were a few last minute details to iron out before the SEALs filed out to cami up. Diamond acknowledged Julia's worried look. "Your ex-partner was a SEAL, huh?"

She stood and nodded. "Conrad Flynn."

"Flynn. I've heard of him. His group did a lot of work in the

Gulf region, didn't they? What made him defect to the CIA?"

That made her smile. If Conrad was listening, he was probably cussing the younger SEAL out. "He's not the best team player."

Diamond chuckled. "Is that why you're not partners anymore?"

Julia gave him a wink. "That, I'm afraid, is classified information."

"Right." His smile faded and he turned serious. "Ms. Quinn, one of my men is in the local news channel's van right now decking out a news camera to hold his weapon so he can enter the house disguised as a cameraman with Heller and assist in the takedown. We'll be coming in through the front, back and upstairs, and if the counterassault goes as planned, my men will locate the hostages and eliminate the tangos before Raissi can clear his throat for his speech. If he or any of his men try to flee, the FBI snipers will take them out as they exit the house. Have confidence."

Julia couldn't hide her lack of it. "Lt. Diamond, Raissi's too clever to fall for the cameraman angle. He'll demand Heller bring in the camera and he'll have one of his own men videotape the interview."

"We'll be ready for that too," Diamond said.

Agent Buchanan stormed into the tent, assaulting the door flap so hard the lights hanging above their heads swung back and forth. "Sorry, Ms. Quinn. Jurgen Damgaard has extreme confidence in your abilities, but even he and Susan Richmond couldn't get the okay from my boss to let you interfere in this rescue. Are you satisfied now?"

Julia bit the inside of her cheek and looked at Lt. Diamond. "If I were a man, a former SEAL, like my ex-partner, would you let me participate?"

Buchanan answered, "Absolutely not."

But Diamond smiled at her.

Buchanan looked at his watch. "Our deadline's approaching and I need to be spending my time preparing for the counterassault. If you have valid information to share with me or Lt. Diamond, please feel free to do so. Otherwise, consider yourself done here, Ms. Quinn."

Julia watched him head for the flap. "Can you tranquilize the dog instead of killing him?" she begged. "Please? For

Director Stone?"

Buchanan stopped, looked up at the swinging lights and blew out a long breath. He shook his head, but reached into his back pants pocket and handed Julia one of his business cards. "I like your tenacity. Give me a call if you ever decide you need a career change."

Julia's hopes fell, but she took the card. "Thank you, sir. I'll do that."

As Buchanan exited the tent, she heard him start calling out orders to the gearheads in the blue vans.

"We've got tranquilizer guns," Diamond said to her as he too made his way to the flap. "I'll see what I can do."

Julia felt a spurt of hope again. "Thank you."

After Diamond and Agent Koburn left the tent, Julia examined the plan her brain had been building since midnight. It was dangerous. It was foolhardy. And it was something she had to do.

Glancing at Buchanan's card, she folded it and tucked it into her bra.

No one saw Julia slip the black FBI windbreaker off the back of a chair or a matching baseball cap and the headset from the front seat of one of the blue vans. No one took notice of her snagging two jumbo cinnamon rolls from the coffee table and folding them in separate napkins before sticking them in the windbreaker's pockets. The helicopter bearing Thomas Heller was thirty minutes away and everyone inside the FBI operations camp, including Susan Richmond, was too busy preparing for his arrival.

So no one paid any attention as she ducked under the security tape and walked by the police barrier securing the area south of the front gate. She wound her way quickly through the reporters and onlookers and headed down the gravel road toward the line of trees.

Ignoring the white "Forever Flowers" van parked in the midst of news vans fifty yards away, she entered the woods she had run through the previous afternoon, and once out of view of the road, exchanged her own jacket for the black one, put the headset on and shoved her hair under the cap. She took the tiny night-vision binoculars she'd swiped from Smitty out of her jacket pocket and hung them around her neck. Then she went to find her tote bag still buried by the oak tree.

"Still no answer?" Conrad asked. Smitty shook his head.

Conrad drummed his fingers on the table. "She's always bitching at me about trying to save the world. Now she's doing it."

"She wants to save Director Stone. Not the whole world."

Dropping his head into his hands, Conrad made no comment. He had to get Julia out of there, but he didn't know how.

Smitty spoke up. "We could go in after her. Susan's not expecting us now."

Conrad considered the suggestion, rubbed his forehead. "Getting past security will be about as easy as making the Empire State Building disappear."

Smith held up a finger, stood and moved to a shelf on the other side of the van. Digging through a stack of files, he pulled one out and handed it to Conrad. "I started working on these last week. All that's left is to laminate them."

Conrad opened the file and looked at the fake CIA IDs. He grimaced at the picture of himself, one Smitty had made for the passport he'd used the week before, complete with disguise. He could duplicate it. "You never cease to amaze me, Smith," he said, reaching over to lightly punch Smitty's arm.

"Occasionally, I even amaze myself." He grinned, stretching his arms out and cracking his knuckles.

"What about me?" Ace asked, jumping up. "What do I get to do?"

Smith and Flynn turned to him. "Drive," they said in unison.

Still in the front seat, Cari stared out the window. "I do not think that will be necessary. I see her coming this way."

Conrad leaned back in the chair to see out the windshield and felt himself relax a micron as he, too, saw the slim figure of Julia walking on the side of the road near the tree line. "Finally." He sat back up and pushed the fake CIA badge away.

"Uh-oh," Cari said.

Ace jumped up from the floor. "Uh-oh? What uh-oh?"

Both Con and Smitty were on their feet and pushing Ace out of the way as they scrambled to see what Cari saw.

"I don't believe it," Conrad seethed through gritted teeth. Julia had just disappeared into the woods.

Chapter Forty-Four

At 3:45, Fayez Raissi paced the Italian marble of the kitchen floor and stifled a yawn. He was tired. He had showered and shaved, but even that was not enough to completely refresh him. The only thing keeping the exhaustion at bay was the thought of speaking to the world on national television, immortalizing himself before dying in an explosion of holy retribution. With great deliberation, weighing risk against payoff, he had decided to address America. The day and the hour would be Islam's. In his mind, he saw his dead brothers waiting for him in their heaven, holding out their arms to welcome him in.

Allah is great.

Raissi thought of his son, too young to die and too young to live alone in a country torn apart by war. There were only those two choices for his son and so many other young men. Death by either was inevitable. What was a father to do? Take his son with him? Or leave him behind?

Wiping the tears from his eyes, Raissi pulled in a deep breath. So much was at stake now he had to be sure, as the messenger of his faith and his country, that he didn't lose his concentration. He stopped pacing, gathered his posture erect. Drawing in another deep breath, he closed his eyes and pictured himself completing the final two objectives of his plan. Envisioned himself, tall and proud, speaking not only to America, but to the world, with Muammar, his son, by his side. The newsman, Heller, would be there within a half hour. Raissi would wait until dawn, when Americans were waking up to their morning news, to give them something newsworthy.

Another breath and he focused his thoughts on the speech

itself.

    Keep it simple.
Keep it short.
End with a bang.

    Julia knelt in the woods and uncovered her tote bag from the pile of leaves and brush. Finding her penlight, she turned it on, brushed the last of the wet leaves off the bag and started moving toward Michael's house. She wasn't as worried this time about making noise, but she still moved as stealthily as possible. Buchanan had the edge of the woods and the path to the lake staffed with his men and women for security purposes, and while the windbreaker with FBI in bold yellow letters across the back might keep her from being shot by one of them, she was still treading on very dangerous ground.

    As she maneuvered through the trees, keeping the flashlight's beam pointed at the ground, she thought about the twists and turns her life had taken in the course of the last few days as well as the last few years. There had been a lot of pain and grief, but there'd also been a lot of peace and happiness. She had felt great passion and great heartbreak. She had survived everything the world had thrown at her and, more than survived, she had thrived in her life. She had defended the innocent and worked passionately at keeping her country safe. She knew what it felt like to love and be loved by two good men.

    Listening to the wind whisper in the leaves above her, she decided her life had been a good one overall, and if she had to die in these early morning hours, it would be okay. She would take the chance if she could save Michael.

    She reached under her shirt and pulled the mic off her stomach and the transmitter off her back and shoved them in her bag. She had to do this and there was no way Conrad would understand. "Sorry, Con," she whispered in the dark. She knew Raissi and didn't trust him. The terrorist had cut his teeth on military strategy and had studied the FBI and SEAL team tactics for years. Julia was sure he would wait until Heller got in the door and the SEALs were descending on him and then blow everybody to kingdom come. But she could create a diversion and prevent that, giving Buchanan's men and the SEALs much better odds.

    Her cell phone vibrated on her hip again. Julia shut off the penlight, turned her phone off and slowed her steps as she neared the tree line. Raising the night vision goggles, she looked for security officers and found none in her general vicinity. She checked her watch and saw it had taken almost twenty minutes to cut through the woods. The HRT snipers would already be in position. She was running out of time.

Setting her bag on the ground, she felt for the tools she would need to get into the house and pocketed them. Then she edged closer to the property line, lay on her stomach and watched the area through her binoculars, keeping her body shielded behind a tree. Several human shapes showed up on her lenses in various spots around the property within her view. Like her, Buchanan's team was laying low.

She saw Pongo, standing up in his kennel on alert. He seemed to be looking right at her. She moved closer and heard his soft whine. He definitely knew she was there. The faint smell of cigarette smoke made her shift her gaze to the balcony. One of the glass French doors was open. Raissi's man was enjoying a last smoke, and Julia wondered at his stupidity to expose himself to a sniper's bullet for such a pleasure.

A second later, the secure radio headset she was wearing crackled in her ear. Then a man's voice. "Bluebell, this is Morning Glory," Lt. Diamond murmured. "Do you read? This is a test. Over."

Nick Worley's voice responded, "Roger, Morning Glory. We read you loud and clear."

Diamond continued his test until all SEALs and HRT personnel had responded.

"Take positions," Diamond's voice commanded. "Helo due in four. Bluebell out."

Julia looked through the darkness at the spot, ten feet in front of her, where Pongo now paced, stopping to scratch at the kennel's wire fence. The sound of her pulse pounded over the blood roaring in her ears. She was about to take the biggest chance of her life, and she suddenly felt like she was back in her dream, sinking in quicksand.

Drawing in her breath, Julia forced herself to think of the things she loved.

Music, poetry, sex. Breathe.

Cherry blossoms, emerald earrings, hot showers. Breathe.

Michael's smile. The brush of Conrad's fingertips down my

back. Breathe.

Cognac and poker. April in Paris.

She stopped her mental list and blew her breath slowly out through her lips.

It was raining again, or was the wetness on her face tears? She wiped it away with the heels of her hands and pulled a flattened cinnamon roll out of her pocket. The balcony terrorist had tossed the last of his cigarette over the railing and disappeared back into the bedroom. "Hi, Pongo," she whispered to the dog and laid the roll on the ground.

She definitely had his attention. He wagged his stubby tail and danced in circles, lifting his front legs up and spinning. "Hang tight, buddy."

Pulling her iPod out, she slid it into the pocket of her portable armband. She used this when she was exercising to listen to her music. Now it was going to help her distract Raissi.

She shimmied a few steps back into the woods and ran through the trees ten yards south, using her binoculars to locate the laser beam base unit partially hidden by some landscaping at the southwest corner of the property. The laser unit sent out two electronic beams to the northwest end and was mounted to the post of a solar landscaping light. Julia Velcroed the armband into a circle and lifted her binoculars to the balcony's doors. No sign of the terrorist. He'd probably left his post for a pee or to find another cigarette.

She dropped to her belly and crawled through the small muddy ravine. Coming up to the stones and bushes of the landscaping, she dropped the iPod over the post, knocking the beams out and, hunched over, ran back across the ravine and into the woods.

"What the *hell*," Conrad said, barely above a whisper as he watched Julia run down the hill through his night-vision goggles.

Smitty crouched on the ground nearby. "What's she doing?" It was too dark to see anything without his binoculars which were missing, and Conrad had their only pair of goggles.

"She's setting off the house alarm." Conrad's voice was flat.

"Why?"

Conrad handed the binoculars to Smitty. "To create a distraction. She's going in."

"I knew she would. Didn't I call it?"

Conrad was up off the ground and moving in the blink of an eye. Stealthily, but quickly, he began to move in between trees. Smitty moved behind him. "You can't go after her, Con," he whispered.

Conrad registered Smitty's comment but kept moving. All his senses were trained on Julia. He was never going to get to her before she went in the kennel and his mind was ticking through his options.

"Conrad!" Smitty grabbed his shoulder.

Conrad pulled away, intent on his quest. Smitty tackled him from behind, sending both of them crashing face down in the slimy, wet undergrowth of the woods. Conrad brought an elbow back and caught Smith on the side of the head.

"Ouch," Smitty barked, giving Conrad a hard shove as he moved off of him and stood up. "What the hell's the matter with you? You cannot go after her." His breath was coming fast and he reached down to help Conrad to his feet. Wiping slime off his pants, he rubbed the side of his head with his left hand.

"You don't understand." Conrad took a step backwards.

"I do understand. You love her. But you have to know when to let go, Con. You have to put your emotions aside this time. Julia just made a choice. She's chosen Stone."

Conrad cursed, slamming his hand against the nearest tree. He stood for a moment, letting the fact sink in. Damn, his stomach hurt. It didn't matter what choice she'd made, he wasn't ready to let her go. Not again.

She's mine.

He looked at his best friend. "I don't care who she's chosen. I have to go after her." He stuck his hand out. "Take care, Ryan."

Smitty put his hands on his hips. "Oh fuck, Conrad. You're both going to get blown to kingdom come. Don't do this to me."

"I'll be damned." Conrad stared at his partner. "You have been hanging out with me too much. You're swearing like a true sailor."

"Conrad," Smitty started, but Conrad was already running toward the edge of the tree line. Ahead of them, a floodlight came on. Smitty ran after him.

Neither man was expecting the blows that knocked them

both to the ground. Conrad, his head ringing from the side attack, felt a knee dig into his back as his assailant pushed him face down into the mud and leaves and handcuffed his hands in two swift movements. He'd been so distracted thinking about Julia, he'd been taken by surprise.

"State your names and business," the man said in a low voice next to his ear.

Conrad spit debris from his mouth. "CIA operator Conrad Flynn. Special assignment for Titus Allen, confidential."

Smitty confirmed the same, God bless him, and the man, a SEAL Con guessed, radioed in to his boss.

"Shit, shit, shit," Conrad said into the muck under his face.

"Ditto," came Smitty's reply.

Julia didn't stop to watch the floodlight over the balcony light up the hillside or see the guard slide open the balcony door and raise his AK-47 at the woods where she had emerged and then disappeared again. She sprinted past trees and pushed aside saplings as she ran back up the hill parallel to Pongo's kennel. In her ears, she heard the HRT and SEALs addressing each other, trying to figure out what was happening, and she knew inside the house, Raissi was doing the same.

If he sent his men out to look for her and remove the block from the laser unit, they would be easy targets for the HRT to pick off. If he didn't send them to investigate and remove the iPod, he would leave himself open to attack on the west side even if he left the alarm system activated. If he left the alarm system activated, the constant blare would put him and his men on edge. If he deactivated it, the whole property would be vulnerable to intruders.

As partial chaos distracted both sides, Julia pulled the headset off her ears and laid it on her neck. She cut across the few feet of side yard, hunched over to avoid the camera mounted above the dog kennel and fell on her knees to greet an ecstatic Pongo.

Chapter Forty-Five

The west side of his property had been breached.

Michael, hope racing though his veins, recited the alarm's deactivation code to Fayez Raissi, and watched as the terrorist entered the numbers on the keypad with one hand while pointing a handgun at him with the other. The house's pulsing alarm stopped as Raissi's men radioed in from their various locations throughout the house. They saw nothing, heard nothing to indicate the FBI was moving on them. None knew why the alarm was triggered. Muammar watched the video screens and shook his head at his boss. He spoke to Raissi in what Michael thought was a Pakistani dialect, but his meaning was clear. Nothing unusual showed there either.

"It could have been a raccoon," Michael volunteered, "or skunk. Animals often trip the sensors." But he knew it wasn't a nocturnal animal that had breeched the tripwires.

Raissi ignored him, moving to stand over Muammar's shoulder and studying the video coming in from the cameras. Again he contacted each of his men stationed around the house and again the reply was the same. No one had seen anything.

Moving back to the keypad, Raissi reactivated the alarm. The pulsing resumed and Raissi narrowed his eyes at Michael.

Michael continued to offer reasons. "Maybe a tree branch blew down and is blocking the wire sensors. You'll have to send one of your men out to move it if you want to keep the system activated."

Raissi studied the video monitor for a moment, and even Michael could see there was no tree branch or other object blocking the wires. He guessed one of the base units had been damaged, but if the HRT had taken out one, why not the others? Why were they not storming the house?

"The system could be malfunctioning," Michael said, still trying to divert Raissi's brain from suspecting a failed rescue attempt, and his own as well.

Raissi moved to Brad Kinnick and pulled him up off the couch. Removing a KA-BAR from a leg holster, Raissi sliced the duct tape from Brad's wrists, while holding the gun level with his temple. "You will check the tripwire base units on the west side," he told Brad. "The man upstairs will have his gun trained on you. If you try to run or cause any distraction"—he pointed the end of his gun toward Michael's chest again—"your boss dies, you die, everybody dies. Understand?"

Brad locked eyes with Michael, and he nodded. "I understand."

Agent Koburn kept her rifle's night-vision scope trained on the balcony terrorist even as the men talking on her headset demanded to know what was happening in her corner of the world. The backyard's floodlight was on and she'd had more than one opportunity to take out the gun-slinging terrorist on the balcony's deck but had not been given the okay from her boss to do so. "I saw nothing before the light came on," she spoke into her headset. "Tango on balcony smoked a cigarette, threw it out and disappeared into the dark bedroom. He only reappeared when the floodlight activated. He's antsy now, watching the backyard with his finger on the trigger. He is in full view. Orders?"

Buchanan ordered her to stand down and sweep the yard with her scope to see if she could see any reason for the security light to be on. Elaina did as ordered and just as she was ready to return her rifle scope to the balcony, she saw the back door of the house open. A man, as broad as a linebacker for the Steelers and dressed like a Secret Service agent, stepped out from the shadows and made his way across the yard. Elaina knew in an instant this was security officer Brad Kinnick. She'd seen his picture ID along with the others. On the balcony, cigarette man kept his AK-47 trained on Brad's back.

Her finger itching to pull the trigger, Elaina drew a deep breath and relayed what she saw into the mic of her headset. She identified Brad and described his advance across the property. He scanned the trees, the ravine and the yard before stopping at the southwest corner. As he crouched and examined the laser tripwire base unit, she saw him pull something from the post. He rose, turning the item over in his hands.

Watching him through her scope, Elaina zoomed in on his hands. The floodlight was still on, and even in the far corner of the yard, it gave plenty of light for her to identify the object Brad was looking at. She had an identical one in her backpack.

"There was an iPod in an arm holster hung over the base unit," she told Buchanan. "Kinnick has removed it from the post and is returning to the house."

Diamond's voice now came to Elaina. "Repeat, Rosemary. Did you say an iPod? Over."

Earlier, Elaina had thought she'd heard movement in the woods off to her right. She'd taken her eye from the scope for only a second, but had seen nothing nearby. It was most likely one of her own team members, but Elaina wondered where the CIA analyst, Abigail Quinn, had disappeared to, if she were in the woods with the HRT watching the impending takedown. Elaina liked the spook. In fact, she understood quite well Abigail's need to be off the bench and in the middle of the playing field. She'd always been the same way and on many levels it galled her that she and other women in her ranks were as skilled as the SEALs but could never be one of them. Someday, she hoped to see that rectified.

The appearance of the iPod confirmed Elaina's suspicions. Agent Quinn was indeed in the middle of the playing field. No one but a spook would pull such a stupid maneuver. "I repeat, an iPod in an arm holster." She watched Kinnick disappear into the house. She wondered if Agent Buchanan was thinking the same thing as she was. "Orders, sir?"

Buchanan's voice, calm and clear, came back to her. "Everyone remain engaged but do not move until my command. Helo will land in two minutes. Proceed as planned."

In the distance, Elaina heard the sound of helicopter blades.

She was in.

Julia had given Pongo the first cinnamon roll and cut the outside rubber curtain off at the top of the doggie door before Agent Buchanan had radioed the team's sniper and asked her to scope out the grounds. She'd spit in her hands, rubbed them together and stuck them like suction cups to the Plexiglas door and slid it up before Elaina had responded.

Even through the Plexiglas, Julia had heard the house's alarm blaring a warning. She'd paused, her ears straining to hear movement over the rhythmic alarm on the other side of the second rubber curtain. Cautiously, she'd pulled the inside curtain through the hole and checked for tripwires crossing the entrance. There were none. She'd pushed herself through the doggie door, given Pongo the other cinnamon roll, and shut the Plexiglas to keep him out, letting the rubber curtain fall back into place.

Hearing voices in the kitchen, Julia crouched in the unlit mudroom connecting the garage to the main house. Several of Michael's jackets hung on one wall. A basket of dog toys sat at the end of a barn board bench. Rubber boots and an assortment of Michael's favorite running shoes were lined up on black rubber mats just inside the garage door. A stacked washer and dryer sat silent next to the bench.

Julia listened as one of the terrorists gave someone else instructions and the familiar voice of Brad Kinnick responded. Raissi was sending him out to check the tripwires and see what the problem was. There was rustling by the back door, it opened and the screen door screeched. Julia sat tight, scrunching down and holding her breath. She pulled the headset back onto her head and listened to Elaina Koburn describe Brad's trek through the yard and the identification of her iPod. She heard the screen door screech again. Brad said nothing, but she heard his footsteps as well as the terrorist's leave the kitchen as Agent Buchanan's voice on her headset told everyone to proceed as planned.

Removing her gun from her waistband, she moved quickly and quietly into the kitchen. She slipped past the refrigerator and between the cooking island and the sink. At the back door, she noticed Raissi's man had left a sheet of Semtex on the threshold. Carefully, she removed the blasting cap from the sheet and stuck it in the fridge. She checked the windows and found wires that she knew led to bricks of C-4. These she left alone. It would take too much time and there was too much risk involved in disabling those.

A moment later, she opened the Plexiglas door and brought

Pongo inside. As she descended the carpeted stairs to the basement on cat feet, her hand holding his collar securely, she heard the distinctive *thump, thump, thump* of helicopter blades.

"This was hung on the solar light post," Brad said, holding out something in his hand to Raissi. "It was blocking the sensor for the tripwire."

When Michael saw the iPod his heart slammed like a sledgehammer against his ribs. *Abigail.*

Julia.

What the hell was she doing?

But he knew the answer. She was letting him know she was there.

Raissi examined the iPod and met Michael's gaze for a brief moment. If he thought the arrival of the iPod strange, he didn't show it. He simply dropped it on the desk and moved to the security panel to deactivate the alarm.

In the abrupt silence, Michael heard a helicopter nearing his home. While Raissi reset the alarm, Muammar duct-taped Brad's hands again. Michael caught his security guard's gaze, and Brad winked at him over Muammar's shoulder.

Michael dropped his attention to the carpet and felt his heart continuing to pound like a sledgehammer, its rhythm matching the approaching helicopter's thumping blades.

Julia. Jesus, what was she doing?

Worley and Harris lay on the ground at the edge of the woods, waiting for the HRT sniper to drop the dog.

Worley and Harris were pissed, but neither let it interfere with their concentration. They were supposed to be in the house already, in position, but the little stunt someone had played setting off the security alarm and the floodlights had delayed their secret entrance into the house. Now they'd be a few seconds behind everyone else but it wouldn't matter. Raissi was going down.

IR thermal imaging showed the hostages were in the northeastern quadrant of the house, all contained in Michael Stone's study, and all sitting down. No telltale signs of bombs rigged to their bodies could be seen.

Two human figures could be observed standing and moving

freely around the room. Two more on the main level covered the front and back doors. One upstairs guarded the balcony. Tangos. With guns, but similarly free of body explosives.

Lt. Diamond advised his men of the location and the apparent lack of booby-trapped bodies. The two SEALs shared a quiet high-five.

And then, as the men returned their vigilance to the kennel, the dog disappeared into the house.

Koburn's voice spoke in their ears, addressing Buchanan. "The dog has been taken into the house. Do you copy? Over."

Buchanan was silent for a long moment. "This is Bluebell. I copy. Proceed as planned."

Worley and Harris took off for the kennel. They had just found the cut rubber curtain when a somewhat familiar, but out-of-place voice came over their headsets. They both froze.

"Special Agent Buchanan," the woman's voice said, "listen closely. The odds we talked about are now stacked in your favor. I have removed Semtex from the back door that enters the kitchen, but there are wires across the downstairs windows attached to bricks of C4. Ditto on the basement windows and probably those on the second floor. Do not, I repeat, *do not* send the SEALs in through the windows. Come in through the back door. It's clean and unlocked. Do you copy?"

"Agent Quinn!" For the first time, Buchanan raised his voice. "Get the hell out of there. You are jeopardizing this mission."

"Your mission needs to be a covert operation, no guns going off until your men have Raissi in their sights, no explosions. Do not let Heller approach the house or drop anyone on the roof," she continued. "I'm about to give you all the diversion you need to simply walk in the kitchen door and resolve this conflict. Are you ready? Here it comes."

A microsecond later, the house went dark.

Another microsecond and Buchanan's voice came through loud and clear. "Back door. Go!"

Worley and Harris crawled back out of the kennel and, staying low to the ground, entered the back door.

Chapter Forty-Six

The house went dark.

The cavalry's here, Michael thought.

As a human alarm went up from Raissi's men, Michael rocked his chair from side to side, straining to push it over. Rocking to the right, he tipped the chair off balance and landed hard on the Persian rug.

Worley went in first, Harris to his left. They passed through the kitchen silently, weapons drawn as they moved toward the front of the house. Worley brought his weapon to bear on a terrorist running toward him from the front of the house. "Tango One down!" he yelled as the man's body fell to the floor.

Harris fired at the same time as another terrorist appeared on the steps above them. "Tango Two down!" The terrorist's body rolled down the stairs.

The helicopter bringing Heller was landing on the front lawn and the noise in Worley's headset was deafening. Adrenaline pumped through his body. As he neared the door to Michael Stone's study, he caught another terrorist coming through the door. *Bam,* and the man went down. "Tango Three down!"

Rounding the doorframe of the office, his eyes picked up the light coming from the helicopter's beams through the front window. He had no trouble pinpointing the man he'd studied a picture of an hour before.

Fayez Raissi looked him in the eye and time went into slow motion. Raissi had a large gun in his hand, but instead of pointing it at Worley, he aimed the gun toward a target in the middle of the room.

Bomb. Worley's brain seized on the thought.

Raissi was in his kill zone. Worley squeezed the trigger of his weapon, firing a double burst at the man's forehead.

He was a dead man.

Michael Stone knew he was dead the minute he heard the sound of a gun discharging in the hallway. Rocking himself onto the floor had been his only hope of survival.

He had failed. Raissi pointed the gun at Stone's chest, covered with Semtex, and pulled the trigger. Before the bullet hit him, he saw Raissi's head snap back, brains dislodged and flying over his desk.

He closed his eyes, thinking he heard Pongo bark.

Chapter Forty-Seven

Julia buried her face in Pongo's fur, her breath coming in gasps from the anxiety tightening around her lungs like a steel band. A weapon cracked above her head, making her and Pongo both jump. He lunged toward the stairs, barking madly, but she pulled him back. She felt a tingling sensation in her fingers where they grasped his collar. She forced a deep breath in through her nose, willing her heart to slow down. She would not hyperventilate, dammit, before she got to Michael.

More weapons retorted above her and she instinctively pulled Pongo further back. There was static over her headset and the beat of the helicopter blades were drowning out the shouts coming from inside, but her hope soared as she heard the SEALs call out their death list.

Pressing one of the ear buds of the headset deeper into her ear, she covered it with her hand, trying to hear what the SEALs were reporting. A second later, she heard the words that stopped her heart.

"Michael Stone down!"

Michael Stone down. The words rang in an endless loop in her ears.

Julia ripped the headset off and flipped the generator back on. Then she rushed up the stairs, Pongo racing beside her. Grabbing the doorframe, she catapulted herself down the hallway and into the office.

Oh God, please don't die, Michael. Please don't die.

Agent Koburn heard the count of downed tangos. Heard the call for the medic from Worley and the "clear" announcements from the other SEALs securing the house. All the tangos were dead. All the hostages were accounted for. A demolition team was moving in to disable the rest of the bombs.

Securing her rifle, she started down the hillside. The horizon was just beginning to brighten. The clouds had cleared. Tim Buchanan met her at the bottom of the hill. "What the hell was that?" he said, hands on his hips.

Elaina didn't need to ask what he was referring to. "I don't know, sir." She shrugged. "But it worked."

"Goddamn spooks," Tim muttered as he started jogging toward the house.

Elaina fell in beside him and laughed under her breath.

Julia hit the doorway into the study, taking in the scene in the blink of eye. Dead men lay sprawled on the floor. King, Allen and Kinnick lined the couch, talking loudly in the aftermath of the siege.

In the middle of the room on the floor lay a bruised and bloodied Michael Stone.

Jumping over one of the dead terrorists, Julia flew to his side, falling on her knees next to Worley. He and Harris were cutting the unconscious man loose from the toppled chair. The left side of Stone's face sported an irregular purple and black bruise that was splattered with drops of his own blood.

Raissi's bullet had torn through his left shoulder, missing his heart and a sheet of Semtex by a mere inch. Pongo shoved his head under Julia's arm to sniff at the explosive and his master, but Julia stopped him and pushed him back. At her command, he dropped to the floor and whined.

Julia gently cradled Michael's face in her hands. "Come on, Michael. Stay with me."

Worley grabbed her right hand and pressed it into the gaping wound in Michael's shoulder, telling her to put pressure on it as he removed the blasting cap from the sheet of explosive and pulled the tape strapping it to Michael's chest off. Julia rested her other hand on top of her right and continued to whisper encouragement to Michael as she pressed down, trying to stop the flow of warm blood. Michael's life was draining out between her fingers.

Harris started an IV. A minute later, EMTs, who had been standing by during the counterassault, were ushered in, snaking a gurney through the crowded room. Someone pulled

Julia out of the way and she watched as one medical worker placed an oxygen mask on Michael and began recording his vitals while the other talked to the hospital that would be receiving their patient.

Worley spoke into his headset microphone. "L.T., we're going to need that helo to transport Michael Stone. He's lost a lot of blood."

Julia couldn't hear the response but saw Worley nod to the closest EMT. "You're cleared to use the helo."

The man nodded back and the two medics and Harris lifted Michael onto the gurney. He moaned, his eyelashes fluttering. Julia stepped forward and touched his face. "You made it, Michael. You're going to be okay."

His eyes opened and he struggled to keep them that way. He mumbled something incoherent and Julia pulled the oxygen mask away from his mouth. "What?" she asked, leaning close to his face.

"I'm sorry," he sighed.

Julia smiled at him. "Sorry for what? You did great. Everything's going to be okay."

"For yelling at you," he whispered.

Tears stung her eyes and she brushed his lips with hers. "I deserved it. Now go get yourself fixed up, Stone. We still have some work to do."

The medics replaced the oxygen mask and pushed her out of the way. The floor and doorway were cleared to let the gurney pass and Julia followed it until it was out the kitchen door. When she was back in the office, Worley gave her an antiseptic wipe to clean her hands. Lt. Diamond had entered the room and he, Harris and Belcini were releasing the other three men from the couch.

Brad Kinnick addressed Titus. "Permission to go with Director Stone, sir?"

Allen pulled duct tape off one of his wrists and rubbed it before slapping Kinnick on the back. "Of course," the DCI said. "And let me know if anyone, including Susan Richmond, tries to see Michael before I get there. Don't let anyone in on my orders. I'll have backup for you within the hour and be there myself as soon as I can."

Kinnick gave Julia a nod as he left. She waited for Director Allen to shake hands with the SEALs before approaching him.

He smiled at her. "Ms. Torrison," he said, stepping over Raissi's body and picking up the iPod from Michael's desk. "Your calling card, I presume?"

Julia nodded. "Yes, sir."

Titus held out a hand to her. "You are definitely Conrad Flynn's partner. That was the foolhardiest thing I've seen in a long time, and I enjoyed every minute of it."

Julia saw the questioning glances Worley and the others sent her way, but she nodded and returned his handshake. "Sir," she said, "we still have a serious breach of CIA security. Did Michael explain everything that's going on?"

Elaina Koburn and Tim Buchanan entered the room and Buchanan advanced on her. "You don't have clearance to be in here, Ms. Quinn."

But before he could continue yelling at her, Titus shut him down. "Put a sock in it, Buchanan. She's one of mine, and I'll take care of her."

Buchanan pulled up short, and Titus turned back to Julia. "I know what's going on with Susan. Where are Flynn and Smith? I want to talk to all of you."

Worley rose from the terrorist body he was examining. "Conrad Flynn and Ryan Smith? We caught them in the woods. They were attempting to follow you"—he pointed at Julia—"into the house. We immobilized them."

Lt. Diamond stepped forward. "They handcuffed both men and left them where they found them. I notified Chief Richmond before I came in here of their whereabouts."

"Oh no." Julia exchanged a look with Titus. Daniel King was trying to quietly slip out the door. "Daniel," Titus barked. King froze in the doorway. "Don't go too far. We still need to have that talk."

Senator King nodded and left with his head down. Then Titus addressed Diamond and Buchanan both. "Those men are in danger from Chief Richmond." He motioned to Worley. "Show us where you left them."

Julia followed on Worley's heels, Harris running alongside her, Titus behind her and Agents Buchanan and Koburn bringing up the rear. A minute later all six were standing in the woods.

"They're gone," Worley announced.

"Of course they are," Titus said, looking around.

Julia thought she would scream. She clenched her fists and paced a few feet away, her mind trying to think of what to do, but nothing concrete would come. Her brain was as exhausted and overloaded on adrenaline as her body. She felt like running back to the FBI's operational base, but she knew Susan wasn't there. She'd taken Con and Smitty, and Julia had no idea where.

Two more paces and she threw her head back and yelled at the top of her lungs. "God*dammit!*" Then she kicked the tree, not once, but three times. "I'm going to kill her. She hurts one hair on their heads, and I will kill her!"

Pongo jumped and barked at her, pushed his head into her hand.

Hanging her head, she fell to her knees, grabbing Pongo and hugging him for all he was worth.

"Yes, siree, you are definitely Conrad Flynn's partner." Titus chuckled from behind her.

Julia turned to find everyone staring at her. She took a deep breath and let it out slowly. "Excuse my outburst," she said, getting back to her feet. "It's been one very long, crappy night."

Everyone smiled at her except for Buchanan. "Where would Chief Richmond take them?"

Julia shook her head and started to answer, but her cell phone vibrated inside the pocket of the FBI jacket. She pulled it out and heard a familiar voice.

"Sheba?"

"Ace? Where are Con and Smitty? Have you seen them?"

"Yeah, they went by in the backseat of a Caddie a few minutes ago. Connie was in the window yelling something at me when they drove by, but I don't know what he was sayin'. Me and Cari didn't know what to do, so we tried to follow the Caddie. We lost sight of it a few minutes ago, but I think it's headed to the lake I scoped Big Mike out at when he was running that morning. Y'know where I mean?"

Julia spoke to Buchanan. "Susan's kidnapped them and is on her way to the lake northeast of here. It's about two and half miles if you take the path on the east side of the house. Michael runs that path every morning. If you drive there, it's twice as far because the road to it frames part of this property and a horse farm adjacent to it."

"We can use the other helicopter," he said to Titus. The smaller aircraft that would have dropped Belcini on the roof was still sitting in a field nearby unused.

"I can run it before you even get the helicopter in the air," Worley said. "Just tell me what you want me to do once I get there."

Everyone looked at Titus. "Our object is to save Conrad Flynn and Ryan Smith, but I want Susan Richmond alive and well enough to torture."

The group froze and Titus smiled. "Oh, for crying out loud, get your panties out of a bunch. You don't really believe I would torture her, do you? But, seriously, I do want her alive. So I can talk to her."

Lt. Diamond gave Worley a nod and the SEAL took off. Then he radioed the house and ordered Harris and two more of his SEALs to join Worley.

"Is that another of my long-lost operatives you're talking to?" Titus asked Julia.

"No, sir. Just a friend."

"I'm the wheelman!" Ace shouted in her ear. "Tell him, I'm the wheelman."

"How close are you to the lake?" Julia asked him.

"We're bumping closer every minute," Ace answered. "Wish I had the Jeep. Baby loves this kind of terrain."

"Are there any weapons in the van?"

"This van belong to Conrad Flynn? Sheesh, what a question."

Julia sighed. "Right. You and Cari armed?"

"Cari's double barreling it right now."

Titus motioned for Julia to give him the phone. "Young man," he said. "Do you know how to create a diversion?"

Julia could hear Ace's affirmative reply. Titus motioned for everyone to follow him while he spoke. "Here's what I want you to do."

Chapter Forty-Eight

Steam was rising off the lake as the sun broke over the hill. The light reflected on the water left from the night's storm and the leaves of the trees looked fresh and clean.

It made a cool picture, Conrad thought, except for the fact he and Smitty were wearing flexi-cuffs and facing the business end of a Magnum .44 with Susan Richmond's finger on the trigger.

The partners stood on the lone boat dock, side by side. Conrad's hands were completely asleep and his arms tingled as his circulation continued to be cut off.

But even though he and Smitty were about to die, he was glad Julia was safe. She'd pulled off the stupidest, most asinine move he'd ever seen, but she was alive.

Stone had made it too. With Conrad out of the picture, maybe Julia'd go back to him and live happily ever after.

Over my dead body.

"You're toast, Susan." He took another step back. Smitty did the same. "Even your backup plan failed. Stone and Allen are alive and they know everything. Why kill us now? You're only adding murder to your list of crimes."

Susan smiled at him. "I'm starting over, Flynn, and you're the only one who could possibly track me down. It's time for me to be rid of you once and for all."

Behind her, a helicopter rose over the hill and zeroed in on them. Susan looked over her shoulder at it and while she did, Con whispered to Smitty, "You know how to swim with your arms tied behind your back?"

The look Smitty sent him was total disbelief. "No problem," Conrad said, even though this was a big fucking problem. "Just jump in the lake when I say."

"Looks like our time is up." Susan tightened her grip on the gun. "Back up another step so when I shoot you, your bodies fall in the water."

Conrad took another step, a big step, back. His heel was almost hanging off the edge of the dock. Smitty turned and looked over his shoulder at Con, his face white, his eyes wide. Then he glanced at the water and the mist rising all around them, but he didn't step back.

Smitty was scared shitless.

"Move," Susan ordered him, but he just stood frozen to the dock.

Con saw Susan's cool slip a notch, saw her hand twitch before she pushed the end of the Magnum against Smitty's forehead. "I said, move back."

And then Conrad heard Smitty laugh low in his throat. "No," he said. "I'm done taking orders from you, Susan. You can't order me to my death."

Holy crap, Smitty had just grown a spine. Conrad cleared his throat and yelled at the top of his lungs, "Hallelujah!"

At that moment, the Forever Flowers van came careening out of the woods, doing, Conrad guessed, about twenty miles an hour more than it should have been. It swerved, righted, swerved again. Ace was driving. Cari was hanging out the passenger window, yelling her head off and shooting at the sky with Conrad's favorite HK MP5. "Now who has the big gun?" she screamed at him before ripping off another burst of bullets.

Susan jerked at the distraction and from behind her Cadillac, a SEAL, dressed in camo, rose up, his weapon pointed at her. "Stop!" he called. "Drop your weapon."

Two more appeared out of nowhere, one from behind a rock, one from behind a tree. The helicopter swooped over them to land in an open sandy area.

Susan looked in all directions and lowered her gun.

But she didn't drop it.

The turn she executed was sharp, her gun hand snapping up and pointing at Conrad. As he saw her finger pull the trigger, he pushed off the dock with his toes and dropped like a weight into the water.

In the helicopter, Julia's hand was pressed flat on the door. She saw the SEALs emerge from their hiding places. She saw Susan give up.

And then she saw her turn. Saw Susan raise her gun and heard the gun go off over the sound of the helicopter blades.

Her hand slammed against the door, and she screamed Conrad's name as his body dropped off the dock like a dead man.

Before Buchanan could set the helicopter firmly on the ground, Julia shot out of it, running toward the dock for all she was worth. Tears streamed down her cheeks.

Worley jumped into the lake after Conrad as Susan was disarmed by Harris. He was handcuffing her as Julia approached. Without hesitating, Julia pulled out her gun and stiff-armed Susan in the head with it as she ran by. Susan went down on the dock with a heavy thud.

Passing Smitty, Julia stuck the gun back in her waistband and dove in after Con.

Chapter Forty-Nine

Prague, two weeks later...

Susan Richmond admired the beads made of Czech glass hanging in an explosion of iridescent red, electric blue and pale green around her wrist. She had purchased the trinket on Nerudova Street, a winding walkway of designer shops and cafés in *Mala Strana*, for less than twenty American dollars. It was a nice addition to her collection of jewelry souvenirs from the European cities she had visited so far.

Making her way past Prague Castle, she continued to survey and enjoy the architecturally stunning capital of the Czech Republic. *Stare Mesto*, the Old Town, and *Mala Strana*, the Lesser Town, were equally rich in art, music and culture. A perfect blending of medieval and modern. A mecca for someone with her tastes.

Out of habit, she stopped several times along the way to check if anyone was following her. It was easy after a few weeks of watching and not seeing a tail to grow careless. She was determined not to. Moving around from one European capital to another kept her alert while providing a multitude of places to blend in amongst the thousands of residents and tourists bustling around. Her trail was growing cold to the CIA and that lessened her anxiety, but she would continue to move around for another year, maybe two, before she settled in one place for any length of time.

That was all right with her. At first she had been furious both her plans had failed so miserably. After all the planning and strategizing, to have it end with her on the run was ridiculous. But of course she had planned for that outcome, just in case, and it had paid off. The bribe for the convenient mix-up during her booking. The help of a certain CIA administrator she'd been sleeping with for years to get her out of the country. The promise to a certain dictator that she could supply him and his friends with unending information about the United States' plans for them. All of it had paid off. She had plenty of money to support her travels and plenty of smarts to keep herself alive.

St. Vitus Cathedral, the final resting place of St. Wenceslas, rose up before her and she stopped. The church's immense stature alone was mesmerizing, its doors beckoning her inside.

The smell of Catholicism, burning candles, wood and peace, filled her nostrils as she entered. It had been years since she'd been in any church, but in this place, she fell naturally into the movements and rituals all Catholics learn. She automatically genuflected and made the sign of the cross before entering a pew to sit down.

She allowed herself to daydream for awhile in the safety and sanctity of the cathedral, enjoying the quiet sounds of priest robes and nun skirts and murmured prayers. Tourists came and went. Others—mothers, fathers, friends—came and bowed their heads, lit candles, prayed in pews. Susan closed her eyes and waited for her lover.

She heard the man before she saw him. Heard the brush of his coat on the end of the pew. With her eyes still closed, she smiled. Finally, Jurgen had come. He had been promising to catch up with her as soon as he was sure no one was following him. Susan knew today was the day they would be together again.

Opening her eyes, she took in the brown hair, perfectly trimmed over the collar of the man's black trench coat and felt a spurt of uncertainty. It wasn't Jurgen, but the man was familiar. She fingered the bracelet. Something was wrong. Where was Jurgen?

A second man moved into the pew directly behind her, the lightest touch of his fingers grazing her neck. Cold fear ran down her spine. She glanced around. The church was suddenly too empty.

"Enjoying your vacation, Chief?" the man behind her murmured in her ear.

She went utterly still at the sound of his voice. It couldn't be. For all of her vigilance, she had still become the cornered animal. Forcing herself to breathe, she continued to face forward, daring either man to make a scene.

And then, Julia Torrison plopped into the pew next to her. "Wow, how did you get that nasty bruise on the side of your face?"

"You." Susan couldn't keep the venom out of her voice. "How did you find me?"

Julia smiled. "Your boyfriend ratted you out right before I put a bullet in his head."

Susan's chest heaved as she gulped air. It wasn't so much Jurgen's death that shook her, but the fact she had truly been beat at her own game by one of her pupils. Her mind grasped at straws. "You killed him? You've never even shot anyone."

"Wrong. I shot Benito Raines."

Susan stared at Julia's eyes. She didn't believe she'd killed Jurgen, but there was something there, something more hardcore than Susan had ever seen in Julia before. She looked away, spoke over her shoulder to Conrad Flynn. "I thought you quit the CIA. Why are you tracking me?"

Flynn's chuckle was hot on her neck. "Still have sources feeding you from the inside, don't you? I'll be sure to hunt them down too."

Regaining some of her composure, Susan was still aware of the pulse beating wildly in her head. "The game is over for me, Solomon. You were all just pawns in it and now it's done. I have no interest in any of you anymore. I'm an old woman. I just want to be left alone. You're safe."

Ryan Smith turned in the pew in front of her, resting his arm on the back and giving her a crooked grin. "We'd like to take out a little insurance on that."

The words slipped out of her mouth before she could stop them. "What kind of insurance?"

Flynn's fingers were suddenly around her throat, tightening just enough to make her gasp. She dug at his fingers with her own, the glass bracelet tinkling from her desperate movements.

He spoke in her ear. "Let's go back to your motel room, and we'll talk about it."

Chapter Fifty

Arlington, twenty-four hours later

Michael was barely putting one foot in front of the other, and Brad was having no trouble keeping up twenty feet behind him. He was sweating like a pig, but by God, he was running. The surgeons had done a good job and the wound in his upper chest was healing nicely. Only a pink scar and a little pain when he ran reminded him of his close brush with death.

He had relived the hostage situation over and over again in his mind. Saw himself going down those basement stairs to turn the generator on. Saw Brad with the gun held at his temple. Felt the blow from the rifle.

There were nights when he swore he heard Raissi's voice outside his bedroom door. There were dreams where he stared down a bullet.

And lost.

He would wake, a scream echoing inside his head, and he would think of Julia.

Stopping on the path, he bent over at the waist and rested his hands on his knees. He pulled in several deep breaths and caught movement out of the corner of his eye.

"Damn, and me without my oxygen," the man said, and Michael looked up. Conrad Flynn stood a few feet away, laughter in his eyes.

Pushing himself up, Michael felt anger explode deep in his stomach that the man he hated almost as much as Fayez Raissi had caught him at a weak moment. "Do you have something to report, or are you just here to annoy me?"

Flynn looked toward the lake as he reached in his pants pocket and drew out a multicolored glass bead bracelet.

Throwing it to Michael, he said, "The job is done, *boss.*"

Michael let it drop on the ground near his feet. Feeling the pain over his heart subsiding, he drew in one more deep breath and put his hands on his hips. "Did you kill her?"

Flynn shook his head no. "Jules wouldn't let me."

At the mention of Julia, Michael looked away. "You brought her back, though? Turned her over to authorities?"

"We turned her and Jurgen Damgaard over to Titus an hour ago. He and a few special friends of his met us at the airport. Susan won't get away this time."

It was done. The problem had been eliminated. Michael didn't have to worry about Julia's safety anymore. He could rebuild his Operations group and move forward.

But it ate at him that Titus had used Flynn to bring Susan back. "How many people have you killed?" he asked.

Flynn shot a dark look at him. "You don't really want me to answer that, do you?"

Michael shrugged. "Technically, you don't work for me in any official capacity right now. Technically, on the books, you're still dead."

Flynn shrugged. "Not as many as you think." He shifted his gaze back toward the horizon and squinted. "But enough."

"No surprise." Michael stretched his arms over his head. "Smith has been reinstated as Chief of Operations/Europe, has received a glowing letter of appreciation from President Jeffries, and will be honored with the distinguished CIA Intelligence Medal. Ace Harmon has been cleared of his fugitive status and will receive a letter of commendation from the DCI before the end of the month. Cari Von Motz is working with Titus to secure a tight prosecution of Susan in return for her own leniency.

"Julia has been offered, but has not yet accepted, Susan's position as Counterterrorism Chief, and I've accepted the Deputy Director of Central Intelligence position to replace Damgaard. What about you, Flynn? What are you going to do with yourself now?"

"I also received a presidential letter of appreciation, you know. President Jeffries was quite abundant in his praise of my *honorable* actions."

Michael crossed his arms and waited.

Flynn laughed, shook his head. "No quarter from you, huh?

Actually, Titus and I were just discussing my options at the airport. He said it was up to you whether I still had a job or not. He says he put in a good word for me."

Michael clamped his jaw and looked out toward the lake. He kept his voice level. "He suggested I offer you my previous position as Director of Operations."

Flynn whistled under his breath and then laughed. "You and me together in the same building every day. How long do you think it would take us to kill each other?"

"Do you think you deserve such a promotion? I don't."

"Why do you hate me so much? Is it that whole Navy-Jarhead thing? Did I fuck you over in a previous life or something?" He tapped his temple with a finger. "Oh, right. I forgot. That was *this* life, wasn't it?"

"You are such an ass," Michael said. "What in God's name does Julia see in you?"

"You know, I was just thinking the same thing about you."

Michael's fist moved on its on accord, slamming Flynn in the eye and sending him down on his back in the dirt.

"Damn, that hurt." Michael shook his fingers out and held his left hand out to stop Brad from approaching. "And yet, I'm pretty sure I want to do it again."

"Uh-oh," Ace Harmon and Ryan Smith said at the same time. Taking their matching pairs of binoculars away from their eyes, they exchanged a glance.

"Maybe I better run down there and break this up before it gets out of hand," Ace said.

They were lying in the grass fifty yards uphill from the path watching the scene below. Smitty shook his head. "No way. The first rule of surveillance is to never give your presence away."

"What if they kill each other?"

"It won't go that far. Stone's security officer will stop it if necessary."

Ace brought his binoculars back to his face. "Mikey's a big guy. Think Connie can take him?"

"With or without his gun?"

Ace shot a glance at Smitty again. "Tell me Connie's not armed."

"He's not armed."

"Shit," he said at the obvious lie.

"The man is *always* armed. His hands alone are a lethal weapon."

"Why did Big Mike hit him? I thought he would be happy you guys found Susan Richmond and brought her back to the States."

Smitty shrugged. "My guess is they're talking about Julia."

"Oh. This is going to get ugly, isn't it?"

"Yeah." Smitty dug in his pants pocket and pulled out a small camera. "And I've got video."

"I got a twenty says Flynn wins."

Smitty eyed Ace with disbelief. "You want me to bet against the Great Conrad Flynn?" He laughed, bringing his binoculars back up to his eyes. "You're on." The two shook hands.

"Shit," Conrad spit out, holding a hand over his eye. "What'd you do that for?" He tried to sit up with the little balance he still had.

"Don't go and mess with Julia's head again, Flynn. She deserves better than that."

Michael Stone wasn't as gimped as he'd thought. "Save it." He blinked through his hazy view to gauge how far he had to move to reach Stone's legs. "I'm back in the living world. I'm free to do what I want and what I want is to make up for lost time with her."

Stone took a step closer to him and Conrad flinched at the thought of another blow. When Stone stuck out his hand, palm up, Conrad stared up at him, calculating the sincerity of the offer before he accepted it. Stone hauled him to his feet, but Conrad didn't let go. In the next second he hooked his foot around Stone's leg and pushed him backwards. Stone held on and pulled Conrad with him, twisting and throwing him to the ground.

Damn, for a guy who's been shot recently, he's stronger than I expected. Conrad got in a stomach punch before Stone could block it, and he heard the man grunt, but his satisfaction was short lived as Stone's left hand shot out, looking to make contact with Conrad's face.

Conrad dug his heels in and pushed up, causing Stone's fist to land on his collarbone. Rolling away, he jumped up on his feet, but lost his balance and staggered backwards a couple of paces. Breathing hard, he watched Stone slowly get up on his knees, then his feet.

"You are an arrogant piece of shit," Stone said, between breaths, but he didn't make any move toward Conrad.

Conrad laughed. He and Stone both needed this. Physical release of their hatred for each other. "And you hit like a girl."

As expected, Stone rushed him. He turned sideways just before impact to embed his elbow in the man's ribs, but it was an even trade. Stone sunk his right fist into Conrad's kidney and they both crashed to the ground again.

Five minutes later, both men were panting and dripping sweat as they hung over at the waist, staring each other down. "Give up?" Conrad said, praying Stone would say yes.

Stone wiped at the blood on his bottom lip. "Never."

But Conrad took it as a good sign he didn't come at him. His legs were shaking and he was still seeing two of everything. Maybe it was time for a distraction. "Did Julia...ever tell you...about her childhood?"

Stone blinked and looked away. Conrad recognized he'd hit a nerve. "She didn't share her past with too many people." He coughed between breaths. "She didn't want them to look at her...you know...like a victim."

Stone's eyes narrowed as he met Conrad's again. "But she told you."

Conrad straightened up. "Her real father was never in the picture. When Julia was four years old, Valerie married Jimmy Valhuis. He was abusive to both of them. A year after Val and Jimmy married, Eric was born." Conrad paused as Stone stood up, eyeing him warily. When Stone made no move toward him, he relaxed his guard. "Jimmy didn't usually take his anger out on Eric, but one day, when Julia was eleven and Eric was six, Jimmy came home from the local bar and found the boy in Julia's room playing with her Barbie dolls. He went ballistic and started beating Eric up. Julia was scared, thought Jimmy was going to kill her little brother. Mom was at work, and she didn't know what to do.

"Jimmy kept a piece of metal pipe beside his bed to defend himself, Julia said, in case someone broke into their house in the middle of the night. She ran into the room, grabbed the pipe from under the bed and went to kill her stepfather. He had Eric down on the floor strangling him. Julia walked right up behind him and laid that pipe across the back of Jimmy's head twice, knocking him off Eric, but not knocking him out."

"Christ," Stone muttered, rubbing his forehead.

Conrad continued. "After a minute he gained his feet and went after her. He ended up breaking her arm, but he never touched Eric again. She said from that point on, Jimmy focused most of his abuse on her, and she took it because it was worth the price to keep her little brother safe."

"Jesus Christ." Stone walked several paces away, hanging his head.

Conrad knew exactly how he felt. "Makes you want to hunt the guy down, doesn't it?"

"I can't believe you haven't already."

"Crossed my mind more than once, but it seems like revenge on Jimmy Valhuis is Julia's prerogative. She's a better person than I am. She'll never do it."

Stone shook his head in disgust and wiped his forehead with the sleeve of his sweatshirt.

Conrad wiped his own face off with his hands. "All these years, she's been trying to make the world safer for everybody else and wanting more than anything to feel safe herself. She felt that way with me, and then I betrayed her. I have a lot to make up for."

Stone shook his head. "She's better off without you."

Conrad felt his anger rising again. "You're saying that because you still want her for yourself."

"She'll come back to me if you just leave her alone. I can give her the sort of life she deserves. All she wants right now is some time to sort things out."

"You don't get it, do you? She's not coming back to you. She's not coming back to the CIA *because* of you."

Stone didn't answer, but turned his back to Conrad and started walking back the way he'd come.

Conrad raised his voice to Stone's receding back. "If you expect Julia to come back to you, you're dreaming."

Stone turned on his heel and pointed an accusing finger in Conrad's direction. "Julia blamed herself for your death and you let her. You are a walking, breathing lie, Flynn. Nothing more, nothing less." The finger was in Conrad's face now. "She trusted you. You had this wonderful woman and you tossed her aside like yesterday's paper for your *job*."

The finger turned back to Stone's own chest. "I'm the one who picked up the pieces after you deceived her. I'm the one who held her when she cried. I'm the one who helped her get her life back here in America. Not you."

Conrad wanted to grab Stone's finger and break it. Instead he took a step back. "Will you leave the Agency for her? If she doesn't have to face you every day, she'll take Susan's job."

The muscle in Stone's jaw twitched and he dropped his hand back to his side. "I don't love my job any more than I love Julia, but I won't walk away from the CIA right now. Too many people are depending on me."

Conrad laughed. "Exactly what I told myself when I faked my death. If I didn't flush out the rogue CIA, others were going to die, my country was going to be compromised, Julia's life was at stake." He looked at Stone. "So I saved the day, but I lost something more valuable."

"And now you think you can reclaim it." Stone shook his head. "Love doesn't work that way. Leave her alone."

I can't, Conrad thought. He turned his back on Stone. "See you at the office," he called over his shoulder, "*boss*."

Chapter Fifty-One

Julia's apartment, an hour later.

Julia stepped out of the shower to find a mug of steaming coffee waiting for her. She smiled, took a sip and got herself dressed.

She was so unbelievably tired—jet lag was hell—and yet so unbelievably happy.

Her heart had frozen solid when it looked like Susan had shot Conrad on the boat dock that day. But he wasn't shot, just pulling some stupid SEAL maneuver and giving her a heart attack. Michael had recovered from his gun wound and was back at Langley already in his new position as Titus's right hand man. She, Conrad, Smitty and Ace had been cleared of any wrongdoing. She'd even gone to Ben Raines and made peace with him. She and Titus had set up a deal with the Justice Department to clear Cari's name in exchange for her testimony against Susan, and Julia had helped her fill out papers to become a legal citizen of the United States. Senator King had temporarily left his post until the conclusion of a special investigation into his dealings with Susan.

Susan.

Julia, with Smitty and Con's help, had tracked her down and brought her back to face prosecution. It wasn't as satisfying as Julia had hoped it would be, but she'd done the right thing, no matter what Con said.

And now she was due in forty minutes for a job interview with the FBI. Agent Buchanan had recruited her to work on his East Coast HRT, but his offer was not so different from Abigail's analyst job. Titus had offered her Susan's job and she would have jumped at it if it hadn't meant seeing Michael every day.

She couldn't do that to him. Or herself.

Turning Buchanan down hadn't been hard, and he had offered to feel out his boss about a different line of work for her. Fieldwork, hunting down felons. She was excited and she didn't even know exactly what she was getting herself into, but that wasn't going to stop her.

Grabbing her coffee, she left the bathroom and found Con at her kitchen table, reading the morning news, a plate of bagels on the counter, cut and ready for cream cheese. "Hi, Navy boy."

He looked at her over the top of the paper, and Julia saw one of his eyes was red and swelled. She knew where he'd been and decided not to ask what had happened. He raised the eyebrow over his normal eye. "We just got in from Germany two hours ago and you're dressed to go to work. What are you? Super Girl?"

"Wonder Woman. I have an interview with the FBI this morning."

He whistled under his breath. "The FBI, huh? Sounds important."

Julia smeared cream cheese on two bagel halves and pressed them together. "I'm ready to try something different."

"Like what?"

Julia dug a sandwich bag out of her cupboard and stuck the bagel in it. "I've got the bug again. I think I want to get back in the field."

Conrad lowered the paper and waggled both eyebrows at her. "Need a partner?"

"No." Grabbing her purse off the chair, she pulled out the keys to her Audi and tossed them across the table at him. "But I do need a driver."

Another killer day over in his still somewhat new position as Deputy Director of Central Intelligence, Michael Stone threw his briefcase on the kitchen counter and drew in a deep breath.

Pongo trotted into the kitchen with a brand new rawhide dog bone the size of a small child's leg hanging out of his mouth and dropped it at Michael's feet.

"Where'd you get that, boy?" he said, frowning at the bone. Pongo whimpered and wagged his stubby tail.

Michael continued to frown as he bent over to pet the dog. He had not given Pongo the bone and the only person Pongo had ever accepted treats from, besides him, was Julia.

With a lurch in his heart, Michael stood and, pulling his tie out of the neck of his shirt, took the stairs two at a time to his bedroom.

At the top of the stairs, he felt the hair on the back of his neck rise and he stopped short.

All was quiet. He could pick up no hint of anything out of place or anyone in his house.

But as he crossed into the bedroom, it hit him full force. Lavender. Not just an innocent trace of it. An unabashedly rich essence that made his knees weak.

Abigail.

Julia.

His gaze darted around the room and he called her name hesitantly. He hurried to the French doors and threw them open to see if she was sitting out on the deck.

Nothing.

She was not there. He started for the adjoining bathroom and that's when his eyes saw the envelope on the bed, his name written in her tidy, elegant hand. Snatching the envelope up, he ripped it open. A picture fell out, landing on the bed, while he unfolded the note inside.

Dearest Michael,

Abigail Quinn is gone now but she was real. She was real because you reached out and helped her. Gave her reason to believe in fairytales again. Showed her there was a right way to live and there was something worth living for.

I, Julia Torrison, am forever in your debt. Even though I chose to leave your fairytale world, I'll always carry the perfect love you gave me in my heart.

The picture is to remind you that Abby was real and so was her love for you. Forever, Julia

Michael reached down and grabbed the picture. It was one Liz Scofield had snapped of him and Abigail while they were on the Scofields' sailboat. The two of them were laughing, Abby's face turned up to his as sunlight glimmered on the water in the background. And even though he knew her carefree manner had changed seconds after the picture was snapped, the unadulterated love in her eyes at that moment was like a soothing balm on his wounded heart.

Walking out to the balcony, he stood still and let the moon bathe him in light. Propping the picture on the ledge, he closed his eyes and whispered, *"Julia"*, into the night.

Epilogue

Cozumel, Mexico

Julia watched as Con made his way across the white sand, balancing two tall, gaudily outfitted tropical drinks in his hands. With his dark features and deeply tanned skin, he was beginning to look like one of the natives.

From the moment he'd sallied up to the bar with his signature alpha-male walk, he'd turned heads like light attracting moths. Female eyes appraised him and found him to their liking. Male eyes followed their companions' stares and a sudden wave of testosterone-driven posturing had begun.

Cozumel was beautiful and warm and a million miles from Langley. They'd needed a vacation and some time alone. They both had big career decisions waiting for them back in Arlington, but for this week, they could bask in the sun, snorkel in the ocean, make love on the beach and forget about their careers.

Still attracting attention, Conrad shot her a grin as he worked his way around a group of sunbathers dotting his path. She smiled back, absently rubbing the new silver band on her left ring finger.

Looking down at the book in her lap, she carefully reread a line of prose Emily Brontë had written more than a century before.

Whatever our souls are made of,
his and mine are the same.

Raising her head, Julia felt a warm ripple of familiarity when her gaze locked with Con's.

He's mine, she thought. *All mine.*

About the Author

Misty lives in a small town along the Mississippi River with her husband Mark, her twin sons Sam and Ben, and her big dog Max. She is an award- winning, multi-published author if CIA thrillers as well as paranormal comedy. To learn more about Misty, please visit www.readmistyevans.com. Send an email to Misty at misty@readmistyevans.com or join her Yahoo! group to join in the fun with other readers as well as Misty. http://groups.yahoo.com/group/MistyEvansSuspense.

*When a member of the CIA's premiere counter-terrorism unit
discovers the woman he loves is a suspected terrorist,
he'll go to any lengths to uncover the truth.*

Long Road Home
© 2007 Sharon Long

Jules Trehan disappeared without a trace three years ago much to the dismay of her parents and Manuel Ramirez. A counter-terrorism specialist, Manny has utilized every agency resource in his attempt to discover what happened to Jules, to no avail.

As suddenly as she disappeared, Jules reappears in a small Colorado town. Injured in an explosion, she's hospitalized, and Manny rushes to her side, determined not to ever let her go again.

But Jules has one last job to do or Manny's life will be forfeit. A mission she must complete, even if it means betraying the only man she's ever loved.

Available now in ebook and print from Samhain Publishing.

Enjoy the following excerpt from Long Road Home...

Jules stared out her window, the miles passing in a blur. To Manny she probably appeared as though she were resting, unaware of where they were going, but she was paying attention to every detail of the landscape.

She hadn't seen a sign in miles, but the location of the sinking sun told her they were headed south and slightly east. Likely into New Mexico or West Texas.

"If you want to know where we're going, all you have to do is ask," Manny said dryly.

She twisted in her seat, surprised once again at his perception. "Where are we going?"

"New Mexico." He didn't offer more and didn't look over at her though she was staring hard at him.

She sank lower in the seat, gingerly drawing her knees up to her chest. Her fingers stroked the duffle bag at her side, drawing assurance from the outline of the gun there. If anyone found her and Manny, at least she'd have a way to defend them.

A sharp pain twisted through her chest and robbed her of breath. She sucked in air, determined not to panic as the scenery blurred before her. Damn, her ribs were on fire. She reclined the seat in an attempt to alleviate the growing pressure in her midsection.

The pain eased as she stretched out, and her breathing evened. She pressed her hands to her temples and squeezed her eyes shut, the thudding of her pulse pounding incessantly against her fingertips.

"Speak to me, Jules. What's wrong? Do I need to get you back to the hospital?" Manny's concerned voice seared through her haze of pain.

"No," she said faintly. "I'm all right. Really."

"Where are you, baby? Because you're miles away from here right now."

She cringed, not wanting to voice what she had been thinking. It sounded pathetic and defeatist. But she blurted it out anyway. "I was thinking it should have been me who died. Not Mom and Pop."

To her surprise, he slammed on the brakes and pulled over

to the shoulder. He turned on her, his eyes blazing in the faint light offered by the headlights. "Don't say that. Don't ever say that," he said fiercely. "I thought I lost you, Jules. For three long years I lived with the awful reality you might not be coming home. And then I found you. Don't you dare wish you had died, because I've spent the last three years praying you were alive."

Before she could respond, he put his hand around the back of her neck and pulled her to meet his lips. Her mouth opened in surprise, and his tongue darted forward, gently probing her lips.

It was everything she had ever dreamed it would be. For a moment, she was in high school again, dressing for the prom, depressed because the one guy she wanted to take was eight years older and already out of college. She had closed her eyes and imagined it was Manny kissing her when her date had delivered her to the door with the prerequisite peck on the lips.

He was exquisitely gentle, his lips moving so softly across hers, reverently almost. His fingers worked slowly into her hair, kneading and stroking as he deepened his kiss.

Then, as suddenly as it had begun, it ended. He pulled quickly away from her and ran a hand through his hair in agitation. "Christ, I'm sorry, Jules. You don't need that right now."

She stared at him in shock. With a trembling hand, she raised her fingers and touched her slightly swollen lips.

"Don't look at me like that," he pleaded. He captured her hand and brought it to his lips, kissing it softly. "I'm sorry, baby."

He allowed her hand to slide from his, and she took it back, cradling it with her other hand. What was she supposed to say? She was so damn confused, she doubted she could recall her own name at the moment. For that matter, she really had no idea what her real name was. A hysterical bubble of laughter rose quickly in her throat, and she fought to choke it back.

Manny swore softly then pulled back onto the highway. "Get some sleep, Jules. If you don't, I swear, I'll call Tony and have you transferred to the hospital we'd planned. It's what I should've done in the first place."

"Who the hell is Tony anyway?" she grumbled as she lay back against the leather seat. She shivered slightly, and Manny reached over to turn up the heat.

"Tony is my partner."

"Partner in what? Somehow I doubt you're still in the computer software business." He looked far too dangerous to be a computer nerd. She had never been able to reconcile his image with his profession.

"Rest," he said in a warning tone. "We'll talk when we get there."

"Wherever there is," she said in exasperation.

He smiled.

"What's so funny?"

"You are. You're sounding more and more like the Jules I know all the time."

She sobered instantly, the throbbing in her head resuming with a vengeance. "I'm not her," she said softly. "Maybe I never was."

Manny remained silent, his hands gripping the steering wheel tighter. "Rest."

Not arguing, she turned to the window. She could never go back to that carefree, naïve girl she had once been. She'd seen and done far too much. In a faint moment of shame, she was glad Mom and Pop never got to see the person she'd become. Their disappointment would have been more than she could bear.

She raised trembling fingers to her lips, lips still swollen from Manny's kiss. What exactly were his feelings for her? She'd never imagined that he returned her sentiment, that he might want her just as badly as she'd wanted him, but in the face of the way he'd kissed her, she could hardly ignore the possibility. Had she been blind to the signs?

She thought back, trying to analyze Manny's behavior toward her. As a teenager, she'd idolized him, fantasized about being Mrs. Manuel Ramirez, but she'd been careful to keep her girlish imaginings to herself. She would have died if he'd found out the extent of her infatuation.

Three years ago, she would have done anything for Manny to kiss her like he just had, but now it only complicated matters. No matter how much she wanted him to be more than a big brother protective figure, it wasn't possible. And if he knew the truth about her, he wouldn't want her anyway.

"It's snowing." He turned to her when she looked over. "You used to love the snow."

"Yeah," she said faintly. But she didn't now. It was too easy to be tracked in the snow. She remained silent, not voicing that tidbit of information. Instead she watched the flurry of snowflakes through the windshield wipers.

The heat pouring from the vents and the steady hum of the wipers lulled her into a state of relaxation. Soon her eyes grew as heavy as her heart, and she allowed them to close. Her final thought was that she hoped it wasn't snowing wherever they ended up.

Pretending to be newlyweds is a dangerous game...
particularly if you're falling in love.

Holding Her Own
© 2008 Marie-Nicole Ryan

FBI Special Agent in Charge Caitlin Chaney believes in doing things strictly by the book. It's the only way to prove she's earned her rank despite her father's position in the federal government. Just her luck, she's been teamed with an agent who's known for following his instincts, not the rules. To her way of thinking, Agent Jake LeFevre is a screw up and bound to trash her operation—and career.

Jake is used to running undercover ops his way, and he's not too happy with his new boss—an accountant, no less, whose undercover experience is limited at best. He needs a partner who can hold her own, not a prima donna.

At first the sparks that fly between them aren't the good kind. From the very beginning, their cover as madly-in-love newlyweds at a New Orleans casino is tested to the max. But as they work together to find a missing whistleblower in a money-laundering scheme, their admiration grows to respect—and something more.

Then Jake discovers the casino CFO is someone he loved as a teenager. If the woman recognizes him, things could go sideways, and fast—and in a way that could leave their bodies—and hearts—in pieces.

Available now in ebook and print from Samhain Publishing.

Doing whatever it takes could get them both killed.

Living Lies
© 2008 Dawn Brown

Twelve years after her sister's disappearance, Haley Carling spends her days trying to hold what's left of her family together, running her late father's shop and caring for her alcoholic mother. Then her sister's remains are uncovered in the basement of their old home, and fingers start pointing. At the Carlings.

Dean Lawson, long the prime suspect in the Carling girl's disappearance, is sure he's got evidence proving who the killer is. He's determined to clear his name, and he won't let anything stand in his way. Not even his lingering attraction to Haley.

Haley is just as determined to protect her family from the former town bad boy's accusations. But now someone is stalking her, and Haley realizes Dean's the only one she can trust.

With a killer closing in, Dean wonders if he's made the biggest mistake of his life...a mistake that could cost Haley her life.

Warning: This title contains a mystery to keep you turning the pages late into the night.

Available now in ebook and print from Samhain Publishing.

GREAT cheap fun

Discover eBooks!

THE FASTEST WAY TO GET THE HOTTEST NAMES

Get your favorite authors on your favorite reader, long before they're out in print! Ebooks from Samhain go wherever you go, and work with whatever you carry—Palm, PDF, Mobi, and more.

Samhain Publishing Ltd

WWW.SAMHAINPUBLISHING.COM

Printed in the United States
150116LV00001B/39/P